The Weaver's Dream

Donna Baker

Myriad Books Ltd
35 Bishopsthorpe Road
London SE26 4PA

ISBN 1 904154 16 6

Printed and bound in Great Britain

Chapter One

Fog padded through the streets of London like a slow, predatory animal, claws sheathed for silence. It wrapped sinuous limbs around the shivering bodies of the people, hurrying to get home and shut it out; though many of them, having closed their broken doors, would find it slinking after them through cracks and crannies, slithering around the mould-dampened walls to wait in beds of sack and straw and chill their bones when they finally lay down to rest.

Rebecca Pagnel thought of such people as she drew her two-year-old son into the small house she and Francis lived in near the carpet warehouse. She had had her time of living in poverty, her childhood of near starvation as she stood hour upon hour by her father's loom, drawing for him as he wove the carpet that was their life. She never ceased to give thanks that her life now was easy and comfortable, never forgot her sorrow for those who were still condemned to the conditions she had known – and worse, for here in the London of 1824 she had seen poverty such as even the most abject weaver in Kidderminster had never known.

Here, in the mean streets around Covent Garden, Rebecca had seen little children forced to beg for food that a dog would sniff and pass by. She had seen girls who had barely reached the age of childbearing, their bodies already swollen as they offered themselves to men for a few pence at a time. She had seen old men and women, too frail to drag their twisted bodies further than the doorsteps of the cellars and hovels where they dwelt, reaching out quaking, bony fingers for the bounty only a few would, or could, give.

It was on scenes like this that she closed her door

1

on this murky November afternoon and felt the warmth of the small house enfold her as if it were a cloak of fur. There was a lamp already lit on the little table where she laid her gloves and bonnet, its yellow light driving back the shadows, and as she bent to take off Daniel's coat and hat, the kitchen door opened and Tilly, the little maid of all work, appeared.

'Oh, ma'am, you're back.' She scurried forward, taking the clothes and smoothing Daniel's hair. 'Ain't it 'orrid out there? I said to Sal, the mistress will get lost in this, easy as ninepence, if she don't take care. I'm that glad to see you safe, I am really. And there's a gentleman to see you, ma'am, sitting in the parlour this past hour he's been, and wouldn't take no more'n a dish of tea, no matter what. Sal's all of a dither, wants to know if he's to stay for supper, but I dussn't ask him, he looks at me so . . .'

The voice rattled on, but Rebecca heard no more. A gentleman, in the parlour? To see *her*?

'Are you sure you haven't made a mistake, Tilly?' she asked. 'Surely it's the master he's come to see.'

The small, neat head that had been alive with lice when Rebecca had taken the child in, shook vigorously. 'No, ma'am, it's you he asked for. Shall I take Daniel to the kitchen for his tea, ma'am, while you goes in there? I been in twice to attend to the fire, ma'am.'

Rebecca looked at her and smiled. Tilly, voluble and even saucy when at home with the family she had come to know, was still unaccountably timid with strangers, particularly men. Rebecca had often wondered what had happened to her before she had come to the Pagnels as maid, but she only shook her head when questioned, and her eyes looked so much like those of a terrified wild animal that no one had the heart to persist. But someone, at some time, had done her harm, it was clear, and Rebecca felt a knot of burning anger

2

in her breast when she thought of what it might have been.

'It's all right,' she said. 'I'll go and see who the gentleman is and what he wants. You'll come if I ring, won't you? Though I don't suppose he'll stay long, and I'll have to feed the baby soon anyway. Has he behaved himself while we've been out?'

'Oh yes, ma'am. Slept all the while.' Tilly ducked her head and took Daniel by the hand. 'Come along o' me, Daniel, an' see what Sal's bin making for your tea. Shall I bring you a dish of tea, ma'am? You must be shrammed, being out there in that awful fog.'

'Yes, I would like some, but I'll see who the gentleman is first.' Rebecca smoothed her hair and laid her hand on the doorknob. She had an odd sensation, as if time had slipped back. As if she were once again the maid, bobbing to her mistress, answering the door, scurrying to obey orders. Of course, her situation had been very different from Tilly's – taken from a weaver's hovel to work in the big house of the man whose carpets she had seen on the loom, kept for her first two or three years more or less chained to a big earthenware sink in the dark, cramped scullery that seemed to be permanently piled high with dirty dishes; the lowest scrap of life in a hierarchy of servants, working from before dawn until well after dark, allowed out only to take scraps to the rubbish heap or to go to church on Sunday afternoons.

Memories of those days had taught her to treat her own maid as a human being, with feelings and needs of her own, and Tilly had responded by investing her with a devotion that seemed at times to be almost too much for the skinny frame that no amount of feeding had yet fattened. But she had still not grown in confidence; it seemed that trusting Rebecca, old Sal in the kitchen, and Francis himself had absorbed all her energy, and she shrank from venturing out of doors.

Rebecca turned the doorknob and went into the

3

parlour. It was her pride and joy, this room with its heavy furniture and the polished table at which no meals were ever eaten. She cared for it herself, trusting neither Sal nor Tilly to polish the shining wood or dust the ornaments that decorated the mantelpiece.

The lamp had been lit in here too, and cast a mellow glow which blended with the flickering light of the fire Tilly had lit. An armchair had been drawn up before the fire, its back turned towards the door, and although Rebecca could see a pair of legs stretched out towards the flames she could not see who the 'gentleman' was. She stepped forwards, feeling suddenly nervous, and at the sound of her footstep the man in the chair moved suddenly and rose to his feet, looking gigantic in the shadowed room.

Rebecca stepped back, startled, then took a breath and laughed.

'Mr Pagnell! Why didn't Tilly say – but of course, she's never met you before. Why didn't you let us know you were coming? Does Francis know you're here?'

Jeremiah Pagnel looked down at her gravely. Rebecca had been a maid in his house, first standing in his scullery, then scrubbing floors and peeling vegetables in his kitchen, and finally cleaning fireplaces, dusting, polishing and sweeping in the rooms he sat and ate and worked in; yet he had never noticed her, had barely seen her, until after she had been driven away to London, pregnant with his grandchild.

Since then, he had gradually got to know her, the girl that his son loved and had pursued to London to find and marry. It had not been easy – with the truth of Francis's birth revealed, Jeremiah's wife Isabella had forbidden him ever to enter her house again. And although Jeremiah's brother Geoffrey and Geoffrey's wife Enid, who had raised Francis as their own, had been happy to receive Rebecca as a daughter, she knew there would never be a real welcome for her in

4

Kidderminster while Isabella lived.

Their visits had therefore been few. And indeed, there had been little time for visiting. Jeremiah had made Francis manager of his carpet warehouse here in London, while at the same time Francis was struggling to establish his own small carpet business with Rebecca's brother Tom. And Rebecca had been fully occupied with Daniel, born during that first hard winter together, and now the three-month-old baby, Geoffrey.

Jeremiah had come to London whenever possible and called at the house near Covent Garden, but his visits had been hurried and secret. Even his adopted son, Vivian, who often accompanied him to London, had not known of them. Vivian was closer to his mother than his stepfather and would not have hesitated to make trouble between them had it suited him to do so.

'Does Francis know you're here?' Rebecca repeated. 'Have you been to the warehouse?'

'No, I came straight here,' Jeremiah took her hands in his. 'Rebecca, I have news for you both.'

Rebecca stared at him, feeling suddenly afraid. What news could have brought him here like this, and looking so solemn?

'Is something wrong?' she asked. 'The factory . . . nothing's happened there, has it?' Her imagination showed her the factory in flames, the carpets burned and scorched beyond repair, men and women killed, children dying. But it need not be so dramatic. Everyone knew that times were bad, that trade had slumped, never really recovered since the end of the Napoleonic Wars. Perhaps Pagnel's had gone bankrupt like so many of their competitors; perhaps Jeremiah faced ruin and had come to tell them so.

She saw the warehouse closed and empty; herself, Francis, and Tom dependent on the small two-loom business that had scarcely begun to pay its way. And

5

it wasn't just the three of them; there were the children too, there were Tilly and Sal. And the old weaver, Samuel, who worked with Tom, and his daughter Nancy who helped her sister Bessie in the millinery business she had started . . . None of them yet fully self-supporting, all looking to Francis – and, past Francis, to Jeremiah – for their livelihood.

Rebecca stared up at the big man, feeling the sick fear that her mother must have felt when her husband, Will Himley, came home without a 'piece' to weave for the coming week. Seven days of sardonically named 'play' while their meagre stock of food ran down to nothing and the faces of the children grew more pinched, while they scraped by on her pay from the winding room, the rent unpaid and the fire unlit. There had been no guarantee, in the hardest times, of a 'piece' the next week, or the next, or the next after that .

Were they to be reduced to this again? Was she to join those poor, ravaged women in the street with their shaking hands held out for food or money?

'Please,' she said, 'tell me what's happened.' And she looked up at him with eyes large and dark in a suddenly ashen face.

Jeremiah let go of her trembling fingers and laid his hands on her shoulders. He guided her to a chair, his face concerned, and pressed her gently into it. Then he sat down close to her and took her hands once more in his.

'Rebecca, my dear . . . don't look so frightened. There's nothing to worry about. I'm a fool, I should have spoken differently, I never thought . . . No, there's nothing wrong at the factory, nothing at all. The bad times have hit us all, but Pagnel's will weather it – indeed, our fortunes are already improving and I want to discuss with Francis the possibility of some new designs. But that isn't what brought me here today. And I thought to save my news until Francis could be present to hear it with you, but now— '

6

He broke off as they heard the slam of the street door and the patter of Tilly's footsteps. Her voice sounded high and cheerful as she chattered about fog and coats and visitors; then they heard the deeper tones of a man's voice, calm and soothing as he sent her back to the kitchen. A moment later the parlour door opened, and Francis came in.

'Father!' For many years, he had been accustomed to call Jeremiah 'Uncle' but that time was past and the true relationship acknowledged. He stepped forward with the eagerness that had never left him, save for those weeks when he had thought Rebecca lost to him, and held out his hands, his blue eyes glowing. 'This is a surprise. How are you? And my aunt, she's well, I hope?' The query was delicately put, for Isabella would never have inquired after Francis; if she had been able to bring herself to speak his name at all, her voice would have been hard, the tone bitter. She had never liked him, even while she had believed him to be of no kin. Since discovering the truth, she had hated the very thought of his existence.

'Have you had tea?' Francis went on, hardly expecting an answer to his question. 'Tilly must bring some – Rebecca, my love— '

'I've ordered it already, it must be almost made by now.' They all turned as the door opened again and Tilly staggered in bearing a tray heavy with crockery and a steaming pot. She set it down on the table, gave Jeremiah a terrified glance and bolted from the room. Rebecca busied herself with the cups and saucers, then poured the tea. She passed a cup to Jeremiah, meeting his eyes as she did so. Please, she begged him silently, tell us what has brought you here today.

Jeremiah's expression changed a little, still solemn but now with a touch of reassurance in the dark eyes. He accepted his tea with a murmur of thanks, then turned to Francis.

'It's good to see you again, my boy. You're well?'

The formalities had to be observed, but Rebecca felt her impatience growing again. With an effort, she curbed it. He would tell them, after all. He had not come all this way merely to tease. She had only to wait.

And she had not, after all, too long to wait. Jeremiah seemed as anxious to tell his news as she was to hear it. And after only a few moments, he broke into Francis's enthusiastic account of his latest designs, and said abruptly: 'Forgive me, my boy, but I have something to tell you. Something— ' he glanced at Rebecca ' — which will affect you both.'

There was a moment's silence. Rebecca felt her heart thump. Keeping her eyes on Jeremiah's face, she stretched out a hand to Francis, and felt him take it in his.

'What's happened?' Francis asked quietly, and she knew that he had been struck with the same fears that she had known. 'Father, what's wrong? Do you need help?'

Jeremiah's face relaxed into a smile, but there was still a shadow in his eyes. 'Help? No, my son, I need no help, though it's like you to offer it. This is something quite different from what you both fear. I've already told Rebecca, there is no question of trouble at the factory, our carpets are selling as well as anyone's, our customers know their quality and are willing to pay for it . . . No, this is a family matter. Francis – I have to tell you that your aunt has died. My wife,' he added, as if they needed clarification. 'She died three days ago, of a heart attack the doctor says. The funeral is to take place the day after tomorrow.'

There was a small silence. Rebecca felt Francis's fingers tighten around hers. She gave him a swift glance and saw his face whiten, his eyes blaze suddenly blue against the pallor. She felt the quiver of his hand and enclosed it in both hers, waiting for him to speak.

'My aunt Isabella?' Francis said at last. 'Died?' He

paused, as if seeking the right words, then said, 'I'm sorry. It must have come as a shock to you.'

'It came suddenly, it's true. Nobody had the least idea that her heart was weak.' Jeremiah too paused. 'But shock . . . Francis, it would be hypocritical of me to pretend to much grief. Your aunt and I had enjoyed little friendship, let alone love, for the past many years. Our marriage was never much more than a business arrangement as it was – an empty shell. Nevertheless . . .' he hesitated '. . . there is always some regret for a life cut off.'

'Of course there is,' Rebecca said softly. 'And the house must seem very empty now. And so big.'

Jeremiah shot her a surprised look. 'That's exactly right – it does seem much larger without her. All those rooms – not that we ever used many of them since the children have all been gone— ' He broke off and Rebecca knew that he was thinking, not only of Francis and Vivian and his living daughters, but also of Isabel, his youngest child, who had died of a decline. 'I never went into some of those rooms,' he said as if speaking to himself, 'nor even thought of them. Yet without Isabella in the house, I seem to feel them pressing at my back, demanding my attention. It's as if she haunted me still.'

'Father, she's been gone only three days,' Francis said gently. 'You must give yourself time. It's a great loss. You'd been together for many years.'

'Twenty-eight,' Jeremiah said, as if repeating an oft-learned lesson. 'Vivian was four years old. A handsome boy – I was pleased enough to name him my heir. Until I had a son of my own.' He glanced at Francis. 'I have much to make amends for,' he said in a low voice.

'You have nothing at all, as far as I am concerned,' Francis retorted. 'You always did your best for me – you gave me to your own brother to bring up as his own, you took me into the firm and into your home when I was grown, you came after me to London and

9

gave me help when I wed Rebecca, you've looked after us since. Would I have been able to set up my own business if I'd not also had the managing of your warehouse? Would Rebecca's sister Bess be a milliner today? Would Tom be able to think of marrying his Nancy, which I believe is in his mind? Would little Daniel and Geoffrey— '

'Enough, enough.' Jeremiah held up his hand. His face was smiling but Rebecca, casting him a glance, saw that his eyes were unusually bright. 'Yes. I did all that, but it was the very least . . . I always wanted to do more, but while Isabella still lived— '

'You could do nothing. I understood that. And I ask no more of you now.' Francis disengaged his hands from Rebecca's and laid them on his father's. 'Father, this changes nothing. I don't expect you to go back on your word to your wife. Vivian must remain your heir. If you've come to— '

'No, I haven't come for that, much though I would like to. That has to stand. But there are other conditions that no longer apply.' Jeremiah had been looking down, at the long, young hands that covered his own. Now he raised his head and looked his son full in the face. 'There is nothing to stop you coming back to Kidderminster now, Francis. That's what I've come to ask of you. Come back. Come back and work with me or alone, whichever is your will, but come back to the town where you belong, where I can see you and my grandsons.' He turned his head to look at Rebecca. 'I need you all in Kidderminster,' he said quietly. 'And have done so for this long time. Come back to me, now that you can.'

Jeremiah would not stay the night. He had to leave at once, to be back in Kidderminster in time for his wife's funeral. But before he left, he made them promise to consider a return to Kidderminster. For there was too much involved, Francis said, to make an immediate answer, and Jeremiah agreed that this was true.

'I've always been afraid that it would be so,' he said, pulling at the whiskers that grew grey around his mouth. 'The longer you remained in London, the more difficult it would be to extricate you. One grows roots, even in a place like this. You've made a home here, thanks to Rebecca, you've started a business, you have friends. I can see that it won't be easy to leave it all behind.'

'We'll think about it, all the same,' Francis promised him, and called Tilly to bring Jeremiah's hat and coat. 'We have to talk to Tom and Bessie too. We can't make up our minds without consulting them.'

'Of course not. But perhaps they'll be glad to come back too. It's their home as well.' He looked questioningly at Rebecca. 'Well, we shall see. They've been in London longer than you two – they may have forgotten the town where they were born. And glad to forget too, who knows?'

'Indeed they may,' Francis said soberly when he returned from seeing Jeremiah to the coach. 'Father seems to have forgotten the reason why Tom and Bessie left Kidderminster in the first place. And I hadn't the heart to remind him just now.'

'Oh, Francis!' Rebecca stared at him. 'I'd almost forgotten it myself. But would that old story be remembered now? It's – how long ago? Ten years. The year the wars ended.'

'You think that people will remember Boney's defeat and forget Jabez Gast's murder?' Francis shrugged. 'Maybe so. But memories are long, Rebecca, and there may be some who find it convenient to remember what Tom and Bessie Himley did the night they disappeared from Kidderminster.'

'But they didn't kill him! It wasn't murder – Tom's told us that often enough, and Bessie too. It was an accident – not that he didn't deserve to die, after what he did to Bess— '

11

'And there's nobody to tell the magistrate that but Tom and Bessie themselves,' Francis pointed out. 'There were never any witnesses. Even Vivian, who helped them to get away— '

He stopped and they looked at each other.

'Vivian,' he said slowly. 'Yes, there's another stumbling block. Is Vivian likely to allow them to return to Kidderminster and say nothing? He's always sworn he would make them pay for the money he gave them to escape— '

'Which he could not admit to,' Rebecca said swiftly, and Francis smiled.

'No, he couldn't, could he? But he might find other ways of queering them. Or us.' He hesitated and looked at her uncertainly. 'He's never been entirely my friend, you know. And since he learned the truth about my parentage— '

'But your father has said there's no question of your displacing Vivian as his heir. He made that promise when he married your aunt, and he means to keep it. It was part of their marriage contract.'

'All the same, Vivian may not believe that. An unscrupulous man may find it difficult to understand the scruples of an honest one.'

'And is Vivian so unscrupulous?'

'He might be,' Francis said thoughtfully. 'Yes, he very well might be.'

Rebecca stirred the fire into life and stared into the flames, taken back for a moment to the days when she had stirred the library fire at Pagnel House in Kidderminster. Francis would sit there, watching her, and both would be thinking of the early mornings, when they met by the same fireplace, Rebecca carrying her housemaid's box to clean out the cinders and ashes and lay the new fire, Francis rising before the rest of the family to read quietly – until he had found the shy housemaid more interesting than any book.

Vivian had caught her in the library once, she

remembered, and shivered at the memory. Vivian, dark-eyed and flamboyantly handsome, had fancied his chance with any woman and particularly a housemaid whose position in the house was so fragile, who could be dismissed at a moment's notice and turned out into the streets for very little reason. Most housemaids would have been forced by their circumstances to succumb to him. Rebecca, however, had fought him off and although he had not had her dismissed – perhaps because he relished the challenge of a housemaid who did not succumb – she knew that he had neither forgiven nor forgotten.

Yes, she thought, Vivian was an unscrupulous man. And as he had once held her fate in his hands, so he could now hold that of her brother and sister if they returned to Kidderminster.

'Tom and Bessie don't have to go back to Kidderminster just because we do,' she said. 'Couldn't they stay here, if they want to, and carry on the businesses? Bessie's just getting on to her feet as a milliner, and it's what she's always wanted to do. And Tom and Samuel can go on with the weaving, so long as they have your designs to work from.'

'That's true. But they ought to be given the choice. And for either of them to be afraid ever to go to Kidder . . . it's a sentence hanging over their heads, Rebecca. And Vivian must know by now that Tom works with me. He could bring them to justice at any time – he need only deny their story that he helped them to escape.'

Rebecca sighed. How quickly, she thought, problems multiplied. A few hours ago, she had no more to worry about than the fog. Now difficulties seemed to be crowding in on her, and to this one she could see no solution.

'What do you feel about going back, Francis?' she asked. 'Do you want to – or do you feel we belong in London now?' She looked around the room where they

13

now sat, the cheerful, comfortable room behind the parlour. A fire burned brightly in the hearth, a rug of Francis's design glowed before it and little Daniel played there with a set of wooden bricks. She and Francis sat on either side of the fireplace in chairs that were old enough to have shaped themselves to the human body, as shoes will shape themselves to feet. In fact, most of the furniture in this room was old and shabby – what money had been available for show had been spent on the parlour – but Rebecca was fond of everything there, and knew that they were both far more at ease here than in the formality of their 'best' room.

Here, in her own home, she felt safe, almost invulnerable. Would she – could she – feel as secure if they went back to Kidderminster?

Francis too had been staring into the fire. Now he lifted his head and looked across at her.

'I've thought of going back for so long,' he said slowly, 'that it's become a kind of dream, something I longed for but knew was impossible. And now that it *is* possible – it's strange, I ought to be overjoyed, making plans to leave at once. But I'm not. I feel, well, almost as if I'd rather it *remained* a dream. I feel almost afraid.'

'Surely that's just because it's come so suddenly. You've always seen it as something that couldn't happen for years. Now it's upon you and you feel unprepared.'

Francis nodded. 'Perhaps. And yet . . . Somehow, Rebecca, I feel that this is an important turning-point for us. If we stay here in London, life will go on much as it has done. We'll go on with the plans we've already made.' He looked at her and she saw the familiar glow in his eyes, the glow of a passion that had been growing steadily in him ever since they first began to work together, here in London. 'You know what I want

14

most, Rebecca – the dream I have. Setting up our business in a different way, as I've already done with Tom and Samuel, so that none of us is master, none of us is man – we all work together, sharing our skills and our knowledge, sharing the profits that come from them.' He leaned forward, telling her again the thoughts that crowded his mind, thoughts he had expressed so often and which were growing, developing constantly. 'None of us could manage without the others. Without Tom and Samuel, I'd be no more than Father's warehouse manager, selling a few designs as well. Without me, Tom and Samuel would be no more than weavers, perhaps with a loom of their own, but still dependent on the whims of the manufacturer. But together, together we can make our mark. We can weave our own carpets, sell them to our own customers, develop and expand. So it's only right that we should each share the profits equally.'

'And you really believe that will work in a bigger factory, a factory the size of your father's,' Rebecca said, nodding. 'I believe it too, Francis. It's a dream I share. But my dream goes even further – to weavers who won't live in hovels as my family did, who won't starve if their piece isn't finished by Fall Day, who won't have to scrape for food for their children, scour ditches for water and share firing with their neighbours. All that could happen, Francis, and the masters wouldn't have to live so very much poorer.'

'A lot of people would say it's a dream of Heaven,' Francis said soberly. 'A dream that can never come true. But it can, Rebecca – and we can make it come true. Whether it's here or in Kidderminster, it can all come about. So . . . if we stay here, the warehouse will occupy much of my attention, but the business will expand – at least, we hope it will – and grow into a successful concern, making quality rugs and carpets in small quantities for discriminating buyers. We shall move, after a while, to a better house and bring up our children the best way we can. It doesn't sound such a bad life, does it?'

'It sounds a very good life,' Rebecca said with a smile. 'And if we go back?'

Francis lifted his hands slightly. 'Who knows? Obviously, Father wants me to go back to work in the family business again – but how will Vivian react to that? He was always a little jealous and since he's known the truth – well, I've not seen much of him, it's true, but when we have met he's been hostile. Aunt Isabella was his mother, after all. How will he take my return? I'm not sure we could ever work well together.'

'No. And now that you have two sons, and he still has only daughters . . .' Rebecca thought with pity of Maria, Vivian's wife, still endeavouring to give Vivian the son he craved, growing more and more depressed as each baby proved to be a girl. 'Five of them now. And poor Maria pregnant again, so your father says.'

'And if that turns out to be another . . . I think Vivian will be almost too angry to give her houseroom. Poor little scraps. Oh, they're not ill-treated – he wouldn't open himself to censure by allowing that. But they're not loved – not by their father, anyway.'

'But that's terrible.' Rebecca stared at him, then down at the baby who played at their feet. Instinctively, she reached down to touch Daniel's hair. 'How can anyone not love their own babies?'

Francis smiled. 'It's difficult to imagine, I know. But Vivian is different from us, Rebecca. And he wants a son – he needs one, if the family business is to stay under his control.'

'And couldn't one of the girls run it as well as any man?' she demanded. 'Oh, well, I suppose not. It isn't *done*. But it would save a deal of trouble with all this inheriting and marrying if it were done. And I'm sure many women are just as capable as men of doing such things.'

'They might be, if they didn't marry,' Francis agreed. 'But what woman has time to run a complicated business like carpet making as well as oversee a busy household and bear children? You're expecting too much, Rebecca.'

'Yes, I suppose I am. And all this doesn't help us solve our own problem, does it?' She looked at him, her dark eyes reflecting the dancing gold of the fire. 'Do we go back to Kidderminster and face whatever problems we may find there? Or do we stay here in London and go on with the life we've begun?'

Francis met her eyes and held them for a long moment. Then he shook his head and turned away.

'My love, I just don't know. There's so much to be considered – we can't decide it all at once. And I think I should talk to Tom before even trying to make a decision. He has a right to know what's happening.'

'He and Bessie,' Rebecca said. 'Isn't it strange, Francis – we've been married only a little over two years and already our lives have . . . enlarged, in a way. They're not simply ours any more; they include so many others. Tom and Bessie – they came to London years ago and struggled with poverty until you found them. Samuel, who had done no weaving for years and was almost destitute when you and Tom started the loom shop and took him on. And Nancy, who wouldn't leave her father even when things were at their worst, and is now so happy working with Bess at making bonnets.'

'And like to become your sister-in-law, if I'm not mistaken in the look I've seen in Tom's eye lately,' Francis said with a smile.

'I hope so. She's a nice girl and Tom ought to have some happiness. But what I'm saying, Francis, is that all these people depend on us in some way. We're not really free to decide for ourselves. Any decision we make now must include all these others.'

Daniel dropped one of his wooden bricks on to a

17

finger and began to cry. Rebecca bent and lifted him into her lap, kissing the injured hand and murmuring soft words of comfort.

She was nineteen years old and already aware of her responsibilities; and when she thought back to the weaver's hovel where she had been born, to her early days as her father's drawer, she wondered how she had ever come to be here, the wife of Francis Pagnel, the mother of his children.

And where would life take her next?

'Go back to Kidder?' Tom said doubtfully. He glanced at his two sisters: Bessie, with her yellow hair and slightly prominent blue eyes and the bold look she had always had about her, and Rebecca, still a slender girl in spite of her two children, dark as their father had been and with the same firmness about her small mouth. Will Himley had been a cottage weaver, jealous of his independence, determined never to become a factory man. Too determined, perhaps; for independence had not been enough to prevent him and his wife Fanny dying in poverty from cold and starvation.

'Don't you think it's a good idea, Tom?' Rebecca asked. She passed him a platter of cheese. 'Would you rather stay in London?'

He glanced at her as he cut a slice of cheese and laid it on a thick slice of bread. They were sharing their supper, as they often did. Bessie had finished hers and was trimming a bonnet, while Rebecca held the baby Geoffrey on her lap.

'No, I don't know as I'd *rather* stay here,' he said slowly. 'Kidder's always been home, though it's long enough now since we saw it, Bess and me. But – going back – that's summat different. That needs thinking about.'

'Because of old Jabez, you mean,' Rebecca said quietly, and Bessie dropped her work in her lap.

'Well, of course because of him!' Her voice was high

18

and nervous. 'You know what they think happened – Tom and me did for him. Well, maybe we did but it were an accident – Tom never meant to kill him, he just went for him to get him away from me. Jabez would be alive today if he'd never— ' Her hands shook as she tried to pick up her work again, and she laid it back on her knees. 'But what's the use? No one 'ud believe us.'

'No, I'm afraid they wouldn't,' Francis said soberly. 'They might – but we can't take the risk. But is it any less risk to stay here?'

Bessie stared at him. 'What d'you mean?'

'Well, Tom's working with me quite openly. Vivian must be aware of it, or if he isn't he will be before long. He could as easily set the constables on to you here as in Kidderminster.' Bessie drew her breath in sharply and Francis laid a hand on her arm. 'Don't be frightened, Bess. He's done nothing yet and may not intend to. But we ought to be sure. We ought to *make* sure.'

'How can we do that?'

'I don't know,' Francis said, 'but I think I must go back to Kidderminster, at least for a visit. Perhaps then it will be easier to decide what is the right thing to do – for us all.' He looked at Rebecca. 'Will you come with me, my love?'

'Of course. But I shall have to bring the babies – I can't leave them here. And where should we stay? Your father could hardly— '

'No, we'll stay with Pa – with my uncle and aunt in Church Row.' Francis stumbled over the title; he had been accustomed since a baby from calling his Uncle Geoffrey 'Papa', had grown up looking on him as his father and his Aunt Enid as mother. 'It's time I saw them again anyway. They're ageing fast.'

'I think that's a good idea,' Tom said. 'Get an idea of the lie of the land. Maybe once you see Kidder again you'll not be so keen to go back. I hear things ent too good there these days, no more'n here in London.'

'That's true, I'm afraid.' Francis frowned. 'Business is bad everywhere. That's the trouble with luxury industries, they're the first to suffer when times are hard. Yet there are still plenty of people with money who are ready to pay well for fine quality goods. Not everyone will go to the wall, and as long as we maintain our quality— '

'Which, with your designs and Samuel and Tom's weaving, we will,' Rebecca said.

'—then we shall survive,' Francis finished with a quick smile at his wife. 'After all, we've survived so far.' He glanced at Tom and Bessie. 'You two in particular have survived.'

'It's not been easy, though,' Bessie said grimly, and Rebecca looked at her, noticing again the tired look on Bessie's face, the strain that showed around her eyes and mouth when her face was in repose. Bessie had never really recovered from those years when she and Tom had been forced to live by their wits; she had never confided in Rebecca exactly how they had lived, nor had Francis told her in just what circumstances he had discovered her sister, but Rebecca guessed that Bessie had been forced to sink low in order to live at all.

Now, however, she seemed to have turned her back on her past life and to be happy with her small shop where she and Samuel's daughter Nancy made hats and bonnets. It was hard enough work, and barely paid enough to keep them both, but Bessie was confident that she would soon be able to employ another girl or two, and so expand as Tom and Francis were expanding their own business.

'All the same,' Rebecca said to Francis sometimes, 'I wish she wouldn't work quite so hard. That recurrent fever she gets worries me. It doesn't last long, I know, but while she has it she's miserable with the rash and headache it brings, and it seems to take her longer

20

each time to recover. And I don't believe those potions Sal gives her do any good at all.'

But Bessie seemed well enough now, though she was clearly alarmed by the thought that her and Tom's trouble, although ten years old, might still catch up with them.

'I'll talk to my father when we're in Kidderminster,' Francis said decisively. 'He's a magistrate and he has all our best interests at heart. He won't allow you to be wrongly treated, Tom. And it would be best to have the matter cleared up.'

'Ah, it would that.' Tom looked relieved. He had always hated living under a cloud, and to be wanted for murder – he who had always refused even to pilfer ends of wool from his own employer – had been a shadow over him for too long. 'I'd be glad to get it settled, whether we goes back to Kidderminster or no.'

'That's decided, then.' Francis helped himself to ale. 'Rebecca and I go back for a visit while you stay here and look after the business. And as soon as we can, we'll be back with news.'

'And if you decide to go back and we want to stay?' Tom looked at him with some anxiety. 'You move the business and we has to move with it, willy nilly. That's Bess and Sam and Nancy and me, all of us.'

'I know. And you'll do nothing you don't want to do.' Francis put out his hand and Tom laid his against it. 'Whatever Rebecca and I decide to do won't have any adverse effect on you, Tom. You have my word on that.'

Tom gave him a steady look, then nodded. They shook hands across the table, and Rebecca caught Bessie's eye and gave her a smile.

'You can believe it,' she said quietly. 'Francis never goes back on his word.'

'Let's hope he don't have to,' Bessie said. 'You know what promises are – like piecrusts. Easy broken.'

Rebecca shook her head. She remembered what

Bessie had been like as a girl, bouncing off to the carpet factory of a morning, giggling with her friend Nell and looking out of the corners of her eyes at the men. Life had been an adventure then, even though there had been precious little comfort to be had in the Himley cottage, and Bess had gone off each morning as if today were the day when life would change for ever. As it had indeed; but at night, not during the day, and in a way she could never have imagined.

Bessie's light had dimmed then and it had never really brightened again. And Rebecca looked at her and felt a stirring of the old rage against a system, a way of life, that put girls at such risk, that resulted in such tragedies.

She thought again of the poverty that lay outside in the teeming streets of London, too immense, it seemed, ever to be put right. But in a smaller town like Kidderminster, perhaps such injustices could be overturned. Perhaps there, people with compassion and imagination could bring about a better way of life.

She found herself hoping suddenly that Francis would decide to move back to Kidderminster, and take the whole family with him. Get Bessie into cleaner air; give them all the chance of making a good, healthy life.

Give herself and Francis the opportunity to realise what he often referred to as his Dream.

Chapter Two

Kidderminster had begun to change in the two years or so since Rebecca and Francis had left it. More houses had been built for workmen in the various industries that were growing up – principally that of carpet making, which had flourished here since the end of the previous century. But there were also many smaller concerns: shoemakers, watchmakers, joiners and ironmongers, a number of tailors and straw hat makers and even one or two still making the bombazine for which Kidderminster had once been famous.

'It's growing,' Rebecca observed as they caught their first glimpse of the town across the winter-silent fields. 'There are already streets we've never seen, Francis.'

'It's the same everywhere.' Francis held Daniel up to the window of the coach. 'Look, Danny, this is where your grandfather lives. Villages are becoming towns, and towns growing bigger and more crowded. No wonder people are becoming restless about the parliamentary system. It's quite wrong that a tiny hamlet, with no more than forty or fifty inhabitants, should be able to return two Members, while a place like Kidderminster has none at all. How can improvements ever be brought about while the people have no voice?'

'They have no voice as it is,' Rebecca said. 'My father never had the vote, nor any weaver I ever knew. And those who can vote are often forced to elect a man they don't want, because he's their employer or landlord. Where's the justice in that?'

'There's none at all. Nor ever will be, unless the people themselves take a hand in bringing about reform.'

'As they did in Manchester, five years ago?' Rebecca said, and they both fell silent, thinking of the terrible day that had been dubbed the Massacre of Peterloo. 'Women and children, come out to attend a peaceful meeting, dressed in their best clothes, cut down by the cavalry's swords?' she went on, her voice trembling. 'How can people take a hand, when such frightful things can happen?'

'All the same, it's sometimes the only way.' The coach rattled into the streets of Kidderminster and Francis began to gather up their packages. 'And it does those poor folk no good if we all draw back and do nothing. Reform never comes about by people sitting at home and putting up with injustice.'

They were drawing into the inn yard now, and Daniel was jumping excitedly up and down, anxious to be out of the cramped interior of the coach. Tilly, who had been huddling mute in the corner, clearly feeling miserably ill from the motion and longing for the journey to be over, pulled herself upright and rubbed a hand wearily over her pale face. Rebecca wrapped Geoffrey in his shawl and peered out through the window. She thought of the day she had left Kidderminster, disgraced and in despair, believing she had lost Francis for ever.

'I never imagined I'd be coming back like this,' she said as they climbed out and stood for a moment making sure they had all their possessions safe. 'As your wife, the mother of your children . . . Francis, you don't regret anything, do you?'

'Regret anything? Why, what should I regret – except those months when you were so alone? I would certainly give a good deal for you not to have suffered them.' He looked down at her, then slipped an arm around her shoulders. 'But as for what went before, and what has come since – no, my love, there's nothing to regret. And everything to be thankful for.'

They smiled at each other, sharing one of their

moments of complete communication amidst the bustle and noise of the yard. Then they heard a voice close by, speaking their names, and both turned with pleasure.

'Mother!' The word still came most easily to Francis's tongue as he bent to kiss the woman who had brought him up as her own. 'But what are you doing here on such a cold day? You should have stayed at home and waited for us to come.' He glanced around. 'Isn't my uncle here with you?'

Enid Pagnel shook her head and turned to embrace Rebecca. Her greeting was warm and unfeigned; there was no hostility here towards the serving maid who had married Francis only weeks before the birth of their son. And when she had kissed Rebecca she turned at once to the children, the baby in Rebecca's arms, the excited little boy tugging at her skirt.

'They're beautiful, both of them,' she exclaimed. 'Daniel's just like you, Rebecca, with those lovely dark brown eyes. And Geoffrey— ' she parted the shawl with gentle fingers and peeped at the sleeping face ' — why, he's exactly like you were when you were a baby, Francis!'

Francis laughed. 'Well, we all have to have some cross to bear. Perhaps he'll grow out of it. Now, let's get some conveyance to take our luggage to Church Row. Where *is* my uncle? Has something delayed him?'

Enid shook her head again and Rebecca noticed that she looked tired and drawn, her face showing her age now that her first excitement at seeing them was over.

'He's had a chill lately, and you know how they always settle on his chest. I thought it better for him to wait at home. I ordered a cart to carry your boxes – it's waiting over there. Perhaps Rebecca and the babies would like to ride, and we could walk, Francis.'

'Indeed not,' Rebecca said firmly, before Francis could answer. 'You must ride, Mrs Pagnel, and take Geoffrey for me, if you will. It's no more than a step from here, and Daniel and I will be glad of the exercise – won't we, Danny? You'd like to walk, wouldn't you?'

The little boy nodded eagerly but within a few minutes began to regret his agreement, and Francis lifted him to his shoulder and carried him through the town to where Church Row climbed the hill from the old Bull Ring to the open space in front of the tall red church. Here, in one of the old houses that leaned out across the narrow way, Francis had grown up, known to everybody as the adopted son of Geoffrey and Enid Pagnel.

Francis had known from an early age that he was not their natural son. It had never made any difference to his feeling for them – to him they had always been his parents, Mother and Papa. And when Jeremiah had told him the story of his love for the gentle governess who had been Francis's mother, and the tragic way of her death, Francis had found it difficult to realise that they were in truth uncle and aunt. Geoffrey had suggested that he should now be acknowledged as Francis's uncle; but Enid was all the mother Francis had ever known, and he kept the affectionate title for her, knowing how precious it was to her.

'I wonder what's really the matter with Uncle Geoffrey,' he said now as he strode by Rebecca's side, Daniel perched high on his shoulder. 'These chills and colds of his worry me. I hope it isn't serious.'

'Well, we'll soon see for ourselves,' Rebecca said comfortingly, but she too felt uneasy. There had been something in Enid's face and voice that hinted at more than a chill. And Geoffrey Pagnel had never looked strong. Thin, bent and bookish, he had spent his life in study and teaching in the King Charles I Grammar School, with little thought for anything else save his family. Nobody would have thought that he was brother to Jeremiah, so big and hearty, so full of energy and ambition.

26

The carter was already unloading the boxes when they arrived, and Tilly was staggering to the door with the first of them as Francis and Rebecca came up the street. Francis lifted Daniel from his shoulder and set him down, and Rebecca took his hand to keep him out of the way. The Pagnels' servant came out to help with the luggage, but there was no sign of Geoffrey. Her uneasiness grew.

'Come in out of the cold,' Enid drew her inside and they stood for a moment accustoming their eyes to the darkness while the luggage was stacked around them. 'There should be a good fire burning in the library.' She took Rebecca's arm, urging her gently along the narrow passage. 'And I ordered tea to be made as soon as we arrived – you'll need something to warm you after that dreadful journey. I've always hated coach journeys – not that I've had to travel very much, thank goodness.'

She opened a door and Rebecca went into the small, cosy room where Geoffrey and Enid spent most of their time. It was warm, with a bright fire burning in the grate, and a tray of cups and saucers already on the table. But Rebecca's eyes were not on the tray; instead, she looked at the figure sitting hunched in the chair by the fire.

Geoffrey Pagnel had aged badly since she had last seen him, when he and Enid had come to London only six months ago. His fair hair, then grey, had completely whitened and the pink of his scalp showed through its sparseness. The lines on his face had deepened and his eyes had sunk into dark hollows; yet as Rebecca approached, he raised his head and the same sweet, though now rather weary, smile lightened his countenance.

'Rebecca my dear . . . so good to see you.' He lifted a thin hand and she took it, disturbed by its fragility; she felt almost as if she might crack the bones by holding too tightly. She sank down beside him, trying

27

not to show her alarm. 'And is Francis with you? And the children?'

'Yes, we're all here. And all well. But you – how are you? Mrs Pagnel said you'd had a chill.'

'Aunt Enid, please,' Enid's voice said from behind her. 'And Uncle Geoffrey – isn't that right, Geoff?'

'Most certainly, most certainly.' His voice was thin, as weak as the rest of him. 'Well, I have been a little poorly, but I'm on the mend now, on the mend, aren't I, Enid, my dear? Yes, I'll soon be up and about again.'

Rebecca looked at him, then turned her face up to Enid Pagnel, just in time to catch a strange expression that was immediately replaced by a cheerful smile. Rebecca felt a twinge of fear. Was Geoffrey seriously ill?

But before she could speak, or even think what to say, Francis was in the room, leading Daniel by the hand, and she moved away so that he could greet his uncle. She saw his look of shock, mirroring her own, and gently disengaged Daniel's hand from his father's, so that Francis could give his full attention to the old man in the chair.

'I know what you're thinking,' Enid murmured as they withdrew to the other side of the room. 'But it really has been no more than a chill. They always affect him like this – he'll be his old self in a day or two.'

'Has a doctor seen him?' Rebecca asked, and Enid shook her head.

'There's not much a doctor can do. I know Geoffrey's chest, and what soothes it best. And since he began to suffer with his joints, he does seem to have these attacks more often, but the liniment I make up helps with the pain.'

Rebecca sighed. She knew that Enid was probably right; there was little a doctor could do. Geoffrey had never been strong, and now he was growing old, and there was nothing anyone could do to prevent his ageing. And only a few fortunate people lived into a

28

painfree and healthy old age; most, in her experience, died miserably.

'Let me take you upstairs,' Enid said. 'You must want to wash, and Daniel wants something to eat and drink, I know.' She looked down at the little boy and her face was filled with tenderness. How sad, Rebecca thought, that she had never been able to have children of her own; and how fortunate that she had been able and willing to take Francis and bring him up as her son. Fortunate for both herself and for Francis.

'I must feed Geoffrey, too,' Rebecca said as the baby stirred in his shawls. She felt the familiar ache in her breasts, the tingling that told her that milk was coming, ready for him to suck. 'He loves his meals, Geoffrey does – I've never had any problem feeding him.'

'You feed him yourself?' They were outside the room now; Enid would never have discussed such a matter in the presence of the men.

'Of course. Why not?' But Rebecca knew quite well why not. It was unfashionable in some circles to feed one's own baby – many women employed a wetnurse. 'Aunt Enid, if you could see the conditions poor women live in in London . . . the thought of one of them feeding my baby makes me shudder. And Francis and I don't move in fashionable circles anyway – we're really no more than tradespeople, and happy enough to be so.'

'For the time being, perhaps.' Enid led the way up the steep, narrow stairs. 'But Francis has too much talent to remain a tradesman.'

'I know. His designs are already attracting attention.' Rebecca followed her into the room at the top of the stairs. 'Oh, this is lovely! Is this where we're to sleep?'

'I hope it will be all right.' Enid straightened the bed cover. 'I'm sorry you have to have the children in here with you too, but we have very little room, as you know. I suppose Daniel could have slept with your maid, but she has to share with ours so— '

'It's perfectly all right. We don't mind a bit, having Daniel with us. We have to have the baby anyway, he still needs his night feed. And Daniel will love his little bed.' Rebecca looked around the room with its crooked floor and small windows leaning out over the narrow street. 'You really didn't need to go to so much trouble. Was this Francis's room when he lived here?'

'Yes, before he went to live at Pagnel House.' Enid too glanced around, her eyes soft with memories. 'He was such a good son to me, so affectionate – I was sorry to lose him. But it had always been understood that when Jeremiah took him into the business he would go to live with the family. Like any other apprentice, really, lodging with the master. I knew it must happen, but I was sad when the time came.'

'Of course you were,' Rebecca said gently. 'But you never really lost Francis, you know. He's always thought of you as his mother, and this house as home.'

'I know. I've never doubted his affection.' Enid looked at her. 'And it's easy to see he loves you too, Rebecca. You've clearly made him very happy.'

'No happier than he's made me,' Rebecca said. 'We love each other very much, Aunt Enid.'

They stood quietly for a moment, then Daniel grew bored and began to scramble up on to the big bed. Rebecca laughed and pulled him back, then turned to take the baby from Enid's arms.

'I must feed him now. He'll be crying if I don't. I'll sit here in this chair.'

'And I'll take Daniel downstairs and give him some milk. You'd like that, wouldn't you, Daniel? And perhaps Jenny might have made some cakes for your tea. Let's go and see, shall we?'

'Tilly,' Daniel said, and Enid nodded.

'Yes, we'll see Tilly too – I daresay she and Jenny are getting to know one another.' She smiled at Rebecca. 'Come down whenever you're ready, my dear. I want you to look on this as your home.'

She departed, closing the door behind her, and Rebecca unbuttoned her dress to feed Geoffrey. The baby fastened upon her nipple and began to suck strongly, and she felt the familiar tide of warmth spread through her body as she looked down at the fair head. Feeding her baby never failed to increase her love for him, and she knew a pang of pity for those women who never experienced it. Did they realise what they were missing? she wondered. And what their babies were missing too?

Love, it seemed to Rebecca, must be the most important thing in the world.

The next few days were spent in reacquainting themselves with Kidderminster. Apart from the new streets and buildings which had appeared while Rebecca and Francis had been in London, there did not seem to have been much change. The streets were still filled in the mornings and evenings with people hurrying to work, the sky was dark with smoke from the tall factory chimneys, the air clattered with the noise of machinery. And the River Stour was still coloured with the dyes of the wool which was to be woven into carpets, the brilliant reds and greens and blues swirling away from the skeins as they were dipped into the water on the ends of long poles. Rebecca stopped to watch for a moment.

'I used to see them doing this when my mother was taking me to the bobbin-winding shop,' she told Francis. 'I always thought it looked so lovely at first – all those colours swishing about and merging into each other. Beautiful enough for a carpet design. But you hardly have time to admire it before they've all mixed up and turned into nothing but a dirty-looking soup.'

'You didn't ever actually work in the bobbin-winding shop, did you?' Francis asked. 'I thought you drew for your father.'

'Oh yes, I did, once I was eight years old. Bessie

had been doing it until then, but once I was big enough she went to the factory and I stayed at home. But Mam had to take me with her, and I used to sort out bits of wool and do little jobs like that, or else just sit in a corner. I had to behave myself, though.' She smiled a little ruefully. 'I once almost caused poor Mam to be dismissed – the overseer said she was winding too loose and threw her bobbin down the shed. And I went for him and shouted that he was being unfair – which he was. But you must never talk back to an overseer. Poor Mam had to grovel and beg almost on her knees to keep her job that day.' She gazed down at the murky water and sighed. 'I never forgot how I felt about it. I was very young – five or six, no more. But it all seemed so unfair, and there was nothing to be done about it. And it's not so very different now, is it.'

'No,' Francis said, 'not so very different.'

They walked on in silence, approaching the big carpet shop where Pagnel's best carpets were made. Francis was to meet Jeremiah there and see some of his newest designs being produced. As they came near the big building, the door opened and a tall man with dark curly hair and a florid complexion stepped through it.

Rebecca tightened her hand on Francis's arm.

The man saw them and stopped; then he came forward, holding out his hand.

'Frank, by all that's wonderful! So you really have come back to honour Kidderminster with your presence again.' He grasped Francis's hand and pumped it up and down. 'I thought the lights of London had got you for good this time. And this is your beautiful wife – Rebecca, isn't it?'

He turned away from Francis and stared at her, and she returned his look as coolly as she knew how. Surely he must remember seeing her about Pagnel House, carrying heavy trays to the dining room, bringing hot water for his morning wash, stoking up the fire with fresh coals . . . and surely he must remember that day when he had trapped her in one of the warehouses and tried to force himself on her. And again, in the library at the house. Both times she had been forced to use violence to defend herself, and she knew that Vivian was not a man to forget either defeat or humiliation.

And he had not forgotten. She saw the memory in his eyes, and a look on his face that told her he had not forgiven, either. Vivian Pagnel rarely, if ever, forgave.

'Well, well, well,' he said softly. 'Little Rebecca. Yes, I remember you well. And so now I am to call you cousin, am I?'

'You may call me what you wish,' she said steadily, and he laughed, a harsh, abrupt laugh that sent a chill through her bones. But he said no more, merely turned to Francis with every appearance of friendliness and took his arm.

'You were coming to see the workshops, I imagine? Well, you must come in, both of you. I'm sure Rebecca – *Cousin* Rebecca – isn't too fine to walk around a carpet shop. Her sister worked here, after all – in this very one, I believe. It was Butts your sister worked for, wasn't it, Cousin Rebecca? And let's see, who was the weaver she drew for – Gast, was it not? Jabez Gast?'

Rebecca drew back. How had it happened that she and Francis, absorbed in watching the river and talking, had not realised that they were approaching the building where Bessie and Tom had had that fateful encounter with Jabez Gast? She gave Francis a look of wild appeal, but caught Vivian's eye on her, sardonically waiting, and knew that she could not give him the satisfaction of refusing to go into the building. Instead, she lifted her chin and met his eyes steadily.

'I believe it was,' she answered. 'Though I was too young to know much about it at the time. But I daresay you've had a good many other accidents in the carpet shops since then.'

Vivian lifted his eyebrows and laughed. 'An accident, eh? Well, no doubt you all felt better for calling it that. But it was a long time ago, and who is to say now what the truth was? There were no witnesses, after all.'

'No,' Francis said, 'and therefore no reason for Bessie and Tom not to come back to Kidderminster where they belong.'

Vivian stared at him. 'They're not thinking of that, are they? Oh, I know you're in touch with them in London – the brother works with you, you could hardly expect to hide it. But I never thought that either he or you would have the gall— '

'And why not?' Francis stopped and faced him, withdrawing his arm. 'It was an accident, and as you say yourself there were no witnesses. Why shouldn't they come back? What have *you* got against their return, Vivian? Tom was nothing but a half-weaver and Bessie a draw-girl when they left – what can it possibly be to you?'

Vivian's colour deepened. 'You know what— '

'Yes. You told me, that day when we found Bessie and realised what she'd come to.' He gave Rebecca a quick glance of apology. 'You gave them money to escape, and you thought you'd bought them both. And when you found you hadn't, you nursed a grudge for years. But you surely don't still hold that against them. It's ten years and more ago, for heaven's sake. It's water under the bridge.'

Vivian looked at him and hesitated. To Rebecca, watching the flush on his already reddened face and seeing the tension in his jaw, he seemed about to explode. Then he released his breath slowly, and smiled.

'Water under the bridge . . .' He turned and looked at the Stour flowing past them, turbid with the dyes that had merged into a bruise of muddied colours. 'Yes, you're right, Frank. Of course it is. We'll say no more about it.' He turned and offered his arm to Rebecca, bowing with impeccable courtesy. 'Forgive me. I've been thoughtless – will it disturb you to come into the carpet shop, or would you rather I found someone to escort you home? I would not wish to embarrass you.'

Rebecca looked at him doubtfully, but his dark eyes looked back at her with apparently total candour. There was nothing she could do but accept his arm and murmur that no, she wasn't embarrassed in the least and did not wish for an escort home.

All the same, she could not rid herself of the feeling that there was a hint of something else behind Vivian's candid look – a glint of laughter, perhaps – and a sense that some new idea was forming and taking root.

And a reminder that he had not forgotten those previous encounters of theirs.

'No,' Rebecca said a few days later, 'nothing has really changed.'

She and Francis were eating dinner with Jeremiah. Vivian was present too; Jeremiah had bidden him and Maria for a 'family welcome' but Maria had sent a message saying she was 'slightly unwell'. Rebecca sat quietly, saying little, as her husband and his father slowly relaxed together and Vivian talked urbanely, as if the four of them shared a meal two or three times a week. Jeremiah was clearly relieved by his adopted son's apparent acceptance of having Francis and Rebecca in Kidderminster again.

'What kind of changes did you expect?' He gestured to the butler to pour more wine. 'There's been a deal of new building.'

'Oh yes, we saw that at once,' Rebecca said. 'And new factories too, in spite of the poorness of trade. But for the people who live in those houses and work in the factories, nothing has changed at all. The poverty's still there, as cruel as ever. I thought it was worse

35

in London than it could ever be anywhere else. But coming here again has brought it all back . . . Mr Pagnel, there are people starving here, and nobody seems to care.'

'But of course people care,' Vivian said easily. 'We pay our poor rates, which are high enough in all conscience, they're well looked after in the workhouse, and outdoor relief is given. What more can be done? There are always some who sink to the bottom of the heap, no matter what's done to help them.'

'I'm afraid that's true,' Jeremiah agreed, but Rebecca shook her head.

'It may be true of the real paupers – the ones who have nothing at all. I agree, they do have the workhouse, where they're fed and clothed. It's some of the working people who distress me. Men working such long hours for so little pay that they have to rely on little children to help support the family – and those children working as long hours as their fathers. I *know* about this, Mr Pagnel – I came from such a family. And it seems to me that nothing's improved, nor shows any sign of improving.'

'Rebecca's right,' Francis said. 'We pay our weavers too little, and it's the same in all trades. And live comfortably ourselves – where's the justice in that?'

Jeremiah glanced round the well-furnished room. 'Most of this didn't come from carpets,' he said uneasily. 'A good deal was bought by my wife when we first married. It was her fortune that enabled me to set my business on its feet— '

'And gave employment to these same distressed weavers,' Vivian interposed, 'who might well have died of starvation by now if my mother's money had not been so used. Pay them too little? They should be grateful to be paid at all.'

'Nevertheless, they have a right to be paid a living wage for the job they do,' Francis said. Rebecca saw that he was pale and knew that he was beginning to be

36

angry. She could feel the tension in him and tried to find some way to diffuse it.

'Tell me about the new weaving process,' she invited Vivian. 'It sounds a very romantic story. Francis tells me it was invented by a Frenchman and bears his own name.' Francis had told her a good deal more than that – in fact, she probably knew as much about it as either Vivian or Jeremiah. But asking a man to explain technical matters was, she had found, a quicker way to his heart than through his stomach.

'Jacquard, yes,' Vivian said carelessly. 'Some French weaver, quite a poor sort of fellow, I understand, but he happened to hit on an idea that looks as if it might prove quite valuable. It simplifies the whole process of pattern-making – and at the same time makes it possible to produce a wider range of design. I believe Broom's looking into it, with a view to trying it out. It's never been used for carpet manufacture before, you see, only for silks and such – but there's no reason why it shouldn't do very well.' He turned away as if to return to the subject of the weavers and their wages.

'It uses paper rolls, doesn't it?' Rebecca persisted. 'I can't quite see how— '

Vivian smiled kindly at her. 'No, it must be difficult for you to picture such a thing. But I'll try to explain. You see, the paper, or rather card, punched with holes that correspond with the pattern required, is hung on to a wooden cylinder drilled with – oh – several hundred holes. The pattern's worked out through the holes in the card catching on pegs which make the warps rise to form the correct shed. The holes allow the ends of these pegs, or hooks, to go through, leaving the warps not required to rest in the back of the carpet.'

Rebecca visualised the process, thinking of the years she had spent drawing for her father; hour upon hour, standing beside him, drawing the lashes towards her, inserting first the wooden 'sword' then the terry wire, until her arms, legs and back ached.

'It must make the work a good deal easier for the drawer,' she remarked, and Vivian shrugged and said carelessly that it probably did.

'Not that that will prevent them from expecting higher wages,' he added caustically, but Rebecca was glad to see that Francis did not rise to this. Instead, he asked whether Jeremiah had any plans to install the new process in his own factories.

'No doubt we shall in time,' Vivian answered. 'But Father thinks it's better to wait and see how John Broom manages before taking any risks of our own. And Jacquard does have disadvantages too – it's not the saviour of carpet manufacture, by any means.'

'Oh?' Francis said interrogatively.

'Size is the greatest problem,' Jeremiah said. 'The loom has to be so large, so high, that many of the smaller loom-shops would be quite unable to house it, and it would be totally out of the question in any weaver's cottage. And we rely very much on our independent weavers, as you know. Men like your father, my dear— ' He looked at Rebecca with embarrassment; they all knew that Rebecca's father had died in poverty, from starvation as much as from the growth that had finally stopped him working. 'We should have to build new loom-shops to accommodate these Jacquard looms, and trade simply isn't good enough at the present time. We're all interested in it, but only John Broom has taken any steps towards actually trying it.'

'And he'll be the one to make his fortune by it,' Vivian said tersely.

'Or to earn his bankruptcy by it,' Jeremiah returned with equal curtness.

There was a brief silence. Rebecca wondered if her attempts at tact had not brought about a worse situation than that which she had tried to avoid. But after a moment or two, Vivian laughed and exclaimed, 'Why are we all so solemn? Here are Francis and his lovely bride come back to us and we sit with long faces! Let's toast the pair of them.' He lifted his glass. 'To the Pagnels of London – good health and many years of happiness to you.'

Jeremiah lifted his glass also, and Rebecca met Francis's eyes across the table and saw that he too had noticed the barb that Vivian had included in his apparently sincere good wishes.

The Pagnels of London. Where Vivian had thought them safely ensconced. Where he wanted them to return.

'Vivian tosses aside the plight of the weavers very lightly,' Francis remarked as they returned to Church Row. 'And did you notice how little he sees the unions as a threat? Not surprising, when one considers how trades unions have been treated in the courts, with men transported and hanged – but we can't simply dismiss them out of hand. The feeling's there – it won't go away.'

'No, indeed.' Rebecca remembered her father talking to her about such things. No one had been more independent than Will Himley, to his eventual cost, but he had seen the wisdom of men banding together against the injustice of their employers. 'Yet surely if everyone would accept your idea of the co-operative movements, it would be better.'

'I'm sure it would. And it needn't be restricted to the carpet trade. It could apply to any trade. Everyone subscribes, everyone works and draws a sensible wage, everyone shares in the profit. There would be none of this distinction then between manufacturers and men, with the one living in luxury in a grand house and the other scraping a living in a hovel. Those who worked hardest would be the richest – or better still, everyone would be equally well paid. Not everyone is able to work so hard – they shouldn't be penalised for their infirmities or ill luck.'

'I believe it used to be like that,' Rebecca said as they came into Church Row and began to climb the hill. 'Manufacturers lived close by their weavers, and all in similar conditions. What happened? Why did it change?'

'Greed,' Francis said soberly. 'They kept too much of the profits. Now most manufacturers neither know nor care how their weavers live, and they've even managed to persuade themselves that the poverty they can't avoid seeing is the weavers' own fault.'

They were at the door of Geoffrey Pagnel's house. The moon shone down from a clear sky, lighting the narrow street. As Francis raised his hand to knock, the door swung open.

'Oh, sir!' Tilly exclaimed, her hand flying to her breast. 'Oh, thank goodness you're here. I was just coming out to see if you was in sight yet. Oh sir, I don't hardly know how to tell you. The master – the missus— '

'What is it?' Francis demanded, staring at the quivering little figure. 'What's happened?'

'Oh sir – ma'am – sir— ' But Tilly could say no more. She broke down in a fit of tears, her hands covering her face, her thin shoulders shaking, and Rebecca pushed Francis aside and took her by the shoulders.

'Tilly, what's wrong? Pull yourself together, child, and tell us – is it the master? Mr Pagnel? Has he been taken ill again?'

Tilly nodded violently, then shook her head. She tried to speak but the words were distorted and incoherent. Gently, Rebecca pulled her hands from her face and Tilly looked up at her with tear-blotched eyes, her mouth twisted with grief.

'Is he dead?' Rebecca asked quietly, and heard Francis draw in his breath.

'Oh, *ma'am*!' Tilly cried, and flung herself against Rebecca in an agony of weeping.

A sound caused Rebecca to raise her eyes. Holding Tilly against her, she peered into the shadows of the passage and saw Enid standing there, clad in a wrapper, her face white, her eyes hollow. For a long moment, they gazed at each other, and then Rebecca put Tilly away from her and reached out for the older woman.

'Go into the kitchen, Tilly,' she said, 'and make some tea for everybody. Aunt Enid, come into the library and tell us what has happened. Francis . . .'

'Yes,' he said in a voice almost too low to hear, and as the two women went towards the library he began slowly to ascend the stairs.

'He said he felt a little unwell,' Enid said as they sat with the tea steaming on the table. 'He didn't want food – said he would go to bed and rest. I went up a little later to see how he was . . . and he'd stopped breathing. Just . . . stopped breathing.'

'It was peaceful,' Rebecca said softly. 'He never had to suffer much, Aunt. And he'd been happy, these past few days.'

'Oh yes, he was happy. So happy, having Francis here, and you and the boys. Especially the baby . . . named after him. Little Geoffrey – but he loved Daniel too, of course, he was delighted by him. And he loved you, too, Rebecca. He said to me only today what a fine young woman you are and what a good wife to Francis. You've made his last few days very happy, all of you.'

'And you made his whole life happy,' Rebecca said firmly. 'There can't be many men who have lived so peacefully and cheerfully as Uncle Geoffrey. I haven't known either of you long, but I can see that's true. And now he's safe from all pain and worry.'

'I know – and I'm glad for him.' Enid turned to her, catching at her hands, and her whole face twisted with sorrow. 'But – oh, Rebecca, I'm going to miss him *so* much!'

* * *

41

The funeral over, Francis and Rebecca saw that Enid went to bed early. The past few days had clearly exhausted her and even the children could not raise a smile on her weary face. She bade them a tired good-night and climbed the stairs slowly on Francis's arm. Rebecca helped her to undress and left her, already half asleep.

'She seems to have grown so frail, so suddenly,' she remarked, rejoining Francis in the library. 'It's as if she could only be strong while your uncle was here to be strong for. Now he's gone, she seems so lost – as if she has no purpose any more.'

'I think that's just how she does feel.' He stirred the fire. 'Rebecca, you know she'll have to leave this house now? It belongs to the school – it will be wanted for a new master. Not that Uncle Geoffrey had done much teaching, these past few months, but he was still master of the lower school.'

'What will she do?'

Francis shrugged. 'Who knows? I suppose Father will probably take her in – but their lives have been so different, I wonder if she would ever settle there in that big house. She's been accustomed to such a quiet life and I feel she might be happier on her own, in some small cottage she could make cosy. But– '

'She's going to be very lonely,' Rebecca said quietly. 'She can't live alone, Francis. Not at her age. And she surely isn't strong enough anyway.'

'No, I fear not.' He remained silent for a moment, then looked up and met her eyes. 'Rebecca– '

'It's all right,' she said. 'You have no need to say it, Francis. She would be best living with us – I know that. You're her son – yes, in every way but one, and that has no importance now. And she looks on Daniel and Geoffrey as her grandchildren. She could be happy, living with us and watching them grow up. And I would be happy to have her.'

He reached across to her and took her hands in his.

His eyes were dark with love.

'You know what it would mean?' he asked, and Rebecca nodded.

'Yes, I know. It's been decided for us, hasn't it, Francis? And maybe that's the best way anyway.' She lifted his hand to her cheek. 'There can be no question now of our staying in London. We couldn't ask Enid to live there. We have to come back to Kidderminster now.'

Chapter Three

'So you'm really going to stay here in Kidder?'

Polly picked up her cup and sipped her tea. Her bright eyes twinkled at Rebecca over the rim, and Rebecca felt her mouth twitch in reply. Suddenly all constraint between them was gone. They were no longer a manufacturer's wife and housemaid; they were back in the kitchen of Pagnel House, sharing the chores of cleaning and blackleading fireplaces, carrying cans of hot water to the Family's bedrooms, giggling together when they had a chance and falling into their narrow beds in the attic room they shared, too exhausted even to wish each other goodnight.

'They wasn't bad times really,' Polly said thoughtfully. 'We had a lot of laughs, you 'n' me. It's never bin quite the same since you went.' Her eyes gleamed again with mischief as she glanced down at Daniel, playing on the rug. 'Still, you did all right in the end, didn't you? Got two fine and bonny babbies and a husband to look after you. But why come back to Kidder when you could live in London?'

Rebecca smiled wryly. 'London isn't the glittering and exciting place you might think, Polly. There's worse poverty there than in Kidderminster. I've seen it. It's a wonderful place if you're rich – but the poor live in hell, they really do.'

'That's the same all over, I reckon,' Polly said. 'The rich allus rides on the backs of the poor. It'll never be any different.'

'But it ought to be. It could be.' Rebecca bent to lift Daniel on to her lap. 'Every man who helps to make a carpet should have a proper share in the profits. It's only fair.'

'So it might be. But life ent fair, is it?' Polly set down her cup and stood up. 'I'd better be off. I only got till teatime an' if I'm not back sharp Mrs Hudd'll have my guts for garters. Here, when're you going to come and see us up at the House? Even Susan's bin asking.'

'I'd like to come. I'll bring the boys, one afternoon. It's just that— ' Rebecca hesitated, but Polly took her up at once.

'Bit awkward, innit, what with you being sort of related to the master now. One day you're visiting upstairs, next day you're in the kitchen hobnobbing with the servants. I can see that. Well, if you don't want to— '

'But I do want to! Of course I do. Everyone was so good to me – when Mam died, and when I found I was in the family way.' Unconsciously, she slipped back into the speech she had grown up with. 'Polly, you know how I feel about you and Mrs Hudd and the rest – you're my friends. My family, really. I never forgot that.'

Polly grinned her old, impish grin. 'It's all right, Becky. I knows that. I didn't mean nothing. You come round the back door any time, we'll all be glad to see you. Might even give you a pot or two to scrub, just to keep your hand in, like.'

Rebecca laughed. 'Oh, I can still do it, Polly – I haven't forgotten how. But I don't suppose you scrub any more pots than I do these days – in line for Head Housemaid, aren't you, when Susan goes?'

'Whenever that is.' Polly grimaced. 'You know what she is, she'll hang on till that arthritis of hers pins her to her bed for good. And even then, she'll still be able to move her tongue. Well, you can't blame her, 'tis nothing but the workhouse she's got to look forward to and anything's better'n that.'

Rebecca stared at her. 'But hasn't she got money saved?'

46

'Out of the wages we gets? Be your age, Becky. How could Susan ever save enough to keep her in old age? Oh, I daresay Mr Pagnel might give her a present to leave with, but it ent going to buy her a house, is it? You know what it is for the likes of us – or hev you forgot?'

'No,' Rebecca said slowly, 'I haven't forgotten.'

She saw her friend to the door and returned thoughtfully to the fire. The January days were still short and she drew the curtains against the darkness outside. Daniel came to her knee, begging for a game, and she sang several nursery rhymes with him, but for once her mind was only half on her son. In imagination, she was out in the narrow streets of Kidderminster again, hurrying through the desolate streets to comfort her mother when Will Himley died; struggling back through the bitter storm, with Fanny herself almost at death's door.

Francis had helped her then, as far as he could. But the servants at Pagnel House had been her best support on that terrible day, and she felt the warmth of their care in her heart again. Yes, she must go to see them. She ought to have gone sooner. Why had she put people like Vivian and Maria Pagnel first? Why had she allowed convention to dictate to her?

The door opened and Francis came in. Rebecca looked up, her smile lighting her face. Polly was right – she'd been very lucky, luckier than most. She lifted her face for his kiss.

'Well, it's all arranged.' Francis sat down in the chair opposite her and Daniel immediately climbed into his lap. 'We're to have the house in Unicorn Street. It's a fine house, with good rooms, and it's high up so the air's healthy. And there's a garden for the boys to play in.' He bounced Daniel on his knee and the boy squealed with delight. 'You'll like that, won't you, my son? Grass to run about on and trees to climb. We'll look for birds' nests together. And perhaps have a pond, with frogs in it. Isabel and I used to enjoy keeping tadpoles and watching them turn into frogs.'

Rebecca glanced down, thinking of his cousin, who had died on the very day when Rebecca was dismissed from Pagnel House. But although Francis's voice was sad for a moment, he was soon talking again about the new house, and his pleasure was infectious.

'It really is just what we need, Rebecca. Plenty of room for Mother to have her own sitting room as well as a bedroom, and good kitchen quarters – I know that's important to you. And room for visitors, as well.'

'You mean Tom and Bessie. Francis, do you think they'll ever come?'

'I hope so. I'd like to have Tom working with me again – we make a good team. He understands what I want from my designs. And he's too good to be limited to a two-loom shop. He should be in charge of a full ten- or twelve-loom shop. And if we go into Jacquard—'

'You think you will, then?'

'Oh, certainly. Everyone's just waiting to see what John Broom makes of it and he's almost ready to start.' Francis frowned slightly. 'You know, I'm rather inclined to agree with Vivian over this – we ought to be in the forefront, not playing cautious. Jacquard is such an efficient system, and it's already been proven in the silk industry – it must come to carpets. Father is hanging back too much. As Vivian says, the first in the field are the ones to make the fortunes.'

'And what would he do with his fortune?' Rebecca asked with a touch of bitterness in her voice. 'Spend it on finer furnishing for his own house, on elaborate gowns for Maria. While the weavers would still go as hungry as before – more, because the new machines would put some of them out of work.'

'I don't think so. The Jacquard machines still require a weaver and a draw-boy or girl. But I agree, Vivian would be unlikely to think of raising their wages simply because he was making more money from the new system.'

'He'd be more likely to lower them because the work was easier,' Rebecca observed, and when Francis shook his head she added impatiently, 'Francis, don't let him fool you. He seems to have accepted us now, but is that genuine? I don't trust him.'

'Oh, I think he's genuine enough now,' Francis said easily. 'He shows no sign of that jealousy I used to feel in him – he knows his own position is safe, so why should he be jealous? He has his fine house, his wife who virtually leads Kidderminster society, his position in the business— '

'His five daughters,' Rebecca said quietly, and Francis stopped and stared at her. 'Make no mistake, Francis, as long as you have sons and he doesn't, Vivian will be jealous. Hadn't you realised that?'

'No,' Francis said slowly, 'I must admit, I hadn't looked at it in quite that way. Do you really think— '

'Of course. To feel really safe, Vivian needs to show that the business can be carried on by him and his line. Otherwise your father might still bequeath the business to you, or at least to Daniel. He may have promised to make Vivian his heir – but he never promised what would happen to the property in the next generation. Vivian might find himself holding the business in trust for Daniel – and that wouldn't suit him at all.'

'No, it wouldn't.' Francis stared into the fire, his fingers playing absently with Daniel's hair. 'But surely Father would never do such a thing.'

'He might not,' Rebecca said shrewdly, 'but can Vivian be sure of that?' She looked gravely at her husband. 'Be friendly with Vivian, by all means,' she said. 'But don't ever trust him.'

The next day, Rebecca went to see the house in Unicorn Street. As Francis had said, it was ideal for their needs and she wandered from room to room, picturing how they should be furnished. This one for the drawing room, this for the library – Geoffrey had left Francis all his books – this the boys' nursery. And these rooms would be ideal for Enid, spacious and sunny, looking away from the busy streets and out towards green, quiet fields. She stood at the window, gazing out, looking down into the garden and imagining the boys playing there together.

'It's real nice, innit, ma'am,' Tilly said, clumping across the bare floor to stand beside her. 'I never thought as 'ow I'd ever live anywhere like this.'

'Neither did I,' Rebecca said, thinking of her childhood in the weaver's cottage. 'Yes, it is nice, Tilly. And do you think you'll be happy, sleeping in one of those rooms upstairs?'

'Ooh, ma'am, yes.' The girl's plain face shone with joy. 'Why, it's fit for a real princess, that room is. Mind, it'll seem queer sleeping by meself – I don't know as I'll like that. Be a bit spooky, that will, I reckon.'

Rebecca looked at her. Of course, the little maid would probably never have slept alone in a room – from her big, crowded dormitory at the workhouse she had come straight to share a room with old Sal in the small house Rebecca and Francis had rented in London. And few girls of her age would have had the experience of sleeping alone anyway – London was so crowded that most rooms housed whole families, sometimes even with a stranger or two paying a vital shilling a week to share what little space there was. She thought of the 'homes' she had seen, spaces no more than ten or twelve feet square in which women struggled to care for eight or nine children as well as a husband who might come home wet through and dirty after a day's labouring. There must be many girls like Tilly who would find even such a tiny room as the attic bedroom here frighteningly big and empty without someone to share it.

'Sal will be coming too, I hope,' she said. 'And I daresay we'll engage another maid to help you – there'll be more work here than in London. You can share the room with one of them if you'd rather.'

Tilly said nothing, but ducked her head gratefully and Rebecca reminded herself not to forget what life had been like as a servant. She, more than anyone, ought to be able to imagine how Tilly would feel and what her days would be like. It was useless to criticise the manufacturers' management of their employees if she could not treat her own servants properly.

They left the house and began to walk back towards Church Row. The streets were crowded with women coming off the afternoon shift, their heads and shoulders wrapped in shawls against the icy wind. It was almost dark and the few street lights that had been installed a few years ago gave off a wavering yellow light.

'Here,' Tilly said as they picked their way along the littered and slimy footpath, 'the pavements are a funny colour round here. Sort of dark red. And hard – worse'n London.'

'I know. They call them "petrified kidneys". They say you can tell a Kidderminster man all over the world by the way he walks, after treading on these.' Rebecca caught Tilly's arm to prevent the maid stepping into a mass of decaying rubbish, and turned her ankle on an uneven stone, falling against a woman who was hurrying past. The woman dropped her bundle and it burst open on the kidneys.

'Here, hev a care,' the woman exclaimed. 'That's our dinner yer knocking out of me hands. I can't afford to lose good tatties. You'd better help me pick 'em up before some other body gets a free meal.'

'I'm sorry.' Rebecca bent to gather up the vegetables that had rolled over the ground. 'I slipped – I didn't mean to knock against you. Here – I think this was all, wasn't it? Or were there more?'

51

'I dunno, do I? Can't hardly see a thing in this light,' the woman began grumblingly, and then she stopped and lifted her face sideways, peering at Rebecca with half-closed eyes. 'Here, I know you, don't I? Ent you Becky Himley?'

'I was, yes.' Rebecca stared at her. It was difficult to tell what age the woman might be – like so many others, she could have been anything between twenty-five and forty. But surely those dark curls were familiar, and those black eyes? Rebecca imagined them suddenly with a saucy look in them, the kind of sauciness her sister Bessie had had once. And suddenly she knew.

'Nell! You're Nell Foster – Bessie's friend. You used to work with her.'

'That's right. Started in Butts' loom shop we did, same day. I'd bin with Broom's till then but me Dad thought Butts'd treat me better. Some hopes!' She laughed shortly. 'Ent no one treats draw-girls proper – well, your sis found that out, di'n't she?' She peered into Rebecca's face again. 'How is she, your Bess? They say she went to London and wed some fancy gent.'

'She went to London, yes, but she never married.' Rebecca thought of what Bessie had actually become. 'She's a milliner now – has her own little shop.'

Nell pursed her mouth in a whistle. 'Whew! Well, she done all right then, di'n't she? Milliner, eh? Bet she sells some fancy bonnets up there in London.'

Again, Rebecca thought of Bessie, working in her dark little room behind the tiny shop. There was little fancy work about the hats she made; mostly she and Nancy stitched at caps for housemaids or plain bonnets for women who could only just afford the cheapest of new clothes. But she was at least earning money in an open, honest fashion, with no shame attached to it.

'What about you, Nell? Do you still work in the loom shop, or have you a family?'

Nell's mouth twisted cynically. 'You mean there's a choice? Usually both, innit? Work to feed a family – or hev you forgot?'

'No, I haven't forgotten. So you have a family?'

'Three boys,' Nell said with pride in her voice. 'And scallywags, the lot of 'em. But the oldest'll be drawing in a year, so that'll help a bit. Not but what there'll most likely be another along afore then,' she added resignedly. 'But look – I got to get home. God knows what the little devils'll be up to by now, wanting their suppers and all. Give me respec's to Bess when you sees her again.'

She turned away and would have vanished into the darkness, but Rebecca caught at her arm.

'Don't go, Nell. At least tell me where you live – and what your name is now. I'd like to come and see you – Bessie would want me to do that, I know.'

Nell stared at her, then gave that short laugh again. '*You* come and see me? You'm a lady now, ent yer? You wouldn't want to dirty yer fine clothes coming round my place. And my name's same's it was before – Foster. It costs money to get wed, and me and my Bill ent never had enough to spare after we've fed ourselves and the little 'uns.'

'Well, I'd like to come and see you, all the same,' Rebecca persisted, and Nell shrugged and gave her address.

'You won't find no fancy chairs to sit on, mind,' she warned. 'But there, you oughter know all about that, coming from a weaver's cottage yourself. That's if you can remember that far back.'

'I remember very well,' Rebecca said quietly, and let go of the skinny arm. 'I'll come to see you soon, Nell.' But as she watched the woman vanish into the darkness of the narrow lane, she knew that Nell hadn't believed her. And she wondered just how many other people had let her down, to make her so untrusting.

But what reason did any of the weavers, or indeed

any worker in Kidderminster, have to trust those who lived on the profits of their labour? Even a just employer like Jeremiah Pagnel paid wages that barely kept most of his workers above subsistence level. And to those who pointed out the injustices of the system, there was always one answer, the answer Vivian always gave.

'They wouldn't benefit from higher wages if we did pay them. They'd simply drink or gamble the money away and be as poor as ever. The money's better off in our pockets, where it can be spent wisely to build new houses or better roads.'

But as Rebecca and Tilly went on through the littered streets, passing the mean hovels where so many of the workers lived, she could not help wondering just how much of the money was being spent so; and comparing it with the comfort and luxury of the homes of those into whose pockets the profits went.

Homes like that of Vivian and Maria, who lacked nothing. Except the son that money could not buy.

'Do come in.' Maria lifted a languid hand for Rebecca and Francis to take, making no effort to rise from the couch where she half sat, half lay against the cushions. 'It's so pleasant to see you, Francis.' Her eyes moved briefly to Rebecca. 'Vivian's delighted that you've decided to settle in Kidderminster.'

'I'm glad,' Francis said politely, but Rebecca could tell from his wooden tone that he was angered by Maria's coolness. 'It wasn't an easy decision to make.'

'No, indeed. Vivian quite envied you your life in London.' At last, Maria turned to Rebecca. 'And are you happy to be settling in Kidderminster again? It's all rather different for you here now, isn't it?'

Different from being a maidservant, you mean, Rebecca thought, but she smiled and said aloud, 'It's not so very different. A few new streets, some houses – but it's not much over two years or so since I was here, so there hasn't been time for very much change.'

'Only two years? It seems longer. But of course, your little boy is almost three, isn't he?'

Maria's glance was sly, reminding them all of the circumstances of Daniel's birth. But Rebecca had already decided not to allow Vivian's wife to goad her. She smiled and answered readily, as if the inquiry were no more than any friendly remark.

'Daniel will be three next week. They grow so fast, don't they? And how are your little girls?'

Maria's expression tightened and she glanced at Vivian, as if hoping that he had not marked the implication in Rebecca's remark. But Vivian's face was dark, and Rebecca realised that his lack of sons, especially when compared with the two healthy boys she and Francis had produced, was a sorer point than she had understood. She felt suddenly sorry for Maria and wished she hadn't spoken so pointedly.

'I'd love to see them,' she added quickly. 'I suppose they're all in bed now. Do you think . . . ?'

'Oh, I think that would be rather inconvenient to Nanny,' Maria said quickly. 'She has her routine, you know, and I don't like to interfere.'

'It would hardly interfere with her routine if the girls are all in bed,' Vivian said smoothly. 'Why don't you take Rebecca to see them? I'm sure she'd be interested in the nursery too. You'll be needing to plan your own, won't you,' he added, turning to Rebecca, 'and you couldn't find anyone better to help you than my wife. She thinks of little else but decorating the house.'

His eyes rested on Rebecca and she moved a little uncomfortably. She found herself growing more and more uneasy in Vivian's company. His dark gaze reminded her of the day when he had caught her in the warehouse, of the day in the library. She had been only a maidservant then, fair game for the son of the house, and had had cause to be wary. But now . . . Surely as his cousin's wife, Vivian would put away the memory of those days and treat her as he would any other woman in his family.

Surely he would. But Rebecca was still uneasy.

'I really would like to see your children,' she said to Maria. 'And the nursery too. Vivian's quite right – I shall need help in planning our own home.'

Maria shrugged as if the matter were of little concern to her. 'Very well. I suppose there's just time before dinner.' She rose from the couch and led Rebecca from the room and up the stairs to the nursery on the second floor. As they went, Rebecca noticed the luxury of the house. Vivian and Maria had certainly spared no expense in furnishing their home. The walls glowed with colour, dark reds and golds which were repeated in the heavy hangings over each door. The ceilings were rich with ornate plasterwork, and the floors were covered with thick carpets.

All bought from the money earned by weavers, spinners and dyers, she thought, and wondered what Nell Foster would think of such surroundings. She had not yet been to visit Nell, but she could imagine with ease the conditions in which the family lived. And she knew that any one of these carpets, any of the paintings that hung on the walls, any of the heavy tables or chests or overstuffed armchairs, would have kept the weaver and his children in comfort for a year or more.

'Of course, there's still a good deal needs to be done,' Maria said carelessly as they mounted the stairs. 'I'm not really happy with the drawing room. And the fashion for the dining chairs and table we have is past now. I want Vivian to buy new ones, but he's rather obstinate about spending money. You know what men are!'

She laughed, a little high-pitched laugh as if inviting Rebecca to commiserate with her troubles. But Rebecca said nothing. Her distaste for the richness of her surroundings grew. She looked at the gleaming wood and thought of the labour of polishing it, she looked at the curtains and carpets and thought of the sweeping. She looked up the wide stairs and thought of the narrow ones somewhere at the back of the house, where maids scurried unseen by the Family, toiling from dawn until midnight in their efforts to get through all their work, falling exhausted into bed for a few hours' sleep before starting all over again.

'Here we are,' Maria said as they came to a second landing. Here, the furnishings were less opulent, the floor uncarpeted. Maria opened a door and led Rebecca into the nursery where a stout middle-aged woman sat sewing by a fire.

'It's all right, Nanny,' Maria said carelessly as the woman dropped her sewing and jumped up. 'There's nothing wrong. I simply brought Mrs Pagnel – Mrs Francis, that is – to see the children. They're all asleep, I hope?'

'Oh yes, madam. Fast asleep this past hour. I always make sure they keep to their routine, as you know, madam. Though the little one's restless, cutting teeth, she hasn't had a good night's sleep this past week, poor mite.'

'Well, I hope you're not giving in to her, Nanny,' Maria said sharply. 'You know the master's views on that. Children must learn that they can't be attended to every time they demand it.'

'I think I know how to impose discipline in my own nursery, madam,' Nanny said, with a slight edge to her respectful tone. 'I've never had any complaints yet.'

'No, of course not,' Maria said hastily. 'Come in, Rebecca.' She opened the door into the night nursery.

Rebecca followed her inside, Nanny hovering behind them. The night nursery was in fact two rooms, each furnished with two small beds, and the girls lay fast asleep, as Nanny had promised. Two of them dark, like Vivian, two brown-haired like their mother. Rebecca looked at them.

'They're beautiful girls,' she said sincerely. 'Which is the eldest?'

Maria moved to the head of one of the beds and touched the dark curls with gentle fingers.

'Anna. She's eight years old now, a big girl. Susan's six and a half. Lucy's four and a little madam, isn't she, Nanny? Mary's three and little Margaret – she still has her cot in Nanny's room – is just over a year.' She stood looking down at the small faces, and Rebecca saw the love in her eyes, mixed with some darker emotion. Regret that they were all girls? Fears for their future? She felt a sudden sadness herself, and a resurgence of the pity she had felt for Maria. It could not be easy, being married to Vivian.

'Maria,' she said on a sudden impulse, as they stood looking at the baby Margaret in her cot, 'I know you must want a son – but these are such lovely girls, you can't regret having any one of them. And they're all so healthy too – you must thank God every day for their health.'

Maria looked at her, startled, and for a moment Rebecca thought that she had offended her. But after the first moment, an expression of cautious gratitude showed in her eyes, and after a hesitation, almost shyly, she held out her hand. Rebecca put hers into it, and they stood for a moment linked across the cot.

'I don't know what I would do if anything happened to any of them,' Maria said in a low voice. 'But Vivian . . .'

She did not finish, but Rebecca thought she understood. Vivian wanted a son – and each daughter had come as a bigger disappointment. And he would not be Vivian if he didn't blame his wife for it.

Maria stood looking down at the sleeping baby. Then she touched the rosy face, as she had touched each of the others, and straightened up.

'We'd better go back now. Vivian will be impatient

if we're not in the drawing room when dinner is announced.'

They went back down the stairs, descending from the plain homeliness of the nursery to the ostentation of the lower rooms, and as they went Rebecca felt the change in Maria. The soft motherliness disappeared and the hard brilliance returned. By the time they were back in the drawing room, she was as cool as when they had first left it.

Francis and Vivian were lounging in armchairs and rose as the two women came in. There was a slight air of tension in the room and Rebecca glanced quickly at her husband. She saw the touch of whiteness about his jaw and knew that he was annoyed. Vivian, however, was smiling his usual urbane smile and his voice was smooth as he addressed his wife.

'And how are the girls? I hope Nanny gave a good report of their behaviour.'

'They're all asleep and Nanny seems pleased with them.' Maria glanced at the grandfather clock, ticking slowly in the corner. 'I think I should go and make sure the dinner's— '

'There's no need for that. Sibley will announce dinner exactly on time, as he always does.' Vivian's eyes glittered a little as he looked at his wife and Rebecca wished she could think of something to say that would divert his attention. She was feeling more and more sorry for Maria. She remembered the cruel grip of Vivian's fingers on her arms and glanced involuntarily at Maria's wrists, but they were hidden by lace frills. Surely he would not . . .

The door opened and the butler came in and announced that dinner was served. Vivian turned to Rebecca, a different glint now in his eyes, and held out his arm. Reluctantly, she laid her fingers on his sleeve. She knew he was mocking her, reminding her that he too remembered the days when she was a maidservant in his mother's house. But there was nothing she could do about it. And the fact that she was here, going in to dinner on his arm, sitting at his table, must surely be more annoying to him than any subtle mockery could be to her.

'Francis has been telling me about his dreams for paradise here in Kidderminster,' Vivian remarked as they seated themselves and Sibley began to serve them with the first course. 'I daresay you share them, Rebecca.'

'I share his dreams and plans, certainly.' She ate coolly, knowing that he and Maria were both watching to see that she used the right cutlery, and smiled at the irony of it; hadn't she laid the table many times for just such a dinner-party, didn't she know exactly which cutlery should be used? 'I haven't heard him mention paradise.'

Vivian laughed. 'Well, that's what you're talking about, isn't it, the pair of you? Co-operatives, with the workers sharing in the profits? Paradise for them, that is – I doubt if you'd think it paradise, Francis, living in a weaver's cottage while they live like kings. Though I can understand the idea being attractive to Rebecca.'

Rebecca felt a small flare of anger. She glanced at Francis and saw the whiteness around his jaw again. He laid down his knife and fork.

'I don't know quite what you mean by that, Vivian.'

'Why, only that she would naturally want the people she grew up with to be more comfortable. They were her friends, after all – and even though they can be no longer, she must still— '

'Why can they be no longer my friends?' Rebecca's voice cut across his words and Vivian looked at her in surprise, as if she should not have spoken. He spoke impatiently.

'Well, that's obvious, surely. You've moved out of their class. It would be quite unfitting to try to remain

friends with the kind of people you knew then –
wouldn't it, Maria?'

'Quite unfitting,' Maria said.

'Well, I'm afraid I can't agree with that,' Rebecca
said quietly. 'My friends are my friends, whichever
their class. I've already had Polly to visit me— '

'Polly? You mean my mother's maid?'

'Of course. And I shall visit her and my friends in
your father's kitchen. They were kind to me and I
consider them my family. And I shall visit Nell
Foster— '

'Who?' Vivian looked baffled. 'Who in the name of
heaven is Nell Foster?'

'She's the wife of one of your weavers. Well, not the
wife exactly – but they have three children and— '

'You mean they're not married? They have *three
children* and they're not married?' Maria looked as if
she were about to faint. 'Rebecca, you can't be serious
about consorting with such people. Francis, tell her.
You must remember your position now – you're the
wife of a member of one of the most important families
in Kidderminster. You can't bring shame on us by
going about hobnobbing with the lower orders. It
simply isn't done.'

Rebecca looked at her. The moment of closeness
they had shared in the nursery seemed never to have
been. Maria's colour had returned, bringing a flush to
her cheeks that reminded Rebecca of Isabella Pagnel
in one of her rages. But Maria would not give way to
rage. Vivian would never allow it.

'I'm sorry if it upsets you,' Rebecca said. 'But these
people – the lower orders, as you call them – are the
people I grew up with. They're my friends. I can't
abandon them. I won't.'

'And so, presumably,' Vivian said with a hard note
in his voice, 'it's through your encouragement that
Francis has begun to develop these wild ideas. Or are
they your ideas in the first place?'

'They're not Rebecca's ideas,' Francis said. 'But we've talked about them and we're in complete agreement. Vivian, at some point things have changed. Weaver and manufacturer used to live side by side, each in a similar kind of home. Now the manufacturers are rich and powerful, the weavers poor. Yet they work as hard as it's possible to work. Why don't they have a better standard of living? There's something wrong. It can't be just.'

'And what weaver could do what I do, what you do?' Vivian demanded contemptuously. 'What weaver would be able to find buyers for the carpets, arrange delivery, transport, do all the work that's necessary to sell his product? What weaver could even design the carpet he weaves? His job is only a small part of the ultimate production. Why should he be paid more than he is?'

Rebecca felt helpless. There was a flaw in Vivian's argument but he was so articulate that she could not voice it. Then she found the words, but before she could speak Francis had said them for her.

'Because everyone should have a living wage,' he said firmly. 'Because every man should be paid enough to support his family, and not just to keep them from starvation with a roof of sorts over their heads – no, to keep them in a decent home, properly clothed and fed, even educated– '

'*Educated?*' Vivian let out a shout of angry laughter. 'Why, you'll be having them in Parliament next!'

'It will be a long time before that comes about,' Francis said, 'but I'm afraid there will never be real justice until it does.'

'We angered Vivian tonight,' Rebecca said as she and Francis made ready for bed later that night. 'I'm sorry – I'd hoped we could all be friends. And it might make things difficult for you, both working with your father.'

Francis shrugged. 'Vivian has never really liked me.

62

It makes no difference that he likes me less now. We shall have to learn to work together, but it won't ever be easy, thinking the way we do and so differently.'

'He hates your ideas. He'll never agree to the idea of a co-operative.'

'I know. But neither can he be too openly hostile.' Francis sat on the bed to unfasten his boots. 'He can't be sure of my position with my father – or his own. He's jealous, but he's also afraid.' He glanced up at her. 'Does he worry you, my love? There's an odd look in his eyes sometimes when he looks at you.'

'He can't forget I was a maidservant.' Rebecca laid her dress over a chair and came to him, wearing only her shift. She stood before him and placed her hands on his shoulders. 'Francis, you must know what Vivian is – what he has been ever since he was not much more than a boy. Any young maid— '

'He never touched you!' Francis started to rise but she pressed him back on the bed. 'Rebecca— '

'He never had his way with me,' she said quietly. 'But he wouldn't be Vivian if he hadn't thought of it. It's all right – I never gave him the chance.' Seeing Francis's anger, she decided it would be better not to mention those two occasions on which Vivian had trapped her alone. 'And now he can't forget that. But he won't take advantage now – he has too much sense.'

'He'd better not,' Francis muttered. He slid his fingers up Rebecca's arms and she felt the familiar thrill. She sank down on to his lap and he held her close against him, his fingertips moving gently over her skin. 'Rebecca, if I ever thought . . . I'd kill him if he ever . . .'

'He won't,' she whispered, and nestled close against his firm body. 'Francis, you know there's no other man for me but you. Vivian's just *like* that. And maybe he's angry because I preferred you. Which I did, and do, and always, always shall.'

Francis put his fingers under her chin and turned her

face up to his. He bent his head and laid his lips tenderly on hers. His kiss was gentle, as soft as a breeze; but as Rebecca returned it she felt his lips harden and a sudden excitement tingled through her limbs and into her body. She pressed herself closer against him, wound her arms around his neck and let her lips part.

'Don't let's talk about Vivian any more,' she whispered when Francis released her mouth at last. 'He's not important to us.'

Francis leaned back a little and looked down into her eyes. His fingers were unfastening her bodice, their movements quick and unfumbling. He smiled slowly and her heart trembled.

'Vivian?' he murmured, and his hand slipped inside the smooth fabric to cover her breast. 'Who's Vivian?'

Chapter Four

Bess set her last stitch into the bonnet she was making, snipped off the thread and sat back, moving her aching shoulders with a sigh. It was almost dark in the little workroom and oppressively stuffy. She rubbed a weary hand across her face.

'You're looking tired out, Bess,' Nancy said, looking up from her own work. 'Can't you stop now? I can finish this cap and the rest can wait for tomorrow.'

Bess leaned her elbows on the bench and rested her head on her hands.

'I dunno, Nance. Maybe I can. But I promised those caps for Tuesday and if they aren't finished I'll lose the order. And Mrs Fowler's a good customer— '

'We can get 'em done by Tuesday.' Nancy ran a ribbon round the parlourmaid's cap she was sewing and began to stitch rapidly. 'Look, I can do a couple of extra hours in the evening, Dad won't mind if I'm not there, he sleeps most of the time anyway. Just so long as he gets his dinner.'

'And what about our Tom? Don't he like a bit of company?'

Nancy grinned, her dark eyes suddenly mischievous. 'Course he does – but it won't do him no harm to go without for a bit. Men has to learn they can't have everything their own way, and he must see you're tired to death too.' She eyed Bessie with concern. 'What is it, Bess? That old trouble?'

'I suppose so. I just feel hot, like I've got a fever, and I gets this rash and sore throat. It isn't nothing, Nance, it passes after a couple of days, but I allow I do feel bad while it's on me.'

'And ain't none of those potions done no good?'

Bessie shook her head. 'I don't reckon there's anything in 'em to do good, Nance. Just money down the gutter, if you asks me. I shan't waste no more of my pence on 'em, that's for certain. It always goes off after a bit anyway.'

Nancy nodded, but her eyes were troubled. She stitched for a few minutes in silence, while Bessie closed her eyes. Then she said quietly, 'Don't you think it'd be better, Bess, if you and Tom went back to Kidderminster?'

Bessie opened her eyes. 'Nance, we've talked about that — '

'I know you have. Over and over again. But it's not doing you no good here in London, Bess. You're always sickly these days. I dunno what it is, the air or the damp or what, but something here don't suit you. Nor don't it suit Tom. He and Dad – they're working all day at those looms, they're making lovely carpets and rugs, but they both look weary to death and Tom's worried besides. I'm sure he's hankering to go back.'

'We was all right here,' Bessie muttered. 'We was getting along all right till that Mr Pagnel come and took Francis and our Becky back to Kidder. We could have made a good life for ourselves, the lot of us. Now it's all spoilt.'

'But you could have a good life in Kidderminster too,' Nancy said gently.

Bessie shrugged, almost as if she didn't want to be bothered. 'Perhaps. But we aren't never likely to know that, are we? We can't go back to Kidderminster, and Tom and me both knows it. So it don't matter if it's the air or the damp or the stars in the sky that don't suit me in London, I'm going to have to stick with 'em. And that's all there is to it.'

She picked up the bonnet she had been making and set it on the shelf with a row of others, all stitched that day by herself and Nancy. And then she stood and looked at them.

'A milliner!' she said bitterly. 'That's what I thought I'd be. Making fine hats for fine ladies – and here I am, slaving harder than ever, stitching bonnets for old women and caps for housemaids. No, Nance, it don't matter whether you're in London or Kidderminster, when you're folks like us it's just hard work and more hard work, and that's life and we might as well face up to it.'

It must have been at almost the same moment when Tom, too, stretched his aching back and stood back from his loom, looking with satisfaction at the carpet he and Samuel had just finished.

Reaching out, he fingered the glowing colours, feeling the softness of the wool and imagining it beneath the feet of some fine gentleman or lady. Would they ever give a thought to Francis, who had designed the pattern, to the weavers who had set up the loom and sat for hour upon hour creating it? He doubted it, but at this moment it hardly mattered. It was his carpet, his and Samuel's, just for a while.

'Reckon this is the best we've ever made,' he observed as Samuel brushed a few strands of wool from the carpet. 'And finished well before time, too. We're doing well.'

'It's a nice bit of work,' Samuel allowed, coming to stand beside him. 'But I dunno, I can't see why people has to put carpets on their floors. What's wrong with a bit of rag rug like my old woman used ter make? Just as good and don't cost half as much.' He shook his head and Tom grinned. It had always amused him that Samuel could weave such fine carpets without ever appearing to appreciate their beauty. Clearly, however, it did not matter; he knew good workmanship and took a pride in it. Whereas for Tom, it was the production of something attractive as well as functional that made weaving such a satisfying job.

They packed up and went out of the loom shop,

locking the door carefully, then climbed the narrow wooden stairs to the rooms where Samuel lived with his daughter. Samuel went to the cupboard and took out the jug of ale he always kept there for the end of the day and filled two tankards.

'Well, that's another job done. You can deliver that tomorrow, can you? And I'll get the wools sorted out for those other rugs we got to do.'

Tom nodded. He drank deeply from his tankard, then wiped his mouth with the back of one hand. He watched as the older man moved slowly about the small room and saw suddenly how much Samuel had aged since they had begun making carpets together. He was peering more closely at the small jobs he did too, rubbing his eyes as if to clear them of a mist. And the hand he lifted to rub his face was shaking slightly.

He's getting old, Tom thought. How long is he going to be able to manage, working the hours we work, labouring as we do?

A sound on the stair made him turn and he felt his heart lift as the door opened and Samuel's daughter came in. As always, her hazel eyes went straight to Tom and her mouth broke into the wide smile that she always gave him. He grinned back, feeling suddenly happy, and stretched out a hand towards her.

Nancy came over and put her hand in his. He felt the roughness of her fingers, pricked over and over again by the needle, rub against the skin of his palm, and he lifted them against his cheek. She gave him a swift smile and then turned to her father.

'What are you doing now, Dad? You sit down and rest, you bin working all day. I'll get us some supper in a minute – I got a nice pie at the market on me way home.' She looked at Tom. 'Finished that carpet yet?'

'We hev.' He spoke with deep satisfaction. 'And what's more, we both reckon it's the best work we ever done. Could bring us in a good few more orders when the gentry see it. We want a few more designs like that, only I don't know as how we'd ever get time to make 'em.'

'Well, ain't we bin talking about another loom, maybe two or three?' Samuel said. He settled into the old chair where he would spend most of the evening, eating the supper that Nancy prepared and then dozing until bedtime. 'Reckon we could start to think about that now. Maybe you could write a letter to Mr Francis, Tom, and jog his memory a bit. Don't want him to forget about us now he's back in Kidderminster.'

'Letter!' Nancy's hand flew to her mouth. 'If I didn't almost ferget! There's one for you over your place, Tom, come from Kidderminster, and your Bess waiting for you to go an' read it. She's certain sure it's bad news so you better get back there an' find out straightaway. Come just after we stopped work, it did.'

'A letter?' Tom jumped up. 'But why does she think it's bad news?'

'Oh, you know Bess, she's always expecting bad news out of Kidderminster. An' she ain't feeling so good today, neither. That old trouble, touch of fever or summat.' Nancy hesitated. 'If it weren't for that, I'd ask you to come back an' tell us what it is – but I don't think you ought to leave Bess if it is bad news.'

'Go along of him,' Samuel said. 'I can wait for me supper.'

Nancy stood irresolute, and her father flapped a wrinkled hand at her. 'Go on, girl. I ain't a baby. I'd just as soon have a bit of a rest first anyway.'

'Come on, Nancy,' Tom urged. 'Then you won't hev to worry. I don't expect it's bad news anyway, so no sense in fretting. You can be back here in half an hour and tell your Dad.'

'All right.' She picked up a shawl and followed him down the stairs. 'I just don't like leaving Dad too much these days, he looks so tired.'

'He's getting old,' Tom said soberly. 'I was thinking

it just now. I dunno how long he'll be able to go on working, Nance.'

'It'll break his heart if he has to stop. And what would he live on? His savings ain't much – he was out of work too long before you come along. I don't see as how I could bring in much more neither.'

'Well, it needn't happen yet. He can still weave a good carpet. And we're not going to let your Dad starve, Nance. We'll manage somehow.' He stopped and looked down at her. 'Matter of fact, I bin thinking – it's time we got summat sorted out.'

'Sorted out? About Dad, you mean?'

'No, not your Dad,' Tom said quietly. 'You an' me. We're fond of each other, ent we? More'n fond, I reckon. It's time we thought about getting wed, Nancy.'

Nancy's face was lifted towards him. He saw her sudden blush, the widening of her eyes, the parting of her lips. Instinctively, he bent towards her, taking her face between his palms, and brushed his mouth against hers. He felt the tremble of her lips and excitement beat through his body; his kiss deepened and he slid his arms around her body, holding her tightly, feeling the soft shape of her against him.

'Nancy,' he muttered, and ran one hand up the length of her back until his fingers tangled in her hair. 'Nancy, we will get wed, won't we? Soon?' She did not reply immediately and he added with sudden anxiety: 'You do want us to get wed, don't you, Nance?'

She giggled, her breasts quivering against him, and he felt again the surge of excitement. 'Course I do, Tom. It's just – I hadn't expected to be asked, not like this in the middle of the street. Maybe I hadn't expected to be asked at all, in a way. I thought it'd just sort of happen.'

Tom grinned. 'Somebody'd have to say summat, Nance. It don't happen without. But you ent saying no?' He looked at the bright hazel eyes, at the mouth that so often trembled with laughter and was now reddened by his kisses. And he felt a sudden emotion that was more than the desire of a man for a woman's body, more than the affection of a friend. 'Don't say no, Nance,' he said with an intensity that shook his heart. 'Say you'll marry me.'

Nancy smiled at him, and the smile seemed to come straight from her heart and find its way directly to his. 'Of course I'll marry you, Tom,' she said softly. 'But we better stop kissing like this, in the street. We're getting in people's way.'

Tom chuckled and tucked her hand into his arm as they walked on. He felt extraordinarily light-hearted, as if the sun had come out after a month of cold, wet days. He felt curiously strong, as if his body had been given new and better muscles, as if he were able now to face any situation and master it. He felt that the world lay at his feet.

'We'll make a good life, Nancy,' he said. 'You an' me – we belong together. We'll do well.'

'I reckon so too, Tom,' she answered, 'but we got a lot of things to think about. Like whether you're going to go back to Kidderminster or not.'

'Kidderminster?' He stopped and stared at her. 'But I can't go back, Nance, you know that. I told you about the weaver Bess and me— '

'I know, Tom, you don't have to say nothing about that. But Francis and Rebecca are back there, and on good terms with Mr Pagnel, from what they say. Can't they do nothing? Look, it's a long time ago, it was never your fault anyway, and I know you're hankering to go back anyway. I was sayin' so to your Bess only this afternoon – Tom, I reckon she oughter go back too, she's looking real poorly again lately. Are you sure there's no chance?'

Tom shook his head glumly. 'Can't see it, Nance. But let's get home and see what's in that letter. Maybe that'll have some news.'

The air was beginning to cool a little as they hurried the last few yards to the house where Tom and Bessie had rooms, close to the home Rebecca and Francis had shared when they had first married. Tom went in first and Bessie, who had been dozing in a chair by the open window, jumped up. Her face was drawn and Tom looked at her anxiously, remembering Nancy's words. Was she really looking ill, or was it just the heat?

'Oh, Tom – there you are. There's a letter come—'

'I know, Nancy told me.' He took the packet nervously. You never knew what a letter might contain; good news or bad, there was no way of telling from the outside. He turned it over in his hands while Bessie watched with an anxiety that matched his own, and they looked at each other uncertainly.

'For goodness' sake!' Nancy exclaimed. 'Open it, can't you? It ain't going to bite you. Here, give it to me if you're afraid you're going to spoil it.'

'No, it's all right.' Tom tore it open with clumsy fingers and unfolded the sheet of paper inside. He frowned at it, trying to decipher Francis's handwriting. He had learned to read long ago, as a child, but had had little practice for many years and it always took a moment or two to familiarise himself with the letters.

'Well? What does he say?' Bessie demanded. 'Is our Becky all right? When are they coming back?'

'They're not coming back. They told us that months ago, back when Geoffrey Pagnel died.' Tom scanned the page. 'They're well enough. They're talking about installing Jacquard looms – Mr Broom's put 'em in and Francis thinks everyone will be wanting to use 'em now. Our Becky's in the family way again. Oh, and—'

'Becky expecting?' Bessie broke in before he could continue. 'But little Geoff's scarce nine months old. How'd she manage to fall so quick, she was feeding him, wasn't she?'

'Oh, that don't always work, though,' Nancy

said knowledgeably. 'My cousin fell time and again, feeding or not. Some women it don't seem to have any effect— '

'Do you two mind not chattering?' Tom asked, and they both turned in surprise. 'I ent finished reading this letter yet. Do you want to hear what it says, or don't you?'

'Well, what else do it say then?' Bess asked impatiently. 'Surely that's what Francis wrote to tell us, that Becky's expecting? What more can there be?'

'Just be quiet a minute and I'll tell you.' Tom's voice was shaking. The two girls looked at him, then at each other, and Nancy moved to lay her hand on his arm.

'Tell us what it is, Tom. It's summat important, ain't it?'

'It could be. I dunno. Yes, I think it is.' He read the page again, his lips moving with the words. 'It could all come to naught, Francis says. But old Mr Jeremiah's bin asking after you an' me, Bess. He's bin asking a few more questions about what really did happen that night we run away. It looks as if we might be able to go back to Kidder – that's if we wants to.' He laid the sheet of paper on the table and looked at his sister with sober eyes. 'What do you say to that, then, Bess? Do you fancy going back to Kidder – or are you too settled here in London now? It's for you to say.'

Nancy gave Tom a last kiss, then turned and went up the stairs. Her mind, already busy, turned to thoughts of her father's supper. She must give him that before bothering him with anything else. He'd waited long enough, and he was an old man.

'Hullo, Nance.' He was still in his chair, blinking as if he'd been asleep. ''Ere, I must've dozed off for a bit. You bin to Tom's? Not bad news, I 'ope?'

'No, not bad news, Dad.' She went to the cupboard where she kept their food and the few bits of crockery they possessed. 'Look, I brought in a pie for your supper, smells real good too. Here, you get tucked in while it's hot.' She laid the pie on a plate and took it across to him. 'I'll pour you a drop more ale to wash it down.'

Samuel began to munch the pie, making appreciative noises, and Nancy fiddled with a piece of bread and cheese. She glanced at him once or twice, opened her mouth to speak, then thought better of it. Best to let him eat in peace. There'd be time enough for talking afterwards.

The bread tasted dry and the cheese was like soap. Nancy tried to force it down but, hungry though she was, it had little interest for her. Eventually she gave up and left it on her plate, gazing out of the dusty window at roofs and chimney-pots she barely saw, her mind far away.

It seemed a long time since she and her father had come to this street and begun working with Tom and Bessie Himley. Times had been hard for them before that; Samuel, who had worked all his life in the silk weaving shops at Bethnal Green, had lost his job when his employer had died leaving a mountain of debts. The new owner had dismissed all the old workers and brought in younger men and Samuel, along with the mates he had grown up with, had found himself on the street and penniless.

If it hadn't been for Nancy, he would have died in the gutter, but she had taken him into the tiny room she lived in and stretched her own earnings to feed him too. Working from dawn until well into the night as a seamstress, she had seen little of her father, but he had been there when eventually she did creep home, her fingers often raw from the needle, her eyes aching from the close work in poor light. And she had been grateful for his company, for someone of her own.

All the same, her earnings had never been enough to keep them in any but the poorest circumstances, and it had seemed like a miracle when Samuel told her one night that he'd met a young man in the tavern, and been offered a job.

'A job?' Nancy had looked at him dubiously. Was he growing senile at last? 'What sort of job, Dad?'

'Weaving, o' course – what else would anyone arst me to do?' He cackled a little. 'Mind, it ain't silk-weaving but I can soon get in the way of it. Weaving's weaving, when all's said and done, and there weren't none quicker to learn than Sam Clay, no, nor no better worker neither. You wait, Nance, we're on the up and up again, just see if we ain't. Soon be able to buy ourselves a pie for supper when we wants one, an' a sup of ale to go with it too.' He clamped toothless gums together and beamed with satisfaction.

Nancy remembered the doubt she had felt. She had heard tales of wealth before and all had come to nothing. There had been the piestall her father was going to run with a man he'd met in the street, the jellied eels he'd been going to make his fortune with, the old boots he was going to sell from their own damp cellar. None had done anything but cost them money they could ill afford, so that they had gone hungrier than ever and the boots Samuel himself so desperately needed had been sold to pay their rent. At least it had kept him out of the streets and the tavern, and out of trouble; but it had been bitterly sad to think of her father caged like an animal in a zoo, unable to go out because the streets were too icy for old, bare feet.

'So what sort of weaving is it, if it ain't silk?' she asked.

'Carpets. This young feller I met, he's in with another cove what's setting up a carpet-weaving business. They wants a good experienced weaver to take it on, see, and I reckon Sam Clay's just the geezer to do it. And young Tom— '

'Tom?'

'This feller I'm telling yer about. Tom Himley, his name is – he's bin in London a while, picking up odd jobs, but he was a half-weaver in Kidderminster and this other cove, the one with a bit of money, he comes from there too. Pagnel, his name is and that's a big name in carpets.'

'But he's not from Pagnel's, not the big Pagnel's?' Nancy was feeling dazed by this recital. 'He can't be, Dad, not setting up a business with two weavers. Look, you sure he's all right? You don't want to get caught by some fly cove who'll work you to death and then flit. It sounds funny to me.'

Samuel shook his head. 'I knowed you'd say that, girl, but he's on the square, I'd stake me word on that. Tell yer what I reckon— ' he leaned a little closer, as if afraid of being overheard ' —I reckon he's what they call the black sheep of the fam'ly – see? Bin shipped off with a few bob, enough to set up something small, and he's decided to get back into the business he bin brought up in. And why not? He knows it, girl, I've talked to him and I can tell that. Both of 'em knows what they're doing. No, I reckon I'd be a fool to let this chance go by. We might not make our fortins, girl, but we can make a living. And I'll be weaving again.'

Nancy had let it go then, unwilling to deny her father his excitement over being once again a working weaver. But she had still been uneasy about it. And even when she met Tom Himley, she had been reluctant at first to respond to his apparent sincerity.

'It all seems a bit too good to be true,' she remarked as she looked around the rooms they had rented to set up the looms. 'Why my Dad? Don't you want a younger man?'

'We want an experienced man,' Tom said, looking down at her. His eyes were steady in his thin face. He looked as if he'd been through hard times too, she thought, and wondered why he had come to London, why he hadn't himself been working in the weaving trade. 'And we want someone who's willing to work hard. We can take on the younger men later, and your

Dad will help train them. We're going to expand – we aren't going to stay small.'

Nancy pursed her lips. 'Plenty of folk starts off thinking that. How do we know you won't be the same? Big talk don't allus mean big profits.'

Tom shrugged. 'That'll be up to us, won't it? Me, your Dad, and Francis Pagnel. We mean to make a success of it and I don't see why we shouldn't – with a little bit of luck.'

'Ah,' Nancy said, 'luck. That's what we all needs and what precious few of us gets.'

But the little business had thrived, in spite of her doubts, and she knew now that its success had been due to the combination of Francis Pagnel's designing ability, Tom Himley's business sense and her father's expertise at the job he'd grown up with. And while the men had been working hard to build it up, she had met Bess and joined her in the tiny millinery business she had started.

'Not that you'd really call it millinery,' Bessie had said ruefully. 'Not what I saw myself doing – making bonnets for market women and cooks and such. But Tom says you has to start small, and we might end up making hats for a Queen yet.'

'Well, I'd as soon work with you as with old Ma Watson,' Nancy said, for the two girls had become friends now. 'We can have a crack and a laugh or two, even if we do have to work half the night to get an order out. And the money you're offering's better than I'd ever get with her.'

'That's because Tom and me believes in being equal. We saw enough of workers living on air back in Kidder.' Bessie gave her a quick look and turned away, leaving Nancy gazing at her with a curiosity she already knew better than to display. Friends they might be, but there were clearly secrets in the past of the Himleys, secrets they weren't yet willing to divulge.

But that had all been some time ago – why, they'd

been almost two years working with Tom and Bessie for Francis Pagnel. And the brother and sister had gradually learned to treat Sam and his daughter as real friends, and to trust them with the story of their flight from Kidderminster and the things that had happened to them since. Commonplace enough stories, and no unhappier than many Nancy had heard, but she could understand their reluctance to talk about them. And particularly since Tom still went in fear of being arrested and hanged for murder . . .

Her Tom a murderer! Nancy returned to the present with a jerk and looked across the table at her father, just finishing his pie. He had difficulty eating with the few teeth he had left but he always enjoyed a good pie. He lifted his tankard and drained it, wiped his mouth and looked at her.

'Well, girl? What's bin happening? What was the letter all about?'

'It was from Mr Francis,' she said slowly.

'Coming back, is he? Not before time, neither, he's bin away a fair long time. And how's Mrs Pagnel and the little 'uns? I miss that young Daniel in and out of the shop.'

Nancy looked at him, biting her lip a little. How was she to tell him? How would he take the news? Not that there was any real news yet – nothing had been decided finally. Or so the letter had said. But there had been a ring about the words . . .

'Well?' Samuel said sharply, and she found his eyes on her, suddenly shrewd, and remembered that her father might be old but he certainly was not senile. 'Out with it, girl. You got summat to tell us, you better get on and tell us quick. No sense hanging about.'

'You know they're not coming back, Dad,' she said, choosing her words carefully. 'We've known that for months. Mr Francis and Rebecca, they're settled in Kidderminster now. It hasn't made any difference to the business here – they promised it wouldn't and it

78

hasn't.' She stopped again and Samuel's face creased as he concentrated on her words, trying to read the meaning behind them. She looked at him helplessly. 'They've asked Tom and Bessie to go back too,' she said at last. 'Back to Kidderminster. They – Mr Francis wants to take the business there, make it part of the family firm in Kidderminster.'

There was a long silence.

'But I thought he couldn't never go back,' Samuel said at last. 'Tom – ain't he got some sort o' price on his head? Won't he be walking right into trouble if he sets foot in that place again?'

Nancy shrugged. 'That's what he's always been scared of. Him and Bess, they never killed that man, but how could they prove it? It always looked black for 'em. But now it seems that old Mr Pagnel's bin asking questions, saying as how they was wrongly accused and there weren't no proof against 'em and there ain't no reason why they can't go back. And with him being a magistrate and all . . .'

They looked at each other.

'So you reckon they'll go then?' Samuel asked at last.

'I dunno. They ain't decided. They're talking about it now.'

'And you? You're tied up with Bessie now, making bonnets. And I thought p'raps you and Tom . . .'

'Tom wants me to go too,' she said quietly. 'That's if they go – I told you, they ain't made up their minds yet. Nor won't they, for a bit. There's too much to think about.'

'That there is.' Samuel reached out for his tobacco pouch, fumbling across the table almost as if he were blind. 'That there is. There's the business here – what's to be done about that? It's easy to talk about moving it to Kidderminster – what have they got to move? A couple of looms, to a town what's full of 'em already? A couple of men, one of 'em too old to go on much

79

longer anyway, and draw-boys when there's fifteen a penny to be got from their own streets? Mr Francis *is* that business, girl, and he's in Kidderminster already. There's only Tom to go – and if he don't, do you think Mr Francis is going to keep the shop working here just to give him and me a living?' He snorted, but there was something wavering about his voice as he went on. 'No, there might be a lot to think about but there ain't nothing to decide. It's go if we wants to keep our jobs and stay if we wants to starve.' He looked again at his daughter. 'Or weren't we asked to go anyway? Maybe we ain't invited to this party.'

Nancy stared miserably at her father. 'Dad, I don't even know. It was only Tom and Bess mentioned in the letter, I think. But he wouldn't go without you, not without making sure you had a good living. And I told you, he wants me to go anyway, and I won't go without you, so that's all there is to it.'

'And why does he want you to go? To cook his meals for him? To be his draw-girl? To make his sister's fancy bonnets?'

The bitterness in his voice shocked Nancy. Never before had Samuel shown anything but gratitude and respect for Francis Pagnel and Tom. They had taken him from the gutter and restored his self-respect, and he had given them his loyalty in return. Now it was as if they had suddenly become enemies.

'Dad— ' she began uncertainly, but he broke in, his old voice quivering.

'Don't you tell me, my girl! I seen it all before. Didn't I work years and years, from a bit of a boy till I was past me prime, just to be chucked on the scrap-heap and left to starve? They're all the same, these manufacturers. Ride on yer back till a better horse comes along, and then it's off and never worry what happens to them as put 'em where they are now. And your Mr Francis is just the same as all the others, for all he seemed such a gentleman. Did he mention me in this letter of his? Did he arst after you? Did he arst *us* to go to Kidderminster to be part of his fine new business?'

Nancy shook her head miserably. 'But Dad, I told you, Tom wants me to go and— '

'And I arst you,' he said, 'just what is he arsting you to go as?'

'As his wife, Dad. Didn't I tell you that? Tom wants me to marry him. He wants us to be wed.'

Samuel looked at her. An hour ago, he would have received the news with pleasure and satisfaction. Now, all he could say was: 'And did he arst you that before he read his letter, or afterwards?'

'He just don't seem to understand,' Nancy said unhappily. 'He just won't believe there's a job for him in Kidderminster, just like here in London. He's frightened out of his mind he'll be turned off and sent to the workhouse. And nothing I can say will change his mind.'

Tom sighed. 'But there's no doubt about what Francis means to do. He wants to carry on his own small loom shop, weaving special carpets and rugs that won't go to the shops. Special orders for customers who'll be ready to pay more for designs made up just for them. Fashionable ladies will want his carpets for their drawing rooms, just a'cause nobody else will hev one the same. I know it's hard for Sam to understand, when he don't even really understand why folks wants carpets at all – but it's the truth. And Francis and me, we needs Sam to weave 'em.'

'But he ain't the only man what can do that,' Nancy pointed out. 'And he knows it, Tom. Like he says, he's seen it before. He's bin in the gutter and he don't want to go there again.'

'And no more he will.' Tom scratched his head, then put his arm round her shoulders and drew her against him. 'Look, Nance, even if he couldn't work, we'd still

81

look after him, wouldn't we? Can't he even believe that?'

Her face was thoughtful, and when she spoke her voice was slow, as if she were working out her thoughts as she talked.

'I dunno. I think it's a bit more than that, Tom. He's scared of summat else. It ain't just the work. I think he's scared of leaving London at all, and that's what's at the back of it.'

'Scared of leaving London? But what do he think it's like in Kidderminster? Full of bears and wild animals? Cannibals, what'll eat him? Nance, that's daft – there ent naught to be afeared of in Kidder.'

'Ent there?' They both turned quickly to find Bess standing in the doorway. Her face was pale from her most recent bout of illness and she leaned against the jamb as if standing were too much for her. But she shook her head as Tom moved quickly forward to support her, and stayed where she was. 'Ent there nothing to be afeared of in Kidder? I must say I'm surprised to hear *you* say that, Tom Himley. Don't you know you could be strung up for everyone to see, come you go back to Kidderminster?'

'Bess! Now you know that's not true, not any more. Francis told us in the letter. Mr Pagnel says it's all right to go back now, there was no witnesses and no proof, and everyone'll hev forgot that old tale anyway— '

'Will they?' Bessie let go of the door jamb and came into the room. She walked slowly, as if she were unutterably tired, and sank down on the chair, leaning her head back. 'And how can Mr Pagnel be so sure of that? Happen they'll have told him that, just to get you back amongst 'em. It don't tek a magistrate or a judge to say a man has to be hanged for murder, Tom. Sometimes people does it without any say-so.'

Tom felt his blood chill. 'You're talking nonsense, Bess. There weren't nobody loved old Jabez Gast enough to do that.'

'But there might be those who hate the Pagnels,' Bessie said quietly. 'Especially Francis Pagnel. There might be those who'd be willing to pay to queer his pitch, one way or another, and see you as an easy target. And there might be those who'd tek the money for doing it, too.'

Tom laughed, but his laugh was uneasy. 'If you're talking of Mr Vivian— '

'I'm not talking of no one,' Bessie said quickly, glancing over her shoulder almost as if she expected Vivian Pagnel to materialise behind her. 'But that one's got the devil in him and he's got a grudge against you and me. I wouldn't trust him no further than I can throw that loom of yours. And I'm not going back to Kidder to put meself in his power, and that's flat.'

Tom stared at her. 'You won't go back? Not even if Nance and me goes?'

'I wouldn't go back to Kidderminster,' Bessie said, 'if the King hisself asked me to go.'

Tom and Nancy looked helplessly at each other. The street was busy with traffic and horses splashed mud with their hooves, but neither of them noticed.

'What are we going to do?' Tom asked. 'The two of them are as stubborn as pigs going to market. Neither is going to budge – and we can't just go and leave 'em. They ent fit to be left, neither one.'

'And you want to go to Kidderminster, don't you, Tom?' she said softly.

'I do, Nance, and that's the truth. I never wanted to leave anyway, and it were allus a sorrow to me as we couldn't go back, Bess'n me. And now we can – but she won't. And we could do well there. Francis will mek a success of this new idea he has, I know that, and we'd be near our Rebecca and all. It'd be good for all of us.'

'It'd be specially good for Bess.'

'Ah, it would. She ent right in London, never has

been, and she seems to get more sickly all the time. That fever of hers – I don't like it. It's the air here, I'm sure of it.'

'Well,' Nancy said after a moment, 'there ain't nothing we can do but keep trying to make 'em see sense, the pair of them. But I don't hold out much hope over my dad, nobody's ever been able to make him see sense when he don't want to, not since me mum died. I don't see him shifting out of London now. It's like he's grown roots in the place.'

'That's what I reckon it is,' Tom agreed, and then stopped in a corner of two buildings. He took Nancy's shoulders between his hands and looked down into her face. 'And what if he won't move, Nance? What will you do? Will you stay here with him – or come with me? What's it to be – eh?'

She gazed up at him, then turned her face aside as if she could not answer. Her heart was torn between the two men, the one she loved with all the emotion and passion of a woman, the other she felt bound to by the ties of birth and responsibility. She barely recognised the fact that there was love in those ties too; she understood only that she could not leave her father, old and growing frail, to fend for himself in his last years. Her eyes filled with tears and the tears brimmed over and rolled slowly down her cheeks.

'How can you ask me that, Tom,' she whispered, 'when you know you won't be able to leave your sister?'

He dropped his hands.

'Aye, you're right. They've got us in a box, Nance, and no mistake. And both of 'em as wrong-headed as savages. And nothing to be done about it as far as I can see, short of kidnapping 'em both.'

He moved on along the street and Nancy walked beside him. She felt rent with sorrow. It was clear that Tom had never stopped hankering after his home and would have been back in Kidderminster before now if there had been nothing to hamper him. And now, with the chance to return offered him on a plate, with work and a home provided, he was prevented by the fears of Bessie and of an old weaver whom he hadn't even known two years ago.

Or maybe only by the fears of his sister. Sure though she was of his love, Nancy was not sure enough to think that he would have stayed in London for her sake alone. No, it was Bessie who was holding him back, and no wonder. They had been through a lot together, those two.

They came to the house where Nancy lived with her father and stopped at the door. Nancy gave Tom a half-apologetic glance.

'Better you don't come in. Dad's in a funny mood just now.'

Tom nodded. 'He thinks I've let him down.'

'He thinks you're going to,' she amended, and stood close to him, reaching her arms up for a kiss. 'Oh, Tom . . .'

'Nancy.' They stood absorbed for a few minutes, then he lifted his mouth from hers and said huskily, 'You know I won't go without you, Nance. And if you can't go without that old bugger upstairs— '

She smiled, her eyes bright again with tears. 'Tom, I don't want to hold you back — '

'You're not. We'll get there – somehow,' he promised recklessly. 'And if we don't – why, I've managed to live in London a good few years now, I reckon I can go on doing it somehow. Maybe we can persuade Francis to keep on the shop here after all.'

'Maybe.' She gave him a final hug and turned to go into the house. The door closed behind her and Tom waited for a few minutes, as if hoping that she would reappear, and then turned and walked slowly away.

He had barely reached the corner when he heard running footsteps behind him. Swiftly, expecting he knew not what, he turned and saw Nancy, her face white, her eyes wide and dark, her hair flying as she ran towards him with hands held out.

'Nance! What is it – what's the matter?' He caught her in his arms, staring down into her frightened face, and knew what she must tell him before she could find the words.

'It's Dad,' she choked out at last. 'Dad – he's – he's . . .' She caught her breath, then shook her head blindly and blurted it out. 'You don't have to worry about him coming to Kidderminster, Tom. He won't be going nowhere no more.'

Chapter Five

Nell Foster's home was just as Rebecca had known it would be. Yet it still came as a shock to see it – a dirty, damp and crowded basement room with sacking at the window to keep out draughts, a small fire guttering in one corner, and a pile of old blankets and sacks in another. The three boys were huddled round a rickety table, wolfing down gruel which Nellie was ladling out of a blackened pot. The eldest was a puny seven-year-old, the youngest barely toddling. They looked up as Rebecca came in, their grimy faces pinched and suspicious.

Nell, standing at the fireplace, opened her eyes wide. 'So you come! I must say, I never expected it. Thought you'd be too grand for the likes of we now.'

'I'm no different from when I was Rebecca Himley,' Rebecca said, but she knew it was not true. She was different, she must be. She lived in what to Nellie would be luxury, she had warmth and comfort and good food to eat. Her children were fat and rosy, with no gloomy prospect ahead of them of going into a loom shop at eight years old, to stand for hour upon hour wielding the sword and terry wire. They had toys to play with, a rug to roll upon and comfortable beds to sleep in at night.

And even though Rebecca had deliberately worn her oldest and plainest clothes for this visit, she was still dressed like a lady in comparison with Nell.

She stood uncertainly in the middle of the room, feeling suddenly out of place. Perhaps she should not have come after all. Perhaps Nell was thinking bitter thoughts about her: that she had sold herself to the masters, that she had come to gloat, to look down on her less fortunate neighbours. For Nell and her family had once been neighbours, living close by, sharing both their misfortunes and their occasional good luck. And Nell had worked with Bess, come to call for her in the mornings, gone off to work with her as they tossed their heads and giggled, casting sidelong glances at the boys.

And now here she was, that bright, saucy-eyed girl, looking a generation older than her age, weighed down like an old woman by the cares of poverty, child-bearing and continual hard labour. Where had her gaiety gone? And had every bowed, middle-aged woman Rebecca had encountered on her way here through the mean, dirty streets, once been as saucy and optimistic as Nell and Bessie before the world had caught them in its toils?

'I brought you a few things,' she said hesitantly, holding out her covered basket. 'Not much – a few things from the kitchen – some eggs and such . . .' Her voice died away under Nell's sardonic gaze. Acting the grand lady, she thought unhappily. Of course Nell was offended – she had her pride, just as they all had. There was nobody who valued independence as much as a weaver and his family, even though it might cost them dear.

Nell took the basket and looked inside.

'Not much? A few eggs?' she mimicked cruelly. 'There's more good food in here than we sees in a fortnight, and you knows it, Becky Himley. But I ent too proud to tek it, nonetheless. Aye, and I can thank you for it too. It might be just enough to keep the little 'un alive.'

Rebecca flinched at the bitterness of the words and looked at the children again. The smallest one did indeed look frail; his face was shrunken and wizened, like that of an old man, on a head that looked too large for his spindly body. Big, haunted eyes looked out from sunken hollows, and as he grabbed at the hunk of bread his mother broke from one of the loaves Rebecca had brought, his fingers were as thin as those of a skeleton.

'Surely he's ill!' Rebecca exclaimed. 'You must take him to the doctor, Nell.' And then she flushed, realising the impossibility of her suggestion even before Nell, sharing out the rest of the loaf, cast her another cynical glance. 'I'm sorry, Nell,' she said humbly. 'You're right. I have forgotten, a little. Life has been easier for me since Francis found me.'

Nell's face softened a little. 'Aye, I heard a bit about what happened. You must hev bin through the mill when you first got to London. And I ent one to grudge you your good luck – just wish it had happened to me, that's all.' She sighed, looking at the boys who had gulped down the last of their bread and gruel and were now drinking Rebecca's milk from a cracked cup. 'It's a cruel world to bring childer into. But we can't stop 'em coming. It's the way for us all, seems.'

'Have you had more than these?' Rebecca asked, and Nellie nodded.

'Two girls in between. Both went as babbies, and if you ask me they was the lucky ones. You?'

'Two boys so far,' Rebecca said and blushed. Nell's eyes sharpened at once.

'Fallen again, have you? Well, like I say, we can't stop 'em coming. Daresay you'd like a wench this time, dress her up nice and that. Wouldn't mind one meself – they was right pretty, my little Anna and Lizzie – but I was glad it was them as went really. Life's too hard for girls. It's better to be a man.'

She sat down on an old chair and gestured to Rebecca to take the one opposite. 'Tell us about Bess. How's she getting on up there in London?'

'Well enough. She had a hard time at first, till Tom found her.' Rebecca frowned a little. She had never been told quite how Bessie had earned her living in those years before Francis had taken her and Tom from the poverty in which they had lived – poverty as bad as Nell lived in now – and given them a better life. But she had seen enough to guess, and the thought of her sister selling herself to man after man through the days and nights of those long years, sickened her. 'I told you she makes bonnets and hats now. Nothing grand, but she's content enough, when she's well.'

'Sickly, is she?' Nell nodded, as if it were no matter for surprise. 'Well, happen she'll be better when she comes back to Kidder. I heard tell your Tom's coming back, and they lives together don't they?'

'They do, but Bessie doesn't seem keen to come. Tom wants to, and Nancy – the girl he's going to marry. Nancy works with Bess and they both want her to come, but Bessie says she'd rather stop in London. She's afraid of trouble if they come back here.'

'Old Jabez, you mean? That's old history now. And no one missed the bastard anyway – sour old devil. Loom shop were a better place without him in it, and that's the truth.'

'So it might be, but it isn't the way the law looks on it. Murder's murder. But Mr Pagnel says now that there wouldn't be any trouble if Tom and Bessie did come – there were never any witnesses and he's prepared to take their word for what happened.'

'So why's she still afeared?'

Rebecca shrugged. 'I think she's just afraid of change. She's used to London now. She's made it her home. She knows people – if she comes back here, she'll have to start all over again.'

'Aye, and maybe she's afraid her old friends wouldn't want to know her,' Nell said shrewdly. 'We're all different now, Becky – me with my boys, and most of the others in the same boat. And Bessie wouldn't be coming back to the shop. All the same, she'll be lonely there without the rest of you. Tom's coming, ent he?'

'I don't know. I hope so – but he feels badly about

90

leaving Bess. They've been together so long. And Nancy, his girl, works with Bess too. It's a big step for them.' She sighed. 'Oh, I daresay we'll persuade her in the end. She knows Tom wants to come, and she must know he won't leave her all by herself.'

Nellie's youngest child fell from the box he was standing on and set up a yell. She went to pick him up and held him close, crooning softly as he snivelled against her breast, and Rebecca watched her with a sudden fear in her heart. The child was sickly, fragile, in need of far more than the few scraps of food she had brought. What chance had he of surviving in this hovel, its walls streaked with damp and black with mould? Wasn't he doomed to be just another of the many infants who died before their third birthday, another gap in the family that Nell would go on producing?

She had seen it so often before. Her own mother had raised only three children out of the – six, seven, eight? – she had borne. There was always a child dying amongst the neighbours who lived in the huddled cottages. Some were born sickly and died soon, some struggled on like this poor mite, many more succumbed to disease during one of the many epidemics that swept the town. Others died through accident – they tumbled into the Stour and drowned or slipped under a horse's hooves, or fell into the machinery at the factories where they worked. Really, the wonder was that they survived at all.

And even if they did, Rebecca thought with unaccustomed despondency, what sort of life did they live? Nothing but grinding poverty and a death that was due to a combination of hard toil and starvation. And the sicknesses that all knew were due to the work they did in the factories, in air that was filled with virulent dust. What was the purpose of it all?

She looked again at the child in Nellie's arms, now quiet and falling asleep, a dirty thumb stuck comfortingly in its mouth, and thought of her own children. Daniel, so robust and healthy, Geoffrey who was sitting up in his cot now, bright-eyed and laughing. And the one to come, held safely under her heart. And her hand went involuntarily to her stomach, to feel the gradual thickening there, seeking that tiny flutter that would tell her that her baby did indeed live.

'Aye, we're all the same, ent we?' Nellie said, her eyes following Rebecca's movement. 'Don't matter how many we bear nor how many we loses, we can't help wanting them to grow. And yet what hev they got to grow up to?' She glanced around the dank little room. 'Poor little sods. Poor sods, all of us.'

Rebecca felt helpless. She had come to visit Nellie almost as she was learning to visit the other manufacturers' wives, as a social duty and because Nellie had been Bessie's friend. Now she felt as if she had stepped into a deep morass. She could not walk out of here as casually as if she had just drunk tea with a woman as idle as herself, and could forget her until next week. Nellie's eyes, once so bright and flashing, now hard and disillusioned, would appear in her mind as she sat at her table with Francis, eating the meals that Sal and Tilly had prepared. The shrunken flesh of the baby's face would haunt her dreams. The dirt and discomfort of the draughty room would chill her as she sat at her fireside.

'You know there's talk of making things better,' she said. 'Francis is very interested in the idea of co-operatives. Weavers, dyers, spinners all combining to produce the carpets and all sharing fairly in the profits. He's trying to interest Mr Pagnel – Mr Jeremiah, that is— '

'Aye, it would be,' Nellie said with a short laugh. 'You'd never catch that Mr Vivian giving aught away. Hurts him to pay the men their wages as it is. And to think how me and Bess used to fancy him – aye, I wondered sometimes— ' She broke off quickly. 'Well, like I said, 'tis all water under the bridge now. And as for this – what d'you call it? – co-operative idea, why, it's nothing but a dream. No master's going to agree to that and you might as well tell your man to save his breath.' She stood up and carried the baby over to the pile of bedding in the corner, laying him down as gently as if he had been a little prince being put to bed in a cot of gold. 'There, my toad, you just sleep it off. It's the only pleasure most of us has now, sleep. And I'll get your daddy's dinner ready, he'll be home soon.'

Rebecca stood up. 'I'll be going, Nell, I can see you're busy. But I'll come again – if you don't mind. I'd like to see you and the boys.' Her eyes went to the sleeping figure on the sacking and again she touched her stomach. 'Look after the little one, won't you,' she murmured, and slipped away through the cracked and broken door.

Nell stood in the middle of the room, looking after her. Then she glanced down at the two older boys, crouching on the floor playing with a few stones they had brought in. She shook her head slowly.

'Look after the little one!' she repeated. 'What do she think I'm doing but looking after you all? What do any of us do but try to look after each other till we comes to the grave? What else is there?'

Spring came damply in, with the thin chill of February lingering into March and even the beginning of April. A few brave flowers struggled to unfold along the banks of the Stour, but their petals were grimed with soot even before they had properly opened. Nell's boys found them and dragged them up by the roots to take home for their mother, and she stuck them into an old cup with a drop of water from the ditch and set them on the cracked table.

Rebecca's baby was making itself felt now, fluttering with tiny feet inside her swelling stomach. She felt tired, and the sickness which she had suffered only

93

through a few weeks of her first pregnancies seemed to be dragging on longer than usual. The thought of visiting Nellie, of merely getting through the littered and smelly streets to her basement room, was almost more than she could tolerate, but she forced herself to go, taking a basket of eggs and milk and new-baked bread each time she went.

'But the poor little baby looks more sickly every time,' she said to Enid. 'And Nellie gets more and more worried. Her Bill couldn't work last week, he'd hurt his back lifting some bales of wool and had to lie flat for three days. They can't afford to lose money like that. None of the weavers can.'

'Don't they have a sick club, or friendly society?' Enid asked, and Rebecca nodded.

'They do, and of course it helps, but it hasn't enough money to keep a man in comfort.' She sighed. 'Not that a weaver would know what comfort is, anyway – there's none of it in those poor hovels.'

'There must be something that can be done,' Enid said thoughtfully. 'In country areas, the lady of the manor does at least visit the cottages and take soup and such comforts to help the labourers through hard times. But here in town— '

'That's it!' Rebecca exclaimed, lifting her head. 'Or at least, it would be a beginning. If we could persuade the manufacturers' wives to help – if we could show them how the women and children suffer – perhaps some sort of association could be formed.' Her eyes were alight, much as were Francis's when he talked of his Dream. To bring comfort to those cold, bare cottages . . . Her mind was already beginning to work, thrusting up ideas, discarding some, catching eagerly at others. 'We could set up some sort of nursery for the smallest children, so that they needn't spend long hours in winding sheds or dye-houses. We might even teach them a little – start a simple kind of school. We might— '

94

'Wait a minute.' Enid exclaimed, laughing. 'You'll have them in fine clothes and going to Oxford University next!'

'And why not?' Rebecca asked slowly. 'Why shouldn't weavers' children be educated? Why shouldn't they be allowed to use their brains as well as their muscles?'

There was a pause. Enid looked at her.

'You really are serious about this, aren't you?'

'Yes, I am,' Rebecca said soberly. 'Oh, I realise that the idea of a working man's child being educated enough to reach that kind of standard is impossible – though I don't see *why* it should be so,' she added passionately. 'Our brains are as good as our masters', when we're allowed to use them. But that is never going to happen – at least, not for a long time. All the same, we could do much to make things better now. And if the men won't do it – why not the women?'

'Women like Maria? Women who are fond of their creature comforts, the riches that carpets have brought them?' Enid shook her head doubtfully. 'And what of the famous weavers' independence? How will they take to the manufacturers' wives coming into their homes with soup and cast-off clothing, and ideas for nurseries and schools? Won't they be offended, even insulted?'

Rebecca smiled wryly. 'Independence is a fine idea,' she said, 'but it's a luxury, and it's a men's luxury. Women have more sense. They know when to put pride aside. And what woman would put pride and independence before her starving children?'

She rose from her chair, her mouth set with determination, and went slowly upstairs to the airy nursery where her two children spent much of their time. Little Geoffrey was crawling now, and plaguing the life out of his elder brother by constantly making for his toys. Daniel, who seemed to have a bent for architecture, would painstakingly build a large edifice with his wooden bricks, only for Geoffrey to knock it flying

with one swing of his fist. It was hardly surprising that
Daniel would retaliate by hitting the baby on the head
with one of the same bricks, and he was inclined to
sulk when prevented from committing murder.

'Mine!' he protested as Rebecca removed the brick
from his tightly clutching fingers. '*Mine*.'

'Yes, but not to hit Geoffrey with.' She picked the
baby up and carried him to a chair, jiggling him on her
knee. 'And who's a naughty boy, spoiling his brother's
game?' The baby laughed delightedly and she gazed at
him, her heart swelling. How strong he was, how different from Nellie's little one.

How fortunate she was, to be so safe.

Of all her days in Kidderminster, Rebecca loved the
evenings best. Then it was that Francis was home from
the factory and they would sit together after supper to
talk over the day's events and often to look at the new
designs Francis was making for the Jacquard weave
carpets.

'The new loom shop will be ready in a few weeks,'
Francis said. 'And we must be ready to begin work
at once – those high looms have to start paying for
themselves as soon as possible. And designing for the
cards and cylinders is quite different from the designing
we've done until now.'

Rebecca gazed at the sheets of paper he had brought
home, with their complex patterns drawn on them. In
many ways, the Jacquard system made the creation of
a pattern easier, and it certainly eased the laborious
task of the draw-boy or girl – although few manufacturers would change to Jacquard simply to make things
easier for their employees. Indeed, she feared that,
like Vivian, many of them might even see it as an
excuse to lower the wages.

But not all masters were as cynical as Vivian. Francis
and his father were both concerned for the people
who worked for them, both making efforts to improve

conditions, and there would be no lowering of wages or turning loyal workers away simply because a new and easier system had been introduced.

'All the same,' Jeremiah had decreed, 'every man must *work* for his pay. I can't have labour standing idle – that's as bad as slavery is. They're human beings after all, you can't expect them not to take advantage of a soft master.'

'And that's exactly what they'll do,' Vivian said sourly. 'Give them easier work to do and they'll want even less of it. Shorter hours and higher pay will be their call – mark my words.'

'And why should they not ask for shorter hours?' Rebecca demanded passionately. 'They work from dawn until dusk at their looms, no matter how their poor backs and legs may ache from the toil. And the children labour just as long, mites younger than your little Anna, turned out of their beds before you even think of rising, and coming home too weary to eat their supper. They *should* have shorter hours.'

Vivian gave her a black look and seemed disposed to ignore her words, but Rebecca met his look boldly. She knew that, as a woman, she was not expected to have an opinion on such matters, but she had grown up in a weaver's cottage and had known the conditions, and she was not prepared to remain silent. After a moment's hesitation, Vivian replied.

'It isn't easy for you to understand, Rebecca, I know,' he said kindly. 'Your own history . . . and the fact that you were never brought up to view matters from a correct point of view. You see, if the weavers worked shorter hours, they wouldn't earn so much money. How could a man feed his family on less than he earns now? It couldn't be done, you see. We're doing them a favour by allowing them to work the hours they do and so earn a living wage.'

Rebecca leaned her arms on the table. 'Then pay them more. The wage you pay now is no living wage anyway. They take it only because they would starve to death without it.' She paused, thinking of her parents who had died of cold, starvation and disease, thinking of Nell Foster's baby with his shrunken face and body, and added quietly: 'Many of them do as it is.'

Vivian shrugged impatiently. 'Rebecca, my dear, don't you understand – if I reduce the hours and pay more, they will immediately ask to work overtime. They'll become greedy. They'll want fine clothes for their wives, carpets for their own floors— '

'Good food,' Rebecca said. 'Decent houses.'

'The point I am trying to make,' Vivian said with a dangerous edge to his voice, 'is that if I reduce the hours the weavers will immediately increase them of their own volition, so that they will once again – yes, and their wives and children too – be working the same long hours that you complain of now. And I shall be forced to allow it, since our production depends upon it. You see, they *are* capable of working those hours. They're more than capable – they're *willing*.'

'Nonsense,' Rebecca retorted. 'If the men were paid sufficiently there are few who would choose to work the hours they do. No one wants to stand at a loom hour upon hour, day after day, unless he has to. They would be happy to earn more in a shorter period and go home to their families.'

'And then what of our production?' Vivian asked, as if he were speaking to a child. 'Would they also produce more work during these shorter hours?'

'No – but you could employ more labour. Have you not seen the men idling in the streets for lack of work? You know that for every weaver in work there are two or three out of it.'

'And for good reason, too – they *are* idlers. Worthless rogues I wouldn't want to employ shifting bales, let alone doing skilled work.' Vivian glanced at her with increasing irritation. 'And what will happen to our profits? We shall be paying more, far more, for the same production. Will you be happy to see your own children grow thin at the expense of a weaver's? Will you be pleased to see us all move back into weavers' hovels? I think not.'

'And would lesser profits really mean poverty?' she demanded. 'Less fine food on your table, perhaps, and fewer fashionable gowns for Maria. But we could still live well. Vivian – all of us. Man and master, as they used to do, side by side in co-operation— '

'*Co-operation*!' He turned away in disgust. 'I might have known that word would creep in eventually. Do you and Francis talk of nothing else but *co-operation* and *co-operatives*? Does it occupy you during your meals at home, in bed at night?' He spoke directly to Francis, as if Rebecca were not there. 'Can you explain to your pretty little wife, dear cousin, that we need our profits in order to make work for the weavers who are so precious to her? Can you tell her that without profit there can be no expansion? Where would the money come from for the new looms, for instance, for the new buildings needed to house them? Better still,' he added with a brief glance at Rebecca, 'teach her not to interfere in matters that are not of her concern. Or perhaps you would like her to come to Maria two or three mornings a week for lessons in behaviour? We do understand, after all, that she hasn't had our advantages.'

Rebecca drew in her breath. She could feel the angry burning of her cheeks. She opened her mouth but Francis spoke first, quietly but firmly.

'That won't be necessary, Vivian. Rebecca's behaviour does not worry me. She is kindly always to those who warrant it. And now, Father— ' he turned to Jeremiah ' —tell us about your visit to Halifax. Did you meet the Robertsons while you were there? They were very hospitable to me on my visit a few years ago.'

The conversation was successfully turned, but Rebecca was still angry and when she was alone with Francis, before their own fire, she could not help speaking her mind.

'Vivian argues cleverly, but nothing can hide the fact that he sees the weavers as no more than a means to his own prosperity. It's nonsense to say that he needs the profits for housing the new looms – of course he does, but the money isn't coming from his own pocket. Maria has no less money to spend because new looms have been bought.'

Francis smiled and took her hand in his. 'I know, my love, but we must be patient if we hope to change Vivian's mind and attitudes. He's so easily antagonised, and so arrogant that he would never back down even if he knew he was wrong. That's why I prevented you from telling him about your own Association – you were just about to, weren't you?'

Rebecca smiled a little shamefacedly. 'I was. He annoyed me so much. I wanted to show him that some people do care. But you're right. He would have been against it immediately and we would have lost all hope of getting Maria to join us.'

'Well, it's a faint enough hope anyway,' Francis said. 'Maria's unlikely to go against Vivian's wishes, and I'm not sure you'd have her sympathy as it is. She enjoys wealth too much. But you've gained some members already, haven't you?'

'Yes, indeed. Not amongst the manufacturers' wives so far – I was hoping Maria might give a lead there, but I'm afraid you're right about her. Yet several of the wives of managers and chief clerks have seemed interested. Enid and I are inviting them here one afternoon next week for a meeting to discuss what we should do.'

'That's good.' Francis's smile told her that he agreed with her aims, was even proud of her, and she felt a glow of pleasure. How well they worked together, the two of them. For a moment, she wished that she were a man so that she could work even more closely with him – but then I couldn't be his wife, she thought with a quick, inward smile, and being Francis's wife was the best life she could think of.

'And now,' he said, 'let's look at these new designs. I'm not altogether happy with them – how do you think they might be improved?'

Rebecca looked at the drawings he had made, at the swirling colours. The range of designs possible was much greater with this new system, and her interest quickened. She picked up one of Francis's pencils and made a few strokes, suddenly absorbed.

'That would balance it better, I think,' she said after few minutes. 'And if this were in red . . . You could use the same design in several different colours, Francis. One with a blue background, another with green. Didn't you say that the cards can be used over and over again? There would be no variation – you could make miles of carpet, with the pattern identical each time.'

'Exactly,' Francis said, smiling at her enthusiasm. 'And we can duplicate the cards too, so that several looms can be working at once. Something you could never be entirely sure of, with individual weavers.' He looked at the changes she had made in the design. 'Do you know, I believe you have got it just right. Why have you never helped with the designing before?'

'Perhaps because I've never been invited,' she answered with a glint of mischief in her eyes. 'And because I've been busy with other things. Womanly things, as Vivian would have it.'

Francis laughed. 'Bearing children to carry on the dynasty of Pagnel Carpets,' he said, and then sobered. 'Rebecca, you do know that we may never do that. Vivian is Father's heir. If his next child is a son . . .'

'We shall never be anything but the poor relations,' she answered quietly. 'I know that. And when your father dies, is Vivian likely to let you keep your position in the business? I don't think he will.'

'No, neither do I. Although that's no reason why I shouldn't make every effort to contribute to its success while I am a part of it.' He frowned a little, his eyes going back to the design they had made between them. 'All the same, it means that our own business – the one we've begun with Tom in London – is as important to us as ever. And you could be important to its success, Rebecca. You have a talent for design, and it would be a shame to waste it. Do you think you could set aside some time regularly to discuss designs with me, and to make your own? With so small a business as ours, the quality is all-important, and design is what strikes the customer's eye first. You could help us build even more quickly, with your ideas. And we need success, if we are not to find ourselves destitute one day. Not that I imagine Vivian would ever be so unjust,' he added hastily. 'But – his son might be less forbearing. We have to take care of the future for ourselves and our own children.'

'Yes, we do.' Rebecca laid her hands on her stomach where the new baby was kicking more strongly now. A daughter this time, or another son? She was shaken by a sudden wave of love and determination to ensure that this child, with the others, would never suffer the hardship and deprivation that she had known. He – she – must grow up protected from the poverty that had sent its grandparents into paupers' graves.

These were the normal feelings of every mother, she supposed, but her mother, Fanny Himley, had known from the start that they were hopeless. She had told Rebecca once that with every child that was born to her, she had always had the hope – if only briefly – that it would be born dead and so saved the misery of life. 'It would've made it easier for me too,' she had said, her eyes bleak with the knowledge that there would never be anything better for her. 'One less mouth to feed. And them that lived, all except for you and Bess and our Tom, only got sick and died later. What's the point of it all?'

And Bess and Tom had fared no better, as far as she had ever known: forced to flee from home, hunted for murder, hiding in London, scraping a living by means that Bess would never speak of. She had died before she could know that Tom was now working with Francis, and that Bess was a milliner. Nor could she ever have suspected that Rebecca herself would ever be more than a housemaid.

Did everyone have these almost overpowering feelings of protectiveness for their children? Even people like Vivian and Maria, who seemed only to look on their offspring as a means to their own advancement? Rebecca remembered that moment of softness she had experienced with Maria in the nursery; she thought of Vivian's passionate desire for a son. Was his determination to accrue money and profit no more than her own resolve to keep her children safe? And wasn't 'safety' itself a different idea for different people?

To be forced to live as simply as she and Francis did, in this small house at the top of Unicorn Street, would be as unthinkable for Vivian and Maria as to be reduced to her father's hovel again was for Rebecca. And for her father and mother, as for many other weavers and their wives, even that tiny measure of independence was preferable to the idea of complete penury. Her father had valued it even to the extent of resisting Fanny's wish to put Rebecca into domestic service.

'Yes,' she said, 'we must take care of the future for our children's sakes. And we must bring Tom and Bessie back from London. We need Tom – and I can't bear to think of Bessie there, all alone. She suffers with that fever far too often. Somehow we must make her come too. She has nothing to be afraid of here, after all.'

'Nothing,' Francis agreed. 'And I shall tell her so, when I go to London next week. And meanwhile – why don't we look at these other designs? I think you've been hiding your light under a bushel all this time – you have an eye for design which could be very useful to Pagnel and Himley.'

'Pagnel and Himley?'

He nodded. 'I'm not bringing Tom here just to be one of Vivian's employees, Rebecca. I've been talking to Father again and we're in complete agreement over this. I shall continue to work in Pagnel Carpets, with him and with Vivian – but I am to continue too with my own small business, making specialised rugs and small carpets to individual designs.'

'As you and Tom and Samuel were doing in London.'

'That's right. And Tom's missing Samuel badly – and having difficulty in finding a weaver to replace him. Now is the right time for the business to move to Kidder, where there are good weavers in plenty. And we shall set it up properly, with Tom as a partner, not an employee.'

'Pagnel and Himley,' Rebecca said softly. 'It sounds good, Francis. If only my father could have lived to see it . . .'

'It will be the first co-operative,' Francis told her, and she smiled.

'But not the last – whatever Vivian may say. Not the last.'

Francis left for London a week later, slightly anxious about leaving Rebecca who was once more feeling ill. The sickness which had started only a few weeks into her pregnancy and continued through several weary months, had returned and was leaving her weak and unable to take much interest in anything. But she urged Francis to go, telling him that it was normal enough and bound to pass.

'The baby's strong,' she said as the kicks and blows from within made little moving lumps in her stomach wall. 'He's just getting angry at being confined so long. And you know both the boys were late coming – this one will be just the same, you'll see.'

'I hope so,' Francis said worriedly. 'Though I don't want you to have to suffer this a day longer than necessary. And if anything were to happen now— '

'It won't. It's far too early,' Rebecca said confidently. 'And it's important for you to go now – we must get Tom and Bessie here as soon as possible. And my new sister.'

Tom and Nancy had been married for three weeks now. With old Samuel dead, it seemed pointless to wait any longer, and they had written to tell the family in Kidderminster that they would be marrying quietly as soon as the banns could be called. Rebecca had wanted badly to go to the wedding, but Francis had forbidden the journey and, truth to tell, she had been relieved not to have to make it. Instead, she had sent them a loving letter, written by Francis at her dictation, adding that she hoped they would be in Kidderminster soon.

'But it all depends on Bessie, I know,' she said to Francis as she folded the sheet of paper. 'Tom would come tomorrow, and Nancy with him of course, but they won't leave Bessie there.'

And now Francis was going to London by himself, to try to persuade them all to come at once. There was a place waiting for Tom, a home had been found for them nearby, and Bess could live either with her brother or with Rebecca and Francis. And Tom's last letter had been optimistic: Bess seemed to be coming round to it, he said, she had spoken once or twice of Kidderminster and wondered how her old friends were and whether they would remember her.

'Tell her Nellie Foster does and wants to see her,' Rebecca said as she saw Francis off on the coach. 'And there are plenty of others too who remember Bess. She was popular in the loom shop.'

She watched the coach out of sight and then returned home slowly. Her bulk was more than it had been at six months with the other two babies and she had wondered once or twice if she might be carrying twins. That could account for the sickness she was still suffering. And there did sometimes seem to be an excessive amount of kicking, as if there were half a dozen pairs of tiny fists and feet pummelling away at her. Half a dozen! she thought with a sudden lurch of fear. Could it possibly be . . . ? Women did have such astonishing births sometimes. She tried to imagine giving birth to half a dozen babies, one after the other like puppies, and failed. As for caring for them afterwards – feeding them . . .

She was so occupied with her thoughts as she walked back up Unicorn Street that she did not realise that the trap coming towards her had been standing at her own door. It was only when she was almost at the house that she saw the stranger standing there, with Tilly looking anxiously out to see if she was coming.

'Oh, mum, there you are,' she cried. 'I didn't know what to do – the gentleman says he's a friend of the master's and I told him the master's gone to London, but— '

'It's all right, Tilly.' Rebecca looked at the stranger. He was tall, rather broader than Francis, with hair the rich, dark reddish-brown colour of the horse chestnuts her brother had played with as a boy. His dark grey eyes held a smile as he looked down at her, and she felt an instinctive liking for him, although she couldn't help wondering what Kidderminster society would make of such a fashionable creature. His trousers were of the latest style of pantaloon, and his waistcoat brighter even than Vivian was accustomed to wear, especially at this time in the morning. Yet there was nothing foppish about him. The ruddiness of his skin

106

indicated that he spent a good deal of time out of doors, and he looked as if his body would be strong and muscular, as if he were used to hard work. She wondered who and what he was, and then realised with a start that she had been staring. His eyes were on her, crinkled in amusement.

'I hope I haven't called at an inconvenient time,' he said. 'But I've just returned to Kidderminster and since Francis was one of my best friends when I was here, I thought I should call. Not that it's been easy to track him down,' he added with a grin. 'I tried the school but all they could do was direct me here, where his mother lives. They never mentioned that he lived here himself!'

'They're just fools at that school,' Tilly said with fine disdain. 'Don't know enough to give a body the time of day.'

The stranger laughed. 'Then they haven't changed at all.' He glanced down again at Rebecca. 'I used to be at school with Francis, so I know just what the maids there were like.' There was a glint of mischief in the smile now, and she blushed, recalling that Francis had confessed to her his short-lived dalliance with one of those maids, now left to marry a fish-monger. 'Excuse me,' he said. 'My name's Matthew Farrell. I take it you're Francis's wife?'

'Yes.' Rebecca held out her hand and he took it, bowing slightly. 'Francis and I have been married for three years. We've been in London until recently.' She hesitated, realising suddenly that it was not at all the 'done thing' to stand here talking to a strange man on her doorstep, particularly in her now obvious con-dition. 'Won't you come in?' she asked diffidently, wondering if this were the 'done thing' and feeling that it probably was not. 'I usually have a cup of chocolate about this time.'

Matthew Farrell brightened. 'I'd like that very much, if you can spare the time. I'm sorry to miss Francis, but you can give me all his news. And I'm sure I'll see him when he comes back – does he intend to be away for long?'

He followed Rebecca into the house and she took him to the little morning room at the back of the house, where Enid was stitching at some clothes for the new baby. At the sight of the young man, she dropped her needlework and held up her hands. Her face was pink with delight, and Rebecca was glad she had brought him in, 'done thing' or not.

'Matthew! How good to see you. Why, you haven't been near us for – oh, it must be five years or more. Where have you been, you bad boy?'

He smiled, bent over her hand and then took the chair opposite her while Rebecca sat on the sofa.

'I've been a wanderer, I'm afraid. And it's more than five years, nearer seven.' His smile faded. 'I was sorry to hear about Mr Pagnel. You must miss him very much.'

Enid nodded and glanced down at the work in her lap. 'I miss him sorely. But I have so much to be thankful for: Francis and Rebecca and the children. And he died easy. A peaceful end is so much to thank God for.' There was a slight pause, and when she looked up again her face was bright. 'Now tell us about these wanderings. Where have you been, and what have you been doing? Causing trouble, I've no doubt, from what I remember of you at school!'

Matthew laughed. 'You're quite right. I'm known all over the world for a mischief-maker. They won't have me back in America at any price, while as for France . . .' He cast his eyes heavenward. 'And in Italy they mention my name only in whispers. Naturally, I can't tell you why – none of it's fit for ladies' ears.' He stopped and gazed at them in surprise. 'Now, what have I said to make you laugh? None of this is funny, I assure you. It's a very serious thing to be turned away from so many countries. Why, soon there will be no place over the entire globe where I can lay my weary head.'

'And serve you right too,' Enid said with an unsympathetic chuckle. 'Take no notice of him, Rebecca. He was always a dreadful liar and led poor Francis into all kinds of trouble. I'm sure he means to do the same again – we ought to turn him out now, and never tell Francis that he's even been here.'

'You wouldn't do that,' Matthew said plaintively. 'You wouldn't be so heartless. Francis was always my best friend – after you, of course, dear Mrs Pagnel. There was never anybody quite like you.'

Enid laughed. 'Go along with you, Matthew, you'd charm the birds from their nests. Now here's Tilly with the chocolate, so I suppose we must let you stay long enough to drink a cup. And meanwhile, you shall tell us some of your stories, and the truth, mind! No exaggeration.'

'That takes half the fun out of it,' he complained. 'Stories with no exaggeration in them are dull stories . . . I'll tell you about the time when I was in America and joined the circus as a lion-tamer– '

'*No exaggeration,*' Enid reminded him sternly, and he sighed.

'A trapeze artist, then? Oh, very well – in fact, I did little more than help groom the horses. But it was very interesting, all the same, and some of the things that happened to me you would scarcely credit – and they need no exaggeration at all. Let me tell you about . . .'

His voice went on, smooth and pleasant to hear, and Rebecca sipped at her chocolate, hoping it would not make her feel sick, and listened with half-closed eyes. It made a pleasant change to have this exotic visitor to entertain them, and it hardly mattered whether his stories were true or not. She hoped he was going to stay in Kidderminster for a while. Francis would be so disappointed to miss him.

The sound of the church clock, striking the half-hour, startled them all and Matthew Farrell gave an exclamation and drew out a rather fine watch.

'Heavens, I've been here far too long for an unexpected morning call! You must forgive my rough manners – I've been away from civilised society for too long.' He stood up. 'I hope I haven't overstayed my welcome too much.'

'Indeed not,' Enid said, taking up the work that had lain neglected while she listened to the traveller's tales. 'I can hardly believe the clock myself. We're very glad you came – aren't we, Rebecca? And I'm sure we hope you'll come again, when Francis is home. Will you be staying in Kidderminster long?'

Matthew Farrell was already on his way to the door, but he paused and turned to smile at them both. 'Oh, didn't I mention it?' he asked. 'I'm hoping to settle here, for a time at least. I've done enough wandering – and as I told you, there aren't many countries willing to allow me on their shores any more!'

His smile grew wicked and he gave a little sideways tilt of his head before vanishing through the door. The two women stared after him, and then at each other.

'Well!' Enid said. 'Matthew was always unconventional, but he seems to have grown worse. I wonder how Kidderminster society will take to him? He's certainly very handsome – but I can imagine some people looking down their noses at such casual manners.'

And some of them not too far from home, Rebecca thought, imagining the effect Matthew Farrell would have on Vivian and Maria. 'He seems to be rather a nomad,' she said, thinking of the ruddy skin and clear eyes. 'Do you really think he'll settle down?'

Enid picked up the little jacket she was sewing for the new baby.

'Who knows? With Matthew, anything's possible.' She half closed her eyes to thread her needle. 'Don't be taken in by that flippant manner of his, Rebecca. Matthew has a very serious side to him. In olden days

110

he would have been a crusader. He likes to have a cause to fight for. He likes to be using his strength in the cause of someone weaker. If he were to find such a cause in Kidderminster, he might well stay. If not – he'll be off again, searching . . .'

'Searching for what?' Rebecca asked as Enid's voice drifted into silence.

'For what?' The older woman looked at her, almost as if puzzled. 'Rebecca, I don't know what Matthew is searching for. I don't believe he does himself, even after all this time. But something drives him on, it's certain. Something keeps him from a cosy fireside.'

Rebecca looked into the fire. She thought of the tales Matthew had told, the places he had known. His travels had taken him all over the world. Surely he ought to be satisfied now, surely he had seen almost all there was to see. Yet she too had this feeling that he was still restless, that he could not settle yet. And she wondered why.

What was it he sought?

Chapter Six

'Pagnel and Himley,' Francis said, as it seemed he had already said a hundred times. 'Doesn't it sound fine? Don't you like it, Tom? Nancy? Bess?'

He looked at them in turn. Tom, eager, enthusiastic, ready to leave at a moment's notice and begin a new life. Nancy, married to him for only a month, deeply in love although still grieving for her father, ready to go with him. And Bessie . . .

The three of them turned and looked at Bess Himley. She sat at the table, her fingers still busy with her sewing. Her eyes were on her work and she didn't look up, even when Tom spoke.

'It do sound fine, Francis, and I reckon we all owes you a lot for even thinking of it. It were a good day for us when you come to London to marry our Becky. Weren't it, Bess?'

At the insistence in his voice, Bessie looked up at last. She nodded, but there was no answering pleasure in either her eyes or her voice.

'We got a better life now, I'll allow,' she said reluctantly. 'But what's the use of that, when you wants to put a stop to it all and go back to Kidder? And I don't care what you say, Kidder's trouble for me'n' you, Tom. We never had no good luck there, nor never will. I don't want to set eyes on the place again, never.'

Francis leaned forward and laid his hands over hers. 'Bess, I've told you, my father has made certain that you'll never be charged for Jabez's murder. And who else is there to care? It's forgotten.'

'I know one who won't have forgot.'

'Vivian, you mean? What can he do? To bring any charge at all, he'd have to admit that he helped you.

113

He's not going to do that. Bess, I promise you there's nothing to fear from Vivian.'

'He don't need to bring charges,' Bess said flatly. 'He've got his own ways of making trouble, that one. And he would. I know he would,'

'I don't reckon he would,' Tom said. 'I think Francis is right. Mr Vivian's got too much else to think about now than you'n' me. He's an important man in Kidder.'

'Not too important to remember old grudges,' Bess said. She withdrew her hands from Francis's and took up the bonnet she was sewing.

Francis looked helplessly at the other two. Tom shook his head but Nancy firmly removed the work from Bess's hands and put it on a stool.

'Bess, listen to me. Tom an' me, we want to go to Kidderminster. This is a fine chance for Tom, you know that, an' I don't want him to lose it. Pagnel and Himley – how else would he ever get a chance like that? You can't stand in his way. Francis promises there won't be no trouble, can't you take his word? Why should he lie? Why should he want you to go back if he thought there was any chance of trouble? It'd be trouble for him an' Rebecca too, don't you see? He ain't going to risk that, now is he?'

Bessie listened, but still with obvious reluctance. Nancy went on, her voice in turns urging and coaxing. Her hands held Bessie's tightly, not allowing them to be withdrawn.

'An' there's your Rebecca too. She wants you to go back. She come to London to look for you an' she don't want to lose you again, neither of you. She's your sister, Bess, an' she ain't well. Don't you want to go back for her sake?'

'Course I do!' Bessie exclaimed. 'Course I wants to see Becky again – and the little 'uns too. But – I just got this feeling. Kidder never brought me no good luck and I can't see it starting now. I just can't believe it, Nance. I'm *sorry*.' She looked round at them and

Francis was reminded suddenly of a trapped deer he had found once in the woods. It had watched him approach with just that look in its eyes, as if it knew what must happen and dreaded it. He had released it from the trap and, because it wasn't badly injured, let it run free.

Bessie looked like that deer. As if she was doomed and knew it. As if she saw no escape.

We'll never persuade her, he thought.

'Look,' Bess said desperately, 'there ent nothing to stop you going, Tom. You don't hev to hev me with you. I can stay here, I can manage on me own – I did before— '

Tom reddened, opened his mouth and closed it again. Francis knew that he had been about to remind Bess just how she had managed alone, and then thought better of it. Such a reminder would have been cruel, yet it was impossible that it should not occur to all of them.

'All right,' she said, 'I knows what you're thinking. But I got a proper business now, I can find another girl to help me when Nance ent here – two girls, p'raps, three. I got plenty of customers now, I can make a good little business here. Why don't you just go – and I'll come for a visit mebbe. When Becky has her baby.'

There was a small silence. Francis looked at Nancy and Tom. He saw them glance at each other, saw the communication pass between them. Then Tom turned back to his sister.

'I ent going without you, Bess,' he said slowly. 'And Nancy agrees. If you stay – we stay too.' He gave Francis a glance of apology. 'Sorry, but that's how it is.'

'It's all right.' Francis rose to his feet. 'I can see there's no more you can do. But – don't let's make any decisions at once, Tom. I've put a lot of thought into this venture and if there's any way we can work together on it, I'd like to find it. I'll come back tomorrow and we'll talk again. And meanwhile— ' he glanced at Bessie and could not restrain himself from making one last effort ' —do try to think about it again, Bess. There really would *not* be any trouble for either of you in Kidderminster. And Rebecca would so like to have you near. She needs some of her own family at hand.'

'She does that,' Tom agreed. 'You'n' me, Bess, we've had each other. Our Becky ent had no one, not since Mam and Dad died. And she had a bad time too, when she first come to London looking for us.'

'I know,' Bess muttered, and bent her head over her work. 'I know she did, Tom.' She looked up and Francis saw again that hunted look in her eyes and felt sorry for her. 'Look, I'll think about it, all right? I can't say no more'n that – but I'll think about it.'

For the next few days, Francis busied himself with errands his father had asked him to do, as well as discussing with Tom what should be done about their business there. Tom had found another weaver to take Samuel's place, but the man didn't want to go to Kidderminster and was already thinking of looking for a new job. 'He knows this ent permanent,' Tom said. 'Well, I told him when he started. He seems a good enough sort, but who's to blame him if he just don't turn up one morning? He's got his own family to think on.'

'I know. And there's nothing we can do about it till Bessie decides,' Francis said with a sigh. 'Is there any hope there, d'you think?'

'*I* dunno. She ent said nothing yet, just goes about with a long face as if I'd asked her to jump off London Bridge. You wouldn't think it were summat *better* I was offering her.' Tom sounded aggrieved. 'Well, I suppose it ent, to her way of thinking. If only we could make her see— '

'I know. I feel as frustrated as you. And I can't wait

116

much longer – I've been away from Rebecca too long as it is. But there we are – we can't make Bessie go by force. And if she really is worried— '

'I'll have to stop here if she won't go,' Tom said seriously. 'You know that, don't you? I won't leave her – she's had too much trouble in her life, and we've stuck it out together all this time. I'd hev to stop.'

'I know.' Francis looked at him with respect and regret. He had liked Tom Himley from their first meeting, and had grown to value his honest integrity, sustained under almost impossible conditions when he and Bess had come to London years ago, little more than children. There was no sentiment in Francis's wish to have Tom working with him, no family feeling. He wanted Tom for himself, for his own qualities.

The very qualities that it seemed were going to keep Tom here in London.

'Look,' Tom said now, 'I know you won't want to keep the business going here. You wants to take it to Kidder, and rightly so. But if I has to stop – well, I'd like to carry on with it meself in some way. If I could keep the looms going somehow – I'd hev to pay you for them, and I couldn't do that straightaway, but if we could hev some sort of agreement – well, mebbe I could use one or two of the older designs, just to keep me and Nance and Bess going. With the bonnet-making as well— '

'Tom!' Francis gazed at him in consternation. Furiously, he berated himself. How had he not seen the worries that Tom must have – the fears that his livelihood would be taken from him if he did not follow it to Kidderminster. 'Tom, there's no question but that the business will remain here if you don't come with me. It won't be as I envisaged – the first co-operative in Kidderminster – but it can go on as it has been, for as long as it brings a living. And I hope it will do more than that – I hope it will expand. I never had any intention of depriving you of your work, Tom, never.'

'But how can it go on? You said yourself it'd be easier if it was in Kidder, under your eye— '

'Easier, yes. But not essential.' Francis spoke firmly, pressing down his own anxieties. 'Don't have any fears on that score, Tom. And don't worry Bessie about it any more. If she really is unhappy about going back, we can't force her. We shall just have to work something else out.' He smiled at Tom's anxious face. 'You won't be back on the streets, I promise.'

Tom nodded. 'Well, that's good to know, any road up. But I won't say nothing to Jem, not yet awhile. I don't think he'd leave without giving me good warning.'

'Let's hope not.' But it was plain to Francis that a decision must be made soon. He was growing more and more anxious about Rebecca. Her last letter had been cheerful enough, but he detected a hint or two that she was still unwell, and he was becoming very concerned. She had been so well, so blooming, during her pregnancy with Geoffrey. And even with Daniel, alone and frightened as she had been, she had never been quite so sickly as this.

He went about his business in London and completed it, sending several new orders back to Jeremiah. Something, at least, had been accomplished, he thought; though with little satisfaction. And now he could give Tom no more than a day or two before he must go back. He could not wait any longer.

He went to the little house where the three of them lived together, without much hope that anything might have changed and, to his surprise, was met by a smiling Nancy.

'There you are!' she greeted him. 'Come in – we've bin waiting for you. Bess an' me have got a meat pudding boiling, and Tom's brought some extra ale, so we can sit easy tonight.'

Francis struggled out of his topcoat.

'What's happened? You look excited. Has Bessie—'

118

'You go on in.' Half-giggling, she gave him a little push towards the small back room. 'She wants to tell you herself. Not that it'll be much news now!' And she let her giggles break out, smothering them quickly with her hand. 'She'll be wild with me if she thinks I've said anything.'

Catching her mood, Francis gave her a wink and a conspiratorial grin. 'You haven't said a word,' he whispered, and opened the door. 'Well, hallo, Bess – Tom. How are you both? Sorry I haven't been in for a day or two, I've had so much to do for Father.' His eye caught the table, laid with the best cloth and china that the three of them possessed. 'What's this? A feast?' He looked at their faces, Tom's bright with the same pleased excitement that suffused Nancy's, Bess's less excited but flushed and laughing. 'Don't tell me!' he cried. 'Let me guess! Bessie's sold a bonnet to a lady at the court. The King has ordered one of Tom's carpets to spread before his throne. The— '

Laughter drowned his words and Tom stepped forwards. 'It's none of that, Francis, as well you know,' he said. 'It's better'n any of 'em. Bess has agreed to come to Kidder with us, and we'll be ready to go just as soon as you want. Well, allowing for time to sort things out, but shouldn't tek too long. And we'll need to find a place in Kidder to go to— '

'I can do that,' Francis broke in. He looked around at them, delighted, and shook their hands one by one. 'I can't tell you how pleased I am. Tom, it's going to be grand to be working with you again. And Nancy, you'll like Kidderminster, there's real countryside all around, and Rebecca will make you very welcome, I know. And Bess— ' He took her hand and looked gravely down into her face ' —I know this wasn't an easy decision for you to make, Bess. But I'm sure it was the right one. And we shall all do our best to prove it to you and make you happy back in Kidderminster.'

She looked up at him. The flush had left her cheeks

119

and her eyes were shadowed.

'Oh, you don't hev to worry about me,' she said. 'I'll be all right. I allus hev made out in the past. I reckon going back to Kidder won't be so bad. Daft of me to fret about it, I reckon.'

She pulled away and went to the fire, lifting off the heavy pot she used for almost all her cooking – puddings, stews, vegetables, soups. They gathered round the table, still talking and laughing, and Francis ate heartily of the food that the two girls piled in front of him. And never ate better, he thought, even at the table of the richest manufacturer. Or maybe it was the company.

He looked round at the faces of his companions. Simple people, without education – even now, neither of the two women could read, nor write more than their own names – yet full of sturdy independence and an honesty that people like Vivian could never match, never even comprehend. People without pretension, kindly, generous with what little they had, people who had known suffering and did not cause it to others.

It would be good to have them all in Kidderminster. The start of a new era, perhaps, in which men and masters worked together and shared the proceeds of their labours. The era of the co-operative.

The era of his dream.

Rebecca's own dream was starting slowly, but hopefully.

The meeting in Unicorn Street was attended by only a few women, two of whom were herself and Enid. The others were the wives of warehouse or office managers. They sat nervously on the edge of their chairs, glancing sideways at each other, inclined to giggle a little. But when Rebecca began to speak, their smiles faded and their giggles died. By the time she had finished, each one had tears in her eyes.

'But I never realised it was so bad,' Lydia Brewer

said in distress. 'Why has no one told us – why haven't our husbands told us?'

'Because they don't want our sensibilities upset,' Meg Saunders replied, but Rebecca shook her head.

'Oh, they may say that, they may even believe it a little. But don't you think it's also because they realise that once women know about the conditions they'll want them put right? We all know what it is to have ailing children.' She looked at them all, but turning her eyes away out of respect for the babies each one had lost, either in childbirth or infancy. 'If we knew too the conditions our weavers' wives lived in, the poverty and dirt and cold and hunger that kills their families – why, none of us could sleep easily at night. And your husbands know that.'

Anne Curtin stirred in her chair.

'I think you're wrong, Rebecca. I don't believe my husband even *knows* of such things. Why should he? He's never been into a weaver's cottage in his life. He's had no need to. Neither has the husband of any woman here, I'll be bound. They're as ignorant as we were.' She glanced at Rebecca. 'In fact, none of us really *knows*. You've told us, that's all – and you were a weaver's daughter yourself. You're biased.'

The other two looked uncertain, as if half-swayed by this argument, but Rebecca nodded.

'You're quite right to take that attitude, Anne. I might indeed be exaggerating. So why don't we all go and see for ourselves?' She rose from her chair. 'Why not go now? There's no time like the present, after all.'

'Go now? To the weavers' cottages?' Lydia looked aghast. 'Oh, I don't think Amos would like me to do that. The people are so rough— '

'—and there's such disease there,' Meg chimed in. 'Surely it's enough that you've told us, Rebecca. We don't have to actually see it for ourselves – we believe you, don't we, Lydia? Anne?'

'But you don't – not entirely.' Rebecca looked at them. 'Anne doesn't. And she won't until she sees it for herself. *And she's right*,' she added passionately. 'I *am* biased, going hungry because my father couldn't finish his piece in time, seeing my parents die as paupers after a lifetime of hard toil.' Her voice shook a little as she remembered that terrible winter's day when she and Francis had brought her mother home from the bare, cold hovel where her father's body lay slowly stiffening. 'I can't forget those memories, especially as I know they were nothing unusual – such things were happening all the time. And still are.' She paused, looking at the stricken faces before her. 'But unless you see it for yourself, you'll never believe it.'

'Rebecca's right,' Enid agreed. 'And it's not just Kidderminster. It's the same everywhere. Women and children are sick and dying all over the country because their menfolk just aren't paid enough. They can't work any harder to earn more money, because they just don't have the time or the strength. And men are doing nothing about it – so it's up to us women.'

'And we can start,' Rebecca said quietly, 'by forming together and setting out to help. Talking to our men and to our friends. Making them understand just what's happening.'

'Which we'll do a lot better,' Anne Curtin observed, 'if we see it for ourselves.' She gave the other women a challenging glance. 'Well, I'm game if you are. I'll go with Rebecca to the slums and see how the people there live. And if a half of what Rebecca says is true, I'll tell my friends and my husband about it afterwards and do whatever I can to put things right.'

Rebecca gave a sigh of relief. Anne was the strongest of the women there that afternoon, and with her to help set up the association, there was a much greater chance of success.

'So,' she said, 'shall we go to visit the weavers' wives

now? Or shall we go on another day, when we have more time?'

Bill Bucknell left the house where he and Nell Foster lived and walked quickly through the darkening streets. In his chest was the knot of anger that had beaten there in place of a heart for so long, the anger that rebelled against the meagre pay for which he worked so hard, the conditions in which he was forced to keep his family. It was an anger he had expected to carry for the rest of his days, but now, at last, there were signs that times might be beginning to change.

'We won't go on like this,' Bill had told Nell over and over again. 'Working like slaves to make the masters rich, while our own childer starve away. Look at young Sam now, nothing but skin and bone. He needs good meals to fatten him up, and where's he going to get those if I can't get more pay? There ent no more hours left to work.'

Nell had cradled the toddler on her lap. He was weak and ill then, and spent most of his time lying on the pile of sacks and old blanket off-cuts where they all slept at night. He seemed to have lost all interest in food, opening his mouth reluctantly for the gruel Nell spooned in, and as often as not vomiting it back before it even reached his wasted stomach. He stared with dull eyes as his brothers played on the bare stone floor, and seldom cried.

'What can you do about it?' Nell had asked drearily. 'Nobody's going to take pity on us. There's little 'uns dying every day – why should our Sam matter to anyone? Why should they care if we has one less mouth to feed – they'll just say we don't need the pay we gets now. Not that any of 'em even knows what it's like to live on a weaver's pay,' she added bitterly. 'Long as we turns up on time, they don't even bother about us.'

'What about that Becky Himley you said come here the other day?' he asked. 'She ought to know. And

123

she's wed young Francis Pagnel, couldn't she do aught?'

Nell shrugged. 'She's bin here a time or two, and brought us good food too – milk, a few eggs, some fresh bread. Aye, she's helped. And she's got a few of the other women she knows helping too – folk like Amos Brewer's wife, they've got together in a sort of society and they're getting clothes and stuff. But what more can they do? They might talk to their menfolk, but what notice will *they* take? And even old Mr Jeremiah won't go against the rest of the masters and raise pay. They sticks together, you knows that.'

Bill nodded. 'Well, then, there's nothing for it. It's the Union that'll hev to do summat about it.'

'The Union? You mean the Friendly Society? The old sick club?'

'It might hev started out as a sick club,' Bill said, 'but it's a sight more'n that now. It kept a lot of families from starving in the strike in '17, and since then we've got better organised. We can help other workers if need be – word is, there's going to be trouble in Bradford pretty soon. And they'll help us. It's all stick together, like brothers, and if we does that, the masters'll hev to listen.'

Nell had looked doubtful, but at that moment the child had begun to wail on her lap, a thin, keening sound that might have been a scream of pain had he been strong enough, and she had bent to attend to him.

And as Bill walked through the narrow, littered streets on that twilit summer evening, he thought of the way little Sam had finally died. His stunted body racked with a hunger that had sucked the flesh from his bones; piteous, desperate eyes fixed on his mother as he reached out claw-like fingers for the milk she offered him, milk which would not have saved him then even if he had been able to swallow it. The last agony of the swollen belly drawing his bony knees up to his chest.

No child should die like that, Bill thought with that knot of fury tightening in his chest. No child, be he weaver's son or king's.

'Hey up, Bill. Going down the tavern?'

He turned his head swiftly, almost guiltily, towards the man who had hailed him from across the street, then cursed under his breath. George Hodgett, the biggest blabbermouth in Kidder. And he'd hoped that by coming through these streets, he would avoid meeting anyone he knew.

'No, not ternight,' he said. 'Got someone to see.'

'Oh ah?' George fell into step with him. 'Getting a bit late for visiting, ent it? What'll your Nell say, eh?' He nudged Bill sharply in the ribs and chuckled. 'Bet she do' know where thee bist.'

'What Nell knows is her business and mine,' Bill said tersely. 'And I'm in a hurry, if 'tis all the same to you, George. See you tomorrow, mebbe.' He quickened his pace and strode on along the street.

George fell back a step. 'Well, if that's how thee wants it, bugger me if I'll hold you up. Must be important business, that's all I can say.'

Bill was aware of the offence in his voice, but closed his ears to it. Let George Hodgett take umbrage if he wanted – there was nothing to be done about it. Where Bill was going was something that mustn't be told to a soul – that had been impressed on him from the start.

'A secret society is what it says – secret,' Fred Holloway had told him. 'No blabbing it to all and sundry. There's some weavers as is masters' men, and we all knows who they are. Come the day when we takes our rights, they'll get their come-uppance, but we don't want no trouble before that.'

Bill had nodded and given his hand on it, and after that Fred had told him where to come for his initiation. That over, he would be a full member and able to attend meetings and help plan the policies of the Union itself.

125

'The Friendly Society of Operative Carpet Weavers,' he murmured to himself. 'It sounds fine. And when we gets enough money behind us, we can use our power. That'll make they masters sit up!'

He was almost there now. An old house at the end of a dark street, the headquarters of the Friendly Society. It was looked after by an old man who lived with his daughter in one of the basement rooms, and used for meetings. Tonight it appeared deserted and Bill stood uncertainly on the kidney-stones, looking at the darkened windows. A bat flew close to his head and he jumped and swore again.

'That you, Bill Bucknell?'

Startled, he looked around and a figure detached itself from the shadows and came silently towards him. 'Bill Bucknell?' it repeated hoarsely, and he nodded.

'That's me.'

'This way.'

There were no further words or introductions. Slightly nervous now, Bill followed the man into the house. There were no lamps, only the glimmer of twilight from the open doorway. Then the door was closed behind him, plunging the passage they had entered into darkness, and Bill realised that another man had materialised behind him. He felt a sudden lurch of sickening emotion that he recognised, dimly, as fear. Fear . . . He hadn't felt fear since he was a little 'un and caught stealing apples.

'Look, if this is a joke— ' he began, but was immediately silenced by a sharp kick from the man behind.

'That's enough! You ent here to complain. Keep your hand on the wall and just keep walking, slowly. There's steps down, ten of 'em. Start counting now.'

Bill felt cautiously with his toe and began to descend. His mouth was dry now and his heart was thumping uncomfortably. What was going on? What did these men mean to do with him? Where was Fred Holloway – and what did he know, after all, of this 'secret society'? He had only Fred's word that it existed at all. Suppose it was all some trick to get him here, where nobody knew he had come, and then . . .

And then what? His imagination failed him. He fumbled on the steps, lost count and imagined he had one more to go. His leg jarred painfully as he brought his foot down on solid floor.

'All right. Stand still.'

One of his captors was doing something to his head. He jerked away, then found himself pinioned while a thick cloth was bound over his eyes, holding them tightly and painfully shut. He began to protest again and received a sharp smack on the mouth.

'I told yer, keep quiet. All right, Eb, you can light up now, he ent going to see nothing.' There was a sound of tinder being struck and a lamp being lit, but Bill was completely blind. He stood helpless, not knowing where he was, not even sure where the steps were that he had just descended. Miserably, he wished he had never come.

For a few moments, the two men worked in silence. What they were doing, Bill had no idea, but his fears grew. He felt one of them come nearer him, the warmth of his body mingling with the smell of sweat and toil, the familiar weavers' stink of uncured leather and gelatine used to make size, of urine collected from the men for use in the dyeing, of the wool itself. Who were they? He could not recognise their voices from the few words so gruffly uttered. What did they mean to do to him? He gasped and shuddered as something cold touched the back of his neck. A knife? Something bigger?

One of the men laughed shortly, then gave him a shove and Bill half stumbled, half fell forwards. He had an impression of going through a doorway into another room. The atmosphere was different, as if there were more people here. He heard a soft whisper, a muffled snigger.

127

Hands caught him by the arms, and other hands fumbled at the back of his head. The blindfold fell from his eyes and he blinked in a light that seemed bright and painful yet dimmed after a moment or two to a murky twilight, where shadows loomed large and menacing on the walls. He found he was standing before a large table, behind which stood four men, two at each side with a space between them. And in the space . . .

Bill gave a cry of fear and horror, and staggered back, his hands over his eyes.

'Hold up, there!'

Strong arms caught at him, preventing him from falling, stopping him from turning to escape, forcing him to stand and face the ghastly apparition. 'Open yer eyes! You got to look at it. You got to see . . .'

'No!' he bleated, almost beside himself with terror. 'No, I won't look, I won't, 'tis the devil's work, 'tis the devil himself, Old Nick come to get me and I ent ready, I ent going, I— '

'Stop yer blubbing, mate,' one of the men holding him advised, not unkindly. 'We all had to go through it. Stand up straight and it'll be over all the sooner. Now!'

Bill found himself compelled to stand upright. Slowly, he regained control of his shuddering limbs and after a moment or two managed to open his eyes and confront the spectacle again. The horror this time was not so great, though he still wanted to close his eyes, to escape. But as he flinched, the rough hands tightened cruelly on his arms and he took a deep breath and stood more firmly.

'That's better.' One of the men behind the table spoke, but Bill could not look at him yet. At first unable to face the thing at the centre of the group, he could not now take his eyes from it. He stared as if mesmerised, his eyes moving slowly over the ghastly face, half grinning skull, half rotting flesh, down to the

128

neck that was nothing but a column of whitened bone, the shoulders, arms and ribs that were shrouded only in tattered black. He started and saw what was clutched in the bony fingers: the long handle of a scythe.

Death.

'Right. You seen enough.' Bill tore his eyes away and looked now at the men behind the table. All were masked, and in the shadows there was little chance of knowing who they were. He waited, numbed beyond protest now, for what they were going to do to him.

'William Bucknell.' One of the men stepped forwards. He was tall and broad, dressed entirely in black, and he carried a large axe with a blade that gleamed in the flickering light. Was this the blade Bill had felt against his neck? He shuddered again.

'William Bucknell.' It was a fellow-weaver, he was sure, but the voice was muffled and he could not tell whose it might be. 'You are here to take part in the ceremony of initiation into the Secret Society of the Carpet Weavers of Kidderminster. What say you, do you desire to be a brother of this society, do you promise and swear to keep to its rules, to be faithful at all times and ready to answer the Call?'

Bill stared and tried to speak, but could make only a stuttering noise. The voice spoke again, impatiently.

'Well, do you swear? You came here as a man who would be our brother. Will you so? If not, say so now and you can go free, provided you never tell a soul what has happened here tonight. If you do . . .' The axe moved threateningly, and Bill recoiled.

'I swear! I swear I'll never tell anyone, never,' he babbled, and the axe returned to its former position.

'And do you also agree to abide by the rules of this society?'

'I agree. I swear.'

'Then hear this, William Bucknell.' The voice was deep and solemn, intoning as if it were reading a prayer in church. 'Hear and remember, all your life, for this promise will bind you until death.'

Bill swallowed and nodded. He listened to the words as he had never listened before, as if trying to brand them into his memory. Until death . . . His eyes strayed back to the horrifying spectacle behind the table and he felt a sickness rise from his stomach.

'. . . *never disclose to any other* . . .' he heard through the mist of giddiness.

'. . . *uniting to cultivate friendship . . . protect our Trade*
. . . due respect to all our rules must be paid
. . . you will be faithful . . . and all encroachment on our rights withstand.
As Token of our Alliance, give me your right hand . . .'

Bill saw that the figure was holding out a black-gloved hand. Tentatively, he held out his own and found it grasped in strong fingers, grasped as if it would never be let go. He was too afraid to try to withdraw it, and stood linked, silent, fearful.

'*And now, my friend,*' the deep voice continued, '*if you prove deceitful,*
Remember your calamitous latter end!'

The axe shook again, its shadow rising menacingly on the wall behind, and Bill flinched again, half expecting it to fall upon his neck after all. But now the two men who had escorted him there had stepped forward again and stood beside him. There was the clanking sound of chains and Bill realised with horror that they meant to bind him.

'No!' he cried in panic, struggling against them. 'No, I've promised, I've sworn – what more can I do? I'll do all you say, I'll keep the rules, I'll be a true brother, I swear again— '

'Be still,' one of the two growled. 'We ent finished with thee yet. You've to see the President now.'

'The President?' But the chains were binding him now, cutting into his flesh, and he was being urged through another doorway, the man with the axe going ahead and standing close, his weapon unnervingly near to Bill's neck.

In this room there was just one man behind a table. Like the others, he was hooded and masked with black, and his eyes gleamed through narrow slits cut in the fabric. He was seated, but Bill could see that he was a powerful man. And not only in size. Power emanated from him, hung like an aura around him. This was not a man you would cross, even if he were not swathed in black with his head ominously hooded.

'You are here to be admitted to the Secret Society of the Carpet Weavers of Kidderminster. You have heard the rules and agree to be our brother?'

Bill found himself being nudged violently. He nodded.

'Answer.'

'Yes, sir,' he whispered.

'Then swear this solemn oath of allegiance. Place your right hand on your left breast.' Bill found himself unable to remember which hand was his right: he fumbled and found it guided by his guard. 'And your left hand on the Bible.' The Bible lay on the table before him. Trembling, he laid his hand upon it. Visions of being struck down by a thunderbolt rose in his mind, but there was no escape. Haltingly, his voice cracked, he repeated the words of the solemn oath.

'. . . so help me, God,' he finished, and drew a shaky breath. There was a long moment of silence, and then the President stood up behind his table and leaned forward, holding out his hand.

'Welcome to our brotherhood, William Bucknell. May you be a good and loyal member of the society and may we have success in helping the weavers of Kidderminster to gain their just rights. And now leave this place, and remember that you must never, on pain

131

of Death itself, disclose what has happened here to any living soul.' He paused and then repeated, slowly and emphatically: 'Any . . . living . . . soul . . .'

Bill found himself shaking the hand and then being turned by his captors. They led him out through the door and into the other room, now empty. Here they unfastened his chains and dropped them in a corner. Then they tore off their hoods and masks and grinned at him.

'Well done, Bill! You stood up to it well, didn't he, Jem? 'T'ent everyone as gets through it – some of 'em faints clean away. But you went through it like a man and we're glad to have you to stand with us.'

Bill stared at them. 'Fred! And . . . *George Hodgett*! But – I saw you on the way here. You asked me where I was going— '

'And you never told me.' George nudged him in the ribs and he remembered that nudge in the street and the similar dig with the sharp elbow only a short time ago, in this very room. Why hadn't he realised? But you couldn't be expected to recognise a man by his *elbow*, for God's sake . . . 'If you'd let on then, Bill, you'd never hev bin allowed through the door. We got to be sure, see. Anyway, you weren't telling, so that were all right. And now we'm brothers, see, and bound to help each other.' He grinned at Bill's bemused face. 'And now we'm truly off to the tavern. We've summat to celebrate now. And your Nell will smell a rat for certain if you don't go home smelling of ale after all this time!'

Co-operation.

That was the keyword, Francis thought as the coach drew nearer to Kidderminster. Co-operation between master and man, between those who organised the manufacture of the product and those who did the actual making. What difference was there between them, after all, other than a difference of ability and skill? And that difference, as often as not, stemmed from education – who was to say what Tom Himley might have attained had he also been a pupil at a grammar school, had he been given the privileges that Francis and his cousin Vivian had enjoyed?

And now all that was about to change. Slowly, he knew, there would be much opposition to his ideas, as there already had been. Many of the older masters would resist the idea of co-operatives, and indeed a good many of the younger ones too, such as Vivian himself who would fight against the idea of giving up any of his profit so that common weavers could live more comfortably. But there were already a few who agreed with Francis's principles, and there would be more. And the weavers themselves would surely be willing to join, and to work all the harder knowing that there was profit for them too.

Already there was a thriving union, formed from the old sick clubs. And Francis had made up his mind that he must work first with the leaders of that union. If they agreed with his plans, as surely they must, he would have three-quarters of the labouring men of Kidderminster on his side.

And with Tom Himley standing with him too, the future was bright indeed. Not for added riches – not for his own comfort and luxury – but for all those who toiled in the carpet industries, yes, and in others too, all those who lived for nothing but to earn enough pence to stand between them and starvation. All those whose lives were never more than grinding squalor, from the moment of birth until that last desolate tumble into a pauper's grave.

So Francis dreamed as he came back to Kidderminster. And when he stepped from the coach, his eyes were bright, his heart eager to begin. He saw Tom Himley waiting for him, as they had arranged, for Tom had come ahead with the two women, leaving Francis to complete a last-minute piece of business for his

133

father. But now they were all here and the future could begin.

'Tom! Good to see you. And how do you like Kidderminster now that you're back?' Francis was busy overseeing the unloading of his boxes, and barely looked at Tom as he spoke. 'Yes, that's mine too – and that . . .' He turned back to his brother-in-law. 'And how are you settling into the house Rebecca found for you? You're comfortable there, I hope? And Rebecca – how is she? I can't wait to see her again. I suppose she's showing well now – and is she still sickly, her last letter never said.'

Suddenly struck by Tom's silence, he turned and looked into his companion's face. The sounds of the other passengers' chatter, the noise of boxes being unloaded, the stamping of the horses' hooves, all died away. He stared and then took Tom by the arm.

'What is it? Is it Rebecca? For God's sake, man, *tell* me!'

Tom shook his head.

'It ent Becky. She's all right, still a bit sick mornings but well enough otherwise. No, Becky's at home, looking forward to seeing you— '

'What, then? Is it one of the children? Daniel? Geoffrey?' Francis shook his arm. 'Don't stand there twisting your cap in your hands, Tom, *tell* me, whatever it is.'

'It's none of them,' Tom said miserably. 'It's Bess.'

'Bess? Your Bessie? She has the fever again, is that it? She's not – please God, she's not *dead*!'

'No, but she might's well be, I reckon. She ent come with us, Francis. She told us she had a bonnet to deliver – said she'd catch the coach at the next stop, it would be nearer for her than coming back to where we were getting on. But she never did. She sent a note instead. Got someone to write it for her.' He fished in his pocket and brought out a scrap of paper. 'This is it.'

Unbelievingly, Francis took the note and read it.

Then he put out a hand and laid it on Tom's shoulder.

'I can't say how sorry I am, Tom. She really didn't want to come, did she? What will you do?'

Tom shrugged. 'What can I do? We've moved everything here now. It's all arranged. I can't turn round and go back. I shall just hev to hope she goes on all right. She ought to – she've got her bonnet-making. But I can't help thinking of her, all by herself there. We've allus stuck together, me and her. I don't mind telling you, Francis, I'm worried – but like Nancy says, she's a grown woman and must take her own road. I can't look after her if she don't want to be looked after.'

Francis stood with his boxes piled around him, and nodded slowly. The coach had gone now, and most of the passengers dispersed. 'I think Nancy's right,' he said. 'And perhaps Bessie never intended to come at all. Perhaps she only agreed so that you would come back, and always meant to stay behind. She wanted you to do what you wanted, Tom – it would be wrong to go back now, and even more wrong to try to force her to come after all. And we can make sure she's never in poverty.'

'Ah, we can do that,' Tom said, but the heart, the eagerness, had gone out of him. He bent to pick up one of the boxes. 'At least, we hopes so, it all depends on this dream of yours, don't it, and whether it's likely to come true. Dreams don't often, from what I've seen.'

But this one will, Francis thought as he followed Tom to the trap that would take them to Unicorn Street. This is one dream that *will* come true.

I shall make it so.

Chapter Seven

'Lawless Hour!'

The town was alive with the excitement of celebration. Even in the quiet morning room in Unicorn Street, the vibrations could be felt and Francis glanced across the breakfast table at his wife, with some concern.

'You're not thinking of going out today? It would be very unwise.' His eyes rested briefly on her swollen figure. 'I want nothing happening to you, my love.'

Rebecca smiled. With this pregnancy now in its last stages, she had developed a serenity that made her more beautiful than ever. Her skin was smooth, touched with glowing colour, and her hair shone like the chestnuts that could be gathered from the woods. She reached across to touch his hand, and he felt the same thrill, as fresh and tingling as it had been the first time he had touched her. The warmth of desire brushed his skin, and he thought longingly of making love to her again. When this baby was born and in its cradle. When they could be husband and wife once more.

'I shan't go out,' Rebecca said. 'I remember Lawless Hour too well! It was getting rough then, and I hear it's worse now.'

'Matthew's going,' Enid remarked, helping herself to more bacon. 'He told me yesterday. It's one of the things he used to think about when he was away. Wherever he was in the world, however strange the place, he remembered Lawless Hour— '

'—and realised that there was nowhere quite so strange as Kidderminster!' Matthew's voice broke in and they all jumped and looked up as he came into the room, his face alive with laughter. 'Never in all my travels did I find a place where even the most respectable families in town threw apples at the Town Bailiff and his corporation. What a custom! I wouldn't miss it for the world.'

'Well, mind you don't get a black eye from a badly aimed apple or a cabbage stalk,' Francis warned him. 'And serve you right, too. Have you come for breakfast?'

'Not likely. My landlady feeds me far too well.' He sat down and accepted a cup of coffee. 'No, I came to beg a few cabbage stalks of my own from your kitchen . . .' He laughed again at their faces. 'Don't take me so seriously. I promise I shall be very good and merely observe. And I shan't get even the littlest bit drunk.'

'I should hope not,' Rebecca said sternly, though her smile belied her severity. 'And don't come back here and excite the boys with your stories afterwards, either. I don't want them filching fruit to play "Lawless Hour" with for the next month. They can find quite enough boisterous games to play without your encouragement.'

'Leave them alone – they're real boys, full of life and mischief,' Matthew said. 'God preserve us from the little carpet knights they'd be if your cousin Maria had the upbringing of them. I think He knows what He's doing, only allowing her to have girls. And even they are hardly permitted to put a pretty little foot an inch out of place for fear they spoil their frilly little dresses.'

'Maria wants them to be ladies, and so they shall be,' Rebecca said. 'Though I think she may have problems with Lucy – that one has a look in her eye at times . . . And I'm afraid they'll be out of countenance if the next one is a boy.'

'But surely the next one *is* to be a boy,' Matthew asked, as if it were a foregone conclusion. 'Hasn't Vivian decreed it?'

They all laughed, and Francis said, 'Vivian has already decreed it five times, as well you know. Unfortunately, this is one thing my cousin cannot order for himself. And now I think we should stop making mock of him – it's not funny, either for him or for poor Maria. She's already looking frightened, poor woman, in case it turns out to be another girl.' The chimes of the grandfather clock interrupted him and he jumped up. 'Is that really the time? I ought to be gone.' He bent to kiss Rebecca. 'Take care, my love, and send a message at once if anything happens . . . Where are you bound, Matthew? Are you really going to watch this riotous custom, or are you going to stay here and entertain my wife and mother?'

Matthew glanced briefly at Rebecca, meeting those dark brown eyes for a moment. He knew that she would welcome his company. These last few weeks and days of her pregnancy were clearly uncomfortable, and she seldom went out now or had any visitors other than her family. And he wanted to stay – he wanted it very much.

'I'm going to watch your weavers enjoying themselves for once,' he said, rising from his chair. 'I may even throw an apple or two myself. When otherwise does a man get a chance to show his feeling for authority without being arrested for it? No wonder they all take the day off and enjoy every lawless minute of it. But why are you in such a hurry, Francis, if your looms are all stopped for the day?'

'Because, contrary to what most people seem to imagine, a manufacturer does actually do some work around the place,' Francis retorted, aiming a cuff at his friend's head. 'And it doesn't depend on looms running. I shall welcome the peace and quiet. And now stop making eyes at my wife, Matthew, and come along – we'll walk down the hill together and you can go and enjoy yourself while I struggle to make a living for my family.' He strode to the door and called for his hat and coat. 'Don't forget, Rebecca – you're to send a message if you feel in the least ill. Take care of her, Mother.'

Matthew followed him to the door and paused to turn once more and smile at Rebecca. He had seen the brief shadow of disappointment in her eyes when he had said he would not be staying, and the sight had brought a tremor to his heart. Don't be a fool, he told himself harshly. She sees you as nothing more than a friend – amusing company for an hour or two. And that is how it must always be.

Feeling the brightness of the day a little dimmed, he followed Francis out into the street.

'Hallo, they've started,' he exclaimed as the sound of handbells being rung came up the hill from the town. 'Let's hurry, Francis. Don't you remember how we used to slip out from school to see the fun?' He quickened his step. 'Why don't you come too? You don't really have to go to your office, do you?'

'There are a thousand things— ' Francis began, but Matthew interrupted him with affectionate impatience.

'And just how many will you manage to accomplish in one day? Two? Three? A dozen? Leaving a thousand still! Take a day off, like your workers do, and forget you're a solemn manufacturer with all the burdens of the world on your shoulders. It'll do you all the good in the world.' He caught at Francis's arm and dragged him down to the centre of the town. 'Look, they're gathering already. Now don't you wish you'd let me go to your kitchen for a cabbage stalk?'

Francis laughed and gave way, and the two young men hastened down to where the streets were filling with people – weavers, dyers, draw-boys and girls, all thronging the narrow streets armed with cabbage stalks which they began to hurl at each other. As fast as they were thrown, the stalks were caught and flung back, amidst shouts and guffaws from the men and boys, screams of hysterical laughter from the women.

Matthew and Francis stood in a corner, watching, and whenever a stalk came their way Matthew reached out a long arm and caught it, throwing it back into the mêlée.

'It isn't just cabbage stalks, either,' he observed as a battered shoe flew past his ear. 'It's just about anything that can be thrown . . . How on earth did such a custom start, Francis?'

'Heaven knows, nor what it has to do with the election of the new High Bailiff.' Francis ducked as a shower of apples landed at their feet. 'You'd think these children would have something better to do with apples other than throw them about . . . I suppose it has some origin in the old Lord of Misrule tradition. Laws are suspended for a time and everyone, however downtrodden, is given a moment of glory when he can defy any man and think himself a real fellow before he goes back to work and poverty and waits for next time.'

The loud throb and skirl of a fife and drum band struck at their ears and they fell silent and waited as the procession filed by. The band first, then the new bailiff and his corporation, resplendent in their official robes, and finally the constables, on their way to pay their traditional visit to the old bailiff. The crowd of revellers fell in behind them, swelling to a mob as they passed through the streets and drew in the people already there, and as they came nearer to the old bailiff's residence the apple-throwing increased until it seemed that an entire orchard must have been robbed to supply enough missiles.

'We shall be ankle-deep in cider,' Matthew remarked as they felt the apples crunch under their feet, and slipped on the increasing pulp. 'Not that the men will need cider to make them merry tonight – the ale-houses are already doing a roaring trade.'

'Aye, and that's the dark side of it,' Francis said soberly. 'Every year it gets more like a riot – why, only a few years ago there *was* a riot, a serious one when the magistrates tried to put a stop to some of the excesses. Three men ended in jail and there were a good many hurt. And two thousand very sore heads next morning, I should say. Not much good carpet woven, at any rate.'

'But these things shouldn't be stopped,' Matthew said as the procession moved slowly away through the twisting streets. 'They may seem foolish and rough, but they're necessary for people like these. They provide a safety valve. Think of the life of the ordinary weaver, Francis, or indeed any workman. Constant pressure, long, hard hours, an unceasing worry about money and his family . . . were it not for occasions like these when he can let all his anger and frustration loose in one orgy of misbehaviour, he might explode in a much worse fashion. That's why he does it and that's why it's allowed. Authority isn't blind over this – it knows very well what it's doing.'

'I suppose so.' They followed the crowd, watching the antics as men and women, boys and girls, cavorted in a way that would never have been allowed on an ordinary day. 'They certainly seem to be enjoying themselves.'

'Then let them.' Matthew smiled as they passed a doorway with a couple embraced in its shelter. 'And let them enjoy the fairs and other holidays that come their way. They need them and they deserve them.'

'Vivian wouldn't agree with that. He thinks all such days ought to be stopped. The fairs – do you realise we have five fairs a year in Kidderminster, Matthew? The "bannering", when everyone follows the Vicar around the parish boundary and often end up fighting with the men of the next parish intent on their own bannering. The "heaving" at Easter— '

'Oh, I remember that one. Fun for the men on Monday and the women on Tuesday,' Matthew said, grinning.

'The Orange day in July – and just what does a battle

somewhere in Ireland over two hundred years ago have to do with anyone in Kidderminster today, save that it's yet another chance to take a day off and go wild?' Francis shook his head. 'You must admit, Matthew, that Vivian and his friends do have a case. Our weavers have a good many holidays, for all they cry how hard done by they are.'

'And let them go on so,' Matthew advised, 'for if they don't have these opportunities to let off steam, they might explode all the worse, as I just said. And now why don't we do the same? There's an alehouse here, Francis, and I'm thirsty. Let's go in for a jug of good ale and make believe we're weavers too and making holiday with the rest. You run a co-operative, after all – you ought to share in the pleasures as well as the pain.'

Francis gave him a quizzical glance but allowed himself to be drawn into the public house, and Matthew called for two tankards of ale. They sat in a corner and listened to the noise of the crowd outside, and then glanced up as a knot of men surged into the small, smoke-darkened room.

'I tell you, mates,' one of them was saying, 'it won't be long now. They're up to summat – I seen it in their eyes. They mean to dock our money one way or another, and what do it matter what excuse they use? We can't do nothing about it any road.'

'We can,' growled another, whose dark, surly face betrayed a determination not to let any man do him down. 'We can strike.'

'Strike!' the first exclaimed with contempt. 'And ent that what the Wilton men mean to do, and the Bradford combers? What good will it do them – or us? We'll send 'em money, and where'll it all go, eh? Down the nearest gully, that's where.'

'All the same, it'll mek the masters think. And if the boys stand out long enough— '

The first man snorted and then glanced round the

room. His eye fell on Francis and Matthew and he nudged his companions. They fell silent, staring suspiciously until Matthew got to his feet.

'No need to worry, lads,' he said cheerfully. 'We're not spying on you for the masters, and anyway, isn't today a holiday? Why not have a drink with us and forget your problems for an hour or two. It's Lawless Hour and there are no rules, so you can take a tankard from me and no questions asked, isn't that right?'

They stared for a moment, and then he saw the grins slowly break out over the lined faces. 'Aye, that's right,' they said, and then, laughing, 'Aye, right it is and right you are. A sup of ale will go down well, true enough. Hey! Landlord!' And they reached out for their tankards and came over to the corner where Matthew and Francis sat, talking and laughing as if they had known them all their lives. 'A very good health to you, sirs. A good holiday, and a good life.'

'A good holiday,' Francis said, holding up his own tankard, and Matthew echoed his words. 'A good holiday.'

But – a good life? He looked at the faces, old before their time, and wondered. Was life ever really good for the working men of Kidderminster or anywhere else? Or was it just something to be borne, to be tolerated, because there was nothing else to be done?

But before he could come to any conclusion, another face appeared at the door. Tilly – little Tilly, the housemaid who had come to Kidderminster with Francis and Rebecca, who worshipped the two who had taken her from the workhouse and given her a home. White-faced, breathless, her eyes darting about the tavern as if searching, though without any hope of finding what she sought . . . until her gaze settled at last on Francis in his shadowy corner.

'Oh, sir!' she cried, running in and taking no notice of the laughter and sallies of the men. 'Sir, I've been looking all over for you . . . It's the mistress, sir – she needs you – oh sir, she's that bad and Mrs Pagnel says I got to find you, you got to come and I didn't know where to look when they said you wasn't at the loom shop, I didn't know— '

'All right, Tilly, you've found me now.' Francis was on his feet, his ale forgotten. 'It's the mistress, you say? The baby?' Tilly nodded, her face white, her hand pressed to her side and she gasped for breath. 'I'm on my way.' He was already at the door. 'Matthew – you understand— ' His gaze went helplessly to the maid, who had collapsed into a chair, struggling for breath. 'Give her some ale and send her home. I daren't wait . . .'

He was gone. Matthew bent over the housemaid, but Tilly shook her head at him, gasped that she had only a stitch and would be right as rain in a moment or two. He gave her a drink of his ale and watched the colour come back to her cheeks. He would see her home. He could perhaps sit with Francis while Rebecca laboured at her task. He could perhaps be there . . . near her.

It was the least he could do and the most he could do.

Rebecca's third son was born almost a day later, on a fine October morning, with a touch of frost in the air scorching the last green leaves to a dusty gold. But his birth was long and difficult, and he was not the lusty, bawling infant everyone had expected. Instead, he was pale and quiet, needing several sharp slaps to make him cry, and during the first few days of his life it was impossible to tell whether he or his mother were the most exhausted.

'I never felt like this with either of the other two,' Rebecca whispered when Francis tiptoed into the bedroom to see her. 'I don't even have the strength to sit up. And yet he's not even a large baby – it must have been all water, the midwife says.' They looked together at the cot where the new baby was almost completely hidden by a mound of blankets. 'I can't believe that little scrap is the monster who used to kick me so ferociously.'

'He's healthy enough,' Francis comforted her. The doctor had warned him that he must encourage her, boost her spirits and he was trying hard to do so, even though his own heart was heavy with concern. 'And everything's there that should be. All he needs is sleep and good feeding – just as you do, my love. Just close your eyes now, and don't worry.'

'We ought to name him,' Rebecca said anxiously. 'He ought to be baptised. Francis . . .'

He took her hand. 'You're worrying unnecessarily. There's no haste in baptising him. He's tired, that's all. And we've chosen his names already.'

'William Jeremiah,' she murmured with a smile. 'Two good strong names. But is he going to be strong? Francis, I really would be happier if he were baptised at once— '

'There really is no need.' He looked at her apprehensively. The midwife and doctor seemed more concerned for her than for the baby who lay so quietly in his cradle. 'Rebecca, you must stop worrying and rest. He needs you to be strong and healthy – and so do I.'

She sighed, her head turning this way and that on the pillow. 'I feel so weak – so helpless . . .'

'You need to rest,' he repeated, but his heart shook at her pallor. 'Close your eyes – go to sleep.'

Rebecca's eyes gazed up at him, huge, almost black in her white face. 'Francis, you promise me he's going to be all right? You really do believe there's no need to baptise him at once? You're quite sure?'

'Quite sure,' Francis said firmly, and touched her face with gentle fingers. 'I wouldn't deceive you over that, now would I? Little William's going to be as tall and strong as his brothers. But not unless you rest and get your own strength back – otherwise where will the milk come from to make him strong?'

A faint smile flickered across Rebecca's face, and she closed her eyes. Francis stood for a moment, looking down at her with concern. The birth had been worse than she knew – already the doctor had told him that it would be unwise for her to have more children. One more might be possible, he'd said, but even that should not be too soon. And it might even be that she would not conceive again.

'It would be the best thing possible,' he observed. 'But you must take care – great care.'

Francis had gazed at him, numb with sadness. He knew what the doctor was telling him. He and Rebecca should never again share the love that had brought them both such delight, that had bound them so closely together. To do so could bring a risk to her life. And denial was the only certain way of prevention.

Not to love Rebecca ever again. Not to hold that slim, trembling body in his arms, to stroke the smooth skin, to kiss the yielding mouth. Not to caress the rounded breasts, not to bury himself in her warmth, her tender softness. Not to soar again to those shimmering peaks of joy that held them both poised in rapture and renewed their love, time and time again, endlessly, effortlessly . . .

Was all this to be lost to them for ever? And if so . . . how could he bear it? How could he live with her and not long for her touch, her kiss, the consummation of all their mutual desire?

'It doesn't have to mean complete denial,' the doctor said. 'There are ways . . .'

'But none of them certain. And if her life is at stake . . .'

The doctor inclined his head. 'It could be. I can't say that she would survive another ordeal such as this. Her third child . . . it should have been easier for her. And the infant – he's not strong. You have a wet-nurse arranged?'

'My wife likes to feed her own babies.'

'Oh . . .' The doctor's mouth pursed, he shook his head. 'In the case of the first two, yes, for this one I'm not sure . . . she may not be able to produce the milk. I would look for a woman, if I were you. I may be able to help, I know a few who can usually oblige.'

'I know she would like to try,' Francis said uncertainly.

'And there's no harm in that, no harm at all. But this child can't afford to wait, you understand. It will take three days for your wife's milk to appear, if it comes at all, and by then his need will be dire. If there are problems . . . You should have a woman at hand. I advise this most strongly.'

Francis sighed. He knew that feeding her own babies was important to Rebecca. She scorned the fashionable view that it would spoil her figure or that it demeaned her position as Francis's wife, that breast-feeding was something for the lower orders. 'Position?' she had said. 'What is "position"? I grew up in a weaver's cottage, where we had no position at all, and no time to worry about it either. And my mother was glad to suckle me and give me her strength.' She had just finished feeding Geoffrey as she spoke those words, and she laid him in his cradle and looked with tenderness at the small, delicate face, the eyes that watched her so trustfully. 'Feeding our baby is finishing the task that began when you and I loved each other one night, Francis,' she said softly. 'And it tells Geoffrey that I'm his mother. He knows me all the better because I give him my milk, and I am growing to know him too.'

'I suppose it would do no harm to have a wet-nurse at hand, in case of need,' he said now, slowly. 'But I know my wife will want to try to feed him . . . Perhaps the woman could simply take the night-feeds. Could the child accept that?'

'If your wife could accept it,' the doctor said, and

collected his instruments together. 'I'll come again tomorrow. And I'll see the midwife – she'll know who's available for nursing. There are one or two women I know, decent women of clean habits . . . I'll send someone suitable, you may be sure.'

Francis watched him go and came back into his study, his head bowed. Suddenly, their life together which had seemed so bright, so promising, had crumbled about him. Their child's life was in danger, and Rebecca lay ill and exhausted, perhaps never to have another. The life that they had shared, brimming with a tender love that had begun when she was a housemaid, clearing out the library fireplace at Pagnel House, was to lose its expression. Oh, they would still love each other, he had no doubt of that. But the depth of loving would be lost to them and gradually, inevitably, without that intimacy they must drift apart.

Rebecca, his heart cried, and the pain that was so sharp twisted inside him as if it were a long, thin knife that pierced the very depths of his soul.

He sat at his desk, where Rebecca and he had so often sat as they discussed a new design, and rested his elbows on the polished surface. He sank his head into his hands and stared blindly at the half-completed design that lay before him – a design that Rebecca had begun on her own and one that he knew could be her finest yet.

Rebecca. *Rebecca*.

Tom and Nancy arrived just as the sun began to drop from its highest point in the sky and sink like a golden ball towards a glowing horizon. Tom went into Francis's study but Nancy ran straight up the stairs to see Rebecca. She crept into the bedroom, her face wreathed in smiles, and laid a parcel on the bed.

'Just a few things I sewed. Can I look at him?' She peeped into the crib. 'My, but he's tiny! Like a little doll. A real handsome young feller, though.' She came back to the bed and looked down at her sister-in-law. 'Bet you're proud.'

Rebecca smiled faintly. 'I shall be content if he just lives,' she murmured. 'My little William . . . We named him after my father, you know. William Pagnel. It sounds well, doesn't it?'

'Sounds just the ticket. And 'ow about you? Feeling all right, now it's over?'

'Oh yes,' Rebecca said, her voice little more than a thread of sound. 'I'm all right. I'm just worried about him. He's so small. I— ' Her voice shook and Nancy bent nearer, suddenly anxious. 'I'm so afraid he won't live,' Rebecca whispered, and tears flowed from her eyes.

'Live? Course he's going to live!' Nancy's voice was strong and positive. 'Why, he's a Himley, ain't he, and Himleys don't die young.' She stopped, biting her lip as she remembered that Fanny Himley had borne a good many children who did die young. 'Well, this 'un won't, anyway. He might be small, but he's strong, you can see it in his eyes. He's like you, Rebecca, he ain't the sort to give in. He means to live.'

The baby began to wail even as she spoke, setting up a cry that was thin and wavering yet had an edge of determination it it, as if he were annoyed at being kept waiting for his supper. Nancy listened for a moment, and laughed.

'See! He's like all the rest, means to have his own way from the start. Here, you hold him for a bit. Don't suppose you got any milk yet, have you?'

Rebecca shook her head. She held out her arms for the baby and cradled him against her breasts. Instantly, he turned his head and began to nuzzle with his lips, and Nancy laughed again.

'See! He knows already where it comes from. Poor little beggar, he's hungry. Don't they feed you, then?' she crooned, stroking the small cheek with one finger.

150

'Let him suck a bit, Rebecca, it's better than letting him waste his strength crying.'

'But there's no point. There's only watery fluid yet – that's no good to him.'

'Well, I dunno, I always thinks it might be, otherwise why'd it be there?' Nancy helped Rebecca to unfasten her nightgown. 'You just let him have a suck, seeing as he wants it. You having a nurse for him?'

'Yes. The doctor thinks it's best. He thinks I may not be able to feed him myself.' Once again Rebecca's eyes filled with the easy tears of weakness. 'I fed the others so easily, Nancy. It seems so – so unfair – '

'And you don't even know it's true,' Nancy said firmly. 'You have a nurse, Rebecca, but you give him your own milk as well, then he'll be sure to thrive, see? And look at him now.' They both looked down at the small, round head, covered with the faintest of down, nestling against Rebecca's breast. 'He knows what it's all about, anyway. He'll be all right, you see.'

'I hope you're right.' Rebecca touched the pulsating spot on the crown. 'It's all I want now – that this baby should live and thrive. If he does, I swear I'll never ask for another thing.'

Nancy smiled but said nothing. And in spite of her brave words, her eyes were concerned as she watched the mother and her new son. The baby was altogether too small, too pale. And Rebecca looked exhausted. The birth had obviously been a bad one, and it was surprising they'd both lived through it.

It would take them a long time to recover, Nancy thought as she went slowly down the stairs to find Tom. And maybe they never would, quite.

Francis said goodbye to Tom and Nancy with relief. It was a strain, keeping up the appearance of jubilant fatherhood. Not that he'd managed to be jubilant, he thought wryly. Pinning any sort of good humour to his face had been an effort almost too difficult to make, and he was not at all sure that he had managed to hookwink either Tom of Nancy into believing it. He reached out again for the brandy.

When he next looked up, an hour had passed and Matthew Farrell was standing there, gazing at him with concern. He reached across and took Francis's hands in his, drawing a chair close to the desk with his foot and sitting down. The two friends looked at each other.

'What is it?' Matthew asked quietly. 'Enid met me at the door, she says Rebecca is tired but mending well. Is it the baby – something Enid doesn't know? Or Rebecca?' His voice tightened. 'Has the doctor told you something— '

Francis pulled himself together and shook his head. He had already made up his mind that no one must know of the disaster that had befallen him and Rebecca. It was something for the two of them alone. Even Matthew, his friend since schooldays . . . He tried to inject some brightness into his voice. He was a father again, after all! He ought to be happy.

'There's nothing wrong – I'm just tired. Like Rebecca!' He even managed a laugh. 'And of course the baby must give us some anxiety for a few days. It was a difficult birth and he didn't cry as well as he ought to have done. But the doctor assures me that if he lives the week – and there's no real reason why he shouldn't – then all will be well. And Rebecca will recover fast, once she's had some rest.'

'I hope so.' Matthew's eyes rested on Francis's face, and Francis felt uneasily that he had either said too much or not enough. Matthew had always known what he was thinking, even when they were boys. He turned his head away quickly.

'You must have a brandy to celebrate. A third son! Quite an achievement, don't you agree? Though of course, neither Rebecca nor I would have been at all disappointed if he had turned out to be a daughter. We've already been blessed with two fine boys . . .'

His voice trailed off as he realised that not only was he talking too much and too fast, but that there would never be a daughter now, never a little girl to remind him of Rebecca, to sit on his knee and play with his watch, to wind soft arms around his neck . . . He was on his feet, finding a glass, pouring Matthew a drink, and his voice seemed to be running on as if it belonged to someone else. He hardly knew what it was saying, yet he could not stop it. He handed Matthew his glass and drank quickly from his own. At least it silenced that dreadful, chattering voice.

'Francis— ' Matthew began, but Francis shook his head quickly, sharply.

'I told you, there's nothing wrong, Matt. Nothing that anyone can . . . No. *Nothing*.' His voice was rising again and he made an effort to clutch at it. 'It's just been – rather a strain. The whole thing . . . she was never well, you know, never free of that sickness and the birth wasn't easy and now . . .' He took another drink, found his glass empty and refilled it. 'It's the relief,' he said unconvincingly. 'I shall be all right in an hour or two.'

'Not if you go on drinking like that.' Matthew removed the bottle of brandy and set it on a side table. 'And Rebecca doesn't want you going to her side tipsy.' He hesitated. 'I suppose she doesn't want visitors just at the moment?'

'Come and see her tomorrow,' Francis said, his eyes on the bottle. 'I'm sure she'll be feeling stronger then and be glad to see you. She's very fond of you, Matt.'

He stared at the design on his desk, one finger following the lines Rebecca had drawn, almost as if he were caressing it. The finger trembled a little. Matthew watched for a moment and then stood up.

'I see you'd rather be alone.' He came round the desk and laid a hand on Francis's shoulder. 'I'll come back tomorrow,' he said quietly. 'Call me if you need me.'

Francis nodded. But when Matthew had gone, he got up and went a trifle unsteadily to the side table where the brandy bottle now stood. He poured himself another glass, and sank back into his chair.

Never to love Rebecca again . . .

The brief, early frost was over and a mellow light, half pearl, half gold, suffused the air as Matthew walked slowly away from the house in Unicorn Street. But the warmth that had come late in the day would soon disappear as the sun slid early from the sky and an autumn dusk brought a fresh chill and, perhaps, another frost.

He turned his thoughts to Francis, who was sitting alone now in his study, his fingers tracing the design Rebecca had made, his mind slightly fuddled with brandy. What was going on in that mind? Why was he so wretched – for Matthew did not for a moment believe that all was as well as Francis had tried to persuade him. There was something very wrong there, and it was to do with Rebecca and the new baby – yet what was it? If either of them had been in real danger, Francis would have said so – indeed, he was clearly worried about the baby's health. But it was not that which drove him to the comfort of the brandy bottle, of that Matthew was certain. There was something else – something more.

Rebecca?

He thought of that morning when he had first seen her. A bright, smiling figure stepping quickly, lightly, towards him along the street. Dark brown eyes that had looked straight into his, a small firm hand between his fingers.

A breath of fresh air to one who was more accustomed to the languid society miss or the austere matron. A gust of gaiety into a heart that had begun to grow cold.

Matthew came to the river and leaned across the

bridge, looking down into the swirling waters. For once, they were not turbid with the muddied colours of the dyes, floating from the skeins of wool that the dyers held on long poles from the banks. But they were not clear; the Stour never did run clear. It had little chance, flowing as it did through areas that were growing more and more industrialised, with the waste from iron foundries, coal mines and the glassworks of Stourbridge itself, being poured into it before it came to Kidderminster. Perhaps somewhere, many miles to the north, it ran clear and sparkling, but like a child of the streets it had lost its innocence long before it reached maturity.

Matthew had grown up in Kidderminster, living with an uncle and aunt who had taken him in when his own parents died in a fire that had blazed through their house one night. Matthew and his nursemaid had been saved and he remembered nothing of that night, nor his parents. Perhaps it was this that had drawn him to Francis when they first met at the grammar school; two boys who had no memory of their natural parents, two boys who were set slightly apart from the others.

But Matthew had no other family. There had been no cousins, no uncles or aunts apart from the couple who had taken him in. No affection, no rivalry. No loving, no jealousy. Only a dutiful attention to his bodily needs, to his education. And then, when he came of age, a meticulous care that he should receive all the money due to him from the trust that had been set up.

'And then they considered they'd done enough,' he had told Francis a few months ago, when he had first returned to Kidderminster. 'All that was required of them. As of course they had. Nobody asked them to love me as well.' His lips had twisted wryly. 'I can't blame them, it must have been a shock to have a young baby foisted on them when they were looking forward to a comfortable and quiet old age. They were both in

155

their fifties, you know – far too old to be encumbered with a nuisance like me. You were lucky with your parents. I often wondered if you knew how lucky you were.'

It had been common knowledge in the school that Francis was the adopted son of Geoffrey Pagnel, the senior master, and his wife. Nobody had known his true parentage – there had been speculation enough when he had been brought to the house as a baby, but no one could seriously suspect the mild, sweet-natured Geoffrey Pagnel of an illicit liaison and it had eventually been accepted that Francis was the child of an old friend, left orphaned at birth. Which was near enough true, Francis had told Matthew that day – but not quite.

'You're Jeremiah Pagnel's son?' Matthew had echoed in amazement. 'And the governess your mother? So Geoffrey was really your uncle. No wonder there's such a strong resemblance.'

'Not really,' Francis had said. 'My father – Jeremiah – says I look more like my mother.' He pulled a small locket from his waistcoat and opened it. 'See, he gave me this miniature of her only a short time ago, when we came back to Kidderminster.' He handed it to Matthew, who gazed in silence at the small face, the long hair that was exactly the same shade of gold as Francis's, the dark blue eyes and the smile.

'Yes, I can see you're her son,' he said at last, handing it back. 'But I still think there's something of Geoffrey in you. And why not? You're his nephew, after all.' He frowned. 'And what does your cousin Vivian think of this?'

Francis wrinkled his upper lip. 'Vivian has always had a strange attitude towards me – as if he always thought I had the power to usurp him. Or – no – he's far too arrogant ever to think *that* – rather, it's as if he suspected that I might try. And finding out that I was actually Jeremiah's son, whereas *he* is only adopted

156

didn't make his feelings any more friendly.'

'But do most people know the truth? He still seems to be considered the heir to Pagnel Carpets.'

'Oh, he is. My father promised that he should be, when he married Isabella. Even if they had had sons, Vivian would still have inherited the business, because it was Isabella's money that saved it from ruin years ago. She was a rich widow, you know, when my father married her – it was really not much more than a business arrangement, though they did have the three daughters.' A shadow crossed Francis's face as he thought of Isabel, the youngest, who had died. He had never been able to rid himself of a feeling of responsibility for that. 'But he promised that Vivian should be his heir.'

'So Vivian has nothing to fear from you.'

'Except that my sons could take precedence over his,' Francis said succinctly. 'There seems to be nothing to prevent my father leaving Vivian the business, with the promise that it goes to the next male heir – and he can name that heir. Something that seems to have been overlooked when they were drawing up that marriage contract!'

Matthew grinned. 'It all sounds too complicated for me,' he declared. 'I think I'm glad after all that I had no other relatives. Just an elderly aunt and uncle who did their Christian duty by me and then enjoyed a few years' peace and quiet before shaking off their mortal coils. Leaving me free to roam the world and do whatever I liked.'

'Oh, you!' Francis said. 'You're just a parasite. Have you ever done a day's honest toil, Matt? Be honest, now.'

'Indeed I have,' Matthew replied with dignity. 'Toil of the sort you've never heard of, young Francis. Sitting in your comfortable office, drawing pretty pictures – why, you've no idea what goes on out there in the real world.' And he told the enthralled Francis the

157

story of his journeys in America, the trek by wagon across the wilderness through the Cumberland Gap, the Indians who were still a problem to the white settlers who had taken over their country. He talked about the fur-trapping trade in which he had spent a year – the prosperous hunt for the beaver, whose pelt made the hat that had become so fashionable in all the great cities of the Western world.

'There used to be quite a hierarchy involved,' he observed. 'The British at the top of the tree, of course – organising and managing everything. Then the men who plied the canoes that hunt the beaver – they're usually French-Canadians, a rough and ready crew, so fiercely independent that the idea of organising themselves into any cohesive group never occurred to them. And then the Indians to actually do the trapping. They'd sell the pelts for a dollar each – the British sold them on for ten. That's how profits are made!'

'And it's the same in every industry,' said Rebecca, who had been listening with as much interest as Francis. 'Those who do the real work are the ones who earn least. But I thought America was supposed to different. The land of the free, don't they call it? It seems to me that freedom only applies to a few, wherever you are in the world.'

'It's different now,' Matthew told her. 'The Americans do it their way – paddle their own canoes, set their own traps and employ Indians at several times what the British paid. Not that it does the Indians much good – their whole way of life is changing and not, I think, for the better.' He gave Rebecca a reflective glance. 'You're right – they were free before, when it was their own land and they could live in their own way. Now, they're little more than slaves and when they rebel – and they rebel very bloodily at times – they're massacred.'

'But if they don't rebel?' Francis asked. 'If they follow the new laws and work for their masters?'

'Then they live like the working people in this country,' Matthew said soberly. 'And we all know how that is.' He was silent for a moment, then he added, 'To be fair, many of the settlers in America also live very poorly – it isn't all gold-paved streets and prosperity. Many of the pioneers who try to wrest a living from the land die in the attempt. Their crops fail, they suffer disease, poverty and starvation. I met women – women who came from good families, too – who had to cut up their winter dresses to make clothes for their children, who had to work the land by their husbands' sides, with chilblains on their fingers and toes, who had to chop wood and draw water, dig and plough, cope with their children's births and illnesses and deaths, all out in the wilds with no one nearer than twenty miles away. Yes, you have to be very tough to survive America.' He grinned suddenly. 'That's why I came back, of course – I prefer the comforts of home.' And they had gone on then to talk of other things.

Now, gazing down into the opaque waters of the Stour, Matthew thought of those years he had spent in America. Why had he come back? Was it the same restlessness that had taken him there in the first place – the feeling that somewhere in the world was something he needed, something he sought without really understanding what it might be? He had always had the sense that he too was hunting something – not the beaver, which was easy enough to trap and kill, nor the living that could be got from the land, often very prosperously in spite of what he had said to Rebecca. No, what he sought was something more intangible than that – something that he needed to fill an ache of emptiness somewhere deep in the core of him. Something he needed to become a whole person. Something he needed perhaps not to take, but to give. To do . . .

What had made him think he might find it back here, in Kidderminster of all places, when he had searched the world without success?

And yet . . . Something had drawn him back. Something had spoken to him, on one of those starry nights when he lay wrapped in a blanket on the prairie. Something had brought Kidderminster vividly into his mind and that something would not let him rest until he had decided to return.

He recalled that day when he and Francis had gone into the streets, when the folk of Kidderminster had been celebrating Lawless Hour. He had seen it then, briefly, in the haunted eyes of the children. A cold, a hunger, an injustice that ought to be, must be, righted. An injustice that had followed him all over the world so that he was never free of its torment, thrusting itself before him everywhere he went. Demanding that he do something, demanding that he offer himself in some way.

Was this why he was here?

'So Wilton weavers are striking for more pay.' Vivian lifted his chin as if defying a blow. 'Well, what Wilton does has nothing to do with Kidderminster. We pay our weavers the same rate as before, and no arguments.'

'I can't agree,' Francis said. 'What the Wilton weavers do may have a considerable effect on our own men. You may be sure they'll be watching, and if Wilton give in— '

Vivian snorted. 'One business, employing every weaver in the place! Why should the masters give in to – how many? Forty weavers? Pah! What muscle have they?' He leaned back and lit a cigar. 'There's no competition for their labour, nowhere else they can find work. You haven't been to Wilton, Frank – I have. It's a sleepy little backwater, dependent upon its carpets. The men can't survive a strike, they've no support. No, we've nothing to fear from a little skirmish in Wilton.'

'I wouldn't be so sure. The unions are growing stronger – if our men, and others, supported Wilton they

160

might well hold out. And if they do get what they demand – which is no more than parity with our wage, after all – we may find that they like the feeling of power. And who's to blame them? They've had none of it in the past.'

'Which is all the more reason for making sure they don't get the taste for it now.' Vivian drank his port. 'And I'm sure we can rely upon Wilton to do that.' He dismissed the strike and its implications with a wave of his cigar. 'And how's that little wife of yours? Still abed?'

'A little better, thank you. The birth was hard on her. It was too soon . . .' Guilt smote him again, but he could not talk to Vivian about that, nor about the doctor's warnings and the decision he had been forced to make. No one could know about that. 'And Maria?' He was concerned for her, this pregnancy coming so soon after her miscarriage.

Vivian's face darkened. 'Well enough, I suppose. We take care of her, you know.' I'm sure you do, Francis thought, though not for Maria's sake. Until she delivered the child she was now carrying, her value would remain high. If it proved to be yet another daughter, he feared that Vivian would come near to hating her – until she was pregnant again. Poor Maria, treated as no more than a brood mare for the son Vivian so desperately wanted yet seemed unable to father.

And I would have had daughters too, he thought, a dozen of them if it could have spared Rebecca's health. Or no children at all, if it meant I could go on loving her.

'Vivian,' he said, wanting to turn his mind away from the painful thoughts that came into it each time he thought of Rebecca, 'we ought to discuss this strike. I do believe it could spread to Kidderminster – the union is bound to support them. And we can't afford to lose production at this stage, with the introduction of the new looms – we've invested a lot of money, we have to recoup— '

161

'Are you trying to teach me my business?' Suddenly angry, Vivian leaned forward. 'And let me remind you, Frank, it *is* my business – not yours, however entitled you may think you are— '

'I don't claim any entitlement!'

'No, because you haven't a leg to stand on in law. But I know what you think. Oh yes – and I know what you're trying to do, worming your way into my father's – *my* father, Frank – affections, bringing those brats of yours to climb all over him, inviting him to come to your house. Don't think I don't realise.' His face was dark with anger now. 'But you'll get nowhere with your machinations – the business is mine, or as good as. And when it is – finally and completely – you'll be sorry you hadn't worked closer with me. I'm a slow man to forget, Frank, especially my enemies.'

'Vivian, I've never been your enemy— '

'No?' Vivian said, and sent him a look of such dislike that Francis was shaken. He rose to his feet.

'I think it's time I left. Rebecca will be waiting for me.' He inclined his head. 'Thank you for the meal. It might be better if we kept our business discussions to working hours in future.'

'I agree.' Vivian lit a cigar and looked up into Francis's face. He blew a long, slow cloud of smoke and then turned away. And Francis, after standing irresolutely for a moment or two, spun round and left.

He wasn't even sure why Vivian had become so suddenly angry. They always did disagree about the weavers and their union, after all. But, thinking over the conversation as he made his way home, he came to the conclusion that it must be the same old problem – the fact that he and Rebecca had produced three sons, while Vivian and Maria had only daughters.

It was a jealousy that Francis could do nothing about.

William Jeremiah survived his first week, while Rebecca slowly gained strength and recovered from his birth. After three days, she was able to sit up and cradle him in her arms. She tried to feed him, but her breasts were painful and the baby, so eager at first, now seemed unwilling to suck. He lay against her, turning his head away as if the whole business were simply too much effort, and Rebecca's tears fell on his face like rain. She wiped them away from the pale cheeks and handed him back to Nancy, who came every day to help nurse her.

'You'd better give him to Mrs Hodges,' she said sadly. 'I can't do it. Poor little mite.'

'It'll be better in a day or two,' Nancy comforted her. 'I helped with a good few babies while I was in London. It's not always easy to start with. You just keep trying.' She hesitated, looking at the small, pale face. 'Still, p'raps he ought to feed from the wet-nurse as well, or he'll lose strength. But don't worry – I wouldn't be surprised if you aren't feeding him just as well as you did the others, in a week or so.'

Rebecca lay down again and let her tears soak the pillow. She couldn't believe Nancy's optimistic words. Daniel and Geoffrey, both born stronger, had fed at once and with enthusiasm. But little William had to have the nipple forced into his mouth. In vain did Nancy press her finger under his chin, trying to stimulate him; he merely sighed and closed his eyes and drowsed back into sleep, even though a few minutes before he might have been wailing hunger in that thin, weary voice of his.

Would he take Mrs Hodges' milk? At least she was accustomed to suckling and her milk flowed easily. Rebecca wondered what had happened to her own baby. Had it died? If it was still alive, why was she suckling other women's children? Perhaps she had finished feeding it and had kept her milk by this means, like a cow which was milked daily and so continued to fill its udder. Perhaps it was many months, even years, since Mrs Hodges had given birth.

A sound at the door made her turn her head and she found Francis standing by the bed, gazing down at her. There was something in his eyes – a pain that was not due entirely for his concern for her – that caught at the edge of her mind, and she struggled to raise herself in the bed. Immediately, he pressed her back on the pillows.

'Don't try to sit up, my love. I just came to see how you were.' He sat down on the chair, close to her head, and took her hand. 'Are you feeling any better?'

'A little.' She made her face smile at him. No use to worry Francis. 'William had a nice little feed just now, but of course I don't have much milk yet so Nancy's taken him to Mrs Hodges. It was a sensible idea of yours to bring her here.'

His anxious face lightened a little. 'You don't mind? I was afraid it would upset you.'

'Upset me?' Rebecca said lightly. 'Of course not. Why should it do that?'

'Well, I was afraid you would be hurt – you might think I was disappointed in you. Or thought that you weren't a good mother— ' Francis was floundering, embarrassed and unhappy, and Rebecca gave him her sweetest smile.

'Francis, the only important thing is that our son should thrive. And my milk will come . . . it's only three days now, you know there's nothing much for the first few days . . . It's just a matter of getting the baby used to feeding . . . And with William being so small and perhaps rather tired, it's important that he should have nourishment as soon as possible . . .' Her voice died to a whisper of exhaustion and Francis laid his finger on her lips, his eyes dark with concern.

'Don't try to talk. Just lie still and rest. Go to sleep. William's going to be as healthy as his brothers, the doctor says so.' But the worry was still there in his face, and she couldn't believe him. He was talking simply to reassure her – he was afraid.

'Francis,' she said, 'you must tell me if there's any danger. Promise me you'll tell me— '

'I'd tell you at once,' he said. 'You know I would tell you. But I'm sure he's going to be all right.'

'Then is it . . . me?' she asked on a breath of sound.

His grip tightened momentarily on her hand. 'Darling Rebecca, there's nothing wrong with you. You've had a bad time, you're tired, you need a long rest – that's all.' He bent closer to her, touched her face with his lips and then drew quickly away. 'I'm going to take very great care of you in future – very great care. You – you're so precious to me, Rebecca.'

She stared at him, trying to read the truth in his expression, but could find no clue. Yet there was something, she knew it, something he was holding back from her. The way he had drawn back, his lips scarcely brushing her cheek . . . as if he were repelled by her.

The thought was as painful as a stab in the heart. What had she done? Why had Francis stopped loving her?

Was it because she had produced a sickly child, a child who might not live?

Unable to bear the idea, she turned her head away. She could not believe it. Not of Francis, her gentle, caring Francis who had taken her in his arms in his father's library, who had made love to her in the woods, who had gone to London to search for her and stayed there to be with her. He could not have stopped loving her – not simply because of this. He could not.

But, the idea once born, she couldn't forget it. And she kept her head turned away from him, her eyes, closed, while a tear squeezed itself weakly from between her lids and soaked silently into the already damp pillow.

And Francis sat silently, gazing at her, and wishing, praying, that she would turn back to him, wondering why she had turned away. Did she blame him, that she had endured such a terrible birth, that their son was

165

small and frail? Did she think it his fault, for having caused her to bear another child so soon after Geoffrey? For his animal passion, the lust he had thought of as love, that had driven him to possess her body too soon, satisfying himself at her expense?

If she did, he could not blame her. And he wondered if he should tell her now that the doctor had said there should be no more children. That he had made up his mind that it should never be permitted to happen again.

Would she love him the more for such a decision? Or the less?

He could not make up his mind. And at last, after a long, unhappy silence, he realised that Rebecca had fallen asleep. There was no need now to tell her anything.

He sat there for a long time, her small fingers resting in his, looking at the pale, exhausted face, and his heart ached with bitter, unshed tears.

Chapter Eight

October passed in a blaze of colour and, as the dyes swirled beneath the bridge in a motley of orange and gold, it could have been imagined that the river itself was touched with the autumn fires of the trees. But November brought heavy fog, pouring rain and cold, dark evenings. The tawny leaves fell and carpeted the roads with brown slime, and women shivered under thin shawls as they hurried to work, dragging miserable children along with them.

Rebecca was on her feet again, still not back to her full strength but keeping a bright smile on her face whenever she greeted her husband. She was designing again, a little, but most of her time was kept for the three boys – Daniel and Geoffrey, who needed her attention after her unaccustomed sojourn in bed, and baby William, who was growing at last – though still slowly – and had begun to smile and clasp at a finger laid in his tiny palm. And she was now able to feed him almost entirely herself, with only a little help from Mrs Hodges, the wet-nurse.

And Maria had been brought to bed with her sixth daughter.

'Six of them!' Vivian hadn't bothered to try to hide his disgust. 'My God, what did I do to deserve such a wife? And she just lies there, weeping – as if that can do any good. And what use is there to try again? She'll just produce a seventh, to spite me.'

Francis had listened in horror. Did Vivian have no feeling at all for his wife? Had his love turned to hate because of these disappointments? Could that happen to love – could it happen to Rebecca and himself?

Or had Vivian never loved Maria at all, only ever

seen her as a breeder, to give him sons? Perhaps he had never loved anyone; perhaps he was incapable of love.

In either case, Maria was to be pitied.

The strike at Wilton was dragging on. Francis knew that the Kidderminster union was supporting it. Rebecca had started to visit her own friends again – Polly, in the kitchen of Pagnel House, and Nell Foster who lived in the weavers' cottages. Nell's husband – if he could be called such – was much involved with the Union and Nell had told Rebecca that two hundred pounds had been sent from the funds to help the Wilton men. 'And they've already sent more than eight hundred pounds to the woolcombers in Bradford,' she said to Francis when she came back from one of her visits. 'That's a thousand pounds in only six months. A thousand pounds, Francis!'

'More money than sense,' was Vivian's comment when he heard. 'And I've heard about Bucknell myself – a rabble-rouser and trouble-maker if ever there was one. If he worked for us, I'd have him out at once. We want none of that sort at Pagnel's.'

'You're likely to have them, all the same,' Francis observed. 'I've told you before, the Union is growing very strong. Men from every factory are joining now and they're going to gain in power. We can't ignore the trend, Vivian – we shall have to take notice.'

Vivian snorted. 'And *I've* told *you*, Frank, that I don't intend to be dictated to by a rabble of workmen. Nor do I see any possibility that it will ever happen. They're all talk, you know – there's no backbone in them. How could there be – they're uneducated, ill fed— '

'And whose fault is that?' Francis said quickly.

Vivian gave him a scornful look.

'Frank, for God's sake get rid of these romantic notions of yours that the working class is as good as its betters. They're not fit to be educated – they wouldn't be able to take it in, for a start. And they'd misuse any education they did manage to imbibe, by getting above themselves, trying to make the rules in *our* factories, trying to take over. It would mean chaos – anarchy.'

'My co-operative– ' Francis began, but again Vivian snorted his contempt.

'Your co-operative! A plaything, nothing more. You and Tom Himley and a couple of weavers, making a few rugs and sharing the proceeds. It's nothing more than an old-fashioned loom shop, such as any of the old independent weavers might have set up. And that's what it will always be – it's never going to be any bigger, it's never going to get anywhere.'

Francis felt his cheeks flush but before he could answer Vivian was speaking again.

'All the same, you're wise to start up a loom shop of your own, Frank. I know Father's always treated you as an important part of the business here, but he won't be around for ever. And I've several changes in mind, which I shall make as soon as possible once the place is mine. I'm not sure they're changes you'll approve of.'

Francis stared at him. 'Are you saying you'll push me out?'

'Oh come, that's putting it rather crudely,' Vivian smiled. 'All I've said is that you might not approve of the changes I mean to make – so the fact that you have a business of your own must be a comfort to you. Build it up, Francis, that's my advice. It can only do you good – if this co-operative idea of yours works, that is.' His tone expressed his doubt about such a possibility.

There was a short silence, then Francis said carefully, 'This is all looking into the future, rather, isn't it? Father's very well and strong for his age.'

'Mm . . . perhaps. I see more of him than you do, of course. I see signs that he's failing a little.' Vivian smiled again, cheerfully. 'But I expect you're right. He has years ahead of him yet. None of us has any need to worry about that, I'm sure.'

The clatter of the looms filled Rebecca's ears as she stood with Francis and Tom just inside the carpet shop. She watched, fascinated, as the rolls of punched card jerked their way through the high loom, the carpet emerging almost as if it had woven itself. Tom saw the expression on her face and laughed.

'You can't believe as it's your design on those big rolls, can you?' he said. 'Takes a bit of getting used to, I know. Coming out well, too. Take a look.'

Rebecca glanced at her husband and then stepped forwards, letting her eyes move over the bright, swirling colours of the pattern that was being produced with such apparent wizardry. A magic carpet indeed, she thought, and smiled with delight. The design was even better than she'd hoped.

'It's beautiful.' Her eyes glowed. 'Francis, it's beautiful.'

'I know.' He gave her a tender look. 'Your first Jacquard design, and it's a triumph. And only the first of many, I hope.'

'Oh, yes.' Her eyes returned to the bright colours, the reds and greens and blues, surging like the waters of the Stour on dyeing day. She had never expected quite this impact when she saw her first design translated into reality. Now, watching the wools twisting into the pattern she had first seen on paper, she wanted nothing more than to go home and take her colours to produce more designs, designs that would be ever more exciting, designs that would sell all over the country, all over the world . . . She gasped at the wonder of her thoughts, and Francis laughed.

'You see, Tom, she's been bitten,' he remarked. 'I knew it would happen. There's nothing like that moment when one first sees one's own creation take shape.'

'There is,' Rebecca said, her eyes still on the growing carpet. 'There's the moment when a mother sees her baby for the first time. It's like that.'

'And isn't a baby one's own creation?' Francis said softly, so that only she could hear, and she felt his breath on her cheek.

Rebecca stood quite still for a moment. Her heart kicked and then beat raggedly. She looked up into Francis's face, longing to see her own need mirrored in his eyes, and for a moment, in the dim light of the loom shop, she almost believed it was there. But then he turned his head and the light caught his eyes from a different angle and it was gone. And her heart sank.

Before she could speak, however, Tom had directed Francis's attention to something that was happening on the far side of the shop, and the two men hurried over. Rebecca followed more slowly, still looking about her with interest.

It was not the first time she had been into the co-operative's loom shop, but previous visits had been hurried ones and she had not been here at all for the last six months of her pregnancy. Eight months ago, in fact. The Jacquard loom had been installed during that time, sooner than Francis had expected to be able to afford it but, as he had predicted, the quality of their carpets and the designs they were now producing had brought good sales. He and Tom and the weavers who worked with them were confident of success.

And it was certainly a better atmosphere than in many carpet shops, she thought. The men worked cheerfully and well. They looked better, as if better fed, and there was an air of confidence about them, as if they were proud of what they were doing. As if they owned the place, she thought. And so, in a sense, they did.

Her eyes rested on Francis and her thoughts returned to the moment they had just shared beside the big loom. Just for a brief space of time, it seemed that all

171

his old feelings for her were still there, waiting to be expressed. Just for a moment, she had thought him about to express them. But when Tom called him away he had turned from her with what looked very like relief.

What had happened to the tenderness they had shared, the passion? Had she imagined it was there? Did she imagine it still? For she could swear that Francis loved her still, loved her in the old way. Yet if he did . . . why did he never tell her now? Why did he never touch her? Why did he never come to her bed?

Well, it was early days yet, she comforted herself as they turned away from the big loom. William was barely two months old and the birth had been difficult. Perhaps the doctor had suggested that Francis should wait a while. But if so . . . why didn't he tell her? Why let her wait and wonder in this way?

Christmas came, but with it little cheer for the weavers. Bill Bucknell came home to a meat supper, a rare treat for which Nell had scrimped even more than usual during the previous week, and he brought with him some extra ale, a few sweetmeats for the two boys and gin for Nell. They warmed their damp basement room with a fire of wood gathered from the polled willows along the riverbank, and thought about the toddler who had died.

'And well out of it, I reckon,' Bill said. 'This ent no life for children, Nell. No life for no one. I wonders sometimes what we're all here for. Can't be just to mek carpets for the gentry. I mean, it don't mek no sense at all that.'

'I dunno that we're here for aught,' Nell said, drawing a thin shawl closer around her shoulders. 'We just gets born and waits to die, and some of us has to wait longer'n others. You're right – the little 'un had the best of it after all. It's all over for him.'

'If only they hadn't give in, down in Wilton. It's made it worse for everyone – they were asking for the same as we gets, a shilling a yard instead of tenpence. Now the masters have beaten 'em, Kidder masters can say we're overpaid here. We could find ourselves worse off over this, Nell, and God knows how we could manage on tuppence less a week, let alone tuppence a yard.' He shook his head. '1826 looks like being a bad year all round. I reckon we're going to need all the men we can get in the Union.' He closed his mouth suddenly, aware that he'd been about to say something about the secret society, that inner core of the Union into which only the most trustworthy men were admitted. Nell knew nothing of his involvement – knew nothing of the society itself. And that was the way it should remain.

He thought of the meetings they'd had, the plans they'd laid. The Wilton weavers would never have struck without the instigation of Kidderminster – the bigger carpet centre had encouraged the Wiltshire men to demand parity in their wages, and had given both financial and moral support. Once they had achieved this end, they could have banded together and struck in force for higher wages all round. But now Wilton had given in, and the masters were cock a'hoop.

'It ent the end of the world,' Bill had said stoutly at the last meeting of the secret society. 'We can try again. They Wilton codgers caved in, but it don't mean we will, when our time comes. We'm bigger altogether here, we can last out longer if it comes to the push.'

'After sending a thousand pounds to Wilton and Bradford, and all of it wasted?' Fred Holloway had asked bitterly. 'Both those strikes failed, and we're left a thousand pounds poorer. It teks a long time to collect that sort o' money, Bill, and God knows we could all be doing with a smell of some of it. And now I suppose we got to set to and build it up all over again.'

There was a depressed silence as they contemplated

the enormity of this task. Fred was right, a thousand pounds did take a deal of collecting from weavers who needed every penny of their earnings to keep their families alive. Yet there was no possibility of staging a successful strike without money to back up the long weeks – perhaps even months – without earnings.

'I reckon it'll be another two-three years before we can think about making another move,' George Hodgett said at last, and the others nodded gloomily. 'Well, it's a long, slow road, but it's one we got to travel if we ever wants things to get any better. So let's put our hands on it, boys, and seal it in the tavern. Reckon we all needs a sup of ale to tek the taste of Wilton and Bradford out of our mouths.'

The others murmured their assent and began to rise from their chairs. But Bill shook his head.

'No, mates. This is where we puts our money on the table – not on the beershop counter. If we got to start collecting again, we can start here and now, with the pence we'd spend in the tavern. And go home sober to our wives for once. 'Twon't hurt us, and 'twill show willing when we starts to ask the boys for more money. We got a lot of leeway to mek up there – a lot of 'em have lost faith in us and it won't do no good for us to be seen drinking in the tavern straight off.'

The others considered this and nodded reluctantly. What Bill said made sense, though none of them was especially willing to give up his drink. But each man put his hand into his pocket and brought out the few coins he had hoped to spend in the tavern, and Bill gathered them up.

'That'll mek a start, friends,' he said. 'And we'll go on, same as we planned. We'll get more men behind us and we'll go on collecting, till we're ready to start again. The masters may think they've won – but they reckon without weavers. We may not be independent like we used to be, but we ent slaves neither, nor willing to be. We'll show 'em!'

'Ah, we'll show 'em,' they agreed. 'Our time'll come. They ent heard the last of us weavers.' And they had gone out into the cold winter's night, warmed by determination. As George Hodgett had said, it was a long, slow road they had to travel. But travel it they would, for there was no other before them. Not if they wanted conditions ever to improve.

'And they got to get better, some way,' Bill said to Nell as they shared their bleak, cold Christmas. 'Because this ent no way for Christian souls to live – no way at all.'

The Pagnels celebrated Christmas in Unicorn Street, with Jeremiah joining a party which also included Tom, Nancy, Matthew Farrell and Humphrey Price, a clergyman and an old friend of Geoffrey and Enid Pagnel who had come to visit his ageing mother and been prevailed upon to share Christmas dinner with them.

Matthew found himself next to Price at dinner. He observed him with interest. A man with a face like a stone crusader and greying hair. About fifty years old, Matthew guessed, with stern eyes that yet held a twinkle somewhere in their depths. He knew Kidderminster well, he said, having been born and educated here, at the Free Grammar School.

'I'm parson at Needwood now. Near Lichfield. And you? You've lived here all your life?'

'Just as a boy.' Matthew helped himself to vegetables. 'Then I went off and wandered about for a while. Europe, America . . . I came back a few months ago – nearly a year, I suppose.' He remembered that windy March day and seeing Rebecca for the first time, stepping briskly and brightly up Unicorn Street. 'But I'm not sure I'll stay much longer.'

'Nothing here for you? No work for you to do?' The bright grey eyes were on him. Matthew shook his head.

'Work?' he said flippantly. 'No – you see, I have the

misfortune to be slightly rich. My parents died when I was very young and left me enough money to keep me without need to earn my daily bread. Perhaps that's why I go abroad – it's easier, somehow, to work in places like America. I'm not sure my parents did me a favour,' he finished rather wryly.

The clergyman gave him a thoughtful glance but before he could say more, Jeremiah was on his feet and announcing a toast, and there was no further opportunity for conversation. Instead, Matthew found himself playing a game of cards with Tom, Nancy and Enid, and when that was finished the Reverend Price had disappeared.

Rebecca, seeing that everyone was occupied, went in search of Jeremiah. She found him, sitting like a hunched shadow, over the fire in his son's favourite room, the library. She came to sit beside him, pitying him, understanding that he was still haunted by the ghost of his lost love, Francis's mother Mary. His guilt over what had happened to her had not diminished through the years; it had magnified, grown perhaps out of all proportion. There was no way of assuaging it, and now it dominated his thoughts.

'If things could only have been different,' he said. 'If we'd been free to marry— '

'You would never have met her if you hadn't already been married, with daughters who needed a governess,' Rebecca pointed out. 'It's no use to blame yourself like this. It can't help Mary, and it's doing you harm. It's making you ill, and it's all so long ago.'

He turned his eyes on her and she was shocked and saddened by the unhappiness in them.

'Yes, so long ago. All those years, lost to her . . . to me. And all through my own selfish lust.'

He had never spoken to her so plainly before and she was silent, shaken by the bluntness of his language. She looked at him and saw that he was staring into the fire, as if he had forgotten she was there, as if he

176

were talking to himself. Should she answer, should she remind him that he wasn't alone? She hesitated for a moment, then said gently: 'But it wasn't lust, Father. It was love. And without it you would not have Francis. And neither would I,' she added as if it had just occurred to her.

He turned his head slowly and stared at her, and she had a sudden feeling that he did not recognise her. For a moment she was afraid: was Vivian right, was Jeremiah becoming senile? And then the haunted eyes cleared and he smiled and reached out to touch her knee.

'You're right, Rebecca. And without Francis I wouldn't have you to be a daughter to me, nor three strapping grandsons to carry on my name.' And then the shadows came down again. 'Though I shall never be able to do as well by them as I should – my grandsons, my flesh and blood, and can't inherit my business.' His voice was filled with self-reproach. 'And I thought I had made such a success of my life.'

'Oh, Father . . .' Rebecca held his hand in both of hers, helpless to give him the comfort he needed. For what could she say to him? She could not bring Mary back to life, she could not wipe out the past. And without that, she couldn't drive those shadows away. For Jeremiah *had* fallen in love with his daughters' governess, she *had* borne his child and died in doing so. And nothing could stop that guilt invading his mind; nor, apparently, prevent it from growing as he aged and thought of her more and more.

Only his grandchildren seemed to bring him any comfort and it was to Rebecca's home in Unicorn Street that he came most often, bringing small presents for the boys and letting them clamber all over him as he sat before the nursery fire. Baby William knew him already and laughed to see the whiskered face bending over his crib, while little Geoffrey was sturdy enough to push his elder brother aside as the two of them

177

crowded their grandfather's knee to receive the latest toy or sweetmeat.

'You spoil them,' Rebecca would say chidingly. 'They expect a present now every time you come – I want them to be pleased for your sake, not for what you bring them.'

'They are pleased for my sake,' he said, ruffling the two heads. 'Aren't you boys? You don't love me just for my presents, do you?'

They shook their heads, only half understanding but knowing what he wanted them to say, and Daniel said, 'What are you going to b'ing us tomorrow, G'an'papa?' which made both Jeremiah and Rebecca laugh.

'You see!' she said. 'You're just a provider of toys and sweetmeats, and nothing else.' But as she watched the children scrambling up on to their grandfather's knee she knew as well as he did that it wasn't true. This big, ageing man, who had been a figure of awe to her when she had been a housemaid scurrying through her work for fear of being seen by the Family, had mellowed over the years and begun to show a softer, more lovable side to his nature. Not to his employees or to his competitors, she knew – he was as hardheaded as ever in business matters. But within the Family, he had changed.

Why was this? Was it the shame he still seemed to feel over Mary, the governess who had won his heart, or a different kind of guilt over Isabella, his wife? Was it perhaps that, without Isabella, he was able at last to reveal his true nature? Or was it because he could now acknowledge Francis as his son instead of pretending, as he had through all these years, that he was no more than an adopted nephew and of no blood relationship at all?

For he certainly seemed to treasure these children, and his welcome of Rebecca into the family had done a great deal to smooth her path since she had come back to Kidderminster. Not wholly within the family, it was true – Maria still treated her distantly and Vivian's sisters, Edith, Jane and Sarah, spoke to her only if they could not avoid it. None of them could forget that she had once been a housemaid and – worse – a kitchenmaid. She smiled sometimes when she thought that it was more dreadful than they knew, for when she had first come to Pagnel House as a timid ten-year-old, she had been put to scullery work, spending her days at the earthenware sink that was set low especially for the small size of the child who would be working at it. Scrubbing an endless supply of dirty dishes, pots and pans; scrubbing the floor at the end of the day; creeping to bed and, it seemed only moments later, creeping back to begin all over again.

Edith, Jane and Sarah must know that such tasks had to be done, but they preferred not to admit to such knowledge, and they certainly had never expected to be obliged to converse and eat with the weaver's daughter who had toiled in their own mother's kitchen.

Rebecca could imagine their comments when they were alone together, or with their husbands. 'A common servant from some filthy little workman's hovel! How Francis could sink so low – and for Papa to *encourage* him! Mamma was right to dismiss the girl when she found herself disgraced, and right to insist that Francis be sent away when the truth was discovered. They should have stayed away, both of them, and never come back to Kidderminster again.'

No doubt all these remarks and many more had been made in the privacy of boudoirs and sitting rooms. But Jeremiah's presence had silenced their tongues and Rebecca had noticed that the husbands did not seem to share their wives' disdain. Indeed, Sarah's husband Edward had given her several friendly glances and, when not closely observed by his wife, had even smiled and addressed a casual remark to her about the weather or the fineness of the new portrait of Jeremiah which hung on the dining room wall. And Vivian . . .

179

Vivian . . . yes . . . Rebecca sat down in the chair opposite Jeremiah's, watching absently as he played with the boys, and frowned a little. Vivian was something different.

Had he really changed his mind about her? Had he really accepted that she was now one of the Family, to be treated as a sister? Certainly he did not distance himself from her, nor make disparaging comments. He was friendly – but . . .

Was he perhaps a little too friendly?

Rebecca remembered the days when she had worked as a housemaid. Fair game for the son of the house, who seemed to believe that he had not only a right but a duty to seduce every female servant in it, with the exception of the cook, the housekeeper and Susan, the head housemaid and parlourmaid. Few of the girls had escaped his attentions. Some, like Carrie and – Rebecca had always suspected – Polly, had shrugged and made the most of it, coming away unscathed and with a sovereign or two to show for it. Others had been less lucky – there had been more than one girl who had been forced to leave hurriedly before a swelling figure betrayed her sins. As Rebecca herself had been dismissed when she had given way to love.

Vivian had caught her, as he had probably caught every maid in Pagnel House, and tried to force himself upon her. But Rebecca had resisted – with some force, she thought now, recalling the satisfying crack of her toe against his shin – and she knew that it galled him that any woman, even a lowly housemaid, could prefer Francis. All the same, it seemed unlikely that he would have harboured a desire for her through all these years.

No, it was simply Vivian's way of being friendly. The dark glance, the hand lingering on hers, the touch on her arm – they were nothing more than that. And she should be thankful for it, for his antagonism could be dangerous, both to herself and to Francis.

Rebecca's wandering thoughts were recalled to the

present by Geoffrey's squeals as he rode his grandfather's swinging leg, pretending that it was a horse, and she leaned forward to remove him.

'They're getting too excited. Father. They won't sleep tonight. No, Geoffrey, that's enough. You'll make Grandpapa's leg ache. Let's go and see if William's awake, shall we?'

Geoffrey, already walking, struggled from her arms and staggered to the door which led into the night nursery. Together, they all tiptoed over to the little crib and peeped at the baby. He was asleep, his fist curled under his chin, eyelids almost translucent, a few dark lashes spread like tiny fans on his cheek. Geoffrey reached up to the side of the crib and tried to clamber up to see his brother and once more Rebecca scooped him into her arms.

'He's like a monkey, this child. He'll try to climb anything. Look, my love, there's William, fast asleep. Why don't you lie like that, so good and quiet?'

Daniel, standing by the crib sucking his thumb, said, 'Geoff'ey's not a good boy. He c'imbs things.'

'And you don't, I suppose?' Jeremiah said. 'All boys climb. It's natural to them. And some girls too,' he added, and Rebecca glanced at him and knew that he was thinking of his daughter Isabel, who had romped like a boy and never grown up to be a woman.

Poor man, she thought. So much tragedy in his life, so much disappointment. But we can make up for some of it. We can make these last years of his happy, Francis and I and the children.

She touched Jeremiah's arm impulsively. 'Father, you know you are welcome to come here any time you like, to see the boys. They do love to see you. And you are—' she thought of her own father, dead for many years now, worn down by a life of hard work and grinding poverty '—you are their only grandfather.'

'That's so.' He straightened up from the crib where William was beginning now to stir. 'And truth to tell,

Rebecca, I feel more at home here in this simple nursery than in any of the others. Maria – Sarah – their children are so hemmed in by nurses and rules and timetables that I never seem to be able to get near them. And don't know what to say to them when I do. Your boys – they're what children ought to be. God knows they have a lifetime to be men and women – let them be young for as long as they can.'

'I agree. My own childhood was so hard – I want them to enjoy their lives.' She was silent for a moment, then added softly. 'Though it's hard to forget all those little ones who are still living as I did.'

She felt Jeremiah's hand on her arm. 'I know. And I know that you and Francis are both anxious to see conditions improve. So am I, my dear. But it's a long job. Most of the masters take the view that weavers and such will never live any differently, however much they are paid. The whole economy rests on the wages paid at present too – it can't be changed overnight. Why, it would take a revolution to do that!'

Rebecca looked at him soberly. 'And haven't there been revolutions in other countries? Couldn't such things happen here too?'

He looked at her uneasily. 'Those were revolutions against monarchs— '

'Is our present king so popular?'

'No, but— '

'And isn't it possible that a revolution against tyrannical employers could take place, just as against tyrannical kings and queens?' Rebecca bent and tucked the blanket more securely around William's neck. 'Nobody should be too sure of himself these days, Father. With Trade Unions now legal— '

'They have no teeth! Look at the Bradford and Wilton strikes – both failed, both too expensive for the men to keep up.'

'Perhaps,' Rebecca said, looking at the boys who played on the rug at their feet, 'they have only milk teeth as yet. But as they grow older and stronger and learn from their experiences . . .'

Jeremiah followed her glance. 'Yes,' he said slowly. 'I understand what you mean. Trade unions are only in their infancy as yet. But they'll grow, just as these children of yours will grow, strong and healthy – a force to be reckoned with. And then you think we manufacturers had better look to our laurels?'

'I think it might be better still to wonder whether they aren't right to make the claims they make now,' she said, and stretched out a hand to prevent Geoffrey from hurling a wooden brick at his older brother. 'A loyal workforce might be the biggest asset a manufacturer can have in the times that are coming – bigger than any new loom or factory. Men who have been well treated will stand by you.'

Jeremiah stared at her and she met his eyes levelly. He shook his head slowly, as if unable to believe what was happening.

'You're a very uncommon woman, Rebecca. When we talk together like this, I forget that you're a woman at all – you reason like a man. I know no other woman I can converse with so easily, or so sensibly. Where did you learn it?'

She smiled. 'At my father's loom – he used to talk to me about conditions and how they should be changed. He talked about independence – he was proud of being an independent weaver, with his own loom, though it did him little good. But he also talked about men banding together as brothers. The old sick clubs that are now becoming the new trade unions – he saw that happening and thought it must be the salvation of people like weavers and dyers and all the others who work so hard for so little. He never lived to reap the benefit himself – perhaps nobody alive today will live that long – but he believed passionately that it must come.'

Jeremiah nodded slowly.

'And between these four walls, I believe it too. But it may take a very long time.' He touched Daniel's head and the little boy ducked away, laughing. 'Too long even for this little fellow to see the results. There's a long struggle ahead for men like your father, Rebecca.'

'Well,' she said with the ghost of a smile, 'men like my father are used to struggle.'

The baby stirred in his cot and began to whimper. And Rebecca, knowing that he must be hungry, felt the milk tingle in her breasts. She went to the door and rang for Tilly, then returned to the night nursery and unbuttoned her dress.

Jeremiah Pagnel walked heavily down the stairs and out into Unicorn Street. His step was slow, his brow creased with thought. Rebecca was indeed a very unusual woman, and he thought that Francis was a lucky man to have found her. Was she right about the Unions, and about loyalty?

If she was – and he believed she very well might be – could Vivian be made to see the sense of treating his weavers well now, before trouble could brew? And what would happen locally if Pagnel's were to raise their wages, especially with the failure of the Wilton strike still fresh in people's minds?

It wasn't easy, he thought, as he walked back to his own empty home. But was life ever easy?

Matthew Farrell was standing on the bridge when he saw Jeremiah walk past on his way back to Pagnel House. He watched the older man go by, noting the way the broad shoulders were beginning to stoop, the once straight, tall frame slowly but perceptibly shrinking. Jeremiah Pagnel was growing old.

Matthew turned away from his contemplation of the river. It wasn't much to look at anyway – hardly worth calling a river when he thought of some of the great rivers of the world he had seen. The Colorado, the

Seine . . . even the familiar Thames of London, all these were strong, swift rivers that flowed with purpose, that had a job to do. This – he glanced again, disparagingly, at the muddy Stour – this was nothing more than a trickle, a bearer of dirt and human waste from this town to that, gathering more and more filth as it proceeded on its sluggish way. This wasn't worthy of the title 'river'.

Slowly, hardly knowing where he was going, he strolled through the town and out into the fields. Why had he come back to Kidderminster? Why did he stay here? What purpose did his life have that was any grander than the purpose of the Stour?

Few people were about in the fields on this January afternoon. The smoke-hung daylight was already shadowed further by clouds bruised with the threat of snow and in an hour or so it would be dark. There was little incentive to walk on the dank grass when home, even if it were no more than a damp, cold hovel, offered some measure of comfort. But as Matthew walked, deep in thought, he became aware that he was not alone. Another man walked there too. A man of middle height with a face like a stone crusader and greying hair, who turned to look at the town and then caught sight of Matthew, lifted a hand and stood waiting. Humphrey Price.

'It's growing,' he said as Matthew drew near. 'I notice it every time I come back. So must you. It was a smaller town when I was a boy, and cleaner, I fancy. Not so many chimneys.'

He stared over the town again. A few lights were beginning to glimmer through the gathering dusk. 'The last of my family. Only my mother left here now. I don't suppose I'll come back many more times.' He seemed to be wrapped in his own thoughts for a moment, then roused himself. 'And you? It struck me when we were talking at dinner on Christmas Day – you're at a crossroads, aren't you. Dissatisfied with your life as it is, yet you can't see how to change it. You feel without purpose – without direction.'

Matthew looked at him in astonishment. 'How do you know?'

A smile lightened the crusader's face. 'You told me yourself. But you don't have to say any more unless you'd like to. I keep secrets but I never ask for them.'

Matthew continued to stare at him. Had he really revealed so much about himself? He took refuge in a question of his own. 'Were you not happy in Kidderminster?'

Again he was shot a bright, thoughtful glance.

'Happy? What's happiness? Doing what you want to do – or doing what fulfils you?'

'Aren't they the same thing?'

'Not necessarily. You may *want* to go to the city and spend your time whoring and gambling, but would that fulfil you? Would it make you happy?' Humphrey Price shook his head. 'I doubt it, in the end. But doing something which fulfils you – by which I mean satisfies you at your very heart, in your soul – would surely bring its own happiness. A feeling that you were carrying out the task you were meant for. Or perhaps you would rather spend your inheritance in the gambling halls and brothels anyway. I admit the other way might seem harder.'

'No.' Matthew stared at him, slightly shaken by Price's forthright manner. 'No, I wouldn't prefer to spend either my time or my money doing that. But how do I know what I was "meant for"? I don't have a vocation for the Church, I don't want to go into the Army, I don't seem fitted for anything. I seem to be little better than a gipsy, wandering the earth doing a little of this, a little of that and never achieving anything.'

'Then perhaps you're still preparing. You're gathering experience, putting it all together.' The grey eyes examined him. 'You must have learned many things in your wanderings. One day you'll be able to put all those small pieces of learning together and use them. You'll know then what it was you were meant for – why you sought all your different experiences.'

'And meanwhile?' The town was almost in darkness now, a cluster of shadows pierced by faint lights. By tacit consent, they began to walk back across the fields. 'Which path do I take at this particular crossroads?'

'Now on that I can't advise you. I know nothing of you, nor of your situation. But you seem to be searching for something. Is that why you came back to Kidderminster – to find what the rest of the world hadn't been able to give you?'

Matthew frowned at the straggling brown grass under his feet. He thought of the heat of America, the days spent in the saddle riding across the plains, the wagon treks through hundreds of miles of wilderness with the fear of Indian attack ever at his back. He thought of Paris, bright and gay yet with such squalor in its back streets. He thought of his journeys to these places, the weeks at sea, the endless travelling by road.

Had he been searching, all that time? And had he finally been drawn back to Kidderminster in the hope – the belief – that it might have been here all the time?

'Perhaps it was,' he said slowly. 'Perhaps I did come back to find what I was looking for. And yet – although I feel so strongly about the lot of the weavers, there doesn't seem to be anything at present that I can do.' A sigh lifted his shoulders. 'Perhaps the time still isn't right – perhaps I need to go away again. I've been feeling increasingly restless lately.'

'All I can advise you to do, then, is follow your instincts,' Price said. 'I've found they are as good a guide as any other. As if something inside us knows what is right and tries to urge us on. Just do whatever seems to be right for you – and when you're ready, when the right moment comes, you'll know what it is you're meant to do.'

They walked in silence for a few moments, then Matthew turned the conversation away from himself.

'You said you didn't think you would come back to Kidderminster many more times. Doesn't it hold anything for you?'

'Not really. My family have all gone now, I have my life in Needwood, my wife and four children. Why should I come back, other than to visit my mother? And she's old now, almost ready to go herself.' The crusader's profile was very marked as he strode by Matthew's side. 'I have my work to do.'

'And that's what I need. Work to do. But what kind of work?' Matthew sighed restlessly, hardly realising that he had turned the subject back to his own concerns again. 'Kidderminster is a carpet town, and I've no background in weaving nor any of the skills. I could buy into one of the businesses, perhaps, but what satisfaction would that be? And business is poor at present too, with all this talk of lower wages and strikes.' He shook his head. 'The people here face enormous difficulties and I'd like to help them – but that's a task too great for any man alone.'

'But no man need be alone. Aren't there unions?'

'Yes, but they're the working men's concern – they wouldn't welcome a stranger, especially one who isn't even concerned with making carpets.'

'All the same,' Humphrey Price said thoughtfully, 'they may one day need the help of an educated man. They have a long and bitter struggle ahead of them.'

'Even more so, since the failure of the Wilton and Bradford strikes.'

'Yes . . .' They had reached the first of the streets now and paused as if to part. 'This talk of strike,' Price said. 'Do you think it will come to fruition soon?'

'Not soon, no. They need time to recoup their strength – the Kidderminster unions subscribed heavily to the Wilton and Bradford men, they can't afford a strike of their own yet. But in a year or two, perhaps

– especially if the masters take the Wilton failure as a chance to lower wages – yes, I think we may well see a strike here in Kidderminster.'

'And will you still be here then?'

Matthew shook his head. 'How can I tell? A year, two years – it's a long time to wait at a crossroads. I may be back in America by then, or perhaps in some new country entirely. There's a world out there – perhaps there are other things for me to find.'

'Perhaps.' The sharp, iron-grey eyes regarded him speculatively. 'But I think not. Not just yet, anyway. I think you have work to do here, Matthew Farrell. And I don't think you will leave until you've done it.' He held out his hand and Matthew shook it again, impressed once more by its firmness, which seemed to betoken the whole uncompromising character of the clergyman. 'Will you do something for me?'

'If it's within my power.'

'Let me know if it seems that the men are about to strike. As I said, I think the weavers will need help – educated help. That's what was missing at Wilton and Bradford.' He held Matthew's glance with his. 'We could work well together, you and I,' he said obliquely and released his hand. 'Don't forget: Price, Christ's Church, Needwood.' And before Matthew could answer, he turned and strode swiftly away.

Matthew stared after him. His thoughts tumbled about in his head. Was the Reverend Humphrey Price a madman, a fool, or a man of vision? Was he really saying that if the Kidderminster weavers struck against their masters, he would come back and give them his aid?

Was he really expecting Matthew to help him?

Slowly, he turned on his heel and walked in the opposite direction, his hands thrust deep into his pockets against the January cold. Something small and cold and light brushed his cheek and he realised that it was the first flurry of snow. He thought again of the hot

189

sunshine of America, of the bitter cold of its winters.

Matthew lifted his head. The snow fell cold upon his face and he smiled, and walked more quickly now back to his lodgings.

It was time he was out of them, too, he told himself. Time he had a house of his own. Time he started to do something with his life.

Chapter Nine

William Pagnel was two years old, still small for his age and only just beginning to walk, when his grandfather called the first of a series of secret meetings at Pagnel House.

They used the library, where Francis and Rebecca had also met secretly, in the early mornings before the household was astir. Francis sat at the long table and thought back to those days, when everything had been fresh and new. Himself, out of bed at dawn, slipping down to the library to read: Rebecca, newly promoted from kitchenmaid to housemaid, nervous about her new duties and disconcerted to find him there when she came to clear the fireplace. The Family weren't supposed to see the servants about their tasks and it was only with great reluctance that she had been persuaded to do her work with him there, reading at first and then beginning to watch her, beginning to talk to her, beginning to look forward to the fifteen or twenty minutes he could spend with her each day.

And beginning to feel his own nervous excitement at the thought of seeing her. Waking earlier each morning, doing some of her work before she arrived so that they could use the time in talk. Thinking of her through the day; counting the hours until he could be with her again.

When had he first known that he loved her? It seemed to him that she had always been there in his heart, waiting to be discovered. Love had never come suddenly, blindingly out of the blue; it had grown like a seed long dormant, waiting only for the spring sunshine to bring it to flowering life. And he had found that sunshine in the young housemaid, so shy yet with a spark of fire in her dark brown eyes.

But now . . . He sighed. What had happened to that flower, to the innocent love they had shared, to the passion that had bonded them together?

'If you could bring yourself to pay attention, Frank . . .' Vivian said coldly in his ear, and he jumped and remembered where he was. In the library still, but no longer wrapped in the warmth of a young girl's love. Instead, he was surrounded by the carpet manufacturers of the town – men like Ben Humphries and his son James, Henry Brinton, and John Broom who had first begun to use the Jacquard loom. And they had met here secretly to discuss the problems that faced them all – the problems of trade in the depression which had begun almost two years ago.

'We had some good years up till '25,' Jeremiah said when everyone was silent. 'But good years don't last and we all know what it's been like since then. The crash in December of that year affected everyone – I don't think there was an industry in the country that didn't suffer. As we're all still suffering. The question is – what do we do about it?'

'What can anyone do?' one of the smaller manufacturers asked gloomily. 'We just hold on and hope it passes. Otherwise – we go to the wall.'

'Carey Street, you mean?' Vivian said bluntly, 'Well, *I* don't intend to go bankrupt. In my view, the answer's simple. We reduce wages. A penny or twopence a piece, what difference would it make? Little to the weavers, a great deal to us.'

Henry Brinton gave a snort. 'I doubt if they'd agree it meant little.'

'Of course not,' Vivian said impatiently. 'They'd weep and wail and gnash their teeth – but what could they *do*? Nothing, if they want to be paid at all. And they'll certainly not be paid if their masters are forced into bankruptcy. Even the stupidest of weavers ought to be able to understand that simple fact.'

'Not while he watches his children starve yet sees that we still live well,' Francis observed, and Vivian turned on him.

'Trust you to support the lower orders, Frank! Really, I wonder what you're doing here at all. You've no real responsibility at Pagnel's and you side with the men on every issue. I don't know what Father was thinking of to— '

'That's enough, Vivian!' Jeremiah's voice had lost none of its power, even though he was growing older, his hair and whiskers white and his once broad shoulders stooped. 'Francis is here on his own account – he runs a carpet business independently from Pagnel's, if you recall— '

'A *co-operative,*' Vivian sneered. 'He'll probably run straight back to his so-called associates from the weavers' hovels and tell them all our secrets. I really do think you should have consulted me, Father, I would have advised— '

'I don't need your advice!' Jeremiah glowered at his adopted son. 'Remember, I'm still in charge of my own business and have no intention of justifying my actions to you. I'm not in my grave yet. And I'll hear no more of this.' He turned to the others who were shifting uneasily in their seats, embarrassed by this display of family differences. 'Now then, gentlemen, let's return to our discussion. What's to be done about the situation?'

'Let's define the situation first,' said Herbert Mason. The network of worried lines which permanently creased his long, grey face were deeper than ever. 'You mentioned the crash in '25 and the depression that followed. What's the effect of that on the carpet trade? I'll tell you what.' Herbert Mason was always ready to answer his own questions. 'It's left a lot of people with no money to spend on luxuries, and it's left us with huge stocks of carpet we can't sell. Special orders not

193

taken up, regular orders dropped. And we've just gone on, making carpets as if nothing had ever happened. I saw it coming a year ago, eighteen months ago and I said so then, but did anyone take any notice of me? No, you all laughed, said it would never come to that, Well, now I hope— '

'All right, Herbert,' Jeremiah cut in. 'No use crying over spilt milk. We all know the situation now. Large stocks and reduced demand. It's as simple as that. All we have to do is decide— '

'Not quite as simple as that, Jeremiah,' Henry Brinton said. 'Part of the trouble is this new competition we're getting from Scotland and Yorkshire. They've already taken over a lot of the production of Scotch carpeting, and now they're moving into Brussels. Kidderminster's always been ahead of the field in Brussels manufacture, but we won't be for much longer if we don't do something about it. And why are they taking our trade?' He looked around the table and they waited for him to answer his own question, as Herbert Mason would have done.

But Brinton waited too, and eventually someone said, almost reluctantly: 'They charge less. Their prices are cheaper.'

'Exactly,' Henry Brinton said and sat back in his chair.

'So we're back at what I said to begin with,' Vivian declared. 'We have to reduce our prices and to do that we must reduce the wages. It's either that or starve the men we employ by going out of business altogether.' And he turned and stared triumphantly into Francis's face.

'Do that,' Francis said quietly, 'and you'll starve them anyway. Because most of them can barely feed their families as it is. Have you not seen the children in the streets? In the factories themselves?'

'Then they shouldn't have so many,' Vivian said callously. 'Nobody asked that they should father a lot of sickly brats. Most of 'em don't live to grow up anyway – they'd be better drowned at birth, like unwanted kittens, or better still never conceived in the first place.'

There was a short, uneasy silence. Francis looked round the table disgusted by Vivian's words. The carpet masters were looking down at the table, none of them meeting his eye. He felt suddenly sickened. None of them would have spoken their feelings as plainly as Vivian had done, yet none of them refuted his words. He had simply put into speech what they all thought – if they thought about it at all – yet were ashamed to admit.

'Oh, come now,' one of them said at last, 'you know you don't mean that, Vivian. We're all Christian men here, after all. We take care of our workers. But they know the conditions when they come to work for us.'

'They know them,' Francis said, 'but what choice do they have? They are forced to accept them. And then they're forced to try to change them. Why do you suppose the unions have come into being?'

'Greed,' Vivian said tersely.

'No. Not greed. A simple, natural wish to eat enough meat each day to be able to work efficiently, and to feed one's children. Is that so wrong? Don't you feel it yourself? You have as many children as many a weaver, after all.'

He challenged Vivian with bright blue eyes and had the satisfaction of seeing his cousin turn a deep, angry red. If there was one thing Vivian disliked, it was being reminded of his six daughters. And only that morning, Rebecca had said that she was sure Maria was pregnant again. 'And if this one isn't a son, I don't know *what* she will do. Or Vivian, either,' she had added in a tone of foreboding.

'My children,' Vivian said after a moment, 'are none of your business, Francis. And I conceived them in the knowledge that I *could* feed them and care for them.

195

That is what a weaver does not do. He satisfies his animal lust without thought for the consequences. He takes no heed of continence and then expects me and you and every man in this room, to support him in his fecklessness.'

The other manufacturers murmured their agreement, relief in their tones, their shame comfortably mitigated by Vivian's words. Francis looked slowly round the table, sickened once again by their well-fed complacency. Then he rose to his feet.

'If you'll excuse me, gentlemen. I have business to attend to.' He glanced at his father. 'I shall have to leave.'

'I was about to close the meeting anyway.' Jeremiah rapped on the table to silence the murmurs. 'We'll meet again and discuss this matter further. Meanwhile, I ask you all to think most carefully. Let's try to find some other way of surviving this crisis, without reducing wages. Francis is right – the weavers are hard pressed. Nothing is cheap any more and none of them have money to spare— '

'And just as well,' Herbert Mason broke in, 'for they'd only spend it on more ale. Or – worse still – their pestilential union. If they can afford to collect a thousand pounds to send to Bradford and Wilton, as they did two or three years back— '

'And much good that did anyone,' Vivian muttered.

'—then they're *over*paid,' Mason continued. 'A drop in wages might do us all a good turn. Keep them from such dangerous activity.'

'Well, I'm just asking you to think about it,' Jeremiah said. 'We'll meet again soon. We have to stand together on this matter, gentlemen, or the consequences could be serious for us all.' He pushed his chair back from the table and rose to his feet, and the other manufacturers did the same. Slowly, still conversing together, they moved out of the room, leaving Jeremiah alone with his two sons.

The three of them stood silent for a moment or two. Then Vivian gave a short laugh and moved to the window.

'Well, we all know which side *you'll* be taking, Frank. I won't say the word "traitor" but— '

'Vivian, *that's enough*!' Jeremiah spoke with more anger than Francis had ever heard in him. 'I won't have such talk under my roof. I won't ask you to apologise to Francis – even if you agreed to do so, you wouldn't mean it. But I insist that you never use such a word again.'

'I already said I wouldn't,' Vivian said silkily. 'Really, Father, you take me too seriously. Why, Frank and I are the best of friends, aren't we?' He clapped Francis on the back. 'He knows when I'm just funning.'

Jeremiah glared at him and then turned away. Vivian winked, but Francis pretended not to see. He moved towards the door.

'I really must go now. I'll come to your next meeting, Father, though I'm not sure what good it will do. Like Vivian's, their minds are made up. And I'm afraid it will lead to trouble.'

'Trouble? Of what sort?'

'Why, another strike, probably,' Francis said soberly. 'And the next one could last a lot longer. The men are growing more determined and more discontented every day. They won't take a cut in their wages without making a real protest.'

'Let them,' Vivian said coolly. 'It will be Wilton all over again. The masters will win. The masters will *always* win.'

'—and this will be the drawing room.' Matthew led Rebecca around the side of the jumble of half-built walls and foundations and indicated a large rectangular space. 'See, it will have this view across the town which I think is rather fine, don't you? And my bedroom and dressing room will be directly above it so that I can

197

enjoy the same view.' He gazed across the sloping fields towards the roofs of Kidderminster. 'I believe it's almost possible to see your house in Unicorn Street from here. And I'm sure you'll be able to see this.'

'I shall wave to you every morning from my window,' Rebecca said, smiling. 'And I think it's going to be a very grand and beautiful house. It ought to be, after all the attention you've lavished on it. All you need now is a wife to share it with you.'

Matthew smiled a little ruefully. 'Oh, I don't think that's very likely. I don't think I'm the marrying kind. This will be a bachelor establishment.'

'That would be a pity. You should be married, Matthew. You ought to have a wife.'

Matthew turned his head again and looked down at her, his tone light, even bantering, as he replied. 'Find me someone just like yourself, Rebecca, and I might consider it.' And then, more seriously, 'And how is your sister? Is she still set on remaining in London?'

Rebecca sighed and began to walk on along the muddy path that surrounded Matthew's new house.

'It seems so. Her millinery business seems to be doing well, and she has several girls working for her now. Francis and I visited her a few weeks ago and told her that she could make bonnets as well here in Kidderminster as in London, but she won't hear of coming back. It's as if she were frightened – yet there's nothing for her to fear now. Vivian wouldn't cause trouble after all this time. He knows that Tom is here, working with Francis, and he's done nothing. What is there for her to be afraid of?'

'Her memories, perhaps. She was very young when it all happened. She might just be unable to face the place where such horrible things happened to her.'

'Horrible things happened to her in London too,' Rebecca pointed out. 'She's never talked about them, but from things Tom and Francis have let fall . . . Poor

Bessie. She's had a hard life.'

'But she's risen above it. She's made a life for herself in London. I can understand her not wishing to give that up and come back to a place where she was so ill treated, and so frightened, with all the memories it must hold for her.' Matthew paused. 'After all, she hasn't seen death in quite the same way in London, has she? She hasn't been hunted for murder.'

Rebecca shuddered, feeling the old creeping horror, remembering her mother's face when the watchman had come to the house searching for Bessie. Was this what Bessie felt when she thought of returning to Kidderminster – only ten, a hundred times magnified? She looked up at Matthew, seeing the sober expression on his face.

'You understand a great deal, don't you,' she said softly. 'My own sister – you've never set eyes on her, yet you seem to understand her better than I do. Why is it?'

Matthew laughed. 'An illusion, probably! You don't have to believe everything I say, Rebecca – it may sound plausible, but don't forget you do know your sister and I don't – what I say is no more than speculation. I understand women little better than the next man.'

Rebecca said nothing, but in her heart she felt this was not true. Matthew, with all his easy banter and insouciance, had a depth of seriousness that he rarely admitted. But it was displayed in the care he showed for friends like herself and Francis, his concern for the weavers and other workers, his attention to anyone who seemed to need help.

It was a pity that he still seemed unable to find any useful purpose with which to fill his days. The restlessness that had sent him travelling across the world a few years ago had returned eighteen months previously, and he had left Kidderminster to travel again. Rebecca had missed him very much and feared

that he would never come back. But after a while
Francis had received a letter, asking him to set in
motion plans Matthew had made for building a new
house on a plot of land he had bought just outside the
fringe of the town.

And since his return their friendship had grown
deeper. His first call had been to the house in Unicorn
Street, where he had regaled the Pagnels with new
stories of his adventures abroad. He had travelled to
Italy and talked of the trouble brewing in that volatile
land. For all the beautiful art treasures to be found
there, discontent was rife and there were sporadic
uprisings against the repression that prevailed in so
many of the small kingdoms. The Carbonari, or 'Char-
coal Burners', were being hunted in Lombardy and
imprisoned in Austrian dungeons. A revolt had
occurred in tiny Turin, quelled by Austrian troops.
Protestantism was forbidden. The duchy of Tuscany
had become one of the few sanctuaries for the
persecuted . . . The tales went on, pictures of another
world for the two Pagnels who had never stepped outside their own country.

But it was Rebecca who listened most to Matthew's
descriptions. Often, when he came to eat supper with
them, it would be he who came to share the fireside
with her after he had drunk port with Francis. For
Francis tended more and more these days to retire to
his study, to read and work at new designs – designs
in which, it seemed, Rebecca had no part.

As she and Matthew walked down the hill, back
towards the town, Rebecca thought sadly of the distance that seemed to have grown between herself and
Francis in the past few months. Or was it longer than
that? Did it stretch further back into the past – as far
as the months before William was born? It was difficult
to remember just when it had begun, this slow, insidi-
ous estrangement. Difficult to know even now whether
it were really serious.

Perhaps it was nothing to do with her anyway. Trade had been uncertain for months and showed no sign of improvement, the new co-operative was taking time to get to its feet and Jeremiah's age was becoming ever more apparent. Francis was beset with worries and it was selfish of her to be thinking of herself at such a time.

But . . . if only he would allow her to give him comfort, if only he would accept the love she offered so freely still. If only he didn't shut himself away from her heart.

Jeremiah was in the nursery when she arrived home, sharing the children's bread and butter tea. Rebecca came in, warmed as always by the cosy atmosphere, the simplicity of the room and the delight in her sons' faces as they caught sight of her. She sat down by the fire and let them kiss her face until it was wet, and laughed at them.

'And what have you been doing? Has Grandpapa been playing with you?'

'We've been building houses,' Daniel told her, displaying several edifices in the corner of the room, built with the wooden bricks that were the boys' favourite toys. 'That's mine, the best. Geoff's not very good at it yet.'

'Well, he's younger than you.' Rebecca lifted William on to her knee and looked him over. 'And have you been a good boy for Grandpapa?' Her voice was especially tender when she spoke to William. He had still not outgrown his delicacy and was later than his brothers with everything. His walking was still uncertain, his speech restricted to a few words. Yet he was as warm and loving as a puppy, and the thought that he might be destined for an early death would wake Rebecca in the night, twisting her heart with fear. It was then that she most longed to turn to Francis and move her body close to his, to receive the love and comfort she craved . . . but Francis was often not there. And she would know that once again he had sat up late, reading or designing, or perhaps just worrying, and had slept in his dressing room to avoid disturbing her.

Or so he said. Did he not know how much she longed for him to disturb her?

Jeremiah came to sit in the chair opposite her. He stretched out his legs towards the fire, and drew Geoffrey close. He was particularly fond of the middle son, perhaps because he was so like Francis. For so many years, he had been forced to watch from a distance as his son grew up, never daring to show too much affection for him. Now he could live the time over again with Geoffrey, taking the chances that had been denied him. His big hand rumpled the boy's hair as he stared absently at the flames.

The room was very quiet. Daniel had gone back to his building and was busy repairing Geoffrey's rather drunken-looking house. William was dropping off to sleep on Rebecca's lap, his almost transparent eyelids closing over eyes of china blue. Jeremiah seemed lost in his own thoughts and Rebecca let her mind stray back over the afternoon. It had been pleasant, walking across the fields with Matthew, looking at the walls – not much better, at this stage, than Geoffrey's attempts at construction – and imagining the house as it would be. It was such a pity he had no plans to marry. It would be a lovely house for some lucky woman to live in. And Matthew would make such a very good husband . . .

Jeremiah moved and she glanced up. He was staring at a high corner of the room, his eyes almost rolled back in his head. Startled, she followed his gaze, but there was nothing to be seen. She looked back at him and saw that his eyes had closed and his head was jerking slightly. A small patch of spittle appeared at the corner of his mouth. Alarmed, she spoke his name and started to her feet, waking the baby who began to wail. Jeremiah opened his eyes and looked at her in surprise.

'What's the matter?' His voice was very slightly slurred. He frowned a little and sniffed. 'What's that odd smell?'

'I can't smell anything.' She stood uncertainly, holding William against her shoulder. 'There, there, my dove, don't cry, it's all right. Mamma's sorry she woke you . . . Father, do you feel quite well?'

'Well? Of course I feel well.' He stared at her. 'Why shouldn't I feel well? It's just this strange smell – are you sure you can't smell it, Rebecca? I can't think what it is – it seems so strange, yet it's familiar too.' He sniffed again and then shook his head. 'No, it's fading now. It's gone. Most peculiar.' His voice was stronger now. 'Something in the fire, I suppose.' He began to rise to his feet. 'Anyway, I must be going. It's been pleasant here with you and the children, but I have to meet Henry Brinton. Business, you know . . .' He smiled absently, patted the children's heads and fished in his pocket for a farthing for each of them. 'There, now that's for your money-boxes. Save everything you're given and you'll be rich men when you grow up. Rich enough to start your own carpet businesses, perhaps.' He laughed and then grew sober again. 'If there are any customers for carpets by the time you grow up.'

'Oh, Father,' Rebecca said, 'it's not really that bad, is it?'

He sighed and looked at her, and she realised afresh that he was growing old. Too old for all this worry, she thought, too tired. He ought to be resting, he ought to be able to forget it all.

'I don't know,' he said heavily. 'It could be. But I can tell you this – it'll get worse before it gets better. All any of us can do is to hold on. And some of us will fail.' He moved towards the door.

'But not Pagnel's,' Rebecca said pleadingly. 'Surely not Pagnel's.'

'I hope not,' he answered her. 'We all hope not. After all, we have to save it, don't we.' He looked down at the little boys and at the baby in Rebecca's arms. 'We have to save it for them.'

He went out of the nursery and Rebecca turned away from the door. She took William into the night nursery and laid him in his cot, then stood gazing down at him, her heart filled with dread.

What if the business failed, what if Pagnel's went bankrupt as some of the smaller firms had already begun to do? What would happen to her children then?

She thought of Daniel and Geoffrey working at the looms, drawing as she had done when she was only eight years old, their strong little bodies worn and wasted by toil and poor feeding. She thought of William, perhaps never strong enough to labour at any task. And she felt a fire spark into life, somewhere deep in her belly.

No. These children deserved a better start to life than she had had. They deserved a better life altogether. And she, she who had been Rebecca Himley, would see that they got it. No matter what it cost.

'It was really worrying,' she told Francis later, as they sat by the fire together. He had, as usual, moved to go into his study when they had finished supper, but Rebecca had persuaded him to keep her company for the evening. 'I seem to see so little of you these days,' she said. 'And I'm anxious about your father.'

He followed her into the sitting room. Edith had gone to bed early and they had the fireside to themselves. The room was quiet and warm, filled with dancing shadows. Rebecca sat down on the sofa and, after a brief hesitation, Francis sat beside her.

'What are you worried about? He's well, isn't he – or has he told you something? I know he's worried about business, but so are we all.'

Rebecca looked at him. He was thinner, she thought, and sometimes he looked very pale. Were these business worries that he and Jeremiah had both spoken about, even worse than they said? Were they even now approaching disaster? Fear clutched at her throat, but she shook it away with an effort.

'No, he hasn't said anything, Francis. I'm not sure he even realises it. But this afternoon, while he was here with the children . . .' She described that odd little incident when Jeremiah had seemed to 'disappear' within himself, his eyes tipping back in his head as if he were staring at some distant corner of the ceiling. 'I'm sure he didn't hear what I was saying. And he complained about a queer smell. There was no smell, I'm sure of it, Francis. What do you think it could be?'

'What did *he* think it might be? The smell, I mean.'

'He didn't know. He said it must have been something in the fire. But— '

'Then I expect that's what it was. As for the rest, I daresay he just dozed off for a moment or two. It's natural enough, he's growing old now and the room was warm. I'm sure there's nothing to worry about, my love.' He stopped abruptly, realising how unfamiliar those words tasted on his tongue. Was it really so long since he had called Rebecca 'his love'? Had he detached himself from her to such an extent? And yet, she was his love, as much as ever. He could not describe the strength of his longing for her, the force of his love. If only William's birth had been easier – if only the doctor had not given him those warnings . . .

'Well, I hope you're right,' Rebecca said doubtfully. 'It seemed strange though. You haven't noticed it, Francis?'

'Never. He seems as hale as always – wonderfully strong, and with a brain as keen as ever it's been.' Francis spoke bracingly, silencing the doubts in his own mind. Of course Father was well – wasn't he working with the rest of the manufacturers to improve trade, wasn't he one of the leaders of the town? Didn't they all look to him still? He had instigated the secret meetings, the discussions that took place frequently now in his own house. He led them. They listened to what he had to say, they respected him. They needed him. The town needed him.

Francis's thoughts drifted away from Rebecca's worries to his own ever-present uneasiness about the way the carpet trade was going. Everyone was feeling the pinch of poor times, of course, in every trade, but for Kidderminster the situation seemed especially bad. Only two or three weeks ago, Tom had come to him with worry carving deep lines on his face and told him that their best customer had cancelled a large order.

'Cancelled?' Francis had exclaimed. 'But – we're halfway through it. He can't– '

'He has,' Tom said grimly. 'And precious little we can do about it. The firm's gone bankrupt – he's in Carey Street and nothing to pay his debtors with. It's gaol for him, and for the rest of us we just have to make shift the best we can.'

Francis stared at him. The order amounted to three months' work for the co-operative. Half of it completed. Now what were they to do?

'I don't know what to suggest,' he said helplessly. 'Do we go on to finish it, hoping we'll find another buyer – or do we stop and trust that someone will want what we've already made? And how likely is that anyway – the carpet was designed to match the ceiling in the drawing room, wasn't it? Who else is going to want his drawing room decorated in exactly the same way? Who else has a drawing room exactly that size?'

'Aye, it's a problem.' Tom scratched his head. 'The carpet needs to be finished to be worth anything at all. That design's like a picture – get half of it and you only get half the picture. But like you say – who's going to want that picture. No, I reckon we'd be better to tek it off the looms and put it away somewhere. Start on summat we know we can sell.'

'I suppose you're right,' Francis sighed, but it grieved him to see the beautiful design carried away half finished, to be rolled up and left in a corner for who knew how long. And there was the question of money rolled up in it too – money spent on wool, on jute for the backing, on dyeing, on the weaving itself. Money that was lost as long as it lay unfinished, unsold.

He had kept his worries from Rebecca but confided them to Matthew, who was instantly concerned.

'It must be an enormous blow to you,' he exclaimed, and Francis admitted that it was.

'We need that money to finance the next project – nobody pays for a carpet that's not woven yet. It means thin times for us all, if we manage to keep going at all. And we need to make this co-operative a success, Matt – if we fail, the other manufacturers will feel themselves vindicated and such a system will never be tried again. They'll blame our failure on the whole concept, never making allowance for the times we're all going through.'

'Yes, I see that.' Matthew rubbed his chin thoughtfully. 'So what you really need is money to keep you going through this difficult patch.'

'It would certainly help,' Francis acknowledged, 'but where it's to come from I don't know. Loans are expensive, and Father can't help though I know he'd like to – he's having the same problems with his own factory. He's not in trouble – he can ride them out. But he can't afford to help me and Tom.'

'But I can,' Matthew said quietly.

Francis stared at him.

'*You*? But— '

'Why not? I'm rich enough, and I never do anything with my money. Don't even spend it much – I like to earn my living when I'm not in Kidderminster. Well, so why shouldn't I put some of it into your business?'

He grinned. 'I've always wanted to be a master of something.'

'Well, you'll be no master in our co-operative,' Francis retorted with an answering grin. 'We consider ourselves equal, weaver and weaver together. But – if you're really serious, Matt– '

'I'm serious,' Matthew had declared, and they'd shaken hands on the spot. And his money had eased the situation and made it possible for Francis and Tom to carry on.

His thoughts had taken him beyond the walls of the room, and Francis returned now to find that Rebecca had moved closer, laid her hand over his and was stroking his fingers. Very, very gently, her own finger-tips moved caressingly over his hand, whispering across the knuckles, brushing the thin, sensitive skin between them, tingling down the edge of his palm. Her feather-light touch drifted over his wrist and traced the outline of the base of his thumb. Francis felt his heart jerk in his breast. His breath quickened and his blood warmed.

He knew he should draw his hand away. Rebecca's touch was like gentle fire on his skin. The slow pulsing beat of desire was beginning to drum low down in his body, steadily increasing its urgency as Rebecca continued her tender movements. He wanted to turn to take her, take her in his arms, kiss her as he had not kissed her since William's birth. He wanted – oh God, how he wanted! – to love her.

'Rebecca . . .' he muttered, and she turned to him, lifting her face to his. He stared down at it, seeing the glow of the firelight on her skin, the spark of the flame in her eye. Her lips were reddened, slightly parted, the tip of her tongue just visible. He wanted to bend his head to hers, touch that small pink tip with his own tongue, in delicate and loving greeting. He wanted to cover those soft lips with his and drown in her kisses as he had done – it seemed half a lifetime ago. He wanted to feel her body against his, to hold her warm, rounded breasts in his palms, to stroke the smooth, silken skin.

He wanted to *love* her.

'Rebecca . . .'

'Oh, Francis,' she whispered, and moved closer to him, so that he could feel every soft, yielding contour. She lifted her arms and the sleeves fell back, revealing the curve of her elbow, the thin, white skin through which the veins showed a pale blue. Mesmerised, he hardly felt her twist her hands around his neck. His own hands were slipping over the firm, full breasts, down to the waist that was as tiny as ever, even after bearing three children. The feel of her, so long denied him, the scent of her, the warmth of her breath on his face, the softness . . . all served to inflame his desire so that it pounded through his body, roared in his ears, filled his head and his heart with an urgent longing that he could no longer deny.

'Rebecca . . . my love, my love.'

His lips were on hers now, tasting, remembering, savouring. He moved them gently, moulding her mouth to his, letting his tongue meet hers in tiny, flicking, darting movements. His arms were close around her now, gathering her against him, and she came willingly. He could feel her quickened breathing, the soft movement of her breasts against him, hear the tiny whimpers she made as his kiss probed further, deeper. With every sound, every movement, his desire grew until he knew that he must find release in the love that he had denied them both for so long. And he knew she wanted it too – had wanted it for many months. And had never understood his denial.

Why had he never told her? Because she had too much courage – because she would have refused to acknowledge the risk, would have wanted to give him the love he craved whatever the consequences. And he could not have withstood her.

The thoughts flickered through his mind and he knew that he ought to draw back, must draw back. But Rebecca was in his arms, the scent of her was in his nostrils, her hair was against his face, her mouth moving with his. The yearning of over two years' denial, since before William had been born, was drumming through his veins and driving out all possibility of restraint. And he realised that, until this moment, he had never known quite how much he had missed and longed for this celebration of their love. He had never allowed himself to know it.

He drew his lips away from hers, looked down into her burning face. Her lids were drooped over the dark brown eyes as if she were half drugged, her head hung back as if her slender neck could no longer support its weight. Her body lay heavy against him and he held her closely with one arm as he drew his other hand slowly down the line of her cheek and into her throat. Slowly, tremblingly, he began to unfasten the tiny buttons.

'Francis . . .' She fluttered like a bird in his arms. 'Francis, not here. Your mother – Tilly – '

He hardly heard her. He had laid her breast bare and gazed at it now as if all the jewels of the earth lay exposed to his eyes. As tenderly, delicately, as if he were almost afraid to touch her lest she should shatter like a dream, he touched the white skin, the darkened nipple. Rebecca shivered and turned her head suddenly, as if his touch scorched her. And he bent and laid his lips on the smooth curve, his kiss more an act of reverence than an expression of desire.

They lay together, closely embraced, passion replaced for the moment by a deep, sure contentment that at last they had found again the love that seemed to have departed. There was no hurry now, no urgency. Their lives stretched before them like a shining road that led into a bright future. Nothing could now stand in their way.

'Come upstairs, my love,' Rebecca whispered at last, and he drew himself away from her. He looked down into her face, reluctant to let her go even for the few minutes necessary to reach their bedroom. A feeling of uneasiness, that something might happen even now to spoil this new beginning, invaded his mind and he stirred, half inclined to refuse, to take her here and now. But he knew she was right: Tilly or his mother might easily come in at any moment. And nothing must mar their loving now. It was too precious, too new.

He lifted himself from her, and fastened again the buttons that he had undone. Gently, he smoothed back her hair and then drew her to her feet. They stood close and he tipped up her face and kissed it with tiny, pecking kisses that touched her lips, her cheeks, her eyelids and her nose. He took the lobes of her ears between his teeth and nipped them gently. He ran his fingers through the hair that had escaped from its pins, and pulled it down around her shoulders. He held her face framed between his two hands, and kissed her lips hungrily and deep. He held her against him, her face against his shoulder, and laid his cheek against her dark brown curls.

And then he led her from the room. His arm around her waist, he drew her through the door and up the stairs. They reached the landing and he put out a hand to open their bedroom door.

And from the nursery above, they heard a scream.

Instantly, Rebecca stiffened in his embrace. He felt her draw away and pulled her against him, hard, desperately.

'Geoffrey – it's Geoffrey. I must go— '

'Tilly will look after him. Or Nurse— '

'No! He's been having nightmares – terrible dreams that frighten him half to death. I'm the only one who can soothe him.' She tore herself away from him. 'Francis, he dreams that he's *dying*. I have to go, I can't let him suffer so . . .' Half sobbing herself, she

211

was out of his arms and already on the stairs. 'I'm sorry, I'm sorry, but he needs me . . .' Her eyes looked back at him, huge and dark in the candlelight. 'Francis, I have to go . . .'

He watched her disappear into the shadows and then went into the bedroom and set his candle down on the washstand. He looked at the big bed where they had lain together on so many nights, stiffly apart so that he had been unable to bear it and had made excuses to sleep in his dressing room. Where they had once made love throughout the dark, silent hours, and slept at last entwined, one person in every possible way.

He sat in a chair and stared at it. And slowly, as the torment in his body began to subside, he remembered what he had, for a few mad moments, forgotten.

This night could indeed have brought Rebecca back to his arms, brought their love to a triumphant new flowering. But what if it had done more than that? What if his seed had planted a new life deep inside her – a life that could have killed her?

Suppose their fourth child had been conceived tonight? Suppose Rebecca had died in giving birth.

No. His decision had been the correct one. He and Rebecca must never love each other again, not in that way. They had their children, their home, their life together and with that they must be content. He must never, never again allow his passion and his need to overcome him as it almost had this evening.

Slowly, heavily, like an old man, Francis came to his feet and opened the door which led to his dressing room. He undressed and got into the narrow bed that was kept there for the nights when he sat late in his study, working, reading and longing for his wife. From now on, he knew, he would sleep there every night. He would never – *must* never – touch Rebecca's sweet body again.

When Rebecca left the nursery and came down to the bedroom, expecting to find her husband waiting

212

for her, he was pretending to be asleep. He heard her come in, heard her hesitation, imagined her unbelieving glance around the empty room, her hands on the smooth, untouched bed. He heard her open his door and look inside. He heard her voice whisper his name, heard the break that told of tears.

The door closed again and Francis could hear the movements as Rebecca prepared for bed. And then he heard the soft, muffled sound of her weeping.

He was shaken then by a longing more desperate than any he had ever known. To go to her side, to take her again in his arms, to kiss and wipe away the tears, to love her as she yearned to be loved, as he yearned to love her . . . In his agony, he clenched his hands into fists, tore his fingers through his hair, felt his own tears hot upon his cheeks, soaking his pillow. But he did not move from his bed. To go to her now would be to give in . . . and could be more. It could be to kill her.

Oh, Rebecca, Rebecca, he mourned, why did this have to happen to us? Why can't we love each other as we both need? Why does it have to be forbidden?

But Rebecca, weeping in her bed next door, never heard his thoughts. The pain of what she thought of as his rejection was too sharp in her heart. And she could only ask herself, over and over again, why Francis had stopped loving her.

Only yards apart, yet separated by a world of torment, they lay sleepless through the long, bitter night. And neither of them could answer the questions, for neither of them knew just what was being asked.

Chapter Ten

'They'll strike,' Francis said. 'They're bound to, now.'

The words sounded like a knell in Rebecca's ears. She stared at the three men, looking first at her husband, then turning her eyes upon Tom and Matthew. All looked solemn and she felt her heart suddenly beat a little faster. So it had come, the moment they had been half anticipating, half dreading. And Kidderminster would be at war.

The secret meetings between the manufacturers had at last concluded that the rate for weaving standard Brussels carpet must be reduced from one shilling to ten pence a yard. Twopence off every yard woven, adding up to a considerable difference in the wage a man took home at the end of every week. The new price list was issued in March, and immediately there was an outcry.

'It's all a lot of nonsense,' Bill Bucknell told his mates in the secret society, his face flushed red with anger. 'You know what they're trying to make out? That Kidder's falling behind the carpet makers in the north – Scotland and Yorkshire, places like that. They reckon they're making more Brussels there and paying less for it, so if we don't tek less as well folk'll order their carpets from Halifax and such. And then we won't have a job at all, at any price. That's what they're saying, boys.'

'Well, you knows what we thinks of *that*,' Fred Holloway said. 'They ent making that much Brussels up there. And Kidder's the leader of the carpet trade, allus has been, we can set the price any day. We don't need to follow no man.'

There was a murmur of 'that's right, that's right,

well said' from the other men at the meeting, and Bill took the floor again.

'Trouble is, we've been working too hard, mates. There's been a slump, we knows that, and time'll come when it's over and folk can't buy fast enough. It allus happens that way. But just now, the warehouses are bursting with good carpet that we've slaved our guts out weaving, and the masters can't sell. Now, that's their fault and shouldn't be taken out on us – they wanted us to make it. But you see what it means?' He paused, and they looked at him, each knowing the answer but wanting him to voice it. 'It means *they* can keep going while we strike. That carpet's food in their bellies for months to come – and the poor victuals we ate while we were making it have all been forgotten long ago. There's no more living in that carpet for us, mates.'

'No more living at all, by all accounts,' another man said surlily. 'It's just the same as always – them as has the money keeps it, and them as earns it starves. How can we feed our families on tenpence a yard? It were struggle enough at a shilling.'

At that moment the door burst open and George Hodgett rushed in, his jacket half off his back, his hair standing on end. 'Here you all are,' he panted, one hand supporting himself on the door jamb. 'I thought you'd all be at the meeting. Everyone's making for the square – every weaver in Kidder – hundreds and hundreds of them. We got to be there, mates, there ent no time to stand around jawing – come on!'

The Committee scrambled to their feet and followed him out of the door. As soon as they reached the street, they heard the noise of the crowd on its way to the square – the steady tramp of feet on the 'kidneys', the low rumble of voices. Every now and then someone would shout out some slogan or rallying cry, and there would be a few seconds' silence as they listened, and then a great roar of agreement. And the noise grew all the time, as more and more men poured from side streets, alleyways and alehouses to join the throng and add their voices. It was as if the whole of Kidderminster were making its protest.

Bill and the rest of the men who had formed the secret society hurried along, anxious to be in the forefront. As members of the Committee that everyone knew, they had to be leaders here, showing the way. A strike, if it came to it, would have to be carefully managed – you couldn't just leap into a thing like that without considering all the pros and cons. As Bill had just pointed out to his mates, the manufacturers were in a strong position. It wouldn't help the weavers' cause to stage a strike they couldn't keep up, and then have to give in like they had in Wilton a few years back.

The square was filling with men when they arrived, but someone was already erecting a rough platform in front of the Lion Hotel. The Committee made for it and climbed up so that all the men could see them.

'Here, make way for Will Charlton,' Bill said, as the Union President appeared. 'It's him as ought to talk to 'em. Come up here, Will, and let's be hearing you. Or there's going to be a riot here – they're as mad as a nest of wasps.'

William Charlton clambered up on to the platform, followed by the Secretary, Tom Potter. These two men, better educated than most weavers, had been leading figures in the Union – or Friendly Society, as it was still officially called – and commanded a good deal of respect. The crowd fell silent as they stood there, arms raised.

'There must be over two thousand here,' Bill muttered to Fred Holloway. 'The masters surely must see we means business.'

'Don't matter to them whether we does or not, do it,' Fred whispered back. 'They got the whip hand, Bill, and we knows it.'

But Bill wasn't listening. He was paying close

attention to what Will Charlton was saying, in a voice that rang over the silent square. He was talking about the right of a working man, a skilled man at that, to earn a living wage, and the duty of his masters to pay him that wage. 'It ent just a matter of what folk will pay for a yard of Brussels,' he declared. 'We knows that folk who buy carpets can afford 'em at twice the price, if they've a mind. And if they wants good carpet to lay on their floors, when we got naught but a bit of rag rug, they *should* pay a proper price for it. That's only fair.'

He paused while a thunder of agreement rolled around the square, then he went on more quietly.

'All the same, mates, we don't want to rush this business. A strike can hurt everyone. It ent easy – we saw what happened in Wilton and Bradford two-three years ago. Cost a lot of money and in the end the men had to give in. We don't want to make that mistake again. No, we don't jump in with both feet on this.' He paused again and Bill sensed the slight discomfort that was wafting like a pale mist through the crowd. 'None of us wants to starve, does us?' Will Charlton called, and instantly they were all together again with a roar of '*No!*' 'None of us wants to see our wives and children starve?' '*No!*' 'None of us wants to see the alehouses shut down for lack o' business?' And the touch of humour in his voice was echoed in the even greater roar '*No!*' Will grinned and there was a scatter of laughter. 'Right, then,' he said, and now everyone was listening. 'This is what we does . . .'

'Strike?' Matthew said, feeling his nerves come suddenly alive. 'You're sure of it, Francis?'

Francis nodded. 'They're bound to,' he repeated. 'They'll never accept the reduction. How can they? Take off twopence and masters like Vivian and his cronies will think they can take off another penny or two. They'll grind the weavers into dust, and never see what's happening until it's too late. And then . . .' He shrugged, as if anything might happen. As indeed, Matthew thought, it might.

'And the notices are posted now?' Rebecca asked.

'This very minute, I should imagine. Saturday, March 15th – Fall Day.' Francis glanced at the clock. 'The Ides of March – though I don't imagine Vivian thought of that. The men will be reading them now and probably already on their way to call a mass meeting. There are only ten days before the new prices take effect – they haven't much time to decide what to do.'

'It's terrible,' Rebecca said in a low voice. 'The hardship – worse than anything Kidderminster has known yet. And the waste . . .' She stood up and went to the window. 'If only we knew what was happening.'

'Yes, we ought to know.' Francis frowned, then rose. 'I think I should go along – see what their mood is. Maybe I can talk to them— '

He was halfway to the door when Rebecca caught him up and clutched at his sleeve.

'No, Francis! You can't go – you're not well enough. And they may turn on you, they'll be angry, they'll see you as an enemy. Please— '

He shook her off and she turned to Matthew. 'Matthew, please stop him.'

'Rebecca's right. It would be madness to go out there. If they've only just seen those notices, they'll be in an ugly temper and won't be ready to listen to reason, especially from a manufacturer. Stay here, Francis.'

'But I'm not just a manufacturer! I run a co-operative – the first in Kidderminster. They know that. They know I'm on the weavers' side. They'll not harm me.'

'Nor me,' Tom said, getting to his feet. 'What's more, I'm one of them, born and bred. I grew up with Bill Bucknell and his mates, I *know* what it's like to live in a weaver's hovel. If they'll listen to anyone, they'll listen to me.'

But Matthew shook his head.

'I told you, they'll be in no mood to listen to anyone. Look, I've seen this sort of thing before, in America, in Italy – in so many places. Men driven beyond their limits, men blind to all reason. It's not a matter of persuasion when it gets to this stage – it's worse. They can turn really ugly at the slightest provocation – and seeing a manufacturer in their midst could just be that provocation.'

'But I'm not just a manufacturer,' Francis repeated. 'They know about the co-operative— '

'And do you think they really see that as anything important? You and Tom and the men working for you, you're becoming masters all over again. Until you can persuade a few others to set up their own ventures, no one is going to take the co-operative that seriously – and especially not this morning. You're a Pagnel, Francis, one of the biggest manufacturing families in Kidderminster, and that's what they'll see when they look at you, not a friend who wants to help them in their struggle. And Tom, you may have been one of them once but you're a master now in their eyes, co-op or no co-op. They may even see you as a traitor.' He paused, hearing again the words he had just uttered, saying them again in his mind. 'I'll go,' he said quietly. 'I'll go and see what's happening. They'll not touch me.'

Francis hesitated for a moment, then gave in. Matthew, glancing anxiously at him, saw that he was indeed not well. The healthy glow of his cheeks had bleached to a cold pallor, with no more than a bright spot of red. His eyes burned almost feverishly, and he breathed quickly, but whether that was from emotion or fever Matthew could not tell.

Nor did he have time to worry about it now. Already the men might be thronging the streets for a mass meeting. He caught up his hat and made for the door.

But Tom was beside him, his face equally determined. 'I can't help what you say,' he declared, 'this is my business as much as yours – more – and I hev to see for myself. I'm coming too. All right, I'll say naught if there's naught to be said. But I got to be there.'

Matthew looked at him and recognised Tom's right to do as he wished. He nodded and touched the other man's arm.

'I'll be glad to have you with me.'

Rebecca followed them into the hall.

'Take care, Matthew,' she said as he jammed his hat over his thick, chestnut brown hair. 'You may not be a manufacturer yourself, but you're our friend and even that might be held against you. And Tom, don't lose your temper. Matthew's right about the men – they've been pushed too far to see reason, and they could so easily turn against you.'

Tom muttered something and dragged on his coat, clearly embarrassed. And Matthew took refuge, as usual, in humour.

'Of course I'll be careful – have you ever known me take any kind of risk with myself? I'm far too precious – the only Matthew Farrell in the world. I have rarity value, if nothing else.' He grinned and laid his hand on the door handle, then looked at her more seriously. 'I'll be careful,' he promised. 'And I'll come back as soon as possible to let you know what's happening. And you be careful too, Rebecca, and take care of Francis. You're right, he doesn't look well. I think he ought to see the doctor.'

'He won't do that. He says it's nothing, just a cough left over from that bad cold he had before Christmas.' She watched them through the door and down the steep, narrow street, and her heart filled with foreboding.

No good would come of it. No good at all.

The main square was filling with people when Matthew and Tom arrived, but although the men were clearly angry they were not in such an ugly mood as Matthew had feared. The few who glanced round and saw the two men did no more than nudge each other and mutter together, and although they made no greeting, their glances were not unfriendly.

The union leaders were at the far end of the square, mounting a cart so that they could be seen and heard. Tom recognised his old friend, Bill Bucknell, and some of the others – Hodgett, Holloway, Potter. Some of them had grown up with him, others had been weavers who had worked with his father, taking their pieces to the manufacturers on Fall Day, independent weavers who had finally been forced to go to work in the factories. But their sense of pride had never allowed them to see their masters as a final authority. Always, they had kept the knowledge that a man can be wrong, even though he be rich and powerful, and that wrongs can, in the end, be righted.

'And this wrong will be put right,' declared the man who was speaking now, his voice ringing out over the assembly. 'Masters can't go on, grinding poor weavers into the ground, paying them starvation wages and then taking that away too. Their children don't starve, and neither should ours. And they're going to hev to see it!'

A cheer rose from the throat of every man in the square. Matthew listened with disquiet. The men might not yet have reached that stage of vengeful despair that he had feared, but it wasn't far away. And if the manufacturers remained firm – as he had no doubt that they would – the results would be disastrous. For the masters, for the weavers, for Kidderminster itself. Nothing would ever be the same again.

He touched Tom's arm and jerked his head, indicating that they should go. Tom nodded and they slipped away into a nearby alleyway, threading their way through the narrow yards to return to Unicorn Street. Once back in the house, they could talk, and tell

Francis and Rebecca just what had happened.

'So that's how it stands,' Matthew finished. 'They're going to negotiate. They don't want a strike any more than you do – although there are a few rabble-rousers who are keen to stir up trouble. But the union leaders seem reasonable men, and they know what happened in Wilton and Bradford. There's no doubt the union has the money to carry a strike for a while – but no one knows how long it would take, and they're reluctant to take the risk.'

Francis breathed a sigh of relief. 'Thank God for that. And so are they calling for a meeting with the masters?'

'They are. As soon as possible – later today, or tomorrow, as early as it can be arranged.' Matthew glanced at his friend. 'You'll want to be there.'

'Certainly. I *must* be there.' Francis frowned. 'It's hopeful that the men are looking for negotiation rather than action – but I doubt if it'll do any good in the end. You know we've been having meetings for months past, and the reduction has been agreed after a lot of discussion and argument. And almost all the manufacturers in Kidderminster are for it. It'll take more than a few union leaders to change their minds now.'

Rebecca had been listening. Now she spoke, her voice sad with the inevitability of it.

'So you think they'll still strike, in the end?'

'I fear so,' Francis said, a sombre note in his voice. 'Yes, I fear so – very much.'

'We wants to be fair over this, masters,' Will Charlton said. 'We're not taking any sort of hasty action, you've got to allow us that. But twopence a yard just ent reasonable. It's a lot of money for a working man to lose.'

He paused and looked around the room for agreement. Bill Bucknell, standing close behind him with Tom Potter, Fred Holloway, George Hodgett and the

223

others, nodded. But the carpet manufacturers, seated around the long, polished table in Jeremiah Pagnel's library, pursed their lips and shook their heads.

'You men don't understand the difficulties,' Vivian said smoothly. 'Naturally you're concerned about this reduction – we all are. It took a great deal of discussion before we could bring ourselves to impose it. But without it, we would all suffer. There simply isn't the demand for carpet that there was. The whole country's going through a bad time – other industries are suffering just as much. We have to pull together on this, don't you see? We all have to tighten our belts, make sacrifices. It isn't just you weavers— '

'Ent it?' Bill demanded, unable to restrain himself any longer. 'So just tell us what sacrifices you mean to make, Mr Vivian. Difficulties! We understands about difficulties all right. We wakes up to 'em in the morning and we sleeps with 'em at night. As for tightening your belts, the only reason your belts are tight is 'cause your bellies are too full.' He swept a withering glance around the smooth, well-fed faces before him. 'If I takes in any more holes on my belt, it'll meet itself coming back.'

Vivian's face darkened.

'Now there's no need to be abusive— '

'No, there ent,' Will Charlton said quickly. 'Bill, we agreed we'd try negotiation first. There ent no help for anyone in putting their backs up. Look, sirs, we come in a friendly spirit to ask if there ent no other way round this. I know there's a lot of carpet in the warehouses, but that carpet's money to you. You've paid for it and it'll sell eventually. Can't you keep us going on the same money so we can ride it out? I tell you, tenpence a yard's going to mean starvation to some of the men with big families— '

'Then they shouldn't breed so many,' Vivian said coldly. 'And no, we can't carry you. Good God, man, don't you think that's just what we *have* been doing?

For months, if not years? This depression has been coming on for the past twelvemonth and more. And we have our expenses to meet too. It would do none of you any good if I had to sell my house and move into a weaver's hovel— '

'Might do you a bit of good, though,' Bill Bucknell muttered, and Vivian caught the words and glared.

'We don't have to talk to you,' he said abruptly. 'We don't have to listen to you either. In fact, we're wasting our time in meeting you at all. You'd be better going back to your rabble and telling them to get back to work, work that they're very fortunate to have. And tell them also that the price remains as it's been posted – tenpence a yard. Starting on March the twenty-fifth.'

There was a silence in the room. There was no mistaking Vivian's tone; he meant every word of what he had said and would not retract. And Bill, looking at the faces of the other manufacturers, saw that they were all in agreement.

Except for two. Old Jeremiah Pagnel, and the young one, Francis. Jeremiah looked uneasy and tired. Old. And Francis was staring miserably at the gleaming wood of the long table. His face was pale except for two spots of hectic colour, and as Bill watched he put a handkerchief to his lips and coughed.

Bill felt a sick nausea in his throat. Was this the man young Becky Himley had wed, this weakly looking individual who looked as if he'd be better in bed than here with real men? At least Vivian Pagnel had a bit of strength about him, even if he did use it wrong. But this one – young Francis . . .

There was no help there, neither from Jeremiah nor Francis. One was too old, the other too weak. And Bill turned to Will Charlton and the others and curled his lip.

'Reckon there ent nothing for it then, mates,' he said, and they nodded. And Will Charlton and Tom Potter, the union officials, stepped forward and looked gravely at the men who ruled their lives.

'It's a strike, then,' Will said, and his tone was as implacable as Vivian's. 'A full, all-out strike. And then we'll see what you has to say to us.'

'We shall say exactly the same thing,' Vivian replied, not displaying a flicker of emotion. 'You'll starve faster on strike pay than you will on tenpence a yard. But that's your affair.'

For a long moment, they stared at each other, each measuring the other's worth as an adversary. And then, as if at a signal, the weavers turned on their heels and made for the door.

'Stop!'

The voice rang out suddenly through the room, stopping every man in his tracks. Slowly, they turned and Bill saw that Francis had lifted his head and that there was a new look in his pale, set face, a glint of steel in his blue eyes. He had half risen from his seat, as though the effort were almost too much for him, and Bill thought again that he ought to be home in bed. But not, this time, because he was less a man than his cousin.

'Vivian,' Francis said, turning to his cousin and then to the other manufacturers. 'Gentlemen. We can't let this matter go on in this way. We must give it more thought. The weavers are right. Their pay *is* too low. This reduction will force them to become paupers. It's inhuman.'

There was a rustle of embarrassment, a stir of uncomfortable murmuring. But Vivian was neither embarrassed nor uncomfortable. He merely glanced at Francis, sighed and examined his fingernails.

'Really, Frank, this is no time for your radical ideas. You know as well as I do the state the industry is in. We simply can't afford to pander to these people. We have our own livings to consider – as well as the industry itself. If Kidderminster is not to become a centre for unemployment rather than carpet manufacturing, we have to take steps to preserve it for everyone – not just for ourselves. There would be nothing for weavers to weave if we didn't provide it – surely you understand that.'

'I understand it very well,' Francis said coolly. 'And I also understand that every master here could take a cut in his profits that would make this twopence reduction unnecessary. And that without reducing himself to anything like penury.'

There was a long silence. Vivian's face darkened with anger. He cast a swift glance about him at the rest of the meeting. Then he turned his head and addressed the weavers.

'I repeat,' he said, and his voice was as hard, as cold, as implacable as iron, 'you will starve faster on strike pay than on tenpence a yard. And that is our final word.'

Bill's eyes met those of Francis Pagnel once more, but this time they both knew they were beaten. Vivian had the weight of the meeting behind him. And Francis, with his co-operative, was something of a hybrid, neither master nor man, carrying weight with neither side. In that moment, he knew the full despair of helplessness.

'Then that's it,' Bill said quietly, and this time when the weavers turned to the door there was nothing to call them back.

Matthew and Tom were among the first in the square. They found themselves a corner near the carts that had once more been brought there to form a platform, and watched as the union officials climbed up into them. Their faces were grave and it was plain to everyone what the result of their meeting with the manufacturers must be. They lifted their hands, calling for silence, and gradually the crowd quietened.

'Well, men,' Will Charlton began, 'we've been to the masters and asked them to think again. And you

227

must already know what the answer is. There's no shifting 'em, it's tenpence a yard from now on and that's their final word. And we all know what we think of *that*.' There was a roar of agreement from the crowd. 'Well, friends . . .' He looked down at the men nearest him, then away across the vast crowd to those who stood at the back, mere shapes at the far end of the square. He lifted his voice so that all could hear him, and his words rang across their heads and into their ears. 'It's a strike we have, or give in to them,' he declared. 'Now it's your choice, lads. Which is it to be? Will you work for tenpence a yard, or will you withhold your labour as they did in Wilton? You know what it means, you know what happened there. They had to give in, in the end. Are you willing to take that risk?'

'We'll never give in!' someone called, and the crowd roared again. Will gave them time to quieten, then looked out over the crowd again. And then repeated his questions.

'So answer me now, lads. Do we work for tenpence a yard?'

'*No!*' the crowd bellowed.

'Do we strike?'

'*Yes!*'

'Even though we may have to give in, eventually?'

'*We'll never give in!*' they roared, and Matthew found himself glancing at the roofs of the buildings around the square, almost as if he expected the noise to lift them from their walls.

'Then that's it,' Will Charlton said, and his voice held a touch of sadness amidst its grim implacability. 'We go on strike for our twopence a yard, and we stay on strike until they agree to it. And that has been agreed by all here present.'

The crowd almost erupted then. They shouted, laughed, cheered and slapped each other on the back. They danced, where they had room, and staged mock fist-fights and then, when they had had enough, they formed a procession and began to march through the town, exhorting everyone they passed to join them.

Matthew followed soberly, Tom close beside him. It was as if some great national event had been announced, the coronation of a new king, the winning of a war. Instead, these men were facing weeks, perhaps months, of hardship. There was nothing to celebrate – yet he realised that what they were celebrating was the feeling that action was being taken, that they were all together in facing a common enemy. Only later, when the euphoria had died a little, would they begin to recognise the reality of their situation.

The women would realise it at once, he thought, remembering Rebecca's sad eyes at the thought of a strike. The women always did.

A sudden murmur ran through the crowd and he looked up. The procession was beginning to draw near to Joseph's Bowyer's house, and the carpet manufacturer could be seen at the door. He was staring arrogantly at the throng and as Matthew came close he saw to his amazement that Bowyer was brandishing two guns. He watched as the man waved them threateningly in the air, and felt the vibrations of the crowd's anger. A few draw-boys and girls at the back of the crowd began to jeer him and Bowyer stepped forward and levelled his guns at their heads.

'Fire on us, would he!' someone growled. 'Us'll soon show him!' And some of the marchers bent and picked up stones. 'That's it, lads – let him have it.'

A hail of stones flew at the house, some striking windows. There was a crash of breaking glass and someone laughed in triumph. The hail increased. A stone caught Bowyer on the forehead and he retreated to his front door and then, holding up his arm to protect his head, ducked inside. But the marchers saw no reason to stop. They picked up more stones, flung them at the closed façade, broke more windows. They advanced on the house and Matthew began to feel anxious. As he had told Francis and Rebecca, he had seen mobs like this when he had been abroad, mobs who had ended with a lynching. Could such a thing happen in Kidderminster?

Yes. Such a thing could happen anywhere, once men's passions were roused.

'Fire his factory!' someone yelled, and the cry was taken up. 'Fire Bowyer's. Fire them all – all the bloody lot of 'em. They won't pay us, so what's the use of 'em? Fire – fire – fire!'

The situation was very nearly out of hand. Matthew pressed himself against a wall, wondering what he should do. He and Tom had become separated in the crush and he had no idea now where the other man might be. Could he command their attention – and would they take any notice of him if he did? Or would they see him as one of the enemy, friend of the manu-facturers, a scapegoat for all that had happened?

Perhaps he would be the one to be lynched.

As he glanced around, he saw the union leaders thrusting their way back through the crowd. Charlton, Potter, and that other man – Bucknell. As he looked at him, Matthew remembered that he had seen the man before, in the tavern on the day of Lawless Hour, when Tilly had rushed in to find Francis because Re-becca was in labour. All these men had been there, and they'd been discussing the possibility of strike action even then. They'd known that this was likely to happen.

The three men climbed up on the wall of Joseph Bowyer's house and held up their arms, demanding attention, and after some of the more vociferous pro-testers had been calmed down they were able to make themselves heard.

'Lads, lads, don't take on like this. Stoning the mas-ters' houses and firing their factories ent going to do any of us any good. You know what they'll do, they'll bring in the military, and they'll declare our strike illegal. There's other ways to deal with this, mates. What's the use of burning down the factories? Where will our jobs be then? We'll just be giving work to the bricklayers while we starve, and where's the sense in that? Now let's agree to be peaceable, all right? It'll be better for everyone. We don't want none of you hurt or in jail. Is that understood?'

The agreement that followed his words was a trifle reluctant at first, but Charlton pressed home his argument and eventually even the most militant of the protesters were calm and ready to begin the march again. But it did not last long. After a few more streets had been traversed, the men began to disperse, to straggle home to tell their wives and families what was happening. And Matthew too went home; to his own house first, to wash and put on fresh, clean clothes, for he had been considerably jostled during the morning and looked little smarter than a weaver himself. And then to the house in Unicorn Street, to report to Francis and Rebecca.

But there was someone else he must report to as well, he thought as he hurried up the hill. The man he had met in the fields on that cold afternoon, early one winter. The Reverend Humphrey Price, who had asked to be informed if trouble ever came to Kidderminster. Who felt as deeply about the weaver's lot as Matthew did himself, and who had seemed ready and anxious to help.

If he had meant what he said, this was the moment for him to prove it. For the weavers of Kidderminster needed help now as they had never needed it before. And Humphrey Price had struck Matthew as perhaps the only man who could give it.

William Jeremiah, two and a half years old, lay in his crib and smiled at his mother. To Rebecca it still seemed like a miracle. For months she had feared that he would never smile at her, that she had somehow given birth to a being who would never learn to laugh, for whom life would be a solemn affair with never a lightening of his own dark skies.

Yet it seemed impossible – was there ever a child born who did not laugh and smile, who did not for a while at least believe that life was a joyous gift, to be grasped with both hands with the amazing strength of the newborn? Even in the most poverty-struck weaver's cottage, a young baby's smile could lighten the darkness for a while. And yet William Jeremiah, lavished with attention, fed with good milk, kept clean and warm and comfortable for every moment of his short life, had lain as solemn as a judge, watching everything that went on with those dark eyes so like Rebecca's, and with never a tremor of soft lips to express his pleasure or delight.

But one morning his smile had broken over his face like the rising of a new sun and, once discovered, it never left his lips. Rebecca would sit for hours with him on her knee, revelling in his chuckle and doing all she could to keep it, to find new ways to make him laugh. She kissed him, cuddled him, sang to him, showed him pretty baubles, tickled his toes. And William Jeremiah responded with a smile that spread over his round face until it creased, and chuckled with the deep throatiness of an old man, making everyone who heard him laugh in their turn.

She lifted him from his crib now and held him up to Matthew, displaying him with pride.

'Isn't he beautiful? Look at his lovely skin, just like a peach, and his big serious eyes. And his hair's beginning to grow, see – like golden down. He's going to have my eyes and Francis's colouring, won't that look unusual?' She became aware of her other boys, looking up from their game in a corner of the nursery. 'I'm so lucky,' she said softly. 'Three fine sons. And I really was afraid we wouldn't keep this one.'

'Why wouldn't we keep him?' Geoffrey asked inquisitively, coming over to her. 'Does he cost too much? Papa said a dog would cost too much. If we didn't keep Will'am, could we have a dog?'

Rebecca laughed. 'No, not unless Papa says so, and we're definitely keeping William. He's your brother, you wouldn't want to lose him, would you?'

'Got a brother,' Geoffrey said, looking across the room at Daniel. 'Want a dog.'

'Well, you've got *two* brothers, and no dog. And you'll see, when William's bigger and can run about you'll enjoy playing with him just as much as you enjoy playing with Daniel.'

'He's not having my animals,' Geoffrey said warningly, clutching a wooden elephant to his chest.

'He'll have his own toys, but I expect he'll share them with you, and you'll share yours with him,' Rebecca told him firmly. Geoffrey looked at the baby and then at his elephant, set his mouth in uncanny imitation of his mother's, and turned back to his game. Matthew laughed.

'Doubt written in every line of his face! You're going to have some battles there, Rebecca.'

'He's as determined as I am,' she acknowledged. 'But I like that in him. He'll grow up to be a fine man, Matthew, a leader. He already rules his brother, and Daniel's two years older than he is. The problem is to prevent him from getting above himself. His character could be too strong – I'd hate to see him turn into a bully.'

'Bullies are weak, not strong. But you're right to worry about his becoming too dominating. It wouldn't be good for him – but I daresay Francis will take care of that.'

Rebecca was silent. How could she tell Matthew that Francis seldom came into the nursery now, nor even into their own room? That he spent most of his time at home in his study, and slept in the small dressing

233

room? How could she tell him of the gulf that had begun to yawn between them, when she could scarcely believe or understand it herself?

She was conscious of Matthew's glance resting on her, and she bent her face over the baby, pulling gently at the small, curling toes. 'This little piggy went to market— '

'Rebecca,' Matthew said quietly, 'you know I'm your friend, don't you.'

' —this little piggy stayed at home . . . Of course I know that, Matthew and very glad I am of it too. This little piggy – '

'If there were anything wrong,' he said, 'anything you needed to talk about, any help you needed— '

' —ate roast beef, this little piggy had none. And this little piggy . . .' she paused '. . . ran ALL the way home!' The room was filled with William's gurgles, and Rebecca laughed with him. At last she looked up again and met Matthew's eyes squarely. 'That's very kind of you, Matthew. But I can't imagine anything going wrong, can you? Once this strike's over, that is. At least, nothing that *I* could ever do anything about.'

'I didn't mean with the factory— ' he began, and then stopped as if it were useless to go on. And Rebecca felt sorry for him. She knew quite well that he didn't mean the factory. He was worried about herself and Francis. But how could she talk to him, or to anyone else? How could she tell anyone about the night that Francis had turned away from her, about his rejection of her love? How could she even begin to describe this sharp, stabbing unhappiness, the feeling that somehow she had lost his love, lost her way. And, like little Bo-Peep in another of the nursery rhymes she sang to her sons, didn't know where to find them.

'Please don't worry about me, Matthew,' she said quietly. 'I'm happier than I have any right to be. Look at everything I have – a comfortable home, my sons, my husband – I want for nothing. I have no right at

234

all to be *un*happy. And I'm not,' she added quickly. 'I'm not. I'm very lucky.' A shadow touched her mind and she frowned. 'If only— '

'If only what? Tell me, Rebecca.'

'If only Francis were stronger,' she said slowly. 'He seems lately to be – I don't know – almost *fragile*. As if he could blow away in a puff of wind. He gets thinner every day, I swear it. And the worry of the strike seems to make him worse. He hardly rests, you know. And his cough is no better. He's had it since before Christmas.'

'He's never been very different,' Matthew said. 'He was always very slender, however much Enid fed him. And restless always, as if he must always be doing something. The strike's worrying, of course, but I don't really think there's anything wrong, Rebecca. A few sleepless nights, a cough – anyone might suffer from them, they mean nothing.'

'I know I worry too much,' she confessed. 'But I can't help it. Seeing my father and mother die . . . and Francis's Uncle Geoffrey . . . and I have this feeling sometimes, almost like a premonition, that there's someone else I'm going to lose.' Almost unconsciously, she tightened her arms around the baby on her lap. 'I thought it was going to be William, but he seems to be so much stronger now. And if it isn't him— '

Matthew looked at her. Then he left his chair and came to squat on his heels before her, gazing into her face. Gently, he disengaged her hands and shifted William so that he leaned back against his mother's body. Then he took her hands in his and held them close.

'You're the one who is tired and unwell, Rebecca. You still haven't recovered from this little one's birth, you know. It was hard for you and you were so afraid he wasn't going to live, and that fear is still haunting you. That's all it is. There's nothing wrong with William, nor Francis, nor these two rapscallions here. And there's nobody else you're going to lose, except in the natural order of things, and that won't be for a long time yet.'

'Jeremiah?' she whispered, staring at him with huge, dark eyes. 'Enid?'

'Eventually, yes. You know that, Rebecca. But not yet, not for years. Why, they're both as strong as horses. Isn't Jeremiah in the thick of it now, still leading the other manufacturers and trying to make them moderate their views over this strike? Isn't Enid running this house as efficiently as she used to run the school? It's all in your mind, Rebecca. You are the one who needs rest and strength.'

She continued to gaze at him, trying to accept his words. He was right, she knew – Jeremiah was still hale and hearty for his age, though his years were bringing a stoop to his shoulders and whiteness to his hair. But that was only natural. And Enid, who had taken over the running of the house when Rebecca had been brought to bed with William, clearly enjoyed her duties so much that it had seemed a pity to make her relinquish them.

The association Rebecca and Enid had formed with the other manufacturers' wives had proved difficult to sustain. Lydia, Anne and the others were not so free as Rebecca; their husbands would not countenance the involvement with the weavers' problems that Francis encouraged. A little charity work, yes, some hot soup on winter's days, a few cast-off garments. But anything more political would only bring trouble for them and their families.

One day, when she had more strength, she would gather them together again, try to instil her own passion into their hearts. Meanwhile, she had hoped that having more time would enable her to come close to Francis again, to help him in the designing they had once always done together.

It hadn't happened. And her fears and unhappiness

had coalesced in her mind to a terror that she was about to lose someone, something . . . It was fear that she could not lose, could not rid herself of.

'You're not leaving us, are you, Matthew?' she asked at last.

An expression she could not identify crossed his face and he looked down quickly at her hands, examining the fingers as if he had never seen them before. For a fleeting moment, she had the impression that she knew nothing of this man, that there were aspects of his nature that she had not even begun to guess at. Then he looked up again and it was the old Matthew, the one she knew so well who took some things very seriously yet treated his own life as a joke, who laughed his way through life as if it were no more than a game to be played.

'Lose me?' he exclaimed. 'Rebecca, you'll never lose me! Why, you're more likely to wish I would go away and leave you in peace – but how can I, now that you've turned me into a man of property, encouraging me to buy a house and become serious and grave? No, I'm afraid you are encumbered with me for life, Rebecca, and it's your own fault. You'll have to send me away yourself if you are ever to be rid of me.'

He shook her hands and laughed at her, and Rebecca felt a load slip from her heart and laughed back. It was all right. There was nothing ominous, nothing terrible, nothing about to happen.

Matthew scrambled to his feet.

'I'll have to ask permission to leave you now, all the same. I have someone coming to stay with me – the Reverend Price, who I told you about. He's arriving this afternoon and I want to meet the coach.'

'The Reverend Price? Is that the man who was interested in the weavers?'

'That's him. He's anxious to help in the campaign.' Matthew gave her a quizzical glance. 'And with you being a manufacturer's wife, I oughtn't to tell you anything at all about the campaign.'

'Are you involved in it? Really involved?' she asked with sudden anxiety.

'I hope to be.' Matthew's face was serious now, the laughter hidden again, and she wondered how she had ever thought him frivolous. 'I very much hope to be.'

And then, with a quick salute and a pause to ruffle the heads of the two boys, once more busy with their Noah's Ark, he was gone. And Rebecca was left with her baby on her lap, gazing into the fire and wondering.

Just what was going to happen to them all?

Chapter Eleven

*'We crave the candid and humane consideration
so urgently required by an issue of such grievous
and dreadful importance as the condition of the
weavers of Kidderminster. We seek the benevol-
ence of the public to help repel the unjust, cruel
and tyrannical measures of the employers, which
we are determined to oppose in the utmost
extreme, that our humble circumstances, the support of our friends, and the sacrifice of our little
all will allow, and should we meet with that kind
and commiserating aid that we confidently antici-
pate we shall ultimately defeat the base designs of
oppressive influence, and break the galling yoke
of corruptive power.'*

Will Charlton lowered the paper he was holding and
looked around the room. 'How does that strike you,
mates?'

'It's fine wording,' Fred Holloway declared. 'You
done a good job on that, Will. Ought to make anyone
think.'

'And there's more.' Bill Bucknell had been frowning
over another sheet of paper as the men listened to their
president. 'Listen to this.' He read rapidly, savouring
the phrases. ' *"Already reduced to the most wretched
state of poverty . . . bordering on starvation . . . wage
reduction would have the most dreadful consequences . . . the strike is our last effort to prevent
inevitable ruin . . ."* And then we'll add a bit at the
bottom to tell folk that we'll be peaceable right through
the strike. No more stoning or fights.'

'It's good,' Fred said again, and George Hodgett and

the others nodded. 'I reckon that'll get a lot of folk on our side. I hear it's already been in the London papers too. People are going to hear about this, and about what weavers has to put up with.'

'All the same,' Will Charlton said, 'we need more than this. This is just a start. We've got to keep it up. More things in papers, more notices posted. Handbills that folk can send away to mates in other places – Bradford and Wilton, they had all our support last time, we ought to be able to look to them now. And other places too – Halifax, Scotland even. What happens in one place affects those in others. We got to get them working for us too.'

'That minister that come here the other day,' Bill said. 'He said he could write ballads and such. Songs. There's nothing like a song that folk can sing all the time. And he said he'd help out other ways too.'

Fred Holloway pursed his lips.'

'Minister? He's gentry.'

'Ah, and so's his mate, what's his name, Farrell,' George Hodgett agreed. 'And what's more, he's a crony of young Francis Pagnel – and *he's* a master. I don't reckon they're to be trusted. We can handle this ourselves.'

'But Francis Pagnel's not like the rest,' Bill said. 'He set up that co-op, with Tom Himley, him that done for old Jabez Gast years back. And he's married to a weaver's daughter – Rebecca Himley as was, Tom's sister. They're all right, I'd stake me life.'

'Aye, and he stood up for us all right when we went to negotiate,' Fred admitted. 'Set himself up against that cousin of his and all the others. I reckon Bill's right there.'

'Sounds like you're in cahoots with him yourself,' George Hodgett said. 'Sure you're with us, and not feathering your own nest with the masters?'

'That's a slummocky thing to say,' Bill said heatedly. He came to his feet, his face dark with anger. 'You'll

240

tek that back, George Hodgett. I been true to this society ever since the first minute I was enrolled, and don't none of you dare say nothing else.'

'All right, lads, all right,' Tom Potter said soothingly. 'Bill, we all knows you're a true mate and George didn't mean nothing else. Did you, George?' He waited until George had muttered an apology, then went on: 'All the same, you do seem to know a lot about what Francis Pagnel and this Matt Farrell thinks and says. And this Reverend Price, too. How d'you come to be so thick with 'em, Bill?'

'Well, it's our Nell, ent it,' Bill said a little self-consciously. 'I mean, she's thick with young Mrs Pagnel – Becky Himley as was. Comes round to our place, she does, and brings stuff for the childer, things her own babbies hev outgrown, that sort o' thing. And the odd bit food for their bellies. And got some of the other masters' wives helping her, too. Not that they'll do much good – too dainty to dirty their pretty frocks coming down our way, and too feared of their menfolk to do aught useful. But you knows what womenfolk are, they talk, and Becky told my Nell about this Matt Farrell wanting to help the weavers, and this Price, and the upshot of it all was they come round to see me the other night, them and Tom Himley. And I reckon they're fair and square, and we ought to let 'em in. They got education, see. They can say things we wouldn't know how to put.'

'I thought Will's address was good enough for any man,' George Hodgett said, still a trifle belligerently. 'He've got enough education to write summat like that, he've got enough to carry the rest of the strike. Ah, handbills and songs and all, if wanted.'

'Here, I don't know about songs,' Will began, but Bill Bucknell was already speaking again.

'Well, you can turn 'em down if you want, but I reckon this vicar means to help whether we asks him to or no. Us can't stop him writing to the papers and such, and if he's going to do that us might as well hev him working with us.' Bill sat down again, folded his arms and stuck out his feet. He looked around at the assembled men, tilting his head in a gesture of finality.

'I can see you mean what you say,' Will Charlton said at last. 'And it's my belief you could be right. Any road, we ought to talk to these two and see just what sort of coves they are. Can't do no harm to do that, can it? And he's a minister too. Come from Kidder hisself, went to school with the likes of the Pagnels and the Brooms. Get him on our side and we could be halfway home.'

He looked around and the others nodded, with varying degrees of enthusiasm or reluctance.

'So shall I bring 'em along?' Bill asked, and Will nodded.

'Soon as you can get 'em here. If we're going to hev help making out new handbills and such, we ought to hev it as soon as we can.' He paused as the church clock struck nine outside. 'Mek it tomorrow morning, if you can get them here then, Bill. Otherwise, we meet anyway. And now I'm off home. There's a lot to be done and I got to get these notices written out fair for the printer.'

They pushed out of the room, some to go home, others to make for the alehouse. But as Bill set off up the street, he felt a hand on his arm. He turned to find George Hodgett at his elbow.

'I hope you know what you're doing, Bill Bucknell. Getting gentry in to help weren't none of my plan. I thought weavers were strong enough to fight for theirselves.'

'Strong enough don't count at times like these,' Bill retorted. 'We takes any help that's offered and glad to, if we got any sense. And this Price is a good 'un. I knows it. Any road, Tom Himley ent gentry, he's one of us,' he added staunchly. 'A weaver, born in the same yard as my Nell.'

'One of us!' George snorted. 'Might've bin once, but what did he do? Slashed old Jabez Gast and then lit off to London. Do we want a murderer on our side, Bill? Do we?'

For the first time, Bill realised what small, cold eyes George Hodgett had. They gleamed now in the dim light from his lamp as he went on, 'If aught goes wrong with this strike, Bill Bucknell, it'll be your fault. Remember that. 'Cause *I'll* not forget – never.'

'But how are you all going to live?'

Rebecca looked around Nell Foster's cottage. During the past few months, Nell had begun to make it more comfortable, with a few pieces of furniture – old furniture, but fairly sound nonetheless – and oddments of crockery and pots for cooking. There were even a few offcuts of carpet on the floor, brought home from the looms.

Now it seemed as if even these attempts at making a home were to be lost, for if the strike dragged on for long they would have to be sold again to buy food for the children.

Rebecca thought despondently of the wives' group she had formed, and which now looked like foundering. Maria, who could have been such an influence and with whom she'd thought some rapport was developing, had flatly refused to countenance the idea. ('Vivian would kill me', she'd said – and Rebecca had been inclined to believe her.) And now the others, Anne and Meg and Lydia and the few more that they had managed to recruit – each one had come to her, half shamefaced, half defiant, to withdraw. 'It simply isn't possible with the way things are,' they'd said. 'With the men on strike – it would look like a betrayal. We have to follow our husbands.' And although Rebecca had a distinct impression that some of them, at least, would have liked to carry on with their charitable works, she knew that there was nothing to be done.

Women were the slaves of their husbands, she thought. There were few who had a husband like Francis.

And even between herself and Francis, there were still strains and tensions. Still that terrible, unexplained withdrawal, which seemed no nearer being resolved now than it had ever been . . .

'It's one step up and two back here,' Nell said dispiritedly, bringing her back to the present. 'Allus has been for the likes of us – you knows that, Becky. No sooner start getting a few bits and pieces together than you has to watch it all go again. I dunno why we bothers.'

'Because it's all we can do, I suppose,' Rebecca said. 'Either that or give in – and weavers don't give in, do we? My Dad taught me that.'

Nell grinned. 'Ah, so you're still a weaver at heart, Becky Himley. Being a fine lady's all very well, but you never forget where you grew up, do you?'

'Not when you grow up in this sort of home, no.' Rebecca looked around the shabby room, at the green stains of damp on the walls, the sacking that was stuffed into the broken window. 'And I know Francis understands it as well. I've told him – and he saw for himself, when my father died.'

'Ah, it's not like living through it though, is it. He might *think* he understands – but he don't really know what it's like to get up to a freezing morning hours before it's light and go to work with nothing but a cup of water inside you – and that only if you're lucky. Many's the day I've not even had a drink 'cause it's been froze in the pan. He don't really know what it's like to stand twelve, fourteen hours at a loom like me and your Bess used to do, drawing for some old bastard like Jabez who's as likely to beat you as rape you, like he did that night . . .' She shivered. 'No, your man might try to understand, he might think he does, but nobody who hasn't been through it can really know . . . And how is your Bess? Ent she ever coming back to Kidder? I'd like to see her again, we was good mates.'

'I don't think she'll come back, no.' Rebecca sighed. 'She feels safe in London – though why she should, when she wasn't any better treated there than she was here at first, I've never understood. But there is it, she knows her way around there now, and she seems to be getting her business on its feet, and I suppose she's happy. And that's all that matters really, isn't it.'

'No, it ent,' Nell said bluntly. 'Getting fed is all that matters, and keeping warm enough to stay alive in winter. *Them's* what's important, Becky, and if you can afford to think about being happy as well then you've got no real worries. And if your Bess is getting enough to eat and can buy a warm shawl to put round her shoulders, and can lay down in her own bed at nights, I reckon that's all a body can want. That *is* being happy.'

'Yes,' Rebecca said humbly. 'You're right, of course, Nell. I'm sorry – it was a thoughtless thing to say.'

'Don't matter. Anyway, I better get my man's supper started, while we've still got summat to cook and a pot to cook it in.' The abrasiveness left Nell's voice and although she still spoke roughly, it was with better humour as she added, 'Thanks for the things, Becky. You're good to us and I shan't forget it. Don't suppose we'll ever be able to help you out anyway, but you knows— ' A shrug completed her sentence, and Rebecca felt an ache in her throat as she went to the door. She had so much, and Nell so little, and yet here Nell was offering help if it were ever needed!

'Thank you, Nell. I won't forget. And I'll be back again soon, to see how you all are.' She was at the door now and ready to walk up the street, but she hesitated, suddenly nervous. Nell came to stand beside her and took a quick look out.

'Ah, there they are,' she said grimly. 'A lot o' men with naught to do and all day to do it in. That's the

245

worst of a strike, Becky, it brings out the worst in some on 'em. And this lot down here don't want much to bring out the worst in them, I can tell you. Best if I walks along the street with you, I reckon.'

She turned back into the dark little room and caught up her shawl, draping it around her shoulders. Rebecca waited for her, knowing that her offer was sensible. The men who leaned against the walls of the cottages, muttering to each other, looked distinctly unfriendly. They had been there when she arrived and she had been aware then of their hostility, of their eyes following her as she walked up the narrow street. And there were more of them now. It was as if they had called more to wait for her to come out. What did they mean to do?

What *could* they do?

Nothing, she told herself suddenly, and felt a rush of courage. What was it she'd been told when she was a child, coming in crying because the other children had jeered at her over some small trifle? *'Sticks and stones may break my bones, but names will never hurt me.'* These men weren't, surely, going to stone her – the worst they could do was catcall and jeer a little just as those children had years ago? And, it occurred to her, might not some of these men actually have been those very boys who had sent her crying indoors to her mother? Was she going to let them do the same again?

'It's all right, Nellie,' she said as the other girl came to the door. 'You don't need to walk with me. I can look after myself.'

Nell gave her a doubtful look.

'Best if you let me come too. They're a rough lot hereabouts, and in an ugly mood lately. Don't tek much for 'em to turn nasty.'

'And they've reason to,' Rebecca said quietly. 'But I don't need protection, Nell. Go back inside.'

Nell hesitated, but Rebecca gave her a little push and she retreated through the door, though she didn't close it. Instead, she stood half-hidden in the shadows, watching anxiously as Rebecca began to walk up the street.

The men were in a knot at the narrowest part, leaning together as the walls of the cottages leaned together. These were some of the oldest houses in Kidderminster, their timbers rotting in the damp air, bricks falling away to reveal the laths and straw beneath. Once, master and weavers had lived together here, side by side; then, as their prosperity grew, the masters had used the profits to build themselves bigger and better houses on the outskirts of the town, where the air was cleaner and they could look down on the narrow, twisting streets that had grown so haphazardly to form the little community. The old cottages had been left to rot, the weavers paid barely enough to provide for their families, with nothing left over for maintaining their homes. The roofs had decayed, the walls leaked, the floors run with water. They weren't fit for pigs to live in now, Rebecca thought with a tight knot of anger forming in her stomach. And hardly any of the manufacturers had thought to build new homes for their workers, nor even to renovate them. It didn't seem to occur to them that it was any of their business.

She was almost level with the men now, and aware of their eyes on her, hard and cold and angry. And why not? They had plenty to be angry about.

When she had started her walk, they had been clustered on one side of the street, leaning against one wall. Now, lifting her eyes, she saw that they had shifted, some of them moving across the road so that they formed an almost impenetrable barrier across her way. There was just room to pass between them. She came closer, and two of the men moved, barring her passage completely. There was no way through. Nor, when she turned her head, any way back. They had gathered around her and she was surrounded.

'Let me pass, please,' she said quietly.

The men laughed.

'Hear how she talks!' one exclaimed. 'Never think she was from round hereabouts, would you? Fine lady now, are you, Becky Himley? Or should we say *Mrs Pagnel*?'

'You can call me Becky if you like,' she answered steadily. 'It was good enough when I was a girl living here.'

'Ah, but you ent living here now, are you? Moved up the hill to a fine house, married a master. Done well for yourself. Come back to gloat, hev you? Come back to let us all see how well you done?' The voices were joining together now, railing at her, louder as the men pressed closer, thrusting their faces into hers. She could smell their bodies, smell the anger and despair, the reek of poverty, the stench of deprivation. Her fear was pushed aside by an overpowering compassion, a desperate pity that she could do nothing for them.

She looked into their faces and remembered her father, William Himley. Big, hardworking, often short-tempered because he was tired and hungry and worried. Because he had been just too late with his piece for Fall Day, and would get no pay for a week. Because his wife Fanny had fallen for yet another child, was doomed to another seven or eight months of cumbersome pregnancy – if she didn't miscarry again – and then another mouth to feed, if the child survived at all. Because he must watch her drag herself to the bobbin-winding sheds, morning after morning, while he laboured at the loom. Because his daughter Bess and his son Tom had been forced to flee to London, hunted for murder, and he knew he would never see them again . . .

Any one of these men might be her father. Indeed, in that moment, they were each one of them her father, suffering in the same way, as helpless as he, and as deserving of better than this.

She looked into their faces, her glance as straight

248

and direct as a lance, and as she met their eyes their own looks fell and they shuffled uncomfortably. But Rebecca did not want them to be uncomfortable with her. She put out a hand and touched the arm of the one nearest her and he looked up again, startled.

'Jack Greenaway, is it you?' She saw him nod. 'Remember how you used to play marbles with my brother? You gave me a glass alley once – I kept it for months.' She looked past him at the next man. 'Ebenezer, you once taught me to sing a song – my father nearly took the skin off my backside when he heard it. You rogue – I never knew there was anything rude about it.' The man laughed a little, uneasily, and glanced sideways at his mates. 'And you, Joe Beckett, and you, Fred Martin, I remember you too. We were all children together. I remember it all very well. I remember everything.' She paused. 'And I tell people,' she said quietly. 'I tell my husband and my father-in-law and all the family I have. I shall tell my sons as they grow up. I didn't come here to gloat this afternoon – I came to help. And I know there's not much I can do, but whatever there is, I shall do it. I promise you that. And now – will you please let me pass?' In a gesture of frankness, she touched her breast. 'I have a baby at home who is probably crying even now for his supper.'

The men hesitated, glanced at each other and shifted a little. Rebecca waited patiently. She had no fear now of these big, rough-looking men. They were the children she had grown up with, the men who were her father. They would do her no harm.

They parted and made way. And as she moved to pass them, they fell in behind her, and the ones she had spoken to by name walked by her side.

'We'll see you on your way, Becky,' Jack Greenaway said gruffly. 'There's some rough places in this town, and folk are in a funny mood these days. We wouldn't want you getting into any trouble.'

* * *

Humphrey Price threw down his pen and leaned back in his chair. He gazed at the table, littered with quills and shavings, spread with papers that were covered with his sprawling writing, and then glanced up under shaggy brows at Matthew, who sat opposite him. His mouth flickered a brief grin.

'Well, my boy, I think we've got a few telling phrases here and there. Some of it may sink into the right noddles. Let's hope so, anyway.' He picked up one of the sheets of paper and read aloud:

> *'The day was dark and sad and drear,*
> *The midst of March, the present year,*
> *The masters of the Carpet Trade*
> *To their poor journeymen thus said –*
>
> *In the Evening Mail we do declare*
> *That you both drunk and idle are,*
> *Therefore we have resolv'd and say,*
> *We'll have more work and give less pay . . .*
>
> *Potatoes, oatmeal you must eat,*
> *Nor dare to think of butcher's meat—*

What d'you think of that then, young Matthew? And this:

> *See our masters, how they bind us*
> *In the midst of slavery.*
> *See the tyrants, how they drive us,*
> *So – death or liberty.*
>
> *Lift up your heads, ye sons of men,*
> *And have your rights or die,*
> *The rights that our forefathers won,*
> *That was sweet liberty.*

I should think that will strike a few darts too,' he said

with relish. 'I plan to call it "The Carpet Weaver's Lamentation" and I shall send it to *The Times*.'

Matthew smiled, but spoke cautiously. 'Are you sure that's wise, Humphrey? The language is very strong – and the weavers have promised that the strike is to be a peaceful one.'

'And so it is. Not a head has been broken.'

'Not yet. But talk of "having your rights or die" is bound to inflame people. And those who read it will be expecting trouble. You know the Bailiff's already written to the Home Secretary asking for the military to be brought in— '

'More fool him! Why, he's nothing but an old woman – ready to fly into a panic at sight of a mouse running up his skirts.'

'All the same, he *is* the High Bailiff of the town. He can't be dismissed lightly.'

Humphrey shot him a piercing glance.

'Not failing in your courage, are you, Matt? We need to stand together in this. Men like Will Charlton and Tom Potter are well enough in their way, but they don't have the strength that we can bring to bear. Education— '

'They're not badly educated at all,' Matthew protested. 'More schooling than most weavers, and they can string their sentences together too. Look at the address they put out before the strike began.'

'Oh yes, yes, all very well in its way. But they can't do *this* kind of thing.' Humphrey Price gestured towards the scattered papers. 'Broadsheets, ballads, rhymes that men in the street can pick up quickly and easily, tunes they can whistle. Why, these songs will be on everyone's lips in a matter of days – and that's what brings it home to people. Not long, heavy sentences that they have to struggle to understand. Short, pithy sayings that they can all remember, verses that make them laugh at the masters, songs that make them feel strong and brave. That's what we can do, Matt.

251

That's why they need us.' He riffled through the papers again. 'Listen to this:

> Then rise like men in bravery
> To gain the cause or die,
> We will be free of slavery
> And have our liberty.

Doesn't that say all a weaver wants to say? Doesn't it put into his mouth the very words he can't articulate for himself? Matt, these men need champions, you know that. And none have come forward but us.'

'I know,' Matthew said soberly. 'But I'm still afraid . . . I don't want our militance to damage their cause, Humphrey. At present, they have no thoughts of violence. These ballads of yours— '

'Symbolism,' the clergyman said easily. 'It's not *violence* I'm advocating, Matt, not in the earthly sense. All this talk of "slavery" and "dying" – it's not intended to be taken literally. It's attitudes I'm referring to – surely you understand that.'

'*I* might,' Matthew acknowledged wryly, 'though I'm not sure I did until you pointed it out to me! But will the ordinary weaver understand that you're not talking about death or liberty in the literal sense? I doubt it, Humphrey. He'll see it as fighting talk, and a good many of the readers of *The Times* will do the same, if I'm any judge.'

'Well, we must agree to differ on that,' Price said comfortably, and Matthew sighed. Clearly his words were having no effect at all – the clergyman still intended to send his ballads to the country's leading newspaper, whatever Matthew might say. And whatever highflown talk he might indulge in about 'attitudes' and 'symbolism' Matt still had an uneasy feeling that Humphrey Price wouldn't be at all sorry to see the weavers taking a more aggressive stance. More than once, there had been a glitter in his eye when he'd spoken words like 'tyrants' and 'rights' – the kind of glitter Matthew had seen before when men were spoiling for a fight. It was the same glitter the world over, and it always spelled trouble.

Not that Matthew was afraid of trouble. But he had seen enough to know that it rarely solved the problem – indeed, was likely to create more. If you started with negotiation, as the strikers had done, and then went on gradually to more forceful methods, you might get your way before it ever came to a fight. But if you started with a fight . . .

You were likely to end with a war. And everyone would be the loser.

The letter was waiting for her when Rebecca arrived home, and at once it drove all other thoughts from her mind. Almost before she had finished reading it, she was ringing the bell, calling for Tilly, sending her to fetch Enid, to run to Tom's loom shop, to find the master . . . She held the sheet of paper with its few scrawled lines in shaking fingers and, by the time Tom and Francis arrived, was sitting in her chair, trembling and being supported by an anxious Enid.

'What is it? What's wrong?' Francis was at her side, his face white. 'Rebecca, my love, are you ill? Tell me!'

'It's not me – I'm not ill— ' Her voice was cracked and dry, failing after a few words. She shook her head as if unable to say any more, and thrust the letter at them. Francis snatched it and read it quickly, then handed it to Tom and bent once again towards his wife.

'Rebecca— '

'She's dying,' Rebecca said, beginning to cry. 'Bessie's dying – she may already be dead – I must go to her, Francis, I must go to her . . .'

'It doesn't say she's dying. Just that she's ill— ' His voice faded. The letter might not have mentioned the word 'death' but that was certainly what it meant.

Bessie was ill, desperately ill. As Rebecca said, she might already be dead.

'She's dying. I know she is. *You* know she is.' Rebecca looked up, her eyes almost black, glittering like rain-drenched coal with her tears. 'Francis, I must go.'

'Of course.' He straightened up, looked helplessly at the others. 'I ought to go with her. But— '

'I don't see how you can,' Tom said quickly. 'You're needed here, with this strike and all. I'll go – Bess is my sister too and we went through a lot together.'

'If you would.' Francis sounded relieved. He bent again to Rebecca. 'Will that do, my love? Will you go with Tom? I'll make all the arrangements and you'll have every comfort. You can take the mailcoach first thing in the morning, it's the fastest way. I'll see to it at once.' He bent and kissed her head, then hurried from the room while Tom and Enid conferred quickly together, deciding what must be done and taken with them.

'Tilly must go too,' Enid decided, and moved to the door. 'I can look after everything here. I'll go at once and see to her clothes. And you can take some comforts for poor Bess . . . Oh, what a thing to happen! What do you suppose is wrong, Tom?'

He shook his head. 'I don't know, Mrs Pagnel. She's been poorly on and off for years – summat she picked up when we first got to London, I always thought. She used to get this fever and sort of rash. And lately she's been getting thinner too – never looked really right. Always pale, like, and sort of pinched looking, and her eyesight was none so good either, last time I was there. But there weren't nothing you could exactly put your finger on – just that she didn't seem right.' He shook his head miserably. 'We oughter've made her come to Kidder. We could've looked after her then. All those miles away – you don't know what's going on. And it were always my job to take care of her.'

Enid touched his arm. 'You mustn't blame yourself,

Tom. You did all you could – more than a lot of brothers would have done. And Bessie chose to stay in London. You couldn't have brought her, except by force.'

At that Tom grinned. 'You couldn't never force our Bessie to do nothing,' he declared. 'Always did hev a mind of her own. But I reckon that's just Himleys.'

Rebecca looked up. Her eyes were red but she was calm again. She reached out for the letter and read it through once more. Then she looked at her brother and aunt.

'I'm sorry about that,' she said quietly. 'It was – a shock. I'm all right now. I can see to my own packing, Enid, if you'll look after things here. And I'll be very glad if you'll go to London with me, Tom.' Her voice shook again and they knew she was remembering those other journeys to London – when Bessie and Tom had been fleeing for their lives, when Rebecca herself had been turned out of Pagnel House, penniless and with nowhere to go. But the moment was soon over. There was no time now for useless reminiscence. 'The mail-coach leaves at six in the morning, doesn't it? Well, if we're to be ready for it, there's a lot to be done.' She was on her feet, once again in command of herself. 'And Bessie will wait for us. I know she will.'

'Bessie? The little milliner? The whore?' Vivian's brows rose and Francis felt a hot anger rise inside him. Yes, Bessie had been both of those things, but who had been most to blame? Didn't Vivian himself bear at least some of the burden, even though he would never admit it? Hadn't he helped hound the girl and her brother to London when he could have helped them to stay at home, when he could have stood witness for their innocence? For Francis had always suspected that Vivian knew more than he ever admitted about what had happened that night.

'Rebecca's sister, yes,' he said quietly, reminding

Vivian that he was related to Bess Himley by marriage. 'Desperately ill, according to the person who wrote the letter— '

'An illiterate like herself, no doubt,' Vivian said carelessly.

' —and asking for a sight of her sister before she dies. So Tom's gone with her – we decided it would be better for him to go since one of us must stay here, and Bess was – is – his sister too.'

'Oh, certainly. Very commendable.' The matter was clearly of no interest to Vivian, and Francis sighed, wondering why he still expected his cousin to show a little human feeling for others. He never had yet – why should he start now? And especially over Bessie, for whom he had never felt anything other than the passing lust he always felt for a girl ripening into womanhood . . . Disgust rose with the anger in Francis's breast, and he turned instead to his father.

Jeremiah was in his chair. He spent more and more time there these days, but his expression was concerned, even anxious.

'Rebecca's sister? Dying?'

'That's what Frank said, Father.' Vivian's tone was impatient. 'He fails a little more each day,' he muttered to Francis. 'I wish he'd admit it and agree to retire, but no, he insists he can still hold the reins. God knows what damage he'll do us all one of these days.'

'What are you mumbling about, Vivian?' The old man's voice was sharp. 'You're always doing it lately – muttering and mumbling in corners. If you've got anything to say, speak up so we can all hear it.'

'I was merely telling Frank what *The Times* had to say this morning about the strike,' Vivian said smoothly. 'See, they've printed this so-called ballad.' He read a few of the lines aloud. 'Have you ever heard anything so outrageous? "*Slavery – tyrants – death or liberty*" – why, it's a call to arms, nothing more nor less. A declaration of war. And they say this strike's to be peaceful!'

'So what does *The Times* say?' Jeremiah asked.

'Why, exactly what you would expect them to say, of course. The editor has written a piece on it himself. He says – and quite rightly – that such language "cannot be too strongly reprobated" and "does not accord with the weavers' proclaimed intention to conduct a peaceful campaign".' Vivian frowned. 'What I would like to know, is who has written this inflammatory rubbish? It's not a weaver, I'll swear – there's not a man amongst that rabble who could put pen to paper to sign more than his own name, let alone write verse.'

'They're not all uneducated,' Francis said. 'The union officials are articulate enough – look at the address they put out at the beginning.'

'And we don't know that they wrote that. No, there's another hand behind all this and I'd like to know just whose it is.' He looked sharply at Francis. 'That friend of yours – Farrell. I suppose *he* couldn't fancy his talent at versifying? He's just the type to enjoy making trouble – no interest in the trade, nor in Kidderminster itself. He'd do it simply for amusement and then move on when he tired of the game.'

'He's hardly likely to move on,' Francis pointed out, feeling nevertheless that Vivian's remarks might be striking very near home. He hadn't seen much of Matthew lately, and he was recalling his friend's reaction to the strike and to the condition of the weavers. And he'd talked about another man too, some time ago – a Reverend Price, who'd been born in Kidderminster and had a living now somewhere near Lichfield. Could the two of them . . . ? But no. Matthew wasn't a troublemaker. If he were to interest himself in the weavers' troubles, he wouldn't be doing it for sport. And surely no clergyman would involve himself so deeply – especially if he no longer lived in the town . . .

'Matthew was never any use with a pen when he was at school,' he said now. 'English lessons were a torment to him. In fact, he was never a scholar of any kind – he wanted always to be off and out, roaming the fields and woods. I suppose that's why he left Kidderminster as soon as he could and went off to explore the world.'

'And it's a pity he ever came back, if you ask me.' Vivian shot him a quick, sharp glance. 'Just why *did* he come back, d'you know? And why did he decide to stay, build himself that great house? What does Kidderminster hold for a man like that? I'd watch him if I were you, Frank.'

'I don't know what you mean. Matthew's my friend, he always has been. Why should I question his motives in settling here? It's his home, after all. And why should I "watch him"?'

Vivian's mouth curved in its wolfish smile. His eyes narrowed and gleamed. And then he laughed.

'Why, I don't mean anything at all, Frank,' he exclaimed, clapping his cousin on the shoulder. 'Nothing at all. Of course he's your friend. And Rebecca's friend too. And what's wrong with that? Nothing. Nothing at all.'

He held Francis's eyes for a moment or two longer, then laughed again and turned away. A moment later, he was at Jeremiah's side, smoothing out the pages of *The Times* so that the old man could read the editorial for himself.

Francis stood quite still for a moment. He understood very well what Vivian had been trying to do. He was dropping a seed of poison into Francis's mind – poison about his friend and about his wife. It was one of his old ploys, but Francis had seen it done many times before and was determined that it should not work.

The trouble with seeds – even poisoned ones – was that they might lie dormant for a while, but eventually they grew and took root.

Chapter Twelve

'Bessie . . . oh, *Bessie* . . .'

Rebecca stood just inside the room, her hand to her mouth. She felt Tom's arm about her shoulders, holding her close, holding her upright. For a moment or two, she wanted nothing more than to turn her head against his shoulder, close her eyes and blot out the scene before her. But Bessie was there, on the bed, and to do that would have been almost like abandoning her.

She took a deep breath and hurried forwards, dropping to her knees beside the bed. She took the thin, white hand in her own, trying to bring warmth to the chill of the damp skin, reached forward to brush the lank, stringy hair from the pallid face, touched the sweating brow with her lips.

'Oh, Bessie . . . Why didn't you send for us before? Why didn't you let us know?'

Bessie's lips were cracked and dry. They moved slowly, as if speaking were an effort, and her voice was unrecognisable, as harsh as the rustle of dried leaves underfoot on a winter's day. Rebecca was forced to lean close, to make out the words.

'Wouldn't hev done . . . no good . . . I'm for the . . . long walk home now . . . nothing you could've done . . . just wanted to see you again . . . you and our Tom . . . oh, Becky, hold me . . . please hold me . . .'

Desperate with pity and grief, Rebecca slipped her arms around her sister's frail body. It was like holding a bundle of sticks, sticks of thin, brittle glass that would break at the slightest touch. She rested her cheek against Bessie's thin face, feeling the bones of the jaw like the bones of a bird's head, sharp and beaky, and her eyes were hot with tears.

'Tom, find a doctor. She needs help – someone must come, there must be something we can do. We can't let her go like this . . .' She turned her head, looking frantically into her brother's face but in the gravity of his expression she saw no hope. He touched her shoulder and gently, tenderly, she laid her sister back on the hard, narrow bed.

'She's asleep,' he murmured as she stood up again. 'It's the best thing for her, Becky.' The childhood name sounded odd on his lips, as if he were trying to find a past where things like this didn't happen. But they always had happened, in the Himleys' past. Childhood had been no protection for them.

'Oh, Tom,' she whispered. 'How did she come to this?'

Together, they looked around the tiny room. Its small window caked in grime, it was dim and shadowed, but there was enough light to see that its squalor was worse than any either of them had seen before. There was almost no furniture; only a broken-backed chair, a box that Bessie had evidently used as a table, and the bed – a rough, makeshift affair with a straw pallet which even in this poor light it was easy to see was crawling with lice. The smell was that of poverty and dirt: the smell of vomit and excreta, of rotting food, of mice and rats and creeping things.

'This is worse than what we lived in when we first come to London,' Tom muttered at last. 'Even then, even when Bessie was— ' he bit off the words abruptly, but Rebecca understood and bowed her head. She knew what her sister had been reduced to in those early days, knew how she had earned her living for months, years, on the streets of London. But surely now . . .

'Did she go back to that life?' she asked Tom now. 'Is that what brought her to – to this?' She looked again, half fearfully, at the shrunken figure on the bed.

'But why? What happened to the millinery? She wasn't earning her fortune, but she was doing well enough, surely. Why did she need to . . . Why didn't she let us know?'

'She was too scared we'd take her back to Kidder,' he said soberly. 'She was really frightened about that, Becky. And mebbe she thought we'd let her down . . . I dunno. Mebbe me and Nance should hev stayed with her.'

Rebecca shook her head. 'No. We can't live our lives according to other people, Tom. We have to live our own way, every one of us. Bessie had nothing to fear, really, and if she had done what we wanted, she would be in Kidderminster now, safe and well. Or perhaps she wouldn't. Perhaps she might still have had this illness. She used to have that rash, you remember, and that fever – perhaps this is part of the same thing. Perhaps there was no escape for her anyway.'

Tom nodded slowly. 'Ah, it's the life she was forced to lead . . . all those men . . . There's disease in it, Becky. She never had a chance, poor wench. If only she'd never had to come to London in the first place. If only I'd never gone for Jabez the way I did . . .'

'But that wasn't your fault. You had to do it. You tried to protect her, you tried to save her – but she was doomed from the moment she walked into that loom shop and stood as Jabez Gast's draw-girl. It was all set then, Tom, and there was nothing you could do to stop it.' She turned and paced the tiny room, beating her hands together. 'Oh, these horrible carpet factories! They've so much to answer for – so much misery, so much suffering and pain. And all so that people with more money than they know what to do with can have something soft and pretty on their floors. I tell you, if I knew a way to get Francis out of it, I would. But then there would only be something else to make, some other luxury that would fill our bellies while those that made it went hungry to bed.' She came to a halt before him, looking up into his face. 'And if we didn't make them at all, everyone would starve all the faster. What's the answer, Tom? What can be done about it all?'

He shook his head. 'It ent so easy, is it, Becky? Me and Francis, we're doing summat about it, I reckon, with the co-op. Our men ent on strike, nor want to – they has their share in the profits and they can see it's done fair. But it'd tek time to get all the manufacturers working that way, too much time. I dunno if we'll see it in our time, and that's the truth.'

'And meanwhile, men, women and children go on toiling all the hours that God sends, ruining their health and still not earning enough to live as human beings should.' Rebecca walked restlessly to the door and opened it. She stared through, down the twisting, rickety wooden staircase that had led them to this room from a confusion of ramshackle buildings. Down below, amongst rotting timbers and decaying brickwork, there was a maze of slimy, waterlogged alleyways, riddled with cave-like doorways and holes where people lurked like animals, their eyes peering from the gloom with suspicion and distrust.

How had Bessie come to be living here? How had things got so bad for her?

'Becky . . .'

The voice was little more than a thread but Rebecca heard it and came hurrying back from the doorway to her sister's side. Once again, she dropped on her knees beside the pallet, and took the plucking hands in hers, trying to still their ceaseless movements. Bessie was turning her head on the grey mattress, her eyelids flicking open to reveal eyes that were dull and clogged with matter. One of the thin hands struggled feebly in Rebecca's, and she loosened her fingers. Bess reached out trembling, her skeletal hand finding Rebecca's face and touching it, only to fall back as if exhausted by the effort.

'Bessie, Bessie, I'm here – we're both here, Tom and me. Can you see us, Bessie, can you hear us?' She looked round and found a cracked cup standing on the floor, half full of dusty water. She lifted it to Bess's lips. 'Try to drink this, Bessie. It'll do you good.'

'Naught'll . . . do me good . . . now,' the cracked voice muttered, but the water ran into her mouth and Rebecca saw the thin throat move as she swallowed. 'Is it . . . really you . . . our Becky?'

'It's me. Me and Tom, we're both here.' Rebecca cradled the hands in hers and looked across the bed at her brother. 'We're going to fetch a doctor to you. We're going to get you well again, Bess, and take you home. Nobody will hurt you there now. They all want you to come back. Nell Foster – you remember your best friend, Nell? She wants you to come back, she asks me every time she sees me. Nancy wants you – she's having a baby soon, Bessie, and she wants you to help her. And Francis and I want you to come too. We want you to see our little William – named after Father, Bessie, and going to be just like him too, I'm sure. But you've got to get well first, you've got to try . . .' She paused in desperation, seeing the dull eyes close again, the head turn away. 'Bessie, *please* . . .'

'It ent no good, Becky,' Tom said quietly, as Bess's chest rose and fell once more and then stopped. 'She's going . . . I reckon she's gone . . .'

'No. *No*.' Rebecca shook her head almost angrily. 'No, she can't. It isn't *fair*, Tom – she never had a chance. She *can't* die now . . . Look, she's breathing still, I saw her move. Bessie – *Bessie* . . .' She scrambled to her feet, her face pale and set, her soft mouth hardened by determination. 'I won't let you die,' she said intensely to her sister. 'I won't. I'm going to take you back to Kidderminster, where you belong. You are *not* going to die here – do you hear me? You're *not*.'

Bessie gave no sign that she heard, or was indeed

263

capable of hearing. But the chest that had stayed so frighteningly still for that brief moment gave a shudder, and a gasp forced its way from her throat, hissing through dry lips. Rebecca tightened her hold on the thin hands, and bent closer, watching as Bessie continued to breathe those shallow, rasping breaths. She looked up at Tom.

'Find a doctor. One who's not drunk and will come at once. Pay him to come if you must, but bring one. There must be someone out there who can help her.'

Tom turned and fled, and she heard him clatter down the stairs and out into the grimy yard where they had at last found their sister living. She sank to her knees again, gazing into the grey face, concentrating all her powers on pouring strength into the wasted body, on bringing hope and courage to the failing heart. *Get well, Bess*, she prayed, *get well. Try. Try. Try . . .*

By the time Tom returned with a doctor, Bess's breathing was steadier and Rebecca dared to hope that the crisis was past. But the doctor, old and grey, disillusioned by all he had seen in these poverty-stricken warrens, shook his head.

'All you can do is hope that she slips away without pain,' he said. 'Best if she never wakes. Clean her up a bit if you like, and then just sit by her and give her water when she needs it, but there's nothing else that can be done.'

'I don't believe it.' Rebecca stood with her hands on her hips, facing him across the stinking bed. 'She can't die like this. I won't let her. There must be something you can do. There must be some medicine – some potion. If it's a question of money, we can pay, my brother and I.'

The doctor looked at her and shrugged. 'Well, if you're determined, I can give you some nostrum which may help. I've seen cases rally before – but not often, mind you,' he added with a sharp look. 'When they've sunk as far as – your sister, you say?' He gave Rebecca a speculative glance, as if wondering about her own life. 'You understand what kind of disease this is?'

Rebecca nodded. 'My sister has had a hard life. It wasn't her fault that she had to earn her living in the way she did. But I can give her a good home, gentle nursing, healthy air . . . If you can only make her strong enough to travel, we'll take her away from London and make sure she never wants for anything again. If we'd only known before . . .'

'Aye,' the doctor said, 'if only. Two words we can all use, and a more useless wish was never made . . . Well, I'll give you something for her but I don't promise it will do any good. It depends how far the disease has progressed. Good nursing and good food will do as much, if she can only get the strength to take them . . . You realise it will never be cured? It will kill her in the end. You may be doing her no favour by saving her now, if save her you can.'

'I will save her,' Rebecca said steadily. 'And her life will be worth it. I swear it. And I'll nurse her whenever she needs it.' She looked down at the ashen face that had once been so merry, the strawlike hair that had once bounced with curls. 'She's my sister,' she whispered.

'Well, here it is.' The doctor produced a bottle from his bag. 'Give her this whenever she'll take it, and if it works at all she may be strong enough to be moved in a week or two. If not— ' He shrugged and said no more.

Rebecca scarcely noticed his departure. She was bending over Bessie, giving her the first dose from the bottle. And then she straightened up, looked about her and sent Tom for buckets, for water, for firing.

'If there's one thing I know,' she said, lifting the first pan of hot water from the fire they had lit and beginning to scrub, 'it's how to make a place clean. And if we're going to be here for a week, we're going to live properly. Bess will get better faster if she's clean and comfortable. And I mean her to get better, Tom. I'm not going to watch another of my family die of neglect.'

And on the bed, Bessie tossed and moaned. And occasionally opened her eyes and held out a skinny hand and whispered, 'Becky . . . Becky . . . Becky . . .'

'I don't know what it's all going to come to,' Jeremiah said, shaking his grey head. 'The streets are full of them. Weavers with nothing to do. No work to go to. Begging, with model looms in their hands – it's pathetic. Where's my jacket?'

'Here it is, sir, all ready for you.' Polly held the garment out for him to slide his arms into the sleeves. She had been performing this service for her master more and more during the past few weeks – this and more, for it seemed that lately she was the only servant he could tolerate near him. His manservant irked him, the chambermaid did her duties as perfunctorily as she could, and only Polly seemed to strike any kind of accord with him. Perhaps it was because she was the only link now with the old days, when the house had been filled with his family – his wife Isabella, her son Vivian and the others – Sarah, Edith, Jane, Isabel, Francis. And Rebecca.

Polly thought often of those early mornings when she and Rebecca, newly promoted to housemaids, had crept down the back stairs with their brushes and pails to clean the fireplaces. If only she'd known then what used to go on in the library! But Rebecca had been a close one all right – never a hint that Mr Francis was also getting up early and that they were doing a bit more than clear out fireplaces. Not that Rebecca had ever admitted anything, but it had been plain enough later, when her waist had started to thicken and the mistress had sent her packing.

And now here she was, back in Kidder and married to Mr Francis, and with three sturdy boys to show for it and all. While Polly, who had always been careful which way the wind blew when she lay with a man and had taken care to feather her nest, was still no more than an under-housekeeper, for what that was worth. And spending her days helping an old man on with his clothes, where once she'd spent her time helping the young men take them off.

'It'll do no good, this strike,' Jeremiah declared, moving stiffly across to the mirror to peer at his reflection. 'They'll have to give in in the end. Wilton men are getting tenpence a yard, so how can we pay more? We've got to pay the same in both places, or our carpet will cost more to buy and customers will simply go to Wilton to place their orders. It stands to reason.'

'Yes, sir.' Polly knew quite well that he didn't expect any real answer. She was just someone to talk to, a figure to relieve the emptiness of the big house. Only Jeremiah lived here now, alone in the upper rooms, with the servants keeping to their own quarters below stairs. And a sight more comfortable it was there, too, Polly thought with a shiver. Shabby kitchen furniture, to be sure, but there were cushions and bits of rag rug made by the women servants during odd moments, and the range to keep things cosy. Up here, the master seemed to have forgotten about fires, except in the library where he spent most of his time now. The rooms seemed bleak and chilly. They were built for families, for people, for light and laughter and companionship. Not for one old man, alone and lonely.

'Are you going to Unicorn Street?' she asked now, and he nodded. 'Rebecca's not home yet, is she?'

To anyone else, she would have had to say 'Mrs Pagnel' or at least 'Mrs Francis'. But she and Rebecca had been Jeremiah's housemaids and with him she would not pretend – nor did he seem to think she should. He shook his head.

'No, she isn't home yet, though she expects to be soon. Her sister's mending slowly, it seems, and

Rebecca means to bring her back to Kidderminster as soon as she's strong enough.'

'That's good. Pity she didn't come back when the rest of 'em did. She could've been living well here, with your Rebecca or Tom and Nancy. She could've made hats for the local gentry and all. She didn't hev to stop in London.'

'Well, she was afraid . . . We all tried to persuade her that there was nothing to fear, but she had a fixed idea that she would come to harm back in Kidderminster. And what grieves me most is that it was my own son – Vivian, I mean – that she seemed to fear the most. I've never really understood why.' He sighed. 'But she'll come now. Rebecca won't take no for an answer. A very determined young woman, Rebecca.'

Polly chuckled. 'You're telling me! Not but what she allus done her work well when we was in service together. But mek up her mind about summat and there was no shifting her. Allus bin the same.'

Jeremiah nodded. 'Well, I'll go and see the boys. Make sure they're all right, not lacking anything. Mrs Enid's looking after them, of course, but they miss their mother. It does them good to see their old grandfather.'

And it does their old grandfather good to see them, Polly thought, and then was struck by an idea.

'Would you like me to come along of you, sir?' she offered. 'I could help you take them for a walk. I know Tilly's away too. We could go down by the river. Or up the fields.'

Jeremiah looked at her.

'That's an uncommonly good idea,' he said slowly. 'I know Enid finds it difficult to get them out for their exercise. And Rebecca would be pleased. They know you well, don't they?'

'They should do, sir,' Polly said warmly. 'Rebecca always comes into the kitchen for a crack, and brings the little 'uns too. And I've been to Unicorn Street too, more often than I can count.' She grinned suddenly. 'I reckon I can manage that young Geoffrey better'n anyone else. Knows better than to give Polly lip, he does.'

'You'd better let us all in on your secret then, Polly,' Jeremiah said with a twinkle. 'For he's turning into a real scallywag. But I like to see a boy with a bit of spirit – and he's got such a way with him, he could charm the birds off the trees.'

'Oh, he could that,' Polly agreed. 'And now, I'll just run down to the kitchen and tell them what's to do and I'll be ready. Just you wait in the hall for me, sir.'

She slipped away to the basement, thinking how strange it was that she had become on such familiar terms with her employer. She treated Jeremiah these days almost like one of her own family – if she'd ever known what it was to have a family of her own. Family for Polly had been the servants, for almost as long as she could remember. She had come here as a skinny child of eight, to scrub pots and pans at the low sink where Rebecca too had begun her career. Before that, it had been the workhouse – and the memories of that time were something she had very nearly succeeded in pushing out of her mind.

Coming back, she found Jeremiah waiting in the hall as patiently as a child, and a tenderness rose in her for this old man who seemed to have so much, yet had so little. Nobody left to care for him – and who had ever really cared anyway? Not his wife, that cold bitch who had sent Rebecca off to London, not caring whether she lived or died. Not his stepson, Vivian, who cared only that he was heir to the carpet factory. Not his stepdaughters, Edith and Jane, who were both married now and living too far away to visit much. Nor even his own daughter, Sarah, who was too much like her mother and cared only for 'appearances' and 'what people would think'. Huh!

Isabel had cared for him, Polly thought, remembering

269

the daughter who had never grown up. And Francis cared for him, and Rebecca. And the boys – solemn Daniel, mischievous Geoffrey and the baby William. So perhaps he wasn't so badly off, after all.

Plenty of people had less.

And it was good, when they had collected the two older boys from the house in Unicorn Street, to see how he delighted in their company. They walked beside the river, watching the swirling water, and warning Geoffrey not to go too close to the edge.

'The strike's made a difference even here,' Jeremiah said, leaning over the bridge. 'Ordinary times, this water'd be all colours – all the dyes mixed up together, reds, blues, greens, making a pattern like a carpet themselves. Now it's almost clean – or would be, if it weren't for the ironworks upstream. But there's no colour in it.'

'Rebecca used to talk about the colours,' Polly remarked. 'Her mother used to bring her here, on the way to the winding sheds. She said the river looked like a rainbow before the colours got all mixed together.'

'It does, but it takes a child to see it. Now, we just see the dyes.' Jeremiah watched the two little boys scampering along the bank. 'They're fine boys. Francis is a lucky man.'

'Even though he married a servant?' Polly said wickedly, and Jeremiah turned and gave her a severe glance which worried her not in the least.

'You're an impertinent miss. I don't know why I put up with you.'

'Because I'm the only one as'll put up with *you*,' she responded pertly, and he laughed.

'Well, perhaps. And I need a bit of young life about me. How old are you, Polly? Twenty-five? Thirty?'

'As old as my tongue and a little older than my teeth, and that's all you're going to know, sir.' She flicked him an upwards glance, surprised at herself. Was she *flirting* with this old man? Well, and if she was, why

270

not? It didn't do any harm, did it? He was lonely enough and it wouldn't come to anything, he was past causing any trouble. And if it made him feel better . . .

The odd thing was, it made her feel better too. It made her feel more of a . . . person. As if someone noticing her – even needing her, a little – turned her into someone real.

That was the trouble with being a servant. You felt as if you were no more than a shadow on the wall a lot of the time. Someone who disappeared when the lights went out, who had no life of your own, just lived to answer the bell when it rang and bring coal and food and drink when it was needed.

'Geoffrey!' she called, turning away from her employer and beckoning to the two running figures. 'Geoffrey – come away from that riverbank at once. You'll fall in and I'm not jumping in after you, not this side of Christmas. Daniel, bring him back here at once. It's time we went home. Your grandmother will be waiting for you to come in for tea and there'll be no muffins left if we're late.'

You'd think they were her own boys, she thought as the children scurried back. And she thought again of Rebecca, nursing her sister in London and then coming home to these two, to the baby William and her husband Francis. Aye, Rebecca had fallen on her feet all right. She had it all, everything she could possibly want. There was nothing wrong in Rebecca's world. Nor ever would be as far as Polly could see.

'It's all very well to talk about peace,' Bill Bucknell said. 'But the men are getting angry. And the masters hev got the magistrates on their side now, and the London papers and all. They're twisting everything, making us out to be the blackguards in the case. Hear 'em talk, you'd think they were public benefactors, running the factories like a charity to help poor weavers live.'

The meeting was being held in Will Charlton's parlour, which had been cleared of all the knick-knacks and ornaments his wife prized so much, in order to make room for the papers that seemed to increase with each day of the strike. Newspapers, letters, notices, handbills – they lay on every surface, and keeping them in order was a task that occupied Will and Tom Potter for the best part of their time now.

Fred Holloway snorted. 'They always twist things, that sort. Look at this pamphlet. Talks about losing all the Brussels trade as well as the Kidder, if we goes on demanding – *demanding*, you notices – a shilling a yard, just as if it was summat we never had in the first place. How do they put it now?' He scanned the page. 'Aye, here it is – "*thwarting the manufacturers in their laudable endeavours to retain the trade*". Laudable endeavours, my foot! When everyone knows they just wants more money for theirselves. And then what do they say? That we can earn just as much money if we works six days a week instead of four. When we been on twelve-and-twelve almost all our lives!'

'And look what they says about us, the Committee,' George Hodgett said. 'We're a "foolish and well-fed, useless body" who do naught but "talk and prate". I wish I was well fed. I'd like to know what it feels like.'

'Well, Mr Price'll be here soon,' Will Charlton said. 'He'll know how to answer this kind of thing, him and Matt Farrell. In fact, I think I hear 'em now.'

The men looked round as steps sounded outside and a few seconds later the door opened and Matthew came in, followed by Humphrey Price. They nodded to the Committee and sat down on the chairs that had been kept for them, and Humphrey Price drew a sheaf of papers from his pocket.

'I've written a few more ballads here,' he began, 'and a reply to that notice I see you've been looking at.' He started to read and the Committee listened eagerly, nodding their heads at some of the phrases.

272

'. . . "*fallacious arguments . . . false insinuations . . . vile hypocrisy . . . nonsensical rubbish . . .* " I think that should give them cause to stop and consider. They imagine that their high-flown phrases will bamboozle you all for ignorant weavers – this should change their minds.'

'Aye, that it should,' Bill Bucknell said with enthusiasm. 'They'll see we've men of education on our side too. What about the ballads, sir?'

'Ah, yes.' The clergyman riffled through his papers and drew one out. 'This one's called "The Complaint of the Kidderminster Weaver's Wife to Her Infant" – I think it should jerk a few tears in the drawing rooms of London.' He began to read:

> '*Hush thee, my babe! thou wilt not live*
> *The living death such wages give*
> *As tyrants offer. Heav'n's thy home –*
> *Tyrants there will never come.*
>
> *On them and on their children dear*
> *Our blood will be, I greatly fear:*
> *O God! forgive them, lest they rue*
> *The deed they now seem bent to do . . .*'

He lowered the paper and looked around the silent room. The Committee looked at him and then at each other. Bill Bucknell thought of the baby he and Nell had had, the one who had died when he had just begun to stagger. And he knew that each man here had a similar memory: some of them more than one.

There wasn't a weaver in the town who had not seen a child in his family die through poverty; either from starvation, disease or cold. But would the fine folk in the drawing rooms in London know that?

Would they care?

'I've got another here,' Price said, and flourished another sheet of paper. This was a long poem, telling the Dream of a Kidderminster Weaver's Wife – a dream which was not of riches for herself and her family, nor even comfort, but a bitter longing for the 'oppressor's' end – a dream of death in which the carpet master was portrayed as a villain living in a 'rich abode' that was 'enclosed in cedar and painted in vermilion'. The Committee heard it out and then looked again at each other.

'John Broom's house!' Fred Holloway said at last, a trifle uneasily.

'I haven't said so,' Price denied, but they shook their heads.

'You didn't hev to. It's plain enough to anyone that's what you mean. And John Broom, dying that way . . . why, it's nothing short o' murder, the way it's done in the poem.'

'And it could be thought an incitement to murder,' Matthew pointed out. 'We'll no longer be able to claim we're peaceable if this poem is published.'

'It's a dream!' Price protested. 'Nobody can help a dream.'

'They can help writing about it though.' Will Charlton looked dubious. 'I don't know . . . mebbe we'll just send in the other one, keep this 'un back.'

'We can allus send it later on, if need be,' George Hodgett suggested, and the rest agreed, though Bill could see that the Reverend Price looked disappointed. No doubt he'd looked forward to seeing his poem printed in the London newspaper.

'What else are we planning?' he asked, and Will Charlton lifted another paper from the table in front of him.

'The petition to Parliament – we want as many signatures on that as we can get.' He read out a few phrases. 'We're asking for proper laws about fixing wages. It's important – it's folk like us, working men— '

'Artisans,' Humphrey Price put in.

274

'Artisans, that's right – well, we're at the bottom of the pile, see— '

'You don't hev to tell us that!'

' —and we're holding everyone else up.' Will frowned at the interrupter. 'If we don't get treated right, nor will no one else. Reduce our wages by twopence a yard and the next man up the ladder will get his wages cut too – stands to reason. And so on. And that'll spread through all the different manufacturers, and what'll happen to the country then?' He looked round at them all. 'It'll end up hurting everyone.'

'So it's our *duty* to keep on with the strike,' George Hodgett said slowly, and Will nodded.

'That's how we see it. And that's what this petition says.'

'Think Parliament will see it, though?' someone asked sceptically. 'Think they'll even read the words?'

'Well, we can't force 'em, can we? All we can do is deliver it. But I reckon someone'll look at it – there's enough about the strike in the London papers.'

'Why don't we send one to the King as well?' Bill suggested, and some of the others applauded.

'Aye, that's a good idea. Send one to the King.'

'We'll try that later, if Parliament don't take notice.' Tom Potter made a note on his paper. 'Now, what about that new handbill, Reverend?'

'It's here.' Humphrey Price produced another sheet of closely written paper. 'I've made a few points concerning the Wilton weavers – the masters here make great play of the fact that they're being paid at tenpence and therefore Kidderminster weavers should be paid the same rate. But there are less than forty of them, and upwards of two thousand of us.' Bill Bucknell noticed the 'us'. Mr Price really did seem to look on himself as one of the weavers. Showed that you could be gentry and have some feeling for the common man as well. Like Matt Farrell here, and his friend Mr Francis . . . He brought his straying thoughts back

275

under control and listened to what was being said.

'Why should a body of two thousand be ruled by what's being paid to less than forty? Conditions in Scotland, too, are very different from here – why should that be thought relevant to what we need to live on?' Humphrey Price leaned across the table, stabbing the paper as he made his points. His eyes glittered under the shaggy brows and he looked hard at every man in the room. By, Bill thought, he's a good man to have on our side.

'I'll tell you another thing,' Fred said suddenly. 'Wilton weavers get paid out of the poor rate while they're waiting for orders. Out of the poor rate! Treated like paupers, when they're good, honest weavers waiting for the masters to give 'em work. You'll not get Kidder men agreeing to do that.'

'No, you won't.' Bill felt the anger rising in his chest. 'Why, I'd rather starve. Or emigrate. Go to America – Australia— '

'There's ways of getting your passage paid, if that's where you wants to go,' someone said, and they all laughed.

'Well, I reckon that's all we can do for now, lads,' Will Charlton declared. 'We'll get this petition off to London as soon as may be, and we'll have the notices posted in all the usual places. We'll need a few to help us with that. And giving out handbills, too. There's plenty to be done.'

The men got to their feet with a scraping of chairs and a buzz of conversation. Bill found himself next to Matt Farrell. They went out on to the street together and stood for a moment while Matthew waited for Humphrey Price.

'You're a mate of young Pagnel, ent you?' Bill said suddenly. 'Francis Pagnel, that runs that co-op.'

'That's right. We were at school together – we've been friends for years.' Matthew frowned. 'But you don't work for Pagnel's, do you?'

'No – never have. I knows his wife though, her that was Becky Himley. She comes round our place, sees my Nellie and the kids. Brings 'em a few bits and pieces sometimes. She's a good wench, young Becky.'

'Yes, she is.' Matthew's face softened a little. 'She's in London now – her sister's been ill.'

'What, Bess? Here, I never knew that. Our Nellie'll be really cut up about that – her and Bess was good mates, started in the carpet shop together.' Bill shook his head. 'She was always hoping Bessie'd come back to Kidder.'

'Well, Rebecca – Mrs Pagnell – is bringing her back as soon as she can travel.' Matthew glanced round as the rest of the men came out, Humphrey Price with them. 'I'll tell Rebecca I've seen you – your name's Bucknell, isn't it? Will Bucknell?'

'Bill Bucknell. Aye, tell her and tell her my Nellie'll be wanting to see her, ask her about her Bessie. So she's coming back to Kidder, is she? Ah, Nell will want to see her too – they was real mates, them two, allus together.'

He moved away, scarcely hearing the conversation of his friends, surprised at his own reaction. He hadn't known Bess well, after all, just seen her around and that was years ago, before she'd run off to London. Nell had talked about her a bit, giggling sometimes at the recollection of the games they'd got up to. Maybe that was why he felt so pleased – because he knew Bess had been Nellie's best friend, because Nell herself would be pleased. Because just for once things seemed to be going well for at least one person.

They didn't often do that, after all. Usually, life was just bloody unfair, whichever way you turned, when you were only a weaver.

It had become a regular thing for Jeremiah to call at the house in Unicorn Street each afternoon and take the little boys for their walk. Often, Polly would come

277

with him and he found himself enjoying her un-
demanding company. She treated him with the kind of
affection he had become accustomed to with Rebecca
– and which, while Rebecca was away, he missed.

'She'll be back tomorrow,' he said as they walked
down to the river. 'And these young rascals are getting
excited already at the thought of it. Over-excited, their
grandmother says.' He watched benignly as the
children ran ahead, shouting to each other, picking up
sticks to throw into the river or stopping to pick
bunches of wild flowers.

'For Mama,' Geoffrey panted, thrusting a clump of
primroses into Polly's hands. 'You carry them.'

'They'll be dead by the time we get home again,'
Polly protested, but he took no heed and scampered
off again. She laughed and put the flowers into the
basket she carried, then turned to the old man at her
side. 'You've heard from Rebecca, then, sir? Is she
well?'

'Well enough, I daresay. Upset over her sister, as
you might expect. Apparently she was in a very bad
way when they found her. Living poorly too. Rebecca
blames herself for not bringing Bessie back when Tom
came – and I daresay he feels the same. But from what
they've said . . . well, I don't think it'd have made
much difference, between you and me.' He seemed to
have forgotten he was talking to a servant, but then he
didn't seem to think of Polly as a servant much these
days. 'I think she had that disease on her for years,'
he said. 'Marked down from the time she went to
London. Bringing her back here wouldn't have stopped
her being ill.'

'But at least she could hev been looked after,' Polly
said. It was horrible to think of Bessie, forced into a
way of life she loathed and feared, her body misused
and brought to decay – and all because of a weaver
who saw her as no more than a part of his machinery,

278

to toil twelve, fourteen hours at a time at his bidding. And then, when the work was done, as an instrument for his pleasure.

They walked in silence for a while. She glanced sideways at Jeremiah and wondered if he were quite as well as usual. He seemed slower today, heavier, his body that had once been so broad and strong beginning to look shrunken. It was as if he were drawing back into his clothes, like a tortoise drawing back into its shell. He was getting old, she thought, and this strike wasn't helping him. He worried over it. He didn't like walking in the streets now because of the men standing on the corners, watching as he went past. Begging, some of them, with the small model looms they had made to show their trade. Not that there were many people in Kidder to beg from now, for the strike was affecting all the industries. Some of them, she'd been told, had gone to London and were begging there. Perhaps Rebecca had met them, recognised them by the looms they carried.

Jeremiah stopped suddenly and grasped her arm. She looked at him in alarm. His face was pale, his head tipped back a little, and he seemed to be searching the sky, his eyes rolled up in his head. Polly looked up, trying to follow the direction of his gaze, but there was nothing to be seen.

She looked back at him, and he was shaking his head, looking bewildered.

'What is it? Mr Pagnel, what's the matter?'

'Matter?' he said in a strange, vague tone. 'Nothing's the matter, Polly. I just felt a bit – giddy, for a moment.' He sniffed. 'What's that queer smell? I've smelt it before, but I don't know . . .' His voice trailed away and his grip tightened on her arm. 'It's a funny smell . . .' he muttered, and again his head tipped back.

Thoroughly frightened now, Polly looked round for

help, but there was no one to be seen. The boys were at the riverbank about thirty yards away, bending over something they had found. She debated calling them, sending them for help, but they were too young to understand and would be afraid. But something had to be done. Mr Pagnel was in a bad way, no two ways about that, and if he collapsed . . .

'Here, sit down for a minute.' She tried to lead him to a patch of grass, but Jeremiah's body was stiffening in her arms. He jerked against her and then stumbled and she knew he was falling, that she couldn't hold him. The most she could do was try to let him fall gently, but his big, heavy body was moving in great convulsions now and dragging her with him. They fell together, Jeremiah half on top of her, and she felt the spasmodic movements, felt his feet kick, his arms flail, and she knew she could not escape.

Oh God, she thought, what's happening to him? Is it a stroke, or a fit of some sort? It must be a fit. They'd had a footman once did this sort of thing, right as rain one minute and the next he'd be on the floor and foaming at the mouth. They couldn't keep him, he'd had to go – finished up in the madhouse, so she'd heard. But this wasn't a footman, this was Mr Pagnel, Jeremiah Pagnel, owner of one of the biggest carpet manufactures in Kidderminster – in the country. And he was having his fit out here, by the riverbank, where anyone could see him – where his grandsons could see.

His grandsons! Driven by panic, Polly used all the strength she possessed and heaved the body away from her. She scrambled to her feet, panting, and looked down at the jerking figure of the old man. What should she do? He'd hurt himself for sure, twisting about like that – roll right into the river as like as not. She stared wildly around and caught sight of some people, running towards her. They must have seen what was happening, they were coming to help. But where were the boys?

'What's amiss?' The men were close now. They were

weavers, she knew them, and for a moment she had a dreadful feeling that they wouldn't help. 'Here, ent that old Mr Pagnel?'

'Yes, it is – I don't know what's amiss, he's having a fit or something. He was out for a walk with me and the boys— ' again, she looked wildly up and down the riverbank ' —and suddenly he went all queer.' Jeremiah's convulsions were easing now, and as the men bent over him he quietened and lay still. Polly stared at him with horrified fascination. 'Is he . . . dead?'

'No, still breathing, see. Reckon he'll stop like this for a bit and then wake up natural like. My old man did this a time or two, when he was getting near his end.' The man who had spoken stood up. 'We ought to get him home, though. Won't do him no good, laying out here on the cold ground.'

'Can you help carry him? He's so heavy— '

'Aye, we'll need a cart or summat. Or maybe a gate.' The men began to look around for some means of getting Jeremiah home. Unicorn Street would be closer, Polly thought, and again stared about her. Where were those boys?

And then she saw them – no, just one of them. Daniel. Running towards her, arms outstretched, small hands clutching at the air. She saw the expression on his face before she heard his sobbing, the words he could not force past his lips. And she knew, before he could tell her, just what had happened.

She could see it all, as if it had happened before her own eyes. The two little boys, crouching over some new treasure on the riverbank. The muddy, slippery ground, sloping towards the water. Geoffrey, the bold, the curious, edging closer – closer – feeling his foot slip, clutching at the grass to save himself, feeling the grass break away from the earth, feeling it slip through his fingers . . .

She heard the cry, the scream, the terror. And she looked down into the swirling, muddy water and knew.

Chapter Thirteen

It seemed surprising to Rebecca, as she and Tom jour-
neyed home with Bessie, that it was still spring. They
seemed to have been in London for so long – yet it
had been no more than a fortnight. A fortnight of
bitter anxiety and of sheer hard work such as she had
not known since her days as a housemaid at Pagnel
House.

'You're tired out,' Tom had said, looking at his sister's pale face as they walked in Hyde Park one afternoon, having left Bessie to rest. 'What do you think
Francis is going to say to me if I take you home looking
ready to drop? He's trusting me to look after you.
Maybe we should stop on a bit longer – give you and
Bess both time to build up a bit of strength.'

'But I want to be at home – with him and the boys.'
Tears filled Rebecca's eyes at the thought of her sons.
'William had a cold coming, I'm sure of it. And Daniel
– he looked so solemn when I left, I'm sure he'll be
pining.'

'And Geoff? Won't there be aught wrong with him
too?' Tom asked with a grin, and Rebecca smiled reluctantly.

'Oh, I know you're laughing at me, Tom, for worrying about them when they're so well looked after. No,
I don't suppose there'll be a thing wrong with Geoffrey,
there never is. He'll be climbing on everything he can
reach, playing with all Enid's ornaments and generally
making a nuisance of himself to the whole household.'
She sighed. 'I wonder sometimes what is going to
happen to that young rascal. He's so strong-willed.'

'Get along, he's the best of the bunch. He'll go far,

young Geoff,' Tom declared. 'Daniel's a bit too solemn sometimes, he's like an old man. And Will – well, he's just a babby yet. No knowing how he'll turn out. But I'll tell you one thing, Rebecca – they'll all grow up to be fine men. Couldn't help it really, could they – coming from good Himley stock as they do.'

'And what about their Pagnel side? Don't forget they've got Francis's blood in their veins as well as ours.'

'Oh, well— ' Tom flicked a hand as if to dismiss the Pagnel factor in his nephews' make-up. 'If you've got to have a Pagnel as your father, it'd better be Francis. Seems a pretty good combination, anyway.' He drew Rebecca to one side as a pair of horses came galloping towards them. 'That'll be your lads, one day – riding Rotten Row on fine horses!'

'Oh, I hope not! I want them to be honest, industrious, *useful* people – not idle rich, with nothing to do but amuse themselves.' She realised that Tom was laughing at her again. 'Oh, Tom, why is life so unfair? There are these people— ' she gestured at the Londoners who were taking the air in Hyde Park, the women in their flowing gowns, their ruffles and laces that would have looked over-grand at a Kidderminster society ball, the men stiff in breeches and highly polished boots ' —all of them with more money than they know what to do with, and nothing to do but spend it. And then there are people like Bessie, who try so hard and can never raise themselves out of the gutter. And it was as bad for you, all those years you were here together, scraping a living wherever you could – holding horses, sweeping the pavements, running errands. Some so rich, some so poor, and all of it just because of the way they were born.'

'I know. And I dunno what the answer is. Maybe there ent any answer and it's no good searching for it. Maybe we just got to get on with our own lives as best we can. Well, I don't see what else we *can* do, when you comes to look at it – do you?'

'No, I don't. And it all sounds so simple, and yet sometimes it seems so complicated.' They had come to the lake now and Rebecca paused and gazed across the still blue water. 'Tom, let's go home soon. I want to see my boys – I miss them. And I'm worried about Francis. He hasn't been well all winter. I was hoping he would improve once the weather started to get warmer, but he still has that cough . . . There's nothing to keep us in London now.'

She turned and looked into her brother's face. He was tired too, she thought. He had been as anxious as she over Bessie and had shared the work of nursing her. The two of them had become very close during those years of hardship they had shared in London, and he'd been more upset than he'd admitted when she had decided to stay behind when the rest of them had returned to Kidderminster. He'd comforted himself, as they all had, by thinking of Bess building up her millinery business, living in modest comfort in the little house she'd had when they left. To come back and find the truth, to see her in such abject misery, had been a terrible shock.

One neither of us will ever forget, she thought sadly, and touched his arm. 'Let's go home. Let's get Bessie back to Kidderminster.'

'Aye,' Tom said, looking down into her eyes. 'Let's.'

And now the coach was jolting on its last few miles before reaching Kidderminster. The recent dry weather had made the journey much easier by clearing up the mud and puddles of the winter, and the sun shone warmly from a clear sky. It was the kind of day when you must be glad to be alive, Rebecca thought, her heart lifting. The air was filled with the song of birds. She could see them fluttering in the hedgerows, robins with their red breasts like jewels, tits and finches with tiny twigs or scraps of grass in their beaks. A yellow butterfly caught her eye and she watched as it flitted amongst a bank of primroses and violets, purple and gold. Who needed fine clothes when you could see the colours here, for no cost, in the countryside?

The shadows of sickness, of possible death, of heartache, had gone. In less than three hours now, they would be in Kidderminster and she would have her boys once more around her, her husband at her side. And Rebecca leaned her head back on the cushion and closed her eyes, content with the thought. She needed nothing else. What else, indeed, could there be?

'How are we going to *tell* her?' Jeremiah's big body sagged into a chair. He looked up at Francis with blurred eyes and his voice trembled. 'If I could only turn back the clock . . . It was all my fault. I'm an old, useless man, not fit to be in charge of myself, let alone children . . . My own grandson, swept away while I was having a fit – a *fit*! – on the riverbank. Why haven't you had me put into an asylum, Francis, why? It's the only safe place.'

He turned his head away and Francis saw with distress that it was shaking as if he had some kind of ague. He had grown old in the past two days, old and bewildered. He seemed to have shrunk inside his clothes and there were new lines on his face, dragging down the once strong features. His eyes were bleary and watering.

The Jeremiah Pagnel who had commanded respect throughout Kidderminster had become a pathetic old man.

But Francis was too occupied with his own misery to be able to extend much sympathy towards his father. He could think of nothing but his son, little Geoffrey, so bright and lively, so full of mischief and curiosity . . . swept away in the waters of the Stour. Not even a clean death . . .

'I ought to be in an asylum,' Jeremiah said again.

'Father, don't.' Francis lifted his head, aware of the pain in the old man's heart, knowing that it could never be truly eased. 'You couldn't know it was going to happen. You had no warning – you'd never had such a thing before. If anyone was at fault, it was Polly for letting the boys— '

'You can't blame Polly,' Jeremiah said heavily. 'She did all she could. And we always let the boys run ahead. Rebecca does, you do.' He clasped his trembling hands together. 'Polly never took her eyes off them for an instant until . . . Francis, I *fell* on her.' He was shuddering now, great pulsating tremors that shook his whole body, and Francis half started from his seat, wondering in alarm if the old man were about to have another attack. 'The poor girl was squashed almost flat. There was nothing she could do.'

'I know, I know.' Francis sank back, his head in his hands. 'It's just so hard to take in. I still can't believe it. I go up to the nursery and look at his empty bed . . .' His voice shook. 'I look at Daniel, and I don't know what to say. He's hardly spoken since it happened, Father. He thinks it was *his* fault – that he should have taken better care of his brother. And he's only five years old himself. He'll hardly let anyone near William – it's as if he's terrified that if he takes his eyes off him, something will happen to him too.' He looked at Jeremiah. 'Father . . . have you seen a doctor?'

Jeremiah leaned back in his chair, one hand quivering at his brow.

'I've had Curtis take a look at me. He says it's a kind of seizure – epilepsy. It could happen again at any time.' He stared at his son, fear and bewilderment creasing his features. 'It could happen now – on my way home – in the middle of a meeting. I shall never feel safe again, Francis. It's the end of my life.'

'Nonsense, Father.' But Francis spoke without conviction. He ran his fingers through his hair, rubbed a hand over his exhausted face. 'It'll probably never happen again. You were tired – overstrained. It's this strike, dragging on— '

'The strike! I wish we'd never made that wage reduction. Everything's gone wrong since then – Rebecca having to go away to see to her sister, Geoffrey— ' Jeremiah's voice broke and he covered his trembling lips with his fingers. He asked again, pleadingly, 'Francis, how are we going to tell her?'

They stared helplessly at each other. Francis saw his father suddenly, not as his father, nor even as the uncle he had imagined him to be for so many years. Instead, he saw him as the old man he was, an old man buffeted by a storm he had never expected, never prepared for. An old man looking into a future that ran away from him, downhill, out of control; a future filled with fear and dread, disappearing into a menacing fog.

And he could do nothing to help him. Because he needed help too, and did not know where to turn for it.

Matthew paced the library at Pagnel House and wondered what he was doing here.

He had come to see Jeremiah, to try to discover the truth of what had happened. Francis had been able to tell him very little – only that little Geoffrey had been drowned and that Rebecca was on her way home from London, with no knowledge of the tragedy. And then he had begged his friend to go away for a while, leave him alone. And Matthew, reluctant but knowing he must respect that wish, had come away.

Like everyone else, he found it almost impossible to believe what had happened. That bright little life, snuffed out through a moment's carelessness! And not even carelessness, for it seemed that Polly had had no chance to think of the boys in that moment of panic. But he had to know just what had happened, and so he had come here to talk to Jeremiah himself – only to find that Jeremiah had gone to Unicorn Street.

'I'll see Polly then,' he said to the housemaid who let him in, her eyes red with weeping. 'Tell her to come to the library.'

Unable to sit down, he roamed the big room, staring at the books that lined the walls, stopping to gaze blindly out of the window. His mind was filled with thoughts of Rebecca. Even now, she was jolting along the turnpike roads on her way back to Kidderminster, happy to be bringing Bessie home. And to come home to this! His heart ached for her. If only there was something he could do . . . But there was nothing. Nobody could give Rebecca back her dead son, and that would be the only comfort that she would want.

The door opened and Polly came in. Her eyes too were red, her face white, but she seemed composed as she stood before him. He looked down at her gravely.

'I came to find out what happened. Somebody is going to have to meet the coach and tell her. I thought perhaps it should be me.'

Why did he feel he should explain himself to this girl, no more than a servant? But she *was* more than a servant, wasn't she? She was Rebecca's friend. They had been kitchenmaids together, housemaids. If Francis had not married Rebecca, she might be here now, lighting the fire, brushing the hearth.

She would not have been bumping up and down in a coach, coming home to tragedy.

'Mr Francis— ' Polly began, but Matthew shook his head.

'He's in no fit state to tell Rebecca what's happened. He's hardly able to speak himself. And Mr Pagnel— '

'He can't do it,' she said swiftly. 'It would be cruel . . .'

'I know. So that seems to leave me. And I need to know— '

'Or me,' she said quietly.

Matthew stared at her and she lifted her head and met his gaze directly.

'Well, int it my job? I let the poor little scrap run off along the riverbank, didn't I? I was the one should've been taking proper care, of all of 'em. Yes, Mr Pagnel too – I knew he wasn't right. I knew he'd been having queer turns— '

'You mean he'd had these seizures before?'

'Not like that, no.' Polly shuddered. 'But he'd sort of go off for a minute or two – roll his eyes up like he was looking for something up in a corner, and he wouldn't seem to hear what a body was saying. And he'd always say summat about a funny smell, but *I* never smelt nothing. And Rebecca said he'd done it when she was with him too. Well, I reckon it was all part and parcel of the same thing.'

'But you couldn't know what was going to happen.'

'I could've been more careful,' she said stubbornly. 'I could've watched him more.'

Matthew sighed. It seemed that everyone was intent on taking the blame for Geoffrey's death. And no doubt Rebecca would blame herself too, for having gone away and left her sons. But that didn't solve the problem of who was to break the news.

'Tell me just what happened,' he said gently, and then gestured to a chair. 'Sit down and just talk to me. I want to help – I'm Francis's friend, and Rebecca's too.'

Polly hesitated and then did as she was told. She began her story haltingly, her voice breaking as she described how the children had played and laughed their way along the riverbank. He saw the horror in her eyes as she recalled the seizure, those first moments of awareness that something was very wrong, the panic as Jeremiah had collapsed, dragging her with him to the ground. Her frantic efforts to struggle free, her fear that he was dead and then her desperation as she'd looked for the boys and seen only one running back towards her . . .

'Poor little Daniel,' he said softly. 'He must have

290

thought the world was coming to an end all around him. His brother swept away in the river, his grandfather senseless on the ground. And for you— '

'I was all right,' she broke in. 'Nothing had happened to me. I just wish it had.'

'And what possible good could that have done?' he demanded, feeling unaccountably angry.

'It would hev saved a lot of misery, that's what,' she retorted. 'Who would there be to grieve over me? I ent got no family. No one would miss me— '

'That's nonsense! Mr Pagnel would miss you— '

'He'd soon get another housemaid to do what I do for him.'

'The other servants – they're your friends, aren't they? They'd miss you.'

'They'd soon forget. You always do, once a body's been away a while.'

'Rebecca would miss you— '

'Not,' Polly said quietly, 'anywhere near as much as she's going to miss her little boy.'

Matthew was silenced. He looked helplessly at the pale, composed face of the housemaid.

'We're back to where we started,' he said at last. 'I'm grateful to you, Polly, for talking to me. I'll go and see Francis now. I'll tell him I'm going to meet the coach and break the news to Rebecca. It will be better that way.'

'And I,' Polly said, 'will be there too.' She lifted her chin and looked him in the eye. 'I hev to be, Mr Farrell. I was there when it happened, I was in charge of those boys, and I'm Rebecca's friend.' She paused and then added sadly, so quietly that he could barely hear her: 'I *was* Rebecca's friend . . .'

In the event, there was quite a little crowd of people waiting for the coach when it drew up at last outside the Lion Hotel.

Francis, still deeply shocked and white with grief,

291

had refused to stay at home while Matthew met Rebecca.

'I'm her husband. I should be there. She'll need me.' And Matthew had been unable to deny any of this, though his heart ached for both of them. All the same, he insisted, quietly, on being there too. 'I'm your friend. You both need me,' he said, and Francis bowed his head and argued no more.

They did manage, however, to persuade Jeremiah to stay at home. And indeed, it would have been difficult to have brought him, for his deterioration had continued in the days since Geoffrey's death and he now spent almost all his time in the library at Pagnel House, staring into the fire that he insisted be lit in spite of the spring sunshine, and lost in a world of his own.

Polly was torn between staying with him and going to meet the coach. 'I hardly likes to let him be on his own at all,' she told Matthew when he came to see how they both were. 'He's got so queer – forgets who I am, forgets what day it is, forgets where he is sometimes. In his own home! Poor old man.'

They were talking, low-voiced, at the door to the library, while Jeremiah sat hunched by the fireside, apparently unaware that they were there. The old nursery fireguard had been brought in and placed on the hearth, in case Jeremiah should suffer another seizure, and Matthew was torn with pity for this once commanding figure, now reduced by age and shock to such a travesty. He shook his head.

'He'll be all right for a while, Polly. Get one of the other housemaids to come and look after him. You can come out, can't you? The housekeeper understands the situation?'

Polly nodded. 'Oh yes, Mrs Hudd's all right. She's been a good friend to me and Rebecca, always. She'll send young Jennie, like as not, and Mr Pagnel won't hardly know the difference.'

Nevertheless, she cast more than one worried glance back at the house as they left it, and Matthew drove her away in his trap feeling that she'd as soon jump out and run back. And how could you blame her, he thought with a sigh. The coming meeting was one nobody was looking forward to.

There was the usual small crowd waiting for the coach's arrival when they came to the High Street, with the imposing facade of the Lion Hotel dominating the whole of one side of the square. People waiting for friends and relatives, people waiting for deliveries and parcels, people just waiting out of curiosity. Added to them these days were the carpet weavers who were on strike and had nothing to do but lounge against the walls and pillars, trying to interest people in their case and, in some cases, frankly begging.

And everyone, today, was waiting for Rebecca Pagnel to arrive and be told of the death of her little son.

Matthew could see their sidelong glances, their avid stares, as he descended from the trap. Some turned their heads away, pretending not to notice; others watched openly, agog at the spectacle of someone else's misfortune. Matthew cursed the fact that Rebecca was arriving back so publicly, that there was going to be no opportunity to break the news in private. What was it going to be like for her, stepping down from the coach under all these greedy eyes, innocent and unknowing? What was it going to be like for her to receive such news with half the town present to observe her shock?

Polly took one look at the crowd and lifted her chin. Evidently the same thoughts were going through her mind, and Matthew saw her eyes glitter as she stepped determinedly towards the onlookers, clearly ready to deal with any inquisitive prying. At any other time, he would have been amused by the sight of the rabble falling back from her challenging glance. Today, his heart ached at the tragedy of it.

He turned and went into the hotel. Francis was there, already, sitting just inside with a tumbler of whisky on a small table at his side. He looked up as Matthew came in, and his mouth twisted in a small, crooked smile. He touched the glass, lifting his eyebrows slightly, but Matthew shook his head.

'Not for me.' He glanced anxiously at his friend. There was a hectic flush overlying the pallor of Francis's face. 'Francis, do you feel quite well?'

'You mean I'm drinking too much.' There was an unaccustomed belligerency in Francis's voice. 'Well, I'm not drinking too much, and yes, I'm quite well. Is there anything else you'd like to know?'

'No, nothing,' Matthew murmured, much alarmed. He had never heard Francis speak like this before. He sat down and Francis lifted the tumbler and drained it with an air of defiance.

'Well, what are you staring at? You've seen me before often enough.'

'I'm not staring. I'm worried about you— '

'Worried about *me*!' Francis gave a short, unamused laugh. 'I'm the last person you should be worrying about.'

Matthew disagreed, but he didn't say so. He was seriously concerned. Francis was totally unlike himself, his manner bristling with hostility, yet Matthew felt convinced that the hostility was not directed at himself. Rather, it radiated from him like the spines of the porcupines Matthew had seen in America, darting out in every direction, as if it were the whole world he was angry with. He was like a blind man who knows himself to be under attack, lashing out wildly in an attempt to find his target, yet never knowing quite where – or indeed what – his target might be.

Poor Francis. He would never hit his target, for his target was life itself, swirling around him like a mist, as insubstantial and as threatening as a ghost.

The two men sat in silence, with nothing to say to each other. Matthew felt the distance yawn between them like a great canyon – strange how images of America kept occurring to him today – as he searched for words that would not come. It was the first time in his life that he had felt ill at ease with his best friend, and the sorrow of it ached in his breast. It was as if Francis blamed *him* for what had happened, yet he knew that could not be so. Francis blamed no one, not his father, not Polly, not little Daniel. He simply blamed Fate – life itself.

An uncomfortable scapegoat, Matthew thought, for Life could never be brought to book.

A clatter of hooves and rattle of wheels outside drew him to his feet. The coach was arriving! He felt his heart suddenly lurch in his breast, the sickness of apprehension twist his stomach. At any moment, Rebecca would be here, stepping down to her husband's arms, weary and sad from her unhappy journey and unaware that an even greater sorrow awaited her.

He went to the door and watched as the coach came up the High Street. He ached to give her the comfort she would need, the comfort he suspected Francis was unable to give, for he had his own desperate need. But perhaps he was wrong – perhaps in their grief they would be able to comfort each other, as an outsider never could.

'They're coming,' he said in a low voice, and turned to his friend.

But Francis had not risen to his feet. He sat in the chair, his face white, his eyes burning like coals. His body shook and he raised trembling hands in a double fist to his mouth, biting on the knuckles. He seemed to be looking into some horrific scene that only he could see, and it was not hard for Matthew to guess what that might be. He could feel Francis's pain as sharply as if it were a spear in his own side.

He went quickly across to the other man and bent

over him, slipping a hand under his elbow to raise him. But Francis remained passive, a dead weight, neither resisting nor co-operating, and Matthew gave up. He looked desperately out of the open doorway. The coach was almost upon them.

Polly was there, pacing back and forth, her face pale but determined. The crowd of people waiting had thickened: surely there were not usually so many to meet the coach. The square was filled with people – women shopping, men strolling, weavers drawing attention to the strike – the strike! He had almost forgotten it! And every one of these people, he was sure, aware of the tragedy that had befallen the Pagnel family, aware that Rebecca Pagnel was coming home on this very coach.

The clatter was loud in his ears now as the coach came to a halt at last. Matthew gave up trying to move the almost rigid Francis, and hurried outside. He found Polly amidst the throng and stood beside her, his eyes scanning the passengers as they began to alight.

And there, at last, she was. Rebecca, small and fragile-looking, her pallor accentuated by the black cloak and hat she wore. She stepped down from the coach, leaning slightly into her brother's arms, and then looked around.

She is looking for Francis, Matthew thought, and went forward.

Rebecca's eyes lit on him and she gave him a sudden smile, a smile of pleasure and delight to be home again. But the delight would soon be gone, he thought miserably, for the news must be broken at once, and he knew what happened traditionally to the bringer of bad news. Would Rebecca ever be able to forget it – this moment, when her world was still intact, when there were only seconds to go before it was shattered for ever?

'Rebecca— ' he began, but she interrupted him, smiling.

'Matthew, how kind of you to meet me. And Polly too! But where's Francis?' Her voice sharpened suddenly with anxiety. 'There's nothing wrong, is there? The strike's not worsened? Or – he's not ill?' She caught at Matthew's sleeve, gazing up into his face, her eyes entreating him, and he gazed back dumbly, unable to speak. He had the words ready, had been rehearsing them for hours, and now they refused to be spoken.

'*Matthew . . .*' she breathed, and he saw the horror dawn slowly in her eyes and knew he must speak.

And then, before he could take the breath to do so, he felt himself pushed roughly aside. So Francis had gathered the strength after all, he thought, and allowed himself to be elbowed out of the way. And was ashamed to feel a measure of relief that he had been saved from the awful task. It was, after all, Francis's right as husband and father . . .

But it wasn't Francis who stood looking down at Rebecca now. It wasn't Francis who took her hands in his, gazed gravely into those terrified eyes, drew her close for comfort and began to speak the words that she would never be able to forget.

And Matthew could only stand aside, dumb, as Vivian Pagnel took over the task he had set himself and told Rebecca that her son Geoffrey was dead.

'*Dead?*'

It seemed that all Kidderminster stood still. The square was hushed and silent, the crowds paused in their hurrying, the cries of street vendors silenced, the very twittering of the birds on the rooftops ceased. Rebecca stood like a figure of stone, her eyes wide, black in the sudden ivory pallor of her face.

'Dead?' she whispered again and, as if released by a spring, the movement and sounds of the square began again; but softly at first, subdued, as if in respect for the bewildered grief of a mother who has

297

suddenly been bereft of her child.

Rebecca raised her eyes to Vivian's face. Her mind was still refusing to accept the words he had spoken. Even though her tongue repeated that one word, the word so vital to his message, her brain could not appreciate its truth. She shook her head and a flash of anger came into her shocked eyes.

'Vivian, what is this? If it's a joke— '

'It's no joke,' he said quietly, and held her hands against his chest. 'Geoffrey fell into the river when he was out walking with my father. He drowned, Rebecca. It must have happened very quickly – he couldn't have known much.' His eyes were as dark as hers, sombre with the heaviness of his own emotion. 'Rebecca, I'm so very, very sorry.'

'Sorry?' It was as if it were another new word. Irrelevantly, she reflected that she had never heard Vivian say he was sorry for anything. And now – sorry that she and Francis had lost one of their sons? But she brushed the thought aside, angry with herself for thinking it. However much Vivian might envy them, he could never have wished this to happen.

Her mind came back with a jerk to the reality that it had just refused to face. Dead? *Dead?* Geoffrey, her brave, bold, venturesome Geoffrey who had seemed to lead such a charmed life? Even when he had fallen out of a tree, he had suffered no more than a scratch and a bruise or two. And now . . . *drowned*? She shook her head again.

'It isn't true. I won't believe it. It's a mistake.' Her voice was desperate as she heard the words and recognised them as foolish even as they were uttered. For how could such a mistake be made? Yet . . . it must be. It had to be. Her Geoffrey, so young, so full of life and daring, could not die without even being ill, without her beside him to nurse and comfort him. 'Vivian, *please*, tell me it isn't true.'

But the plea, her last desperate cry for the reality

she had believed in rather than the truth she must face, could not be answered. And she knew that to deny it was futile. Her eyes fell and she drooped her head against Vivian's chest, and he held her against him so that she knew his strength and power and felt it flowing into her.

After a few minutes, she gathered her strength and lifted her head again. She looked once more into his eyes.

'Tell me what happened.'

But Vivian shook his head.

'Not here. Come into the inn. Francis is there waiting for you – he would have told you himself, but he's very distressed.' He glanced around at the knot of people who still stood staring, as if the spectacle of another's grief might lessen their own troubles. 'Come inside, Rebecca.'

But she held back, suddenly aware of her surroundings, her eyes moving quickly, almost frantically, over the throng. 'Tom? Where's Tom? And Bessie – she's still not strong— '

'I'm here.' Tom's voice sounded beside her. He looked gravely at his sister. 'Matthew's told me the news. Becky, I don't know what to say, I . . . He was such a brave little chap . . .' His voice faltered and he dashed a hand across his eyes. 'Matt's taken Bessie into the inn,' he said in a low voice. 'Best do as Mr Vivian says and come in yourself, Becky.'

She nodded automatically, and glanced up again at Vivian. She felt a strange new emotion towards him – a gratitude for the comfort he had given her, tempered with bewilderment that he should offer it at all. Hadn't he always despised her, hadn't he always scorned Francis for marrying her? But perhaps she had been wrong about that, wrong all the time. Perhaps beneath that careless, taunting facade there lay hidden a softer, gentler personality.

But Vivian was frowning now, looking from Tom to

herself as if there were something he did not understand.

'Bessie?' he said. 'Do you mean your sister? Am I to understand that you've brought her back to Kidderminster?'

Tom nodded. 'She was so ill. She's still not strong, but we thought it was better to bring her back than try to nurse her there. She needs good air and good food and proper, loving care – she'd get none of those in London.' He looked directly at Vivian. 'We saw no reason why she shouldn't come back.'

Rebecca heard the note in his voice and felt a sudden qualm of fear. For a while, beset by anxieties which seemed more vital, she had forgotten Vivian's enmity towards Tom and Bessie – forgotten the old story of their escape from Kidderminster and the part he had played in it. But why should she have remembered, or even thought the memory important? Tom had been back in Kidderminster for a long time now, and Vivian had done nothing to carry out his threats of bringing him to justice. Nor could he do so without revealing his own involvement. So why should Bessie's return change the situation?

Yet in some dark, subtle way, she saw that it had. Vivian's face had darkened, as if he were in the grip of some deep, grudging anger, as if his manhood itself had been called into question. Her qualm grew into real fear, and she lifted a hand to her mouth. And at the movement, Vivian's eyes came back to her face, the brief anger disappeared and the grave sympathy returned. He took her arm, and she remembered with a rush of anguish why he had come to meet her. And she turned towards the inn door, thinking now only of her husband Francis and their lost son; the gay, careless life that had been extinguished in the swirling, coloured waters of the Stour.

* * *

Spring became summer and wore on through a dusty heat that Rebecca scarcely noticed, sunk as she was in her grief. The savage pain that had caught at her breast when Vivian first told her of Geoffrey's death, had been dulled for a while by shock, then returned to tear at her body through endless days, eternal nights. She sat hopelessly by her window and stared out over the shimmering town. Even the brightest sunshine was dimmed by a shadowy darkness that gripped with bony fingers at her heart and mind. There seemed to be little comfort anywhere.

And she found it impossible to turn to Francis for support. His own despair matched her own and they seemed to be floundering in different worlds, sharing the same pain yet unable to use it to comfort each other. Sometimes, at first, they tried to talk, but each was too ensnared by anguish to be able to recognise or comfort the other.

Francis blamed himself bitterly. Over and over again, he berated himself for neglect, saying that he should have taken notice when Rebecca had told him of her fears about Jeremiah, saying that he ought never to have allowed the old man to take the boys out, even with Polly. Useless for Rebecca to try to convince him that he was not to blame, that nobody left at home was to blame. Useless for her to blame herself, saying that she should never have left, that she should have sent Nancy with Tom. Useless for her to expect comfort from Francis, when he so desperately needed it himself yet would not allow himself to accept it.

Useless, all of it. Useless almost to go on living.

Her only link with sanity, with happier days, were the two boys left to her, Daniel and William. She would sit for hours in the nursery, watching them play, sharing their simple meals, dressing them in the morning, preparing them for bed. But even the boys were no longer the same. Daniel's solemn gravity, that had amused them all so much, had deepened to a sorrowful pensiveness. And William, so slow to develop, seemed to have been set back six months or more. He reverted to his baby habits, sucked his thumb and scarcely spoke. He looked about him as if constantly searching for something he had lost.

And without Geoffrey's bright, mischievous gaiety, the whole house was a quieter, sadder place.

Meanwhile, in the town, the strike continued, but even there it seemed as if the heart had gone out of the men who had started so bravely. The battle had caught at the imagination of the whole country, with letters appearing in *The Times* arguing about the wage it was possible for a weaver to earn. Thirty shillings a week claimed by one, one pound twelve shillings by another, and by a third only one pound five . . . Ledgers were quoted for past years, and James Bowyer who had once threatened the weavers with guns even divided his weavers into two categories, the 'industrious and steady' and the 'idle and dissipated'. Those too old or infirm to keep up with the 'industrious' workers were classed with the idle which thus became by far the largest portion, and he declared that while the idle certainly had the ability to work fast, most of them would not bother. 'They will not work at all, as long as they have money or credit,' he finished, and many of the manufacturers agreed with him.

'But the weavers are still gaining support,' Francis said one day when Rebecca had roused herself to try to take an interest in the subject that had once aroused such passion in her. 'They're conducting themselves with a dignity that people are forced to respect. Organised and peaceful – even Vivian has had to admit that. And there's talk of a general trades union being formed, one that would support whichever workers were being wrongly treated by their masters. Which, of course, Vivian does *not* wish to happen.'

'I wish you would stop this constant war with Vivian,' Rebecca said listlessly. She was dandling little William on her knee, and her voice was distant, as though she had little interest in what she was saying. 'He's not the man we thought him, Francis. He has a gentle, kindly side that we never let ourselves see before. I truly believe that if you let yourself see him as a friend, he would be one to you.'

Francis turned his head to gaze at her in astonishment. Had she really forgotten all the jibes Vivian had made, the times when he had sneered at them both, the sarcasm, the outright unfriendliness? Had she forgotten Vivian's thinly veiled threats against Francis's position with the business? Had she forgotten those times, never quite spoken of but strongly suspected by Francis, when Vivian had behaved in a less than gentlemanly manner towards the young housemaid under his father's roof?

'We see in other people what we want to see,' she went on, almost dreamily. 'And we've always – yes, I share the blame – we've always chosen to see Vivian as an enemy. Yet he's been so good to me since . . . since . . .' Her voice failed her and Francis felt the ache in his own heart and turned away. A bitterness rose within him. How could he ever forget, how ever live again, if she must constantly remember, constantly remind him?

And yet, he must admit the truth of her words. Vivian had indeed shown a kindlier side of his nature to Rebecca and had appeared able to comfort her when Francis felt trapped by his own despair.

'Perhaps you're right,' he said at last. And then, in an effort to change the subject, 'How is Bessie now? She looks better.'

'I think she is. She's strong enough to take a walk every day, and I think it does her good. She talks of starting her millinery again, here in Kidderminster, and I think it may be a good thing for her.'

'Millinery! But she doesn't need to work, now that she lives with us. I can take care of all Bessie's needs.'

'All her material ones, perhaps,' Rebecca answered. 'But material needs are not all we have, Francis. Even women like to feel they are useful, you know.'

He looked at her, struck by the lost quality in her voice, and not for the first time, wished passionately that they had never stopped their loving. If only it had been possible, after Geoffrey's death, to take her in his arms and comfort her. If only it were possible now. But they had drifted too far apart. The loving touch had been neglected and now fallen into disuse, and he did not know how it could be revived.

'Rebecca, my love,' he said with difficulty, 'you never feel that you are not useful, do you? You know that I depend on you still? That life without you would be . . . insupportable?'

Rebecca lifted her eyes and looked at him, and the sadness in those great, dark pools was shocking to him. He gazed back, knowing that she needed his comfort, needed it desperately. And knowing that he could not give it.

Once, he could have done so, he thought wretchedly. Once, in an early morning in a cold, dawnlit library, when a young housemaid had knelt before the hearth and brushed away the ashes. He could have done it then.

Why not now?

'Well, it's good to see you again, Bess.' Nell Foster, thinner than before with eyes that looked old, sat on her doorstep in the dusty sunshine. 'Not looking so bad, either. Got over that sickness, hev you?'

'More or less.' Bessie sat down beside her with a sigh. She wasn't yet as strong as she had been – perhaps never would be – and the walk in the heat of the afternoon had tired her more than she expected. She leaned her head on her hand and watched the children playing desultorily on the cobbled yard. They looked as listless and drained of strength as Nell herself, as all

304

the women who sat on doorsteps with nothing to do.

'Times ent so good,' she said, and Nell shook her head.

'Strike's dragging on till we're all sick to death of it. Aye, sick to death – and that's the truth!' She laughed without humour. 'Plenty of poor scraps hev give up the ghost over this already, and plenty more will before it's done. Well, you knows what it's like in these parts, Bess, even if you hev been living the gay life in London.'

Bess's mouth twisted wryly. 'Not so gay. It's no better in London than it is here, Nell. I don't reckon it's any different anywhere for the likes of us. Seems to me it's the way most people has to live. There ent many like our Becky that falls on their feet.'

Nell shook her head. 'I reckon you're right there, Bess.' There was a short pause, then she said. 'And there's going to be worse to come. Real trouble, I mean. Well, there's already bin a bit. Some of the men are for going back to work. Did you hear about Jim Male and his missus? Set off in a trap with all they had, meaning to get work in Bewdley, and a gang of weavers went after 'em, pelted 'em with stones and horse dung and smashed all their things. And there was Bet Tasker, made to throw a boy in the river when he'd been working. Weaver against weaver.' She shook her head. 'I never thought that was what these unions and such were supposed to be doing.'

'They're bringing in strangers too, so Francis was telling us,' Bessie said. 'Brought a whole load of 'em up the canal to work down at Bowyer's. That won't go down well.'

'Like I said,' Nell repeated, 'there's going to be trouble.'

Bessie thought of her words often in the weeks that followed, weeks that saw more and more violence in Kidderminster. Weavers were brought before magistrates and fined or imprisoned. Men and women who had wanted nothing but peace and a chance to feed and shelter their families were driven by hunger and despair to attack their masters. Punishment lessened nobody's resentment, and the bitterness grew on all sides and crept like a poisonous miasma through the streets, so that even Rebecca, who had walked so proudly through any yard, was cautious about venturing out alone. Nobody was safe; nobody was quite responsible for what they did.

'The whole of Kidderminster is going mad,' Francis said sadly. 'And yet the men are well supported – subscriptions come in from all over the country. Their cause is seen as a just one by many.'

'But not by the masters.' Matthew stirred in his chair. 'And in the end, it is the masters who have the power. What does Vivian say about this?'

'You'd better ask my wife that,' Francis said with an unaccustomed edge to his voice. 'She sees more of my cousin than I do.'

Matthew glanced at Rebecca, who sat sewing on the couch. She met his eyes calmly and said, 'Francis believes that Vivian calls here too often. But he comes in a friendly spirit, and in that spirit I receive him. It's no more than that.'

'And his attitude towards the weavers? The same as always, I imagine?'

'We never discuss the weavers,' Rebecca said, and returned her attention to her work.

'It makes me uneasy, this sudden friendship,' Francis confided later. 'But what can I do? Rebecca meets all my objections with the same reply, that Vivian has a better side to him than we suspected, and that we should never turn away friendship. And how can I tell her she's wrong? How can I tell her that I've never known Vivian to do anything without advantage to himself? She knows it already – she simply says that he's changed.'

'As a snake changes its markings or a leopard its

spots,' Matthew agreed. 'But what advantage can Vivian find in becoming Rebecca's friend? He has no hope of destroying her loyalty to you – anyone can see that's unshakeable. And I can see nothing else.'

'Nor can I,' Francis admitted. 'And yet . . . sometimes I catch a certain look in his eye . . . as if he's watching some plan evolve. And it worries me. But there— ' he spoke more briskly ' —perhaps I let my imagination run away with me. And I certainly have more to worry about at present. The situation's not good, Matthew.'

'But the co-operative is continuing to work?'

'At present, yes. Most of the weavers believe it's the way of the future. But how long that will last, I just don't know. They may turn against us at any time. We can't be sure of our immunity from this strike, Matthew. Nobody can.'

'Even though we're on their side,' Matthew said quietly, and stared out over the hot, dusty town. 'Even though we want nothing more than to see them fairly dealt with . . .'

Chapter Fourteen

'So it's twelve and twelve again.'

Bill Bucknell and the rest of the Committee were meeting for the last time. The strike had ended in disarray. Dragoons had been called in and the turbulent streets of Kidderminster quietened by the threatening presence of the military. The masters had offered each single man twenty shillings and each married man thirty shillings to return to work at the reduced prices. The Committee had had no hand in the decision then made; the weavers had held their own meeting and agreed to negotiate on that basis. And then, as a final stroke, Will Charlton had been sentenced to a fine of two hundred pounds or two years' imprisonment for his part in the affair.

'But they'll let him go free if we dissolve the Committee,' Holloway said soberly. 'And the way I see it, lads, is – well, we don't have much choice in the matter.'

'We don't hev no choice at all,' Bill said. 'We can't see Will go to jail, and we can't afford to pay his fine neither. We hev to disband. Forget it. And after all we bin through, too.'

They sat silent and dispirited. Whatever they did, the men would return to work next morning. Nineteen weeks had gone by, nineteen weeks of hardship, and nothing to show for it. Nothing had been gained.

'And a hell of a lot lost,' Tom Potter said. 'We used to hev a good working relationship with the masters. We might hev worked all the hours God sends and bin paid poor for doing it, but we knew what to expect and so did they. There was a sort of *respect* between us. Now all that's gone. The men look surly when they meets a master in the street, and the masters looks the other way.'

'Aye, you're right,' Fred Holloway agreed. 'Something's gone from Kidderminster these past few months. Something I don't think we'll ever see come back.' He looked around the room and sighed. 'Well, this is it, lads. The last meeting. We've been starved into giving way just like they said we would. They've beaten us.'

The men nodded, shook hands and prepared to leave. An air of gloom hung over the room where so many meetings had been held, so many plans made. They filed out, silent, each one deep in his own thoughts.

'I tell you what, Bill,' Fred Holloway said as they walked along the road together. 'I reckon we'd have done better not to have listened to that man Price. Led us astray, he did, with all his pamphlets and his poetry. You know they're going to prosecute him?'

'Aye, I heard. And it'll be jail for him, without the choice of a fine. And a stiff sentence too – the magistrates will come down hard on him. No chance of a fair trail here in Kidder!'

'Well, they might have it somewhere else. Yes, I reckon we should've put the brakes on him a long time ago. Oh, he meant well, no doubt about that – he was on our side from start to finish. But all those poems and letters – bound to put the masters' backs up, they were. We should have realised it and not let him have his head.'

Bill nodded. 'All the same, the men looked up to him – one of the gentry on our side, it were summat we all needed. And a clergyman and all – give us the feeling we had right on our side. Mebbe he did go a bit too far in the end, but I reckon we still got a lot to thank him for.'

'I don't reckon we've seen the last of this affair,' Fred said soberly. 'I reckon it'll all blow up again someday. The men don't like what's happened. They'll work for a while because their bellies are rumbling, but when they can look about 'em again they'll start to get restless. There'll be another strike, or something very like it, in less than two years from now. And then maybe the Committee will be needed again. Mark my words if it's not.'

Once again, the early morning streets of Kidderminster were filled with the clatter of boots on the 'kidney' stones and the chatter of men, women and children on their way to work. Once again, the rattle of looms filled carpet shops that had been silent for many months; once again, the river ran with colours from newly dyed wool. And once again, as if the semblance of new life in the town had brought new life to all those who lived there, Rebecca lifted her head and looked about her.

Geoffrey was dead, and nothing would bring him back. But her other boys needed her. And she was still a young woman, not yet twenty-three. And there was still much to be done.

'Why did you all stop?' she demanded, calling her friends together for a meeting of the wives' association she had set up in what seemed to be another lifetime. 'Those poor women in the weavers' cottages – they've had to watch their children starve all these months, while you did nothing to help. Why? I thought you believed in the cause.'

'Yes, and we believe in our marriages too,' Lydia told her. 'Think, Rebecca – we'd have had to go against our own husbands. I can just imagine my Amos's reaction – why, he would have beaten me senseless and locked me in my room. And what good would that have done the weavers' wives?'

'And why did *you* do nothing?' Anne demanded. 'I don't recall seeing you down the weavers' yards, Rebecca Pagnel.'

Rebecca felt the heat of anger in her cheeks.

'You know full well why,' she said shortly. 'My son . . . you *know* why, Anne.' She gazed at her friend, her eyes filling with the tears that still came too readily whenever she thought of Geoffrey, struggling in the cold, murky water. But Anne looked back and her eyes were cold.

'We've all lost children, Rebecca,' she said bluntly. 'And had to carry on just the same. So has every weaver's wife in those cottages you talk about so much – as you should know, having grown up in one. How many children did your mother have? Nine, ten, eleven? And how many did she raise?'

There was no need for Rebecca to answer that. She bit her lip and cast down her eyes. But Anne went on.

'And did she stay at home from the bobbin-winding one day more than she had to, whatever happened? Did she sit by the fire bemoaning her lot? No – she went out just the same, because her other children – and you were one of them, Rebecca – needed her. And I don't doubt she was just as sad by the death of every child as you've been, as I was when I lost my Margaret through scarlet fever, as Meg here was when her twins died in their cots, both on the same night.' She paused, and her voice softened. 'Rebecca, I don't want to be harsh. We all know what it's like. But you can't scold us for being cowards when you did nothing yourself. Our troubles are with us – we can't defy our husbands. Yours are in the past and can't be altered.'

There was a long silence. Rebecca felt the tears, hot in her eyes and on her cheeks. Geoffrey, Geoffrey, her heart cried . . . but she knew that Anne was right. Nothing could alter the fact of his death. And mourning, while it must be done, should not have been allowed to get in the way of her other tasks.

Other children had died while she grieved for Geoffrey. Children who had not fallen into rivers or caught scarlet fever or just faded away in their sleep. Children who had starved; who had died for want of a cup of milk or a crust of bread.

'I'm sorry,' she said at last, and looked at each of her friends in turn. 'I'm truly sorry. I've been thinking only of my own troubles. And Francis is different from your husbands – I can see how difficult it would have been to oppose them. But now— ' Rebecca straightened her back and faced them ' —now, there must be something we can do. And we can do it together. We can start again. Now that the men are back at work, we can help their wives once more. And this time, we'll give real help. Soup kitchens – you can tell your husbands they're needed to get strength back into their weavers so that they can work better. Milk for the children. Clothes. They're all still virtually destitute, needing every penny they can earn to pay their debts and feed themselves. We'll go to all our friends, tell them the industry will never get back on its feet without such help. Winter's coming and the people need firing, they need good hot food inside them and warm clothes to keep them warm or more and more will die during the cold weather. Tell your husbands that! And tell them that unless they keep their workers' strength up, production will fall again. And after five months' standstill, the town cannot stand that, however much carpet there may have been in the warehouses when it all began.'

Her voice rang clear and true, as it had not done for many months. The other women stared at her and their faces broke into smiles. They laughed with excitement and began making plans. Once again, they looked to Rebecca for leadership. And once again, she gave it.

Vivian, passing the half-open door of the drawing room on his way to visit Francis, paused and listened. He heard Rebecca's voice leading the others, heard her crisp comments, heard the positive tone once more in her voice.

'Go home and tell your husbands what we mean to

do,' Rebecca said commandingly, and the other women laughed. 'And see if they dare to beat you and lock you up!'

Vivian stood very still for a moment. Then he went on his way. His brow was furrowed with thought, his eyes narrowed. And his mouth was thin and hard.

Life was beginning again for Kidderminster. But few were finding it easy. And Bess, still pale as a wraith, sat by her window in the house in Unicorn Street and wondered aloud whether it had been worth all her suffering to stay alive.

'You should hev let me go when I was half dead, up in London.' she told her sister. 'Let me go the rest of the way. What was the use of saving me just to go through it all again some day? And I will, you know – no one ever gets better from what I got. It rots you, rots your guts, rots your liver and lights, rots your brain. And that ent nothing to look forward to, I can tell you.'

Rebecca gazed at her in distress. 'Bessie, don't say such things. You're better now, there's no certainty that the illness will come back. The doctor said— '

'That doctor's a fool. A quack. I'd hev got better this time without his help. But I wouldn't hev got better without yours – coming and looking after me, feeding me up, cleaning up me mess.' Bessie looked at Rebecca and her ravaged face softened. 'Here, don't look like that. I'm not really sorry you come. It's good to be back with you and our Tom again, even if it won't be for long. I just wish I could be a bit of use about the place. I never bin a lady of leisure before – don't think it suits me.'

Rebecca laughed. 'Oh, we'll find you something to do if that's what you want. Why, you can— ' She broke off as the door opened and her husband came in, with Matthew close behind him. 'Francis! You're home early. Bessie and I were just having tea.'

314

'I know. That's why I brought Matthew with me. He says he's famished for tea. He's been looking round the factory with me and Tom and we've exhausted him.'

'All that hard work going on,' Matthew said, accepting a cup. 'It's nearly as bad watching as doing it. I ought to know something of what happens.' He looked across at Bessie and smiled. 'And how are you, Miss Himley? You're looking a great deal better now than when— ' He stopped but Rebecca said the words for him, firmly.

'Better than when we brought her home from London. It's all right, Matthew – I know why you feel it might be indelicate to say more. But I've stopped hiding from the truth now. I know nothing can bring my boy back— ' her voice faltered for a moment, but she went on courageously ' —and I mean to go on with my life. just as Bessie means to go on with hers, don't you, Bess?' Determined as she was to be brave, she caught thankfully at the opportunity to change the subject. 'She was just telling me she'd like some kind of occupation.'

'Well, I'm sure there are plenty of things you could do, Bess.' Francis said. 'Sewing – you were good at making hats, weren't you? The children are always needing new things, I'm sure my mother is forever making them clothes. Perhaps you could take up some musical accomplishment, or— '

'My stars!' Bessie exclaimed. 'Anyone'd think I was a proper lady. I'm not used to sitting about making fancy bits and pieces, Francis – it was bonnets for working women I made, none of your frills and fripperies. Anyway, I don't know as I want to go back to that sort of work. I'd like— '

'But Bessie, you don't have to work. You're welcome to live here with Rebecca and me – you don't have to feel you must pay your way. And I can give you an allowance, you needn't feel you're penniless.'

'I needn't feel I'm dependent, either,' Bessie

retorted and Rebecca was reminded sharply of her father, talking fiercely about the independence of the weavers. 'Look, I just don't take to heving nothing to fill my days. I want something to *do* – something to make me feel useful.' She paused. 'I bin useless long enough. I want to be someone what *matters*.'

'You do matter— ' Rebecca began, but Matthew lifted a hand and silenced her.

'I know what you mean, Bessie,' he said quietly. 'I felt the same for a long time. Oh, I know – I'm rich, I can do as I like, go where I please. But for years I had nothing *real* to do. The only time I felt I was any use was when I was in America and worked with horses and cattle, driving them across the plains. Every man's equal out on the prairie, and the Indians take no account of white man's wealth.' He glanced at Francis and Rebecca. 'You two have always had something to do – yes, even at eight years old, Rebecca, you mattered. You mattered to your father who would have had to employ another child if you hadn't been there to draw for him. You mattered to the Pagnels and their servants, because you were part of the household with a job to do. And then you mattered to Francis and the boys, and many other people, and still do. And Francis, you mattered to Geoffrey and Enid, to Jeremiah, to the business. To Tom and Nancy. And most of all, of course, to Rebecca and your sons. But Bessie and I – we've been like ships drifting without an anchor, swinging this way and that and never knowing what rocks we were going to fetch up against next.'

He stopped and grinned a little self-consciously. The others gazed at him. At last, Rebecca found her voice.

'But you do matter, Matthew. You matter very much to us, and you matter to the weavers. Look how you've helped them. Look how much they think of you.'

'Now, perhaps,' he said. 'But it took a long time to come about. And I realise now that it's what I've been searching for all along. To know that I matter in some way, however small.' He turned back to Bessie. 'And you feel the same. You need to know you matter.'

'Aye,' she said, gazing at him. 'That's right, Mr Farrell. That's just what I need.'

'Well, then,' he said, 'since we understand each other so well, why don't we agree to matter to each other. You to me, me to you.' He laughed at their astounded faces and said 'If you'd consider being housekeeper to a rather irresponsible bachelor . . . well, I'd be glad if you'd give me a try, anyway.'

There was a long silence. Rebecca stared at Matthew, then at her sister. She saw Bess turn first white, then red. She saw the sudden light in her eyes. She heard the quick intake of breath.

'*Housekeeper*?' Bess breathed. She looked at Matthew as if she were within sight of the Pearly Gates themselves. 'Me – a *housekeeper*? Why, I – I dunno – I've never done anything like that – I never even bin in service. It's Becky here knows all about that, I— '

Matthew burst out laughing. 'And are you suggesting I should offer your sister a job? What do you say, Francis, will you allow your wife to come and keep house for me? No, Bess, it's you I want. And you'd soon learn. Rebecca will teach you all you need to know, won't you, Rebecca?'

'Yes – yes, of course I will. Gladly. But – Bess, are you sure? Are you strong enough? I don't want you to overtax yourself, you've been very ill— '

'And I don't want a new housekeeper for at least six weeks,' Matthew declared. 'Which gives Bess plenty of time to gather more strength and learn what's necessary from you and Enid. That's if she wants to.' He looked at Bess, laughing at her. 'Well, Bess? What's it to be – do you want to be my housekeeper? Do you want to matter to me?'

'Oh yes,' Bessie breathed, gazing back with stars in her eyes. 'Oh yes, Mr Farrell – please.'

* * *

'So the prodigal has been presented with her fatted calf,' Vivian commented. He picked up a sample of carpet, a new design which was being woven for one of the large London stores. 'Do you think she'll make a good housekeeper?'

Francis shrugged. 'Who knows? She's willing enough. And Matthew's not an exacting employer. They'll do well enough, I daresay.' He glanced at his cousin, hesitated, and then gave voice to something that had been troubling him ever since Bessie had been brought back from London. 'You won't make difficulties, Vivian, will you?'

'Difficulties?' Vivian raised his eyebrows. 'Whatever do you mean, Frank? What sort of difficulties might I make?'

'I think you know what I mean,' Francis answered steadily. 'Difficulties for Bess, coming back to Kidderminster – after the way she left.'

'Oh, that!' Vivian laughed. 'All water under the bridge, dear boy. Anyway, I could hardly make trouble now, after having accepted Tom Himley's return. One assumes that it was he who wielded the weapon . . .' He grew thoughtful, then added as if to himself, 'Not that I've forgotten the money I gave those two, which was never repaid. Nor the trouble I went to on their behalf.'

And on your own, Francis thought, having for some time had a very good idea as to why Vivian had helped the Himleys to flee. But aloud, he said merely, 'If it's a question of the money, Vivian, I'll repay you myself gladly. I know Tom would like to, anyway, and no doubt Bess herself wouldn't wish to be in your debt a day longer than— '

But Vivian waved an impatient hand. 'Forget the money, Frank. It's not important and I don't expect you to pay the debts those two incurred. In fact, young Himley did offer once to repay me, but . . .' He smiled slowly. 'It suits me better to have the debt unpaid. I can always call on him then. And his sister too – though what use she'd be to me, or to any other man, God only knows. Only a fool or a suicide would want what she's got.'

Francis looked at him with distaste. He wondered if Rebecca had ever heard Vivian speak like this. He concluded not, or she would never have allowed herself to become so friendly with him. And there was no doubt that they had become friends, unlikely though that might seem. Ever since that day when she'd come back from London and Vivian had broken the news about Geoffrey . . .

'Tell me what you think of the new design,' he said, nodding towards the sample Vivian was turning over between his hands. 'Has it come out well, do you think? Will it find a good market?'

Carpets, he thought. The only thing he and Vivian had in common, the only ground on which they could meet. The tie which had existed between them since childhood and would bind them together for the rest of their lives.

And which had brought Rebecca into his life too – for if it had not been for the trouble that had driven Bessie and Tom from Kidderminster, Rebecca would never have come to work at Pagnel House and he would never have met her.

Never to have met Rebecca . . . It was unimaginable. And as he stared at the carpet in Vivian's hands, carpet that had been designed by him and Rebecca together, Francis knew that however far apart they might have drifted, his love for her was as strong, as unshakeable as ever.

'Libel,' Francis said, laying down the paper. 'That's what it's to be. Thirteen counts of "Inflammatory Libel". He hasn't a chance, Matt.'

'I know.' Matthew sat forward in his chair, staring gloomily at the carpet, barely seeing the design that he

319

had watched come from the loom, woven especially for his own home. 'It's gaol or perhaps even transportation. And he's got a wife and four children over in Needwood. All for publishing a few hotheaded pamphlets.'

'Rather more than hotheaded,' Francis observed. 'He attacked almost everyone, from Joseph Bowyer to the High Bailiff. And he didn't mince his words. I'm not surprised his victims are retaliating.'

'A lot of it was true,' Matthew said defensively. 'Couched in somewhat abrupt language, perhaps but— '

'Oh, come,' Francis said with a smile, 'some of those pamphlets were nothing short of abusive. You see what they're alleging – that he "provoked enmity on the part of the weavers towards their master and thereby prolonged the strike and caused serious risk of violence". And I'm afraid it's true, Matt. Humphrey did go rather far – with the best of intentions, I agree, and I'm sure the weavers looked on him as a champion. But I'm not sure he was really a help to their cause.'

'Well, whether he was or not they'll support him, as he supported them, I'm sure of that. Where is the trial to be held? Not too close to Kidderminster, I hope – there are far too many manufacturers sitting on the magistrate's bench.'

'In Hereford,' Francis said, consulting his paper again. 'Getting on for fifty miles away. A long way for weavers to walk.'

'All the same, I think they'll do it. You used the right word for how they feel about Humphrey Price. To them, he's a champion; and they'll not forget him. Not the weavers of Kidderminster.'

'You seem to think a lot of them,' Francis said, looking at his friend's face, intense with emotion. 'Yet a few years ago, you barely knew they existed.'

'I've changed since then. I seem to have . . . found something, something I was seeking. A cause, perhaps

320

– yet more than that.' Matthew looked up and fumbled for words in a way that was quite unlike his normal self. 'These people – they *matter*, in the way that Bess was saying she needed to matter. They're not just workers, slaves to the masters, to be paid barely enough to keep them alive and working before being thrown aside. They're human beings, as worthy as you and I – more so, perhaps, many of them.' He rose and began to walk about the room. 'You know, Francis, I believe there is something wrong, something rotten about the whole system under which industry works in this country. People who have done nothing to earn their wealth, who receive it simply through being born to wealthy parents – who in turn never did anything to earn it – seem to believe that this makes them in some way *better* than their fellows who have nothing.' He stopped and stared at Francis. 'Can you understand this? Does it make any sense at all? My child has a full purse, so he's a better, more worthy human being than yours, who runs the streets barefoot and in rags? And we make sure that it stays that way, too. We exclude them from education, we see that they grow up as ignorant as the day they were born, so that we can point at them and tell each other how much better we are than they, with our fine clothes, our comfortable homes, our schooling. Well, don't we?'

'Up to a point, yes. But Matthew, the carpet manufacturers aren't aristocracy. They weren't born rich. They built up their businesses and they work to keep them going.'

'And they work to raise themselves in the society they've created! Oh, they'll never climb into the more rarified atmosphere of the really rich, but they can pretend, to themselves and to each other, that they're almost as good.'

Francis was silent. He had to admit that it was true. His cousin Vivian and Vivian's wife were prime examples, with their fine house, their dinner parties, their snobbery. And there were plenty of them.

'Your Rebecca,' Matthew said, and there was a tremor of intensity in his voice, 'is more a lady than any of those doxies, tricked out in their vulgar jewels and silk dresses, could ever be. She is living proof of all that I say. And her brother Tom is not far behind.'

'And Bessie?' Francis asked with a glint of humour. But Matthew was not, for once, in frivolous mood.

'Bessie is living proof of what we do to our fellow human beings with our selfishness and cruelty. Yes, Francis, *ours*. That poor woman has suffered a living death for years, and all because of the conditions manufacturers impose upon their workers. And she isn't the only one – don't tell me you're not aware that even now there are still little girls in carpet factories, yes, in Pagnel's factory too, who are being raped and beaten by weavers on this vicious twelve and twelve system that keeps them in each other's company until all hours. Don't tell me you don't know that it goes on even now, Francis, that and all the other degradations of poverty and hardship.' He came to a halt before the table at which Francis sat and thumped his fist down so hard that a cup leapt from its saucer and was smashed on the floor. 'That's what Humphrey Price was talking about when he abused Joseph Bowyer and the rest. *That's* what he was fighting. The twopence a yard was merely a symbol. It was oppression and cruelty and downright *evil* that Price was fighting, yes, and I was proud to fight alongside him. And still would, in the dock, if they'd arrested me too.'

He stopped, breathing hard, still leaning on the table staring into Francis's face. There was a long silence.

'You're right,' Francis said at last, quietly. 'You're completely right. And I've known it – yes, I've known it for a long time. But I have been trying to do something about it, Matthew. The co-operative – it's always been my dream to make the weavers' lot better by making them a part of the whole production, by giving them a share – their rightful share. And you know we're hoping to open a school, and Rebecca is helping too, with the wives' association she's formed. Things will improve, Matt – but it takes time. It's always a slow process, bringing about change.'

'Change for the better, yes,' Matthew said. 'Change for the worse seems to come about with very little effort . . . I'm sorry, Francis, I know you and Tom and Rebecca are doing your best and I shouldn't have shouted at you. Indeed, it wasn't you I was aiming my remarks at – it was all those others out there – men like your cousin Vivian, well fed, sleek and smooth with their wives behaving like princesses. It makes me so angry!'

'Yes, I do see that,' Francis said dryly, and Matthew laughed. 'So – what are you going to do next?'

'Next?' Matthew shook his head. 'This is where all my fine words begin to let me down, Francis. What can any of us do next? The strike's over and the men defeated, and they'll have no heart for further strife for a long time now. All they want to do is get food into their children's bellies and a secure roof over their heads. And at tenpence a yard, that's going to be even harder than before.' He sighed. 'I suppose you – we're – doing the best we can by expanding the co-operative. I'm glad I came in with you on that, Francis. At least I feel there's some part of this industry that isn't contaminated. That some of the carpets I walk on haven't been woven from children's tears.'

'And Price?'

'He'll go to gaol,' Matthew said simply. 'But he'll come out again – eventually. And then . . . well, maybe we'll fight again.' He looked at Francis and although the anger had died from his eyes, there was an iron implacability in them that caused Francis to believe every word he spoke. 'The weavers' war isn't over yet, Francis. And the greatest battle is yet to come.'

Chapter Fifteen

Holy Thursday, 1829, and it was Fair Day on Bromsgrove Green.

The open space was crowded with booths, rocking horses and swinging boats. Long tables were covered with sweetmeats, pies and pastries, cakes and cold meats. The tooth-puller was attracting a giggling, nudging crowd who watched with fearful delight as less fortunate friends presented themselves to his ministrations. A travelling doctor treated a queue of patients, and old women sold herbal concoctions and potions guaranteed to bring love and happiness. Gipsies told fortunes, sold pegs and flowers, dealt in horses or donkeys and smiled slyly upon the townsfolk who looked on them with wary fascination.

People came from country areas for miles around. If the distance could be walked, they walked it, bringing children in their arms or on their backs. They met friends they had been meeting for years at the fairs, yet never saw at any other time. They exchanged news and gossip and jokes, and they went home refreshed, with something new to occupy their minds until the next Fair Day came around.

Polly met an old friend of hers, a woman who had been a child in the workhouse with her. Taking their accustomed route around the Green, they met as they always did, beside a gingerbread stall. They took their biscuits to a nearby bank and sat on the grass, watching the people and chatting while they ate.

'So how's it all going, Joanie? You wed that farmer yet? He been after you long enough.'

Joan grinned. She'd lost another tooth since last summer, Polly noticed, and it didn't do much for her looks. If she didn't take the farmer soon, he'd start looking for a younger, prettier piece.

'He's getting warmer,' she said. 'Asked me again last week. Told me I could hev my own dairymaid, and hens my own, and all the butter money. I think I might take him.'

'I should think so too!' Polly felt a warm envy stir inside her. All this offered on a plate, and Joan was still keeping the man dangling. 'I dunno why you haven't done it sooner.'

'Oh, you gets more if you keeps 'em waiting a bit.' Joan bit into her gingerbread and winced. Another tooth giving trouble? Polly felt a devilish desire to pull her down a peg or two.

'Tooth-puller's here, if you needs him. It's old Joshua this year – they say he's a right butcher. You can hear the screams from here if you listen.'

Joan looked at her and turned a little pale. Then she snorted and said, 'That's not the tooth-puller, it's those childer on the swinging-boats. Anyway, I don't need him. It were only a twinge.' She bit again, defiantly. 'Here, how's that old man you looks after?'

Polly grimaced. 'Getting worse. Hardly knows who he is now and only knows me one time in four. I hev to be after him all day long, making sure he don't damage himself some way. Proper sad, really. And yet there's days when he's as sane as you and me.' She paused, thinking of Jeremiah as he had been that morning. 'And those times is worse,' she said in a low voice. 'That's when he remembers – and thinks about things. And he blames himself for it all.'

'Well, maybe it was all his fault, whatever it was.'

'No. Not all of it. Not any of it, really. He just did the best he could. And if it turned out wrong— ' She shrugged. 'Anyway, it didn't all turn out wrong. Mr Francis has had a good life. And as for the little 'un – little Geoffrey— ' she shuddered briefly ' —that were my fault as much as his. More. I didn't hev no fit.'

'What about Mrs Pagnel – Mrs Francis? Took it bad, didn't she?'

'And how else would she take it?' Polly demanded. 'Coming home from London only to find her babby's dead . . .' She shook her head, remembering the shock on Rebecca's face as Mr Vivian had taken her gently in his arms and told her. Poor, poor Becky. As if she hadn't had enough troubles in her life. It had been too cruel.

'Hold it against you, did she, you being there like?' Joan's eyes were sharply inquisitive.

'I don't know. I wouldn't hev blamed her – but she's never said nothing like that.' Rebecca had said little about anything since that day, to anyone, as far as Polly could make out.

Except, strangely, Mr Vivian. And that *was* a queer thing. Because Rebecca had never liked Mr Vivian when she was housemaid up at Pagnel's. In fact, Polly would have said she was scared of him. But it was different now, Polly supposed, being family as it were.

'People say she went funny in the head,' Joan remarked casually, and immediately Polly leapt to her old friend's defence.

'Funny in the head! No such thing. She were just upset, as any mother 'ud be. And she's in mourning – you knows folk like that keeps it up for months, not going nowhere or seeing no one. And then heving her sis here to look after and all . . . Anyway, what if she don't feel like making merry for a bit – it's natural enough, and don't mean to say she's gone off her head, nor nothing like it, so mind!'

'All right, all right.' Joan held up her hand. '*I* never said it. I'm just telling you what other folks say— '

'Well, if you hears anyone else say that you can give 'em a split lip from me,' Polly said grimly, and dusted crumbs from her skirt. 'And now I'm going to hev a look round the fair. You're welcome to come if you wants, but if not— '

'Course I wants to come with you, Poll. We allus do, don't us?' Joan scrambled up and took her friend's arm. 'Here, you don't want to go taking umbrage over a thing like that. We allus been friends, ent we? Ent nothing happened to alter that.'

Polly pursed her lips but did not draw away her arm, and they set off together, back down the bank to where the fair was in full swing. They stopped to look at a stall that glittered with cheap, gaudy jewellery and Joan lifted up a brooch.

'Here, what about this, Poll? Look nice on a wedding dress, don't you reckon? How d'you like to be my chief bridesmaid, eh?' And she squawked with laughter.

Polly smiled reluctantly. She was fond enough of Joanie, and probably all the more so because they didn't see each other very often. And it was good to have a friend from the old days to have a jaw with. No – it wasn't worth quarrelling with her over a bit of silly gossip.

Fair Day on Bromsgrove Green and Daniel was there, with Tilly and his brother William, nearly four years old now and as lively as Daniel was solemn. But the two of them were bright-eyed and eager enough to sample the delights of the day.

'No more goes on the swinging boats,' Tilly said at last, after what seemed like hours of pushing on the wooden cradles, while the boys heaved on their ropes to make their craft swing higher. 'You'll be sick of it. I know I am. Come and 'ave a look at the menagerie.'

They abandoned their ship with some reluctance and followed her over to the pen where a few captive foxes and badgers slumped sad-eyed and listless in their cages. A couple of goats started to chew at her skirt and she pulled away quickly.

'Donkeys!' William exclaimed. 'Ride on the don-keys!'

'You'll fall— ' Daniel began, but Tilly drew a penny

from her pocket and gave it to him.

'You can both 'ave a ride, your ma said so. S'long as the donkey don't run,' she added to the gipsy boy in charge. 'And don't tyke 'em too far, see?'

He grinned. 'Not likely, for a penny.' He threw the boys up on to the back of one donkey, Daniel sitting behind William with his arms firmly around William's waist. Then he gave the donkey's rump a slap and the animal set off, plodding slowly away with William clinging to its mane and squeaking with joy, and Daniel looking as grim as if they were charging into battle.

'Poor little sod,' Tilly muttered to herself. 'He looks as if he's forgot how to enjoy hisself.' She watched for a moment, then noticed a friend of hers, a nursemaid who worked at the house of one of the other carpet manufacturers. They waved and the girl came over.

'Got your little 'uns here? They likes the animals, don't they? Mine won't come away from the goats, and hev you seen the man with the parrot and those little monkeys? Real creepy they are, looks at you just like a baby with them big brown eyes, and— '

She was interrupted by a shriek from the other side of the green and then they heard the galloping hooves of the donkey, returning at a speed he had probably not achieved since he was a foal, accompanied by shouts and curses from his owner while the shrieks went on, growing louder and louder as the donkey approached.

'Daniel! William!' Tilly stopped listening to her friend and ran forwards, her heart thumping violently as she tried to see what was going on. The galloping donkey had a small crowd around him now, and it was impossible to see whether the two boys were still on his back or not. Suddenly sick with fear, she pushed her way through the people, elbowing them out of the way. 'Let me through! Let me through! I got to see – outa me way – *please* let me through, it's Mrs Rebecca's two, if anything 'appens to them— '

They parted good-humouredly and let her through. And she saw then that the boys were safe, still clinging to the donkey's back. William was flushed and laughing, his eyes alight with mischief. But Daniel was white. As white as a sheet. And his eyes were large and dark and haunted.

He looks scared out of his wits, poor mite, Tilly thought, and ran to lift him down.

'There now, Danny, it's all right, nothing's happened, you're quite safe.' She held him close, crooning to him as if he were a baby. 'There, there. It's all right. It's all right.' She looked up at the gipsy boy. 'What 'appened? What scared 'im?'

The boy shrugged. 'Search me, miss. We was just coming down to the river when he started screaming like the devil was after him. Looked as if he was seeing a ghost, he did. I dunno what it was – bit funny in the head if you asks me. There weren't nothing there that I could see.' He turned away, losing interest, and the crowd began to melt away too. Clearly nothing had happened, no blood had been spilt nor heads broken. Nothing to laugh at at all, in fact. There were a few murmurs of 'mammy's baby' and then they dispersed.

Tilly ignored them. She held Daniel close until he stopped trembling, and then she walked the two boys away from the animals and led them to a gingerbread stall. She wasn't supposed to buy them food at the fair, but she reckoned this was an emergency. Daniel needed something to take his mind off what had happened.

For Tilly knew quite well that something had happened, and she knew what it was. Daniel had come to the river, quite unexpectedly. For just a brief moment, he had thought himself back on that day when he and Geoffrey had run beside the river, crouching on the bank to look at some small treasure. For just a brief moment . . . just as long as it took to begin to scream.

330

Poor little sod, she thought again, and gave him his gingerbread.

Fair Day on Bromsgrove Green, and all those who could be merry were determined so to be. And for some, indeed, the hardships of the Great Strike, as it had come to be called, were over and in the past, and they looked and hoped now for a time of prosperity and peace. Yet the ripples of discontent had spread far and wide. Support had been given by other weavers, and even by other industries. There was a fear that if the masters won this battle, the disease would spread to other trades, and every working man would find his wage reduced.

Bill Bucknell, watching his children scamper about the fairground, thought about the last days of the strike.

'And all for naught,' he said bitterly to Nell. 'Ten pence a yard, just as they said in the beginning. And how many folk starved and died for the cause, and most of 'em childer or old and sick? Ah well, they be out of it, if that's any comfort.'

Nell sighed. Almost a year had gone by, but Bill could not forget, could not put it behind him. Even on this day of holiday, his mind was still tormented by the injustice of it all.

'How long must Mr Price stay in prison?' she asked.

Bill's mouth hardened. 'Till they pass sentence. And then for however long the judge says. Could be months – years.' He scowled at a gipsy who was begging him to cross her palm with silver. 'Lucky face! I wish I did hev a lucky face. And I wager Humph Price wishes he had one too.'

He thought again of the long march of forty-five miles that he and many of the other weavers had undertaken, in order to attend Price's trial in Hereford. 'They'd never hev treated him fair in Worcester.' The whole affair had brought about another strike, short-

331

lived and not supported by all the weavers, so many of them too starved and poverty-stricken now to risk any more loss. But enough to slow down production for a few days, enough to allow Price's supporters to be there at his side during the trial.

'I still don't properly understand what they got against him,' Nell said, watching her boys grab a swinging boat as soon as it was free and scramble aboard. 'I mean, he never actually did anything, did he? He never hurt no one nor stole nothing.'

'No, but he wrote a lot of poems and stuff, and they reckoned that encouraged – *incited*, they called it – anyway, it was why some of the weavers got above themselves and started throwing stones and knocking folk about towards the end.' Bill kicked moodily at a tuft of grass. 'Well, you knows as well as I do that's just rubbish. They'd have done that anyway, they was just looking for an excuse. Wasn't Price's fault.'

'So why— '

'Look, they're all gentry, that lot, ent they – magistrates, justices, lawyers. And the manufacturers ent far off it. They sticks together. And they reckoned Price, being Church, ought to be on their side. Far as they're concerned, he's a traitor and they mean to mek him suffer for it.'

'Well, I think it's a shame,' Nell declared roundly. 'He's a good man, Mr Price, and kind too. Give our Sam a penny once, he did, just 'cause he passed him in the street. Sam wouldn't let go of it till he went to sleep that night. Wouldn't even spend it.'

The boys came down off the swinging boat and looked longingly towards the gingerbread stall. Nell glanced at Bill as if wondering if he would say he'd spent enough that day. Fairs were expensive if you let the children have all they wanted, and Bill had had to go without his ale this week to afford it. But he grinned and put out his hand, ruffling the younger boy's head.

'All right, then. One piece and then that's it for

today. There'll be another fair in June and if anyone gives you pennies before then, you can put 'em away and pay for your own gingerbread!'

The boys laughed and ran off, clutching the money gleefully. And Bill stared over the Green to the factory chimneys, more of them each year despite the manufacturers' claims that times were hard.

Hard times, he thought bitterly. They didn't have any idea what hard times were, up there in their comfortable houses. And what would have happened to them all by the time the next fair came along? Probably nothing. Humphrey Price would be in gaol, Bill and his mates would be slaving at their looms as they had always done, the masters would be feeding well as *they* had always done, and nothing would really have changed.

Except that the resentment seething in so many men's breasts would be a little hotter, a little harder, a little closer to another outburst of passion and hate.

And then anything could happen.

Fair Day at Bromsgrove Green. And Vivian had been persuaded to come by Maria, heavy now with her seventh child, surrounded by the six daughters she had produced, all dressed alike in frills and sashes. A sight that made people smile and even Vivian relax his sombre countenance a little.

Maria walked by his side, her hand on his arm. He glanced sideways at her and wondered if at last she might be carrying a son. If not, he knew it would be his last attempt. The thought of making love to her again, lying with that sagging body, trying to rouse his own desire, was more repugnant each time. And all the more so because Maria did no more than lie there, enduring his attentions, plainly thankful when it was all over and hoping as much as he hoped that this time she would be pregnant, that the longed-for son would arrive and Vivian would trouble her no more.

Did any man have a wife who could also be his mistress? Vivian wondered. What was the difference between wives, who seemed able only to see their marital duties as just that – *duties* – to be observed whenever their husbands deemed it necessary, and to bring about the creation of children; and mistresses, who did all they could to avoid the begetting of children and took pleasure, even joy, in the physical acts that would normally bring it about?

Naturally, he would have been shocked if Maria had suddenly begun to behave as a mistress, flirting with him in their bedroom, moving with the sensuality that his current mistress displayed, using his body for her own pleasure as well as his. And none of his mistresses would have been of any use as a wife – all were of a class that Vivian and his family and friends would have thought quite unacceptable. But was it possible that sometimes, just occasionally, there was a woman born who could fulfil both roles?

Once again, as had happened more and more often just lately, Vivian found his thoughts turning to Rebecca. There was a woman who had stepped out of one class and into another – his own. And there was something about her – always had been. Even when she was no more than a housemaid, working in his father's kitchens, clearing the fireplaces, bringing hot water, helping to make the beds.

Vivian thought of the times he had seen her flitting about the house, slender as a wand, pale and quiet, yet with great dark eyes that were filled with secrets. And a mouth that told its own story, with full, red lips that were made to be kissed. And to kiss . . .

How was it he had never managed to possess that elusive figure? It had been easy enough with the other maids. They had all succumbed eventually, some of them to be tired of quickly, others lasting a little longer. Polly, now, who was still there, looking after his father. She'd been one of the longest lasting and she'd never made the mistake of becoming pregnant either, not like some of the careless hussies. And Polly had never cared much for him, he knew. They had enjoyed their pleasures together and he had paid her well. She'd had sense, that one, known that if she didn't play his games he would have her dismissed, and she'd made the best of it and done well.

But Rebecca . . .

He thought of the times when he had caught her, believed he was to triumph at last. Once in the warehouse, once in the library. She'd fought him on both occasions, fought like a little hellcat, scratching and tearing, but if she'd only known it, that had added to his enjoyment. He would have liked to subdue her at last, he thought. But on both occasions she had got away, leaving him all the more determined. And then, to his astonishment, she had been sent away. Pregnant – by his cousin Francis! Not the innocent virgin he'd imagined after all, but a whore like the rest of them.

Vivian had never expected to see her again after that and it had been a double shock when Francis not only set off in search of her, but married her. And brought her back as his wife, when Vivian's mother had died. No longer a waif of a housemaid, seldom lifting her great dark eyes, but a woman, a wife and mother, grave and composed and yet with a spark in her eye, an inner fire that Vivian recognised and responded to, even as he wondered if Francis had any idea what he possessed.

Was Rebecca that rarity, a wife and a mistress to her husband?

Vivian bought his daughters some gingerbread, to be taken home and eaten, not devoured here on the field as if they were common children.

'You've seen enough now,' he said as they lingered by the swinging boats. 'We only came to look, for a little while. I haven't time to stay any longer, and your mother's tired.' It was safe enough to say that. Maria was always tired. And no wonder, with six daughters. But that was her affair. She need only to have presented him with a son, or two, for safety, and he would have troubled her no more. That was all he had ever asked. Little enough, one might suppose. And instead, he had all these daughters and the expense that they would bring him as they grew.

While Rebecca had sons.

Three, so far, even if one had been lost. And no doubt would have more. Although . . .

Lifting his youngest daughter into the trap that waited for them at the side of the field, Vivian wondered again about Rebecca. There had been a look about her lately, a kind of simmering fire, that told him that she was hungry. A hunger that he recognised; a hunger that he could feed. But wasn't Francis doing that?

He remembered the day when Rebecca had come back to Kidderminster, to hear the news about Geoffrey's death. Francis had been too shocked to help her then and Vivian had stepped into the breach. Why he had done it, he was never quite sure, except that if he hadn't that scoundrel Matt Farrell would have done, and Vivian knew that this was an important moment, and one that he should not let pass.

The man who had offered Rebecca comfort when she most needed it would not be forgotten. She would owe him a debt that might not be reclaimed for years, but that could be called in later, with interest.

Vivian had no idea how Rebecca could pay that debt. But he liked the power that debts brought. And he had never quite forgotten that Rebecca had escaped him in the past. Or that her sister, that strumpet Bess Himley, had got away with murder and now come back to Kidderminster bold as brass, to flaunt herself like a lady.

Perhaps the time was coming when all their debts would be paid.

* * *

Fair Day on Bromsgrove Green. But Rebecca was not there. Instead, she stayed at home, the curtains drawn, her hands idle in her lap and stared into the empty fireplace.

Francis found her there when he came home for his dinner at three o'clock. He came quickly across the room and knelt before her, taking her hands and looking into her face. But Rebecca's expression did not change. She looked at him almost sightlessly, and he felt a chill pass over his body.

'Rebecca! Rebecca, my love, why are you sitting in the dark like this? And you're cold – your hands are like ice. Why didn't you call someone to light the fire?'

She looked at him then and he was shocked by the bitterness in her eyes.

'Light the fire? Francis, if there's one thing I can do it's light fires. I don't need to call someone to do that for me.' She sighed and attempted to draw away her hands. 'Perhaps that's what I ought to be doing – the housework. It's what I was born to, after all. I should never have tried to step out of my class, I should have stayed where I was meant to be. People are right when they say it only brings trouble.'

'They're not right! Not for you, anyway.' Francis felt his anxiety grow like a hard knot on his chest. It was weeks since Rebecca had slipped back into this depression and he'd really believed it was at an end. 'You've been so much better since you started working for the weavers' wives again,' he said. 'And – what happened to Geoffrey was nothing to do with you being what you are – you weren't even here.' He shook her hands, trying to regain her attention. 'Rebecca, I can't bear to see you like this. It's nine months now since Geoffrey . . . You must try to look forward again, just as you've been doing. You must try to live. For my sake and Daniel's and William's. We need you, Rebecca.'

She turned back then and looked sadly into his eyes. Her own were as dark as chestnuts, great pools of sorrow. And Francis felt a stab of despair. Surely there was nothing, nothing, that could assuage the depths of the unhappiness she was suffering. If there were, he told himself, if there were anything at all he could give her, she should have it. If there were anything he could do, it would be done.

'How can you say you love me?' she asked at last. 'Francis, you have never loved me since William was born. You have hardly even kissed me.'

Francis stared at her. His heart grew cold. He thought of all the times he had longed, almost beyond endurance, to take her in his arms and love her through the night, to show her how much he desired her, to share the passion he felt for her, to rouse her to her own ecstasy. He thought of the lonely nights when he had slept in his dressing room, afraid to go near his wife; the restless yearning as he tossed sleepless in the narrow bed, thinking of her in the next room, in the wide bed where they had shared so much loving. He thought of the times he had turned away because even to look at her would have undermined all his vows.

'Never loved you?' he said in a shaking voice. 'Rebecca, I have *always* loved you.'

But she looked at him with doubt in her eyes, doubt and sadness and a great, hungry yearning.

'Rebecca,' he said desperately, 'you don't understand. When William was born— ' No. He could not tell her. She would never accept the danger. 'You are my life, Rebecca, my whole life – you must believe that.' He gripped her hands, looked intently into the great dark eyes. 'Rebecca, you must believe that . . .'

'Then show me,' she said quietly, and he knew there was no escape. 'Show me, Francis.'

'Rebecca— '

'*Please*,' she said, and her grip was now tighter than his, her fingers twining in his with a strength he had hardly known she possessed. 'Francis, don't you see how lonely I am? How unhappy I am? I sit here hour

338

after hour, day after day, thinking about poor little Geoffrey, how he must have felt when he slipped into the river, what his last moments were like . . . I can't get it out of my mind. And it's no use for people to tell me that I must stop thinking about it, that I've got to think about the other boys. I can't. I've tried – you know I've tried. For a while I even believed I was getting better. But it's no use. This terrible blackness comes over me and swamps everything else, and my mind just won't do it. Don't you think I *want* to forget?' she demanded passionately, suddenly shaking off Francis's hands and rising to her feet. 'Don't you think I want to stop those dreadful thoughts – don't you think I want to stop hearing his cries, feeling his poor little body struggle, the water filling his lungs, the dreadful choking, the— ' Her voice broke and she turned away, covering her face with her hands. Francis moved to take her in his arms but she threw him off. 'Does anyone really suppose that I want to live my life with this in my head every waking moment, and worse dreams when I dare to go to sleep? Does anyone really believe that if I knew a way to forget, I would not take it?'

'Rebecca . . .' he whispered, appalled by the desperate passion in her voice, by the picture she had given him of her mind. How she had been suffering! And he had never dreamed . . . Sunk in his own misery, he had never fully realised the extent of hers.

'I carried that little boy inside me for nine months,' she said in a low voice. 'He was part of me. His body was my body. When he died . . . a part of me died too.'

'Oh, my love,' he said helplessly. 'My dearest love.'

Rebecca turned and looked into his face.

'I needed you then,' she said simply. 'And you weren't there. Why did you abandon me, Francis?'

He thought of saying that he had never abandoned her, that he had been there every day, trying to comfort her, sharing meals with her, sitting with her in the evening, driving with her in the trap. But he knew that he could not dissemble. He had abandoned her. He had left her alone to suffer in her mind, in her emotions, when her need for him had been greatest.

'Rebecca,' he said quietly, 'please believe me when I tell you that I never meant to – to abandon you. I have never stopped loving you – never stopped wanting you.' He moved closer, laid his hands on her arms and looked into her eyes. 'You have no idea how much I have wanted to come to you, night after night. You have no idea how much I have longed to hold you close to me and love you as we used to do.'

'Then why— ' she breathed.

For a moment, he almost told her. The longing in him, to share the burden that he had carried for so long, that belonged to them both, was almost too much for him. He felt the trembling of his body as he opened his mouth, and knew that she trembled too. She was close to him – so close. The heat of desire swept over him and he closed his eyes, swaying a little, knowing that if he took her in his arms now he would love her, love her until the sun went down the sky, love her until the next day's dawn and beyond.

Memories of past loving swamped his mind, memories of Rebecca beside him in the big double bed, her slender body vibrant with love, her lips returning his kisses. Memories of the closeness between them, expressed and deepened by the loving they shared. If only he could recall those days and nights, if only he could create them again. But the risk was too great. Better to have Rebecca drifting away from him, better if Rebecca must be sad, than to have her dead through desires he could not restrain.

Slowly, heavily, he took his hands from her arms and turned away. And knew that there was no need for words. His last glimpse as he left the room was of Rebecca, standing alone, stricken, abandoned, bereft;

believing him cruel and heartless, when in truth he had never loved or desired her more.

Chapter Sixteen

'The Dream,' Francis said, 'is beginning to come true.'

Rebecca turned her head to look at him. She could see the pride glowing in his eyes. And indeed, she thought, he had much to be proud of. The Co-operative of Pagnel & Himley was at last overcoming its early struggles. It had found its own place in the retail market, even had its carpets exhibited to some acclaim in London, and was showing an encouraging profit. And now it had opened its first school.

Tiny enough, to be sure, with less than a dozen pupils so far, all of them children of the weavers who were part of the venture. But, as Francis said, it was a beginning. And those children, able to read and write, capable of adding a few figures together, would come to the factory later with a better will to work and a better ability to operate the more complicated procedures that Francis said were sure to come.

The Dream. It was something they still shared, in which they both still passionately believed, which kept them bound together almost as closely as the love that seemed to have slipped so inexplicably away from them. Once again, bewildered pain caught at the edges of Rebecca's mind, as a beggar might catch at her skirt, and she pulled away from its clutching fingers as she would never have pulled away from a beggar. She had been through too many nights of torment, longing for his love yet unable to ask for it, unable to risk another rejection. Now she was thankful for the Dream to keep him by her side – that and the two boys who remained to prove that there had once been, and perhaps lingered yet, deep inside, a love that had surmounted all other obstacles.

'We'll build houses too,' he said now as they watched the children lining up to file through the schoolroom door on their first morning. 'Decent houses for weavers to live in, where they can make a proper home and live with a measure of comfort. Warm and dry, so that they don't have to feel ashamed and humiliated by having to live like rats in a hole.' He looked down at her, suddenly contrite. 'I'm sorry, I didn't mean that you— '

'It's all right, Francis.' She shook her head. 'That's just what we were like – rats in a hole. And what so many weavers are like now. And not only weavers – the workers in any industry are the same.' She watched as the last boy went into the school and the door closed behind him. Did that boy realise just how lucky he was? And yet, was there any reason why he should think himself lucky anyway – didn't everyone have the right to learn how to spell his own name, how to add his own wages together? Weren't she and Francis simply doing something that ought to have been done years ago – from the very beginning?

They turned away and walked slowly through the streets. Little clouds of dust rose around their feet, and the ditches that were usually waterlogged were not even damp. Even the wells had begun to dry up, Francis said, and Rebecca made a mental note to put water on the lists of needs which the wives' association tried each week to review. People must be having to buy it, at a penny or more for a bucket, and that green and undrinkable from some murky pond. It was the same in every hot summer, and followed inexorably by some epidemic of disease.

'There's Matthew,' Francis said suddenly. 'Matt! Where have you been? It must be a month since we saw you.'

Matthew crossed the narrow street, his step as springy as ever, humour glinting in his eyes, dressed

344

as if he were about to attend a society ball. Rebecca looked at him with amusement. Who, looking at him now, would suppose that he had driven cattle across the plains of America, fought off Indian attacks, even worked night and day to help the cause of poverty-stricken weavers in an English provincial town? Who, seeing him at those activities, would suppose he could look so foppish and elegant? Yet she knew he would not look out of place in either context. Matthew Farrell was a man who could fit in anywhere, and yet always stand out.

'I've been to Needwood, helping Humphrey to settle back into freedom. You know he was released a few weeks ago?'

'Of course.' Rebecca shivered. 'A year in Stafford Gaol – how did it affect him, Matthew? Did he suffer much? Prison is a terrible place, especially for a man like Humphrey Price.'

'He seems to have taken his treatment quietly, almost as if he were a martyr. And that's just what he was, too.' Matthew's sunburnt face flushed with anger. 'Never allowed a single privilege, forced to go to bed at six every evening as if he were a child, not once allowed the use of a candle – and never heard to complain. After all his work on the weavers' behalf, he would ask nothing at all for himself. He simply suffered it all, with a patience not many men would have shown. *I* certainly would not have done.'

'He's a true champion,' Francis agreed. 'And the weavers know it. They've not forgotten him, Matthew.'

'No, nor the vindictive masters who sent him to gaol. There'll be trouble again in Kidderminster, Francis, mark my words. The battle of the Great Strike might be over, but the war's not finished. It did a lot of harm, that struggle.'

'You don't think they'll strike again?' Rebecca asked anxiously, and both men turned and looked at her.

Matthew glanced at Francis and then spoke soberly.

'There's no knowing what they'll do. There's a lot of bitterness amongst the weavers. They're frustrated because their struggle got them nowhere, and they're resentful because the masters still seem to have the whiphand. That feeling is damped down now, like a volcano – and one day it will erupt. And that day may not be so far away.'

Rebecca shivered. 'Not more trouble,' she whispered, and thought of the last time, the Great Strike which had brought so many troubles with it. It was during that time that Jeremiah had begun to suffer his seizures, that little Geoffrey . . .

But none of those things had been due to the Great Strike. They might well have happened anyway.

Except that, had it not been for the strike, Francis might have had time to go to London and fetch Bessie back to Kidderminster. Jeremiah, left unworried by the problems that had beset him, might not have been attacked by his fits. And Geoffrey might never have fallen into the Stour.

Who could know?

Sometimes, it seemed to Rebecca that it was better not to know the future. Better to be protected from such foreknowledge.

She felt Matthew's eyes on her, and looked up into his face, meeting his gaze. He seemed to understand what she was thinking and his smile was reassuring. He shook his head slightly.

'We can't fight life, Rebecca,' he said gently. 'We have to take it as it comes, good or bad. We can't direct it to our own wishes – all we can do is make the best of what it hands us.'

'I know,' she said, 'but it isn't easy.'

'Has it ever been easy?' he asked, and she thought of her father and mother, their toiling, their troubles and hardships, and shook her head.

No. Life was never easy, for anyone. So why should

346

it be easy for Rebecca Pagnel? Who, even with her troubles, had still been more fortunate than most weavers' daughters.

'So what do you think might start the trouble again?' Francis asked. 'You seem to have the ear of the weavers, Matthew. You're very nearly as much a hero to them as Price is. What's the word now, do you know?'

Matthew shrugged. 'I only know that there's a deal of bitterness. But where trouble might come from, God only knows. It could be anywhere. It's as if Kidderminster were a pile of dry kindling, waiting for a spark, and that spark might come from anywhere.'

'William Cooper, for instance?'

'Cooper? The man who's begun to make common goods?' Matthew pursed his lips in affirmation. 'If I hear correctly, he's paying his weavers less than the standard Brussels.'

'He does, since it's a poorer quality. And talks of reducing it yet further.' Francis looked troubled. 'The Union is afraid it will mean a general reduction, with other masters taking advantage, and they've advised his men not to accept but I believe some of them have done so.'

'Yes, that could easily be a spark,' Matthew observed. 'The other weavers won't like that.'

'That's the trouble. There's been a meeting called in Park Butts tomorrow morning. I'd like to be there – but it wouldn't do, they still see me as a master, in spite of the co-operative. In fact, I sometimes feel I'm in a strange position, neither fish nor fowl. It'll take time, I suppose, for people to get used to the system.'

'It will be easier when more manufacturers begin to use the co-operative ideas,' Rebecca said. 'But there always have to be pioneers, Francis. You're like the frontiersmen Matthew tells us about in America – pushing back the boundaries.'

Matthew laughed. 'And the unions are the Indians,

waiting to attack, I suppose!' He gave Francis a nod. 'I'll attend the meeting tomorrow and come to tell you about it afterwards. You'll be anxious to know if Cooper's wage reduction does prove to be the spark that lights the kindling.'

They walked slowly on, each deep in thought. Rebecca was aware that Francis was concerned about the latest developments and she hoped that there would not be more trouble. His health had been so much better lately, with the warm, dry weather, but she knew that any anxiety might bring on his cough again and with it the troublesome chest pains that seemed now to take little account of weather. Once, it had been a winter illness – now it seemed likely to strike at any time. And Francis needed all his strength to fight it.

Nothing could lessen this concern she felt for him. No, it was more than concern. It was love, the same love that had drawn them together, kept them together in London and at first here in Kidderminster. And that made the growing distance between them all the more strange. They still shared the same dreams, the same concern for their weavers, the same hopes that one day things would be better for the poor who worked so hard for so little. They shared the love for their sons, the grief for the one they had lost . . . So what had happened to the passion they'd also shared, the love they'd expressed in so many intimate ways? And if it really had, for some reason she had never understood, been destroyed – what was that look, that hunger, she saw even now in Francis's eyes . . . ?

When Vivian came to the house later to see Francis, Rebecca was alone. Tilly showed him into the drawing room where she was having tea, and he accepted the offer of a cup. He sat down, stretching his legs out, lifting one dark eyebrow at her as she poured.

'This is pleasant,' he remarked. 'I could almost imagine myself a gentleman of leisure. It's not often I see you idle either, Rebecca.'

'It's not often I am. There's usually something to be done – the boys taken out for a walk, a design to discuss with Francis – a visit to the factory, perhaps.' She spoke deliberately, knowing that Vivian disapproved heartily of her involvement with the co-operative. He could just, albeit rather grudgingly, accept one of her designs for his own factory, though he disliked seeing her come to watch it being woven; but her frequent visits to Pagnel & Himley he considered unwomanly and undesirable, and had not hesitated to say so.

But Rebecca had simply smiled and refused to take offence. And she suspected that Vivian would have been surprised if she had. The friendship that had grown between them was an odd one, its warmth mixed with outspokenness on either side, and neither would back down from a stand once made. Rebecca had sometimes wondered how it was that she could see Vivian as a friend, after his treatment of her as a housemaid and his threats against her brother and sister. But those things had happened long ago. Since then, he had held her in his arms and comforted her over the death of her son. And although he seemed to have little time for Tom or Bessie, he had never carried out his threats. The killing of Jabez Gast seemed to have been forgotten, and it was too late for him now to remind the authorities, even if to do so would not have meant confessing his own part in their escape.

As if he had been reading her thoughts, Vivian said casually, 'And how is your sister? Housekeeping for Matt Farrell now, I hear.'

'Yes, that's right,' Rebecca said steadily, though her heart lurched a little. But he was looking at her with such an open, candid gaze that it was difficult to imagine that his question could be anything other than casual.

'Happy, is she? Gaining strength after her illness?'

'Yes, she is. It's a quiet life and that's what she needs after all her troubles. Matthew's household isn't large and she's no fool. She's making him a good house-keeper.'

'That's good. I'm glad.' He reached out and took a small cake. 'And your brother, Tom, he's doing well too, isn't he. Partner in a thriving little business – though I still think the co-operative idea is a foolish one. It will never last. Weavers are as greedy as the next man— '

'The next man being a master, I suppose,' Rebecca said swiftly, and he laughed.

'Ever the little firebrand! Well, we all have our faults, though I'm not sure that working hard to ensure success is necessarily a fault. And the weavers would be in pretty poor case if we didn't . . . But that's an old argument between us, Rebecca, and I didn't come here to argue.'

'Why did you come, then?' she asked bluntly, pouring a second cup of tea, and he laughed again.

'Such pretty manners! I came to see Francis about these new problems with the Union. It seems to me that if we manufacturers don't hang together, we're going to set ourselves up for more trouble – but you don't want to hear about that. Tell me about yourself. How are you these days?'

His tone had softened, become concerned, and she felt a grateful warmth in her cheeks and wondered yet again why it was that Vivian, of all people, seemed to feel more deeply for her in her loss than anyone else. Perhaps, as he had said, it was because he too had, effectively, lost sons by having had only daughters. But it couldn't be just that. Being disappointed by the birth of a daughter could in no way be likened to losing a child in a tragic accident.

Whatever the cause, she had no doubt that Vivian's concern was genuine, and she answered him as she could never have answered Francis.

'I'm better, I think. I still have moments – whole days sometimes – when everything seems dark and hopeless, as if I'm in some black place, a pit with sides too steep and slippery to climb out of. I suppose it's despair.' She spoke quietly, staring at the cup in her hand, her skin cold as she thought of those times. And in particular, the time when Francis had come upon her sitting alone when everyone else was at the fair, when he had seemed about to come so close and then abandoned her. 'I seem to have no one to turn to then,' she said. 'No one who can give me comfort.'

'You have me.' Vivian set down his own cup and saucer and reached across the little table. He touched her hand and she looked up, into eyes that were dark with concern. 'You can always come to me, Rebecca.'

They stared at each other and then Rebecca looked swiftly away. What was she doing, confiding like this – implying that she could not talk to her own husband? Especially when she knew that even now there was little love lost between Francis and Vivian. Quickly, she raised her cup to her lips and Vivian's hand dropped away.

'I'm sorry, I'm intruding. I didn't mean to do that, Rebecca.'

'I know. And you're not intruding.' She felt a sudden contrition. 'I value your friendship, Vivian. Perhaps I can't talk to Francis because his own sorrow is so great. It brings it all back, and I can't bear to see him suffer.' She thought for a moment. 'And perhaps he feels the same about me, so we don't talk to each other and . . .' And we drift further and further apart and there seems to be no way we will ever come together, she thought, and felt the sadness ache in her throat.

'Let's talk about the Union,' she said, brushing her hand across her eyes. 'You know I'm interested. And I don't mind an argument – especially if there's a chance of changing your mind!'

'You'll argue long and hard before you manage to

do that.' Vivian rose and walked to the fireplace. He looked down at her, unsmiling. 'I don't intend to countenance another strike, Rebecca, and neither do the other manufacturers. If there's any chance of that, we shall clamp down immediately. We've had the military in before; we'll bring them again. And this time at the beginning, not when the strike's dragged on for nearly five months. If they didn't learn their lesson last time, they will this. And I mean that, Rebecca – so tell your friends down in the cottages to take care.'

Rebecca looked up at him. She saw the dark implacability of his eyes. There was no doubt at all that Vivian meant what he said. And she felt suddenly afraid.

'It's trouble for us all,' Fred Holloway said as the Committee gathered, ready for the meeting. 'The men have had enough. There's some of 'em won't stand for no more from the masters, and they've got strong voices – they'll carry the rest of 'em, like as not.'

'After last time?' George Hodgett shook his head. 'I do'know. There's plenty remembers what a hungry belly's like, and it were long enough last time. The masters won't give in in a hurry, knowing they only got to stand firm.'

'Aye, it's a bad business.' Fred looked towards Bill Bucknell. 'What do you think, Bill?'

Bill shrugged. 'Could go either way, but I reckon they'll be for a strike again. They're angry and getting angrier the more they talks.' He looked at the men filling the open space before the platform. There was a low rumble of voices, a rumble as if the earth itself were joining in the debate, and the air was tense. 'I reckon we ought to get this meeting under way. There's some of 'em out to mek trouble and we don't want it here.'

The others agreed and Fred rose to his feet and lifted

his arms above his head, calling for silence. Slowly, as if reluctant to stop their own discussion, the men grew quiet. They lifted their faces towards the platform, and Bill was reminded of that other meeting two years or more ago, when the Great Strike had begun.

Five months of hardship and poverty had begun that day, ending with violence and the Dragoons being called in. Was it all to be done again?

It seemed that it was. The men were angry right from the start, and unwilling this time to consider negotiation.

'It didn't do us no good last time,' a big man in the front row declared. 'They wouldn't even listen. We had to go on strike in the end, so why not do it to start with?'

'That didn't do us much good neither, as I remembers it,' someone else shouted. 'What did we get out of that, eh? Half a year with no pay. Who says this is going to be any better?'

'Ah, we all knows who you are! One of them as has already taken Cooper's cut. Get back to your loom, we don't want none of you here. Go and earn your fourpence a yard, for that's what it'll be afore this lot's finished with us – that's if they pays us at all.'

The voices were growing more angry with every word. Bill could feel the fury rising from the crowd like a cloud of black, foul-smelling smoke. He stepped forward, hardly knowing what he could do but aware that something must be done to calm the men before worse happened. But the voices were taking over now, bawling from every part of the crowd, demanding action, refusing to listen to any kind of reason.

'Mates— ' he began, but his voice was drowned in the outcry. 'Mates, listen to me— '

'We done enough listening! We wants action now – real action. We got to show they masters just what weavers is made of.'

'It's a strike! A strike of common goods weavers. Let Cooper and his cronies see we ent going to be put upon no more.'

'Aye, that's it!' The cry was taken up generally. 'A strike! A strike!'

Fred made himself heard again at last, and his voice rang across the crowd. 'Very well, mates. If that's your vote, so it shall be. A strike of common goods weavers. But let it be orderly. No violence. No stoning like we had last— '

But once again, his words were lost, and indeed no man could have quelled the uproar that drowned his pleas for restraint. He lowered his arms and fell silent, watching helplessly with the rest of the Committee as the weavers turned and made their way back into the town. It was as if they had stopped thinking as individuals, as if they had become one being, a huge, uncontrollable animal that directed the mob with one purpose, a purpose that infiltrated every mind present.

And that purpose was revenge.

All the pent-up resentments and frustrations of years welled up this morning in the breasts of weavers who had never been anything but peaceable. All the impotent anger of men who had been forced to watch their families starve, seen their own children die from hunger and cold and disease, came together this morning in one great explosion of rage. All the despair, the grinding desolation of men who had seen no hope from the cradle to the grave, fused and became the spark that would set off the conflagration; the last rumble, somewhere deep under the earth's surface, that would bring about the eruption of the slumbering volcano.

Bill and the rest of the Committee looked at each other.

'Naught we can do now,' Fred said heavily. 'They won't be stopped. We'd better go along, see if we can keep the peace but— '

'Peace?' Bill said. 'There'll be precious little peace

354

left in Kidder after this morning's work. We lost 'em, Fred.'

'Aye,' Fred said, and his voice was low. 'I think we hev.'

They climbed down from the platform and turned to follow the crowd, and as they went Bill caught sight of a familiar figure approaching from a far corner. He stopped and waited.

'The meeting was soon over,' Matthew Farrell said, coming alongside. 'They're not willing to talk this time, I take it.'

'You teks it right. It's a strike again, and they're out for trouble too. God knows where they're heading, but they all seems to hev the same idea.' Bill looked gloomily after the great body of men still pouring away towards the town. 'Must be nigh on a thousand of 'em there. Half the weavers in Kidder. And they're not all common goods weavers, not by a long chalk.'

'They're heading for Cooper's factory,' Matthew said. 'What do you suppose they mean to do?'

'I do'know. I do'know what they means to do.' Bill began to walk faster. 'Here – we can cut through here, get there ahead of them. I tell you, Matt, this lot means trouble. I don't like it . . .' He began to walk faster, to run, and Matthew ran with him, feeling his anxiety. What Bill was worried about, he wasn't sure, but he recognised the mood of the crowd. He had seen it before, seen the fire in their eyes, heard the raggedness in their voices, smelt the stink of violence in their sweat.

He had seen it in Spain, in Italy, in America. In any country where passions might run high and angry. In any crowd that might at any moment erupt into frenzy.

In any lynching mob.

They arrived at the entrance to Cooper's factory only seconds before the leaders of the mob. And there was Will Cooper himself, brandishing an iron bar, stubborn and defiant. The crowd came to a halt before him, shouting and jeering, their words impossible to hear but their mood unmistakable.

'They're threatening him,' Matthew said. 'This is looking bad, Bill.'

'Aye, I know.' They stood watching for a few moments. 'But there's naught anyone can do about it now. They've got the bit between their teeth – there'll be no holding 'em.' He shivered suddenly. 'There's going to be bad work done over this, Matt. And it's been coming a long time – ever since the strike. That was never finished properly and there's been bad feeling hanging about ever since.'

'You're right.' Matthew thought of Vivian's triumph over the way the weavers had been forced back to work, with no concession made to their needs. Five months of hardship, and they had gained nothing. It was not to be expected that men who had watched their families suffer, their children die, would easily forget. It was not to be expected that they would forget at all. 'And by the way things are going now, it looks as if mob rule's going to have its way.'

The crowd were pressing close to Cooper now, their faces ugly with rage, and he was backing slowly away. He had lowered his iron bar and his stance, instead of defiant, was submissive. He held one hand before him as if to ward them off and an expression of fear came into his eyes. The expression of a cornered animal, seeing no way of escape.

'All right!' he yelled at last as they pressed him against his own factory wall. 'All right, there'll be no more common goods made in this factory – not till we get something sorted out, anyway. I don't want trouble – I just want to make a living— ' he was interrupted by jeers ' —for you as well as me,' he shouted but once again, his words were lost in the noise. 'Look, lads, you come back to work tomorrow and there'll be no more said, now I can't say fairer than that, can I?'

'You can't say fair at all, Will Cooper,' someone

bawled, but the crowd had lost interest in him now. A new murmur had started and was rapidly gaining ground. They were turning their attention to the black-legs.

'Tight Edwards – he were one of them!' A howl of fury went up as a knot of weavers gathered around a big, burly man who was standing near Matthew and Bill. Matthew recognised him as a local prizefighter, often to be seen knocking an opponent to the ground in a bare-fisted fight of a Saturday evening, and spending his winnings afterwards in the tavern. 'You took Cooper's money when the rest of us stood out – you went back to work for him when us was standing by the Union.' They had hold of him now, shaking him, pushing him from one to the other, punching him in the face and about the body. And Tight, who had battered so many men into unconsciousness and laughed at the sight, was now forced to fight for his life, lashing out with his great fists at anyone who came within range and yet unable to stem the tide of blows and kicks that rained upon him. Gradually, he was forced to his knees and could do no more than hold up his hands like a woman, cringing from his attackers, begging for mercy.

Matthew started forwards but Bill Bucknell caught his sleeve and held him back. 'You can't do no good. They won't listen to reason now and they'll just turn against you as well.' And Matthew knew he was right. He had seen it before. But he knew too that he could not stand by and do nothing. He could not watch help-lessly as Tight Edwards was thrust to the ground, beaten and kicked until he lay as still as any of his fist-fighting rivals.

Before he could intervene, however, the High Bailiff of Kidderminster himself was on the scene, elbowing his way through the crowd. Dr Custance was a surgeon and clearly angered by this demonstration of violence. He knelt beside the still figure but before he could

357

begin an examination he too was attacked, and Matthew leapt forwards, catching men by their collars and hurling them to one side as he thrust his way through the milling crowd.

'Leave him alone! Let him see to the man. Do you want him to die – and have his murder on your consciences?'

The men stopped and stared, and one or two of them laughed. An ugly, mirthless sound.

'Well, if it ent one of the masters! And what be you doing here – come to gloat, in all your fine clothes and all? Yah – get back to your grand house up on Mount Pleasant, and hev your dinner, never mind us poor weavers starving to death down here to mek your life easy.'

Matthew ignored them. He knelt beside the unconscious man and turned the battered head so that Custance could judge the damage. But again, they were prevented. A hail of stones hit them about their heads and shoulders, and Matthew felt a boot kick violently against his side, knocking him to the ground.

For a few moments, he was certain that his last hour had come. He lay breathless on the cobbles, his arms above his head in vain protection, aware that he was tightly surrounded. Kicks rained upon him; he had no idea where they might be coming from and each one was a fresh assault, a new area of pain, rolling him helplessly this way and that, causing his body to jerk and twist, forcing cries from his throat that he could not control.

Not that anyone could hear them. The voices of the crowd had turned into a deafening animal roar of pure menace, an almost tangible thing that surrounded him, eddied about him, forced its way into his ears and mouth, vibrating through his agonised limbs.

How long could any man live through such an assault? The smell of fresh blood was in his nostrils. His blood? Tight Edwards's? George Custance, the

High Bailiff's? It hardly seemed to matter any more.

'Here, let us through.' A new voice had joined the uproar and it came close. 'Stand back, there. You're doing murder. Let's get these men out.'

Matthew opened his eyes and saw a constable looming above him, with a soldier close behind. Some of the crowd resisted them and there was a further scuffle, but it was less convincing now and after a few minutes the mob fell back and the two men, assisted by Bill Bucknell, were able to get Matthew, Custance and the prize-fighter away. They were carried to a quiet corner and laid on the ground.

'This one's in a bad way – half dead, I reckon. The other two ent so bad.' Matthew felt hands running over his body, and knew that there must be bruises. 'No bones broken here, I reckon. Can you hear me, mister?'

Matthew opened his eyes. The constable was looking down at him, and he could see Bill's face wavering behind. Gradually, his sight cleared and steadied, the sky stopped reeling and his feeling of nausea receded a little.

'I can hear you,' he whispered at last. 'I'm all right, I think. Just a bit – knocked out.'

'That's all right, sir. You stop there a bit, till you feel better. Reckon we come along just in time. Dr Custance ent so bad, neither, but I can't say same for old Tight. Reckon he've seen his last prize-fight.'

'Dead?' Matthew asked, turning his head and looking with horror on the bloody pulp that was Tight Edwards' face.

'No, not dead, but halfway there. Mind, he might get over it but I don't reckon as he'll be fighting again. Or doing aught much,' the constable added. He looked over his shoulder at Bill Bucknell. 'You a friend of this gentleman's?'

'In a manner of speaking.' Bill gave Matthew a half

apologetic glance, as if to excuse his presumption. 'I'll get him home, shall I?'

'Best place to be.' The constable himself had received some rough treatment, Matthew noticed as he struggled to sit up. His jacket was torn, his collar bloodied and a black eye was beginning to swell. 'Me and the sergeant here'll see to Dr Custance and Tight.' He glanced back at the street, almost empty now, where the riot had taken place. 'Seems to hev quietened down now, any road. Don't reckon they'll be any more trouble, not now Will Cooper's give in.'

'Let's hope you're right,' Matthew said as Bill helped him to his feet. 'Let's all hope you're right.'

But as he made his slow way home, leaning on Bill Bucknell's shoulder, he felt a slow, cold doubt in his heart. The mood of the mob that morning had been too angry, too consumed with resentment and fury and the lust for revenge, to be satisfied with the beating-up of two or three men. It was death the mob was after now, and if they were quiet at the moment it could be no more than the lull before the storm.

And when the storm broke finally, there would be no holding it.

'But how did it happen? What were you doing there? Why did you need to follow them, when you must have known there would be trouble?' Rebecca moved about the room, her hands clasped together, her face white as she berated Matthew. She stopped and looked at him, lying there in his chair, his head bandaged, one arm and hand bound, a bruise discolouring his jaw. 'You could have been killed,' she said and her voice trembled.

'But I wasn't killed. And truly, I'm not much hurt. All this is no more than a bruise or two.' He shrugged and flinched at the movement. 'I shall be as right as rain in a day or two.'

'Well, see that you are. And don't go out looking

for trouble. Not every weaver knows that you helped them during the strike, and to them you're a "master" just because you look like one.' She frowned at him. 'You'll help no one by getting yourself hurt.' And then, 'Oh, Matthew, Matthew! Why don't you just *look after* yourself?' she said, pacing his drawing room while he lay in his chair watching her. Her hands beat together, and she hardly knew why she was feeling so agitated. Except that the shock of dismay and fear she had felt when she heard that he had been hurt, had still not receded. It caught her again, wrenching at her heart, twisting her stomach with dread.

'Why don't you take more care? Going to these meetings when you know the weavers are in an angry mood, interfering when that horrible Tight Edwards is in trouble— '

'How do you know he's horrible?' Matthew interrupted. 'He's a prizefighter, I know, but he may be the gentlest of creatures at home, kind to his wife, loving with his children— '

Rebecca threw him a withering glance. 'Tight Edwards, kind to his wife? *Loving* to his children? Matthew, you forget that I grew up in the streets where Tight Edwards grew up. I knew him when he was a boy, and he was horrible then – a blustering bully, always ready to pick a fight, and always making sure he won. And how did he make sure? By picking someone smaller and weaker than himself, that's how. And that's how he managed to grow bigger and stronger than the other boys too. He robbed them of their bait, he took the few pennies they had and he fought them for anything he couldn't steal from them. And you risked your life to help *him*.' Suddenly she was on her knees beside him, her hands gripping his. 'Matthew, promise me you'll do no such thing ever again. Promise me!'

She raised her face to his, and saw the widening of his pupils as he stared back at her. For a long moment, they remained quite still, gazing at each other. Rebecca felt his fingers curl around hers, warm and strong, slightly rough against her own tender skin. The muscles of his thighs tensed under her arms and she was suddenly aware of the power of him, the sheer physical strength. But more than that, she was conscious of a different sort of power that emanated from him – that crackled between them. A power of personality, of emotion that flowed from one to the other, a distinct and unobstructed channel of communication that needed no words, nor even a touch to set it in motion.

'*Matthew* . . .' she whispered, and tried to draw away her hands, but they would not move.

Matthew stared down into her eyes. She felt her heart tremble in its beating, felt the quiver of her pulse. It was suddenly difficult to breathe, and her face felt hot, as though she stood too close to a blazing fire. With an effort, she closed her eyes, and felt him disengage one of his hands and lift it slowly to stroke her hair back from her brow.

'Rebecca . . .' he murmured huskily, and she turned her face against his hand and felt her lips part. 'Oh, my God . . . Rebecca . . .'

'Matthew – please . . .' But the words were no more than a breath of sound, so soft that she was never sure whether she actually uttered them. And before she could say more, his lips were touching hers, brushing her mouth with the delicacy of a butterfly's wing, his tongue no more than a flicker of sensation against her softness. His hand slipped round to the back of her head, holding her still, while the other, still holding her hands, stretched the length of his fingers against her wrist. She turned her palm and twined her fingers with his, seeking his lips again as he withdrew slightly, aching for the sensation she had so briefly experienced.

'Matthew . . .'

But he had drawn away, and Rebecca opened her eyes in question. His hand was at his own head now, shielding his face from her gaze, and she tried to draw it down, needing to see his expression. 'Matthew, what is it? What's happening?'

For a few moments, he did not speak. When at last he did, his voice was rough, almost angry.

'Don't you know, Rebecca? Don't you understand? Are you telling me you've never understood?'

She shrank from the tone of his voice. 'Matthew, no, I don't understand. Tell me . . .' She looked at the hand that still held hers, grasping it almost cruelly, as if he had forgotten what lay curled in his palm. 'Matthew, you're hurting me.'

He looked down then, staring at their clasped hands as if he had never seen them before. Then he unfolded his fingers and lifted her hand to his lips, touching them gently.

'They're all crushed. Why didn't you tell me before?'

'I didn't notice.' She wanted to keep her hand at his lips, but he placed it on the arm of the chair. 'Matthew, tell me, please.'

'What is there to tell?' His voice was suddenly light, casual. 'You were anxious about me and you came to help, like the good friend you are. And I must be feeling a little weak and light-headed – perhaps the damage was more than I thought – and lost control of myself for a moment. For which I do most sincerely apologise.' He placed his hands under her elbows, urging her to rise. 'Rebecca, don't kneel there like that. It isn't *seemly*.' His mouth twitched as he spoke the word that had often been a joke between them. 'If one of the servants were to come in— '

She looked at him and then got slowly to her feet. With a little hesitation, she went to a chair nearby and sat down. But her eyes were still fixed on his face. There was more to it than that. Surely there was more to it than that.

'Matthew— '

'That's all it was,' he broke in, his voice rough again.

363

'There was nothing more than a momentary aberration. You understand that, Rebecca? You have to understand that.'

There was a note almost of pleading in his voice, and she battled with herself for a moment, longing to argue with him, to tell him that there *had* been more, he knew it and she knew it, and they ought to discover what it was. And then she heard Francis's voice in the hall, and the world rushed in upon her again.

Francis! She stared at Matthew with sudden shock in her eyes and saw him nod, grimly.

Francis. Francis, her husband, whom she loved. Whom, for just a few minutes, she had forgotten as completely as if he had never existed.

Francis, who for a few seconds she had betrayed.

'Oh . . . !' Rebecca whispered, and bent her head to her hands.

Matthew leaned forwards, and the roughness had left his voice now. It was intent, serious, emphatic. 'Rebecca, you mustn't blame yourself for this. We were both upset – such things happen sometimes. They mean nothing. Do you understand? You have nothing to reproach yourself with, nothing to feel unhappy about. You've done nothing wrong. *It meant nothing.* Only friendship. You understand that?' His eyes were on her, burning her skin, willing her to accept what he said. 'You understand, Rebecca.'

'Yes,' she whispered at last. 'I understand.'

'Friendship,' he insisted. 'Only friendship.'

'Yes,' she repeated slowly, 'only friendship.'

Chapter Seventeen

The quiet of the rest of the day lulled them all into the hope that the crisis was over and the weavers would return to work. After all, hadn't they got what they wanted? Will Cooper had promised to stop producing the cheap 'common goods' and go back to weaving real carpets, which could command a market and bring a better wage for his men. Blacklegs like Tight Edwards had been meted out some rough justice which should give others food for thought in the future. And the Union was strong again and perhaps could stand up to the masters now and force them to negotiate.

But there was still an undercurrent of resentment, a thread of anger that ran through the town. And Bill Bucknell, eating a hasty meal with Nell, was anxious to be out again and seeing what was to do.

'It's not going to end there,' he told her, wiping his plate with a hunk of bread. 'There's plenty of lads who see what happened today as a good day's work. Going for Will Cooper like that – they're saying we ought to hev done such things before. Saying we were too kind – we should hev taken the law into our own hands during the strike.'

'But the Committee allus said it ought to be peaceful,' Nell said.

'That's it. And that's the way we still feels about it. But a lot of the men don't see it like that no more – and who can blame 'em? They remembers their little 'uns that took sick and died, like our little Sam, and they remembers that they still never got that tuppence a yard made up. I reckon there'll be trouble tonight, Nell, and I'd better be out there to do what I can to stop it getting too bad.'

'Well, you tek care.' Her eyes were anxious as he rose from the table. 'I wish you wouldn't go, Bill.'

'I got to. You knows that.' He hesitated, then came across and gave her a clumsy kiss. 'You don't hev to worry about me, Nell. I can look after my skin all right. Ent no one going to hurt Bill Bucknell.'

He gave her a grin and pulled open the rickety door. And Nell sat in her chair and listened as his footsteps clattered outside on the 'kidneys' and then faded. The street seemed suddenly quiet, as if it were completely empty.

She got up and went to look outside. There was no one there. The women who would sit at their doorways on a fine summer's evening were not there. The children who would be playing in the gutters had disappeared. The men who would cluster around the alehouse door on the corner were somewhere else.

I might be the only person left in the whole world, she thought with a sudden feeling of dread. And wished that the night were over. Or never begun.

The High Street was not quiet. All evening, people had been gathering there. First a few knots of weavers who grouped in corners, muttering to each other in low voices. Then larger groups, who had met elsewhere and came with heavy tread and louder tones. Gradually, the square filled, the separate knots came together and the crowd grew bigger and more threatening. The air was heavy with the lingering heat of the August day, and the ominous feeling of thunder in the air.

But the thunder that threatened tonight was not thunder from the skies. It emanated from the shifting mob, from the men who moved from one group to another, talking in rapid voices, making urgent gestures. It emanated from the collective murmurs of the crowd, a low, pulsing hum that filled the air and seemed to rise from all around, from the earth, from the walls, from the gathering dusk itself. It emanated from the sense that hundreds of individual minds had fused together in one collective consciousness, one single mind with one single purpose. And the purpose was menace.

Bill Bucknell came to the edge of the square and stood still for a moment, watching. He felt the threat in the air, sensed the uneasy, shifting mood of the crowd, saw the darkness of their purpose like a cloud hanging over the town. He felt the cold dread creep over his skin like a film of ice, and his heart shrank.

'There'll be ill work done this night,' a voice said in his ear, and he turned to find Fred Holloway beside him.

'Aye. Just what I was thinking.' They stood silent for a moment, watching the growing throng, listening to the rumble of voices that grew as more and more men poured into the square. 'And ent naught we can do to stop it now, Fred.'

Fred shook his head slowly. 'No. The time's past for that. They'll not listen to anyone now who don't tell 'em what they want to hear.' Bill caught his sideways glance. 'You and me'd be best out of this, Bill.'

'You don't think they'd go for us? Committee men?'

'Who's to say? A mob like this ent like men in their senses. They're like to go mad tonight and anyone who don't go mad with 'em is going to be a target. I don't see George Hodgett here, nor Tom Potter nor Will Charlton neither.'

Bill looked around. It would have been impossible to say who was here and who was not. The crowd filled the square now, a heaving, thrusting, faceless mass of humanity. George, Tom and Will could be amongst them, could be only yards away and never seen, never heard. They could be part of this seething mob, urging them on or imploring them to stop, and never be known. Fred was right – the Committee was powerless in this situation. And maybe he was right, too, to say that this was no place for them. They would be better off away from it.

'But we don't hev no choice now,' Bill said. 'Look around you, Fred. There ent no way out.'

The narrow streets that fed into the High Street and the square were choked with men, all eager to be in the thick of whatever was going to happen, all adding their own discontent to the ever-increasing roar of voices. And now they were no longer satisfied with complaining. They were beginning to act.

Close to Bill, a man bent and picked up a stone. He hurled it at a gas-lamp and scored a hit. The glass of the lamp smashed, and the light went out.

A cheer went up from all those who had seen it happen, and the next moment they were all doing it. Stones flew through the air and many of them hit their targets. Gas-lamps went out, lamps were smashed, lamp-posts torn up. Windows in the shops and hotels around the square were broken, at first accidentally by stones which had missed their mark, and then simply because they were there and there were no more lamps to smash. The mob cheered at each fresh sound of breaking glass, they urged each other on and soon they were moving out of the square, squeezing themselves into the twisting streets that led away from the centre of the town, shoving and pushing on their way to the home of William Cooper.

''Twas him as started it all,' Bill heard them declare as they struggled along. 'Let's give him what for. He thought he'd got away with it easy this morning, that he did. We'll show him! We'll show him weavers ent to be trifled with.'

'We'll show 'em all,' others replied. 'All the masters – Brinton, Broom, the whole damned lot of 'em. We'll rip 'em apart, they and their looms, and then where'll they be? Eh? Tell us that!'

Where will any of us be, Bill thought, as a cheer went up that seemed fit to lift every roof in Kidderminster. He looked at Fred and they both shook their heads. There was nothing they could do. And they couldn't even get out of the mob now, for there was no way clear. They were carried along, willy-nilly, as if they were autumn leaves under the sweeper's brush.

When they came within sight of Cooper's house the mob was already there, wrenching up the 'kidney' stones from the pavement and hurling them at the windows. Bill saw a scared face appear at a window and then vanish quickly as others saw it too and set up a howl before concentrating all their energies at the window where it had been seen. A hail of stones smashed against walls and windows, the glass was smashed and missiles flew through the gaping holes. Bill imagined the manufacturer and his family cowering inside, afraid to move yet afraid to stay, wondering where they could escape from the maddened horde outside. He felt no sympathy for them, but he knew that the attack, justified though it might seem to the weavers who had been goaded beyond endurance, could do no good in the end. If only there were some way to stop them, some way to make them see sense . . .

But there was none. And he could only watch helplessly as the hours passed in a seemingly endless procession of more rioting, more damage, more frenzied fighting, abuse and even looting.

An ill night's work indeed, he thought.

The messenger came to Unicorn Street just before midnight.

Rebecca was just preparing for bed. All evening, she and Francis had sat listening anxiously to the commotion that floated up from the town below. Several times, Francis had made as if to go and see what was happening, but each time she had stopped him, begging him not to go, convincing him that there was nothing

369

he could do. 'You would only put yourself in danger,' she said. 'They're beyond reason now, they'd turn on you and tear you to pieces like savages. Don't go, Francis, please.'

And he had given way and stayed with her, unable to concentrate on the game of cribbage she suggested or the new designs they might work on, unable to think of anything but what might be happening in the town.

'There have never been such riots before,' he said. 'Even in the strike . . .'

And she had nodded and said she knew. But there was nothing they could do about it now. Nothing.

Several times, he had suggested she should go to bed, but Rebecca had refused. 'I would never be able to sleep. The noise . . . And I'd be afraid of you slipping out.' But at last she had agreed to go, on his promise that he would stay in the house. And then, just as she began to undress, she heard the sound of the door knocker being pounded and Francis's voice at the door.

Hastily, Rebecca fastened the buttons she had begun to undo, and ran to the top of the stairs. She leaned over, looking down into the hall below, and saw Francis looking up at her.

'What is it? They don't want you to go? Please, Francis, you promised— ' A new idea came into her head and she found her hand at her throat. 'It – it isn't Matthew?'

'No, nothing to do with Matthew.' There was a queer expression on his face. 'It's nothing to do with the weavers. It's Maria.'

'*Maria?*'

'Yes. Her time's come, and there are difficulties.' He glanced again at the messenger, and Rebecca recognised him now as one of Vivian's footmen. 'They want you to go. Maria's asking for you, it seems. I've told him you're just going to bed, you can't possibly— '

'But of course I can go!' Rebecca flew into the bedroom, came out again with a cloak. 'Is there anything I need to take?'

'I can't imagine Vivian and Maria lacking anything, can you?' Francis remarked with a flicker of humour. He was putting on his boots as he spoke. 'I'll come with you. There's no knowing who might be about tonight.'

Rebecca waited impatiently and at last they set off, stepping briskly out towards Vivian's house on Mount Pleasant. The dull roar of rioting rose towards them from the town and Rebecca glanced uneasily around and drew her cloak closer about her. The night was warm, yet she shivered and Francis put his arm around her.

'Are you sure you want to go, my love? You're not too tired?'

'Of course not. And if Maria's asking for me— '

'Yes. Though I hadn't realised you and she were such good friends.'

'Neither had I.' It hadn't struck Rebecca until that moment, how strange it was that Maria should ask for her. For the older woman had rarely missed an opportunity to emphasise the differences between them. Rebecca's background, her upbringing, her years spent working as a servant, the fact that her first child had been conceived out of wedlock – all these were darts in Maria's quiver and used regularly to make Rebecca feel uncomfortable, and unwelcome in her home. And Maria had never joined Rebecca's wives' association, nor shown any interest at all in her ideals. Yes – it was strange that Maria should be asking for her now.

And yet . . . there had been that moment of accord, when Rebecca and Francis had first come back to Kidderminster. That moment in Maria's nursery when they had looked down at the sleeping children together and Rebecca had seen a softer side of Maria, a motherliness that was seldom apparent. They had been close

371

then, friends for a few moments. In that brief space of time, she had caught a glimpse of something that could exist between them – perhaps already did, on some deep, unexpressed level.

They were at the house now and admitted by a housemaid who looked tired – as well she might, Rebecca thought, with her knowledge of what a housemaid's life was like. The poor girl had without doubt been up since six that morning and had been kept on the run ever since. Her feet probably ached and her back too, and all she wanted was her bed. And little chance of getting it this night, Rebecca thought, as she gave the maid a sympathetic smile.

The library door opened and Vivian appeared. He came towards them, his face grim.

'Vivian! How is she?' Rebecca went quickly towards him but he gave her scarcely a glance. He addressed himself to Francis.

'This is a bad business, Frank— '

'You mean she's in danger? The child— '

Vivian gave him a blank stare, as if he hardly knew what Francis was talking about. Then he shook his head impatiently.

'Not Maria! This rioting in the town – you know they've gone completely mad, rampaging around the streets and totally out of control? I've advised the magistrates to send for the military, but you know what they are, afraid to make any decision, hoping it will all die down. Die down!' He spat the words contemptuously. 'It'll die down when they die, and not before. God knows how we bred such a rabble of malcontents in Kidderminster. We gave way to them, made life too easy, that's what it is, and now— '

'*Vivian!*' Rebecca was at his side, her face pale with anger. 'Vivian, I've been called here to see your wife, not discuss the troubles of the carpet manufacturers. Please tell me how she is and where she is, so that I may go to her.'

Vivian looked startled for a moment. Then he bowed and held out his arm as if he were taking her in to supper.

'But of course. I apologise for keeping you standing. She's up in the master bedroom, of course, where one would expect my son to be born. No— ' in response to her quick glance ' —he isn't here yet, but he's certainly on his way. And she'll be glad to see you, I know, she's been calling for you this past hour.'

They reached the top of the stairs and he released her arm.

'This is as far as I go. It's no place for a man, in there.' He cocked his head and listened as a low moan issued from within the bedroom, rising to a howl of pain. 'Matters seem to be progressing well enough,' he remarked, 'though she made a deal more noise with the last one. Still, there's time yet . . .' He gave Rebecca a satisfied smile and turned to clatter back down the stairs.

Rebecca stood quite still in front of the door. Then she took a deep breath, turned the handle and went in.

By midnight, the situation in the town had gone beyond any man's control.

Rioters rampaged through the narrow streets, breaking windows, smashing lamps, kicking in doors. They roamed from one manufacturer's house to another, hardly caring which it was as they threw stones and refuse and even tried to start fires. The constables were helpless against such savage violence, and when Dr Custance tried to talk them into calm and the Town Crier read the Riot Act to the mob, they were attacked, stoned and forced to flee for their lives.

Nothing like it had ever been seen in Kidderminster before. Fred Holloway and Bill Bucknell, together with the rest of the Committee, met in a deserted warehouse and debated what to do. But they could come to no conclusion. There was no reasoning with men in this mood. It could only be hoped that the night would pass without murder itself being done.

'Billy Boycott's talking of getting together an armed band, to get them off the streets,' George Hodgett said.

'Arms? You mean guns?'

'And swords and things, anything, I suppose. That's what it's come to, see. It'll be Peterloo all over again, see if it ent.'

Bill shook his head. 'That was different. A peaceful demonstration. There ent nothing peaceful about this lot.' He ducked his head as they heard another crash of breaking glass. 'I'm surprised there's a window left in Kidder to smash.'

'Something's going to hev to be done,' Fred Holloway said, and they looked sombrely at each other. 'I reckon Boycott's right. They got to be stopped somehow.'

'But guns!' Bill said. 'That's murder.'

'If they kills anyone, but who's to say they will? And it might be the only way to stop worse happening in the end. Don't you reckon there's going to be murder done anyway, way it's going?' They listened again to the uproar. 'Know anyone who's got weapons, Bill?'

'You mean you want *us* to go in on Boycott's side? With the magistrates?'

'This ent a strike,' Fred pointed out. 'This ent the Union. And we don't want to get tarred with this brush, Bill. All right, so they ent allus played fair with us – but this ent no time to be settling old scores. We got to do summat about this now, and we has to keep the Union's name sweet or we'll find ourselves outlawed again and then we won't be able to do *nothing*. So – do you know anyone who's got weapons and might be ready to come and use 'em?'

Bill hesitated. There might have been a few in Kidderminster with firing pieces, pistols or muskets perhaps left over from one of the wars. But would they be ready to come out now and use them to threaten their fellows? Even in the cause of law and order?

He thought suddenly of the man he had walked and talked and stood with only that morning. The man who had helped in their struggle before and who wasn't afraid of a fight.

'There's Matt Farrell,' he said reluctantly. 'I heard he's got pistols, brought back from Americky. But he was pretty knocked about this morning, I don't know if— '

'Go and ask him,' Fred said, and then as Bill hesitated again, added impatiently, 'Bill, if we don't do summat they're going to end by firing the whole town. This ent our weavers doing this – this is men who just likes a fight, men who've got nothing to do but cause trouble. I seen 'em in the crowd, leading 'em on – John Crowe, Sim Treadwell and their cronies. They never seen the inside of a loomshop in their lives, wouldn't know what to do with a bobbin if it hit them on the nose. They just likes trouble, and if they ent been in the shops looting yet, they soon will be. They're no friends to us, Bill, and we got to stop 'em. *Now* will you go and fetch Matt Farrell and his pistols?'

Bill stared at him, then turned and ran. He too had seen Crowe and Treadwell and his like, but it hadn't dawned on him that they were leading the riot, he had simply thought that they were joining in. Now he saw the truth of Fred's words. Crowe, Treadwell and the others were known troublemakers, always out to cause aggravation. Seeing the weavers holding their meeting, sensing the anger and despair, they had been quick to take advantage. A meeting could easily be turned into a riot, a riot into a rampage. And shops could be looted of so many things: food, clothes, whatever you wanted. To see you through the winter. To be sold, slowly so as not to rouse suspicion, to bring in money to take you to the alehouse . . .

Fred was right. They had to be stopped. The weavers, maddened by their own despair, must be rescued from such evil intent.

Bill turned and ran, along the streets that led from the town centre, along the alleyways that led to the outskirts of Kidderminster, along the pathways that would take him to Matthew Farrell's house on its little hill, overlooking the town.

'Rebecca . . . I'm so glad you've come . . .'

Maria's voice was less than the faint stirring of the breeze on an almost still summer's afternoon. She lay, white-faced, almost bloodless, in the wide bed, her body misshapen under the sheets that covered her. The room was hot and airless, smelling of sweat and sickness and something sharper that Rebecca recognised as fear. And there was something else too; a smell that she knew instantly she had encountered before, in the tiny hovel where her father had died, in the kitchen at Pagnel House where her mother had taken her last wavering breath, in the squalid attic where Bessie had held her hand and drifted away beyond her reach.

The smell of death.

Rebecca dropped her cloak and hurried to the bedside. Maria's hand lay limp upon the coverlet and she took it in both of hers, cradling it between her palms, willing her own strength into the exhausted frame. She looked down with pity and concern at Maria's weary face and then met the eyes of the midwife, sitting at the other side of the bed.

'How long has she been like this?'

The woman shrugged. 'Since dinner-time, madam. Eight hours, nine. It started well enough, then everything seemed to stop, it's like she was blocked somehow.'

'But this is her seventh child! It ought to be easier— '
She remembered William's birth and how difficult that

had been. And Maria was older, already worn out from child-bearing. Did she have sufficient strength to carry her through this? She looked down again at the almost transparent skin, the closed, blue eyelids, and felt a tremor of fear.

Quickly, she dropped to her knees beside the bed.

'Maria! Maria, can you hear me? It's Rebecca. They said you wanted me – they said you were asking for me . . .'

'Rebecca – yes.' Maria's head turned on the pillow. Her hair was loose, tangled and matted with sweat, and the pillow showed damp, greasy marks from her constant tossing. 'I asked them to bring you . . .' There was a faint strength in the movement of the fingers held so closely in Rebecca's hands. 'You're the only one . . . the only one who understands. The others . . . they left me here . . . alone . . . Jane and Sarah, they won't come near me, they're afraid . . .' A long pause, as if she were gathering strength, and then with an effort, a slightly stronger voice. 'I'm going to die, Rebecca . . .'

'No!' Rebecca was surprised by the strength of her rebuttal. 'No, Maria, you're not going to die. We all think that when we have a baby. It's bad now, but it'll soon be over and you'll have your— ' She wanted to say 'son', for she knew that this was what Maria wanted, what she needed to absolve her from further misery such as this. But how could she promise such a thing, even in this extremity? 'Your new baby,' she amended. 'And you'll love it just as much as you love the others, you know that's true.'

A shadow of a smile flickered on Maria's white lips, but before she could say more her body jerked and twisted on the bed, her hand gripping Rebecca's fingers with a strength that it seemed impossible she should possess. Her face distorted and a scream broke from her throat; a hoarse, guttural scream that rose to a high, piercing agony that seemed to drive a sword

377

through Rebecca's eardrums. The pain racked her for a minute, two minutes, three, an eternity . . . and then she relaxed, her body sagged again on the bed and she lay breathless, panting, and moaning softly.

Rebecca stared with terrified eyes at the midwife. This was surely more than the usual pangs of labour? And Maria had been enduring this agony for eight, nine hours? No wonder she thought herself dying.

'Can't we do anything for her?' she asked in a low tone. 'A drink – something to give her strength. There must be something— '

The woman shook her head. 'She can hev a drink, drink all she likes, but there's naught else. You knows yourself, missis, there's naught can help a woman in labour, she just got to go through it. Give her summat to ease the pain and it teks away the strength as well. She needs the pain to get the babby born, and that's the curse we all has laid on us.' She reached for a glass of water and held it to Maria's lips. 'There you are, madam, tek a sip of that afore the next pain comes and— '

But the water was dashed from her hand as Maria arched her back in another wave of agony, and this time it seemed even worse than the one before. Rebecca clutched her hands, not even noticing the grip of the fingers on hers, concerned only for the distress of the woman who had so often tried to humiliate her. And those humiliations seemed now so unimportant, so petty.

And then there was no more time to think. The pains were coming fast now, one hard on the heels of the other so that for Maria it must seem that there was no respite at all, not even the tiniest space of time in which to gather her failing strength. Rebecca and the midwife worked with her, holding her hands, letting her brace her feet against their arms, feeling her toes curl and pinch their skin as the agony swept over her.

They exhorted and encouraged her, desperately afraid
that her strength would not hold out, desperately afraid
that she would give up and die before the baby could
be born. It was so near, so close, and yet that final
thrust seemed unable to come. As the midwife said, it
was as though she were blocked. As though the child
were too large, or twisted in some way, lying across
her body so that it could not be born, could never
escape.

'What is it?' Rebecca panted. 'Why won't it come?
What's wrong?'

The midwife lifted the sheet and examined the
writhing body as best she could, then looked grave.

'It's as I thought, missis. The babe's in breech position. Feet first. I thought so when I felt her early on,
but often as not they moves round and gets in the right
position. But this one . . .' She shook her head. 'I wish
I'd tried to move it meself, but it's dangerous, and now
it's too late.'

'Too late!' Rebecca stared at her. 'But – it's *got* to
be born!'

'Aye, it'll be born, in the end.' But the midwife's
tone was ominous, and she said no more. Nor was
there any need.

Rebecca looked down at the figure on the bed. Maria
looked scarcely human now, her swollen body no more
than a convulsing mass of torn, aching flesh. It seemed
impossible that she could survive this ordeal, and
Rebecca could only hope that it might soon be over,
her pains vanquished by the death that must come as
a saviour. The screams had died away to a constant
keening sound that was almost worse, a thin, heart-
rending wail from a throat too weak to utter more, a
body that was close to its final fading.

'Maria,' she whispered, kneeling by the bed so that
her mouth was close to the sweating face. 'Maria, listen
to me. It's Rebecca here. Maria, be brave for just a

379

little longer. Your baby's nearly here. It can't be much longer. Just hold on, for just a little while. For me. For Rebecca. Please.'

Maria turned her head. There seemed to be a brief lull in the pains, and she opened her eyes, eyes that were dull yet held a spark of recognition. She looked into Rebecca's eyes and, amazingly, smiled a little.

'Rebecca,' she murmured.

'Yes. You asked me to come.'

'I wanted you here . . .' The voice was faint but lucid, and Rebecca felt a stirring of hope. 'You understand . . . you're not frightened . . .'

Not frightened! Rebecca thought wryly, but she kept her smile on her face and the reassurance in her voice as she said quietly, 'There's nothing to be afraid of, Maria.'

'You . . .' The words were barely audible. 'You seem to have it all, Rebecca . . . I was jealous of you, always . . .'

'Jealous? Of me? But— '

'I hated you because you had all the things I wanted . . .'

'But— ' Rebecca thought of the hardships of her life. She shook her head, but Maria was speaking again, her words no more than a stirring of the foetid air of the bedroom.

'Every time I looked at you and Francis, I thought . . . she has it all. She has love . . . and the sons Vivian wants as well. But mostly . . . love . . .'

Rebecca looked into her eyes then, eyes that were clouding over with pain and exhaustion and the closeness of death. And she felt a sudden humbling of her heart. For Maria, with all her apparent pettiness, all her constant reminders of Rebecca's background, had seen the truth and understood it, and her behaviour had come from the gnawing knowledge that she would never have what Rebecca might easily have come to take for granted.

Love. Her own love for Francis, and his love for her. A love that might seem to have strayed from its path, lost itself in misunderstandings and preoccupations, but which must win in the end, for surely nothing could kill or bury it for long.

The kind of love Maria had never known.

'Maria . . .' she whispered, and held the limp, cold hand more firmly in her own.

And then, as she watched, the swollen body twisted once more. Maria tore her hand from Rebecca's grasp and flung her arms up, as if begging for mercy. A final scream tore raggedly from her throat, her whole body arched and it took the combined strength of Rebecca and the midwife to hold her on the bed.

'I can't!' Maria screamed. 'I can't – I can't – I can't . . .'

And then there was a rush of blood and flesh and water, and all was over.

Matthew paced his drawing room. His head ached, his arm throbbed, but he scarcely noticed them. His whole attention was focused on what was happening outside his house, down in the town.

If only there were something he could do. He was beset by the idea that something vital was happening tonight, something that affected his future as much as that of any of the weavers who had lost all sense and reason and were rampaging through the streets, not caring what damage they did, what pain they caused.

Bessie came in and gave him an anxious glance. She had refused to allow anyone else to look after him, sending the maid back to the kitchen when she found her bringing him brandy, and tending him herself. Ever since he had come home with his bruised head and bandaged arm, she had fussed about him like a mother, until Matthew had protested and finally sent her out of the room.

'I tell you I'm all right, and will mend a lot faster if

I'm left alone. Now please – I'm not accustomed to being pampered. Go and look after yourself instead. You're looking pale.'

'It's worrying over you,' Bessie declared. 'More trouble than a cartload of monkeys, you are. I don't want you sneaking off back to town the minute my back's turned.'

Matthew sighed. 'Very well, I promise not to go out without asking your express permission . . . *Now* will you go away?'

Bessie grinned and went to the door. 'All right. But if I hear this door open I'll be back to fetch you in again. And if anyone comes, I'll be opening it – not that dozy Hester. She'd let you do anything you liked, left to herself.'

Well, I *am* the master, Matthew thought as she disappeared. Or at least, I always thought so until Bessie arrived. But he smiled to himself, enjoying the repartee that he and Bessie indulged in. He guessed that there hadn't been much fun or humour in her life since she'd left Kidderminster. And not a lot before. Yet Rebecca had told him that her sister had been full of fun as a young girl, always laughing and giggling with her friend Nell Foster. And he had set himself a kind of challenge, to bring the fun back into Bessie's life, rekindle the merriment in those once-bold eyes.

A sudden hammering on the front door brought him wheeling, and he was in the hall almost before Bessie, her face grim, had the door opened. He stared in astonishment as Bill Bucknell tumbled in, and drew him quickly into the drawing room, barely noticing that Bessie followed them.

'What is it? What's happening?'

Quickly, almost incoherently, Bill told him what was going on, what was required. Matthew drew back, staring at him.

'*Guns*? They're calling for arms – the magistrates? Are you sure?'

'Billy Boycott himself's put the word out.'

'And the Committee are with them in this?'

Bill shook his head. 'I don't know about the Committee – it was just Fred Holloway and me. But we reckon summat's got to be done, to stop 'em before things gets any worse. It ent just the weavers, you see.' He explained about Crowe and Treadwell and their cronies. 'If you and a few others we know we can trust could just sort of *frighten* 'em into going home quiet like . . . Well, there don't seem to be nothing else to do, see.'

Matthew turned away, thinking deeply. He could see the line of Bill's reasoning. Better a few shots fired over the heads of the crowd by a man who wished them well, than a massacre such as had happened in Manchester a few years ago by the military. And there was no doubt that the military would be called in. They'd been here before, after all, towards the end of the Great Strike. And if they came now they would show little mercy to men who had rioted through the streets and brought terror to the whole of Kidderminster.

But Bessie's thoughts were concerned only with her master.

'You're never asking Mr Farrell to go out with a gun and start shooting people, Bill Bucknell! Why, that's nothing but madness. Look at him – do he look fit to go out shooting? And suppose summat happens to him – what are *you* going to do about it?' She turned to Matthew. 'You ent going. You ent fit to go.'

Matthew glanced absently at her. She went close to him and laid her hand on his arm, and he removed it, gently but firmly, as if she were a kitten climbing on his clothes. He turned his head to Bill.

'I'll come. Now, stop fussing, Bess – this is men's work and nothing to do with women. Fetch my coat.'

'But sir – Mr Farrell— '

'*Bess!*' he shouted, turning on her with such speed

that she staggered back in shock, 'For God's sake, woman, do as you're told for once, will you? Stop treating me like a naughty boy and remember just who and what you are – and *fetch my coat!*'

Bess stared at him, her mouth open. Then her eyes reddened with tears and she turned abruptly and pushed her way past Bill Bucknell and out of the room. Matthew watched her go but his eyes were blank, as if his mind was far away. He turned back to Bill, speaking rapidly.

'I'll fetch my pistols. Wait here a moment.'

Within five minutes, he was ready. Quickly, he checked the ammunition. He glanced briefly at Bessie, who was trying valiantly to control her tears, and patted her shoulder.

'Now don't worry, Bess. I'll be back before you know I've gone, and I don't suppose I'll have fired a shot. You just stay here and get something ready for us to eat when we come back – quelling riots is hard work!' He grinned, but Bessie could give him no answering smile, and a moment later he and Bill were outside, setting off through the darkened streets.

'All the same, I hope this is a good idea,' he murmured to Bill. 'Where are Boycott's men meeting?'

'Down by the Lion, where the coaches comes in.' Bill ducked down through an alleyway little wider than his own shoulders, a crack between two rows of houses. 'This is a quick way through, and none to see us.' From somewhere near at hand, they could hear the roar of the rioters as they stormed through the streets, now totally uncontrolled, led by shouts of vengeance that came from clearly drunken throats. Matthew shivered. There was something about this that was worse than any mob he had ever encountered, whether in Spain, Italy or the wilds of the American frontier. Somehow, in those countries, it seemed more natural – frightening still, but to be expected. Here, in England, in tiny, industrial Kidderminster . . .

384

It was out of place. Alien. And therefore all the more terrifying.

They came out of the alleyways into the square by the Lion, at the top of the High Street. The gas lamps had all been smashed, and the only light was that of the moon. It shone down with a serenity that seemed wrong on this tumultuous night. And it shone upon a thousand or more men, a heaving mass of bodies that struggled and fought and caroused, men who had lost all reason, who hardly knew why or who they fought any more, who would go on to the death unless stopped and stopped soon.

It was right that arms should be used, Matthew conceded, staring at the ghostly throng. It was the only solution.

He followed Bill to the small group that were gathering under the eye of Billy Boycott, the magistrate, and they stood silent while he gave them hasty orders.

'No one's to be shot, understand that. Fire over their heads and try to shock them into some sort of sense. We've got to get them off the streets and into their homes – maybe in the morning they'll see reason. There'll be enough to do then, tidying this lot up. There's been a deal of damage done this night.'

The men nodded, and Boycott climbed up to a hastily erected platform and began to yell for silence. At first, his words went unheard, then the men nearest turned to listen and jeer, and before long he had the attention of most of the men in the square.

'Listen to me!' he bawled, his strong voice carrying on the night air. 'Listen and listen well. You've done enough damage tonight. I want you to go home and not come out until morning – and then come peacefully. And mark this! I'm not asking you – I'm telling you. Go home now and stay there. Otherwise the military will be here and they'll have voices that speak louder than mine.'

There was a brief silence. Then a jeer rose out of the

crowd, and the cry was taken up and quickly spread.

'Go and boil your head, Billy Boycott! We needs it for a suet pudding.'

Boycott stood for a moment watching as the rioters began to stamp and yell. A 'kidney' stone, dragged up from the road, flew through the air, narrowly missing his ear, and smashed the last unbroken window in the hotel behind him. And as if it were a signal, was quickly followed by others.

Boycott dropped quickly from the platform and nodded to his band of volunteers.

'All right, lads. Fire.'

Matthew glanced around. The faces of the men with him were hard and grim. He saw them lift their guns and point them towards the sky.

He raised his pistols high and fired. The salvo seemed to rock the heavens. The crowd was silenced momentarily, and then a howl of fury rose and filled the night.

Bessie heard the first shots as she ran into the square, shoving her way between the men who milled about there. They barely glanced at her, merely pushing back with an oath or two, their attention fixed on the men who stood around the makeshift platform, their guns still smoking from that first volley.

Her heart sickened as she caught sight of Matthew. A hundred thoughts crowded into her mind, a hundred pictures . . . Matthew, killing someone, Matthew dragged off to prison, flung into the squalor of the town gaol . . . Matthew, hanged outside the prison wall for everyone to see . . . Scarcely aware of what she did, she thrust through the crowd, only one aim in her mind – to prevent the catastrophe that would rob her of the only employer who had ever treated her like a human being.

Only a few men stood now between her and Matthew. Panting, breathless, her face streaming with tears, she struggled to squeeze her way past their unyielding bodies. She saw him look almost incredulously at his pistols, as if he could not believe that he was here in Kidderminster, firing above the heads of a crowd, a crowd whose aims he shared, whose needs he understood. And then, in the hush that followed those first shots and that first roar of fury, she heard the order given again and knew that the horror had scarcely begun. And she launched herself forwards, desperation bringing strength to her body, determination thrusting like a wave before her so that the last few men fell back as if stunned by some invisible force.

Matthew did not see her. Did not feel her presence close to his side. He saw nobody, was aware of nobody close to him. His attention was fixed on Billy Boycott, on the order that must come again. He knew only a sense of doom, of inevitability, as if it had been written long ago that this moment must come, as if somehow he had always known it.

'Fire again.' Boycott was no longer mincing his words. The weavers must see that he meant business. 'I want them off the streets,' he said on a growl. 'Fire again.'

Matthew reloaded, raised his guns with the others and laid his fingers on the triggers. And as he gave the final squeeze, felt someone thrust hard against his body. His arm flew out, his gun jerking, out of control. The explosion shook his wrist and amidst the noise and the confusion, he heard a shout, a woman's scream and a cry of pain.

Appalled, he lowered the guns and stared around him. And saw a body lying on the ground, only a few yards away.

Bill Bucknell. In that moment of sickness, Matthew knew that he had shot Bill Bucknell.

Chapter Eighteen

'Dead!'

Rebecca, white-faced, weary, sick with shock, sank into a chair near the door. Francis was by her side at once, his arm about her shoulder, and she leaned against him, feeling suddenly too weak even to sit up without support.

'Dead . . .' Vivian said again, and his tone was strange, almost angry, as if Maria had done it to spite him. As if, in her final moment, she had in some way triumphed over him, revenged herself for his treatment of her. Slowly, he crossed the room and then, reaching the fireplace, wheeled to face them. 'And my son?'

It was almost, Rebecca thought, as if he were determined that in this she would not win, not defeat him. But upstairs in the hot and stinking bedroom, it had been more as if Maria had died because of the truth, because to live with it was beyond her strength.

'Dead too.' She lifted her head and looked across the room. 'And it was a daughter.'

'A *daughter*! Another girl!' Vivian looked baffled, as if he could not believe this last stroke of fate. Yet would it not have been even more cruel if it had been the longed-for son who lay white and waxen in the crib upstairs? Rebecca shook her head and let it droop again. Perhaps he too was suffering from shock. Perhaps it was unfair to blame him for his reactions now.

She rose and went over to him, laying her hand on his arm. He was bereaved, he needed sympathy and love. And who else would give them to him?

She remembered the comfort he had given her in her own bereavement. It had been Vivian who came to meet and comfort her, when Francis had been overwhelmed by his own sorrow. It had been Vivian who broke the news, gently and kindly, who took her in his arms, who let her weep on his shirt-front. Vivian who gave her strength.

Didn't he deserve her comfort now?

'Vivian,' she said gently, and he turned his head and looked down into her eyes.

Rebecca felt a shock like a small blow to her breast, driving the breath from her body. The eyes that looked into hers were dark, with torment, shadowed with thoughts she could only guess at. What was he feeling? Was he overcome with grief for the wife who had tried so hard and faithfully to give him his son? Was he sorrowing for the lost child, realising only now how very precious to him all his daughters were? Was he regretting the times when he had dismissed them as of no account, no more than an everlasting drain upon his purse?

The simple facts were that he had lost a wife and child, and needed comfort. And once again – who else was there to give it him?

'Vivian, my dear,' she said quietly, and drew him down on to the couch beside the empty fireplace. And held his head against her breast.

The clatter of horses' hooves woke those few townspeople who had managed to sleep at all, on that sultry August morning. And Nell Foster, who had not slept, came to her door to look up the narrow street and see what was to do.

Other women were at their doors too, and men who had come skulking back from the riots in the early hours. Their eyes were turned towards the end of the street, where it joined a larger way, and after a few moments they were rewarded by the sight of a troop of cavalry, the men stiff and proud in their uniforms, the horses glossy and well groomed, their tack as polished as the riders' boots. And each man armed and looking ready to use his weapons.

'Soldiers!' Nell breathed, and her hand fluttered to her throat.

The woman next door turned. 'Aye, they've brought in the Dragoons again. And much good it'll do 'em. The men won't be beat by them, just because they've got flashy uniforms and swords. Things hev gone too far for that.'

Nell looked at her. Lizzie Brown had always been a fool – only seeing what she wanted to see, never accepting the truth even when it stared her in the face. 'How can weavers stand out against soldiers?' she demanded. 'What d'you think they can do, strangle 'em with the wool? Don't be daft, Lizzie. You know what happened in Manchester a few years back. Peterloo, they called it, because it was as bad as Waterloo – a massacre of folk who couldn't do nothing to help theirselves.'

'I don't know nothing about that. I just knows my Sam won't let no fancy soldier order him about. Nor your Bill, I shouldn't hev thought. He been out all night too, ent he?'

'Yes,' Nell felt a pang of disquiet. She had been expecting Bill back at any moment, had spent the night worrying about where he might be, what he was doing. He'd been against the fighting, had gone out to try to stop it. He would never have gone on the rampage, rioting and looting as she'd heard the other men had. So – where was he?

Why hadn't he come home?

Lizzie Brown was watching her, curiosity bright in her eyes. 'Ent naught wrong, I hope?' she enquired sympathetically.

Nell turned abruptly to go back into the cottage.

'No. Naught wrong.' But even as she spoke, she had a hollow feeling that the words weren't true. And before she could drag the door shut behind her, there was a commotion outside and she came out again, reluctantly, knowing already that there was something

391

very wrong indeed and that she would have to face it.

A small crowd of men were coming down the street. They looked like ragamuffins from some band of travelling tinkers or vagabonds, dishevelled and bruised, one or two of them with black eyes and swollen noses, all with torn, dusty clothes. They were swaggering as if they had achieved something to be proud of that night, yet their eyes were shifty and shamefaced and they slunk into their cottages like dogs expecting to be whipped.

The women watched as their menfolk came home. And Lizzie Brown and Nell Foster watched too, side by side, waiting until there were only three men left.

'So there you be, Sam Brown.' Lizzie's voice, cocky with pride a few moments ago, was now harsh and nagging. 'And just what d'you think you've been doing all night? *I've* heard all about it – drinking and rampaging and breaking windows. Just like a lot of little kids!'

'Not much play about this night's work, Lizzie.' But the man's denial was little more than an automatic response. His eyes were on Nell, and she felt an increase in her anxiety. Where was Bill?

'Sam— ' she began, but he turned away as if he could no longer meet her eyes, ducking his head, and now her anxiety was beginning to turn to fear.

'Sam!' She caught his sleeve. 'Sam, what's happened? Where's my Bill? He didn't want no riots – where is he?'

He looked at the other men and Nell followed his glance, seeing their eyes slide away from hers as if half scared, half ashamed to meet her gaze. Something had gone very wrong, it was plain, and her heart sickened.

'You got to tell me! He's hurt, ent he? In prison. They took him in mistake for someone else. He never done nothing, not my Bill.' She tugged at Sam Brown's sleeve, her nails tearing at his flesh through a rip in the material. '*Tell me!*'

'All right, Nellie, all right.' He tried to remove her

hand but she dug her fingers in like claws, convinced now that something was terribly wrong, afraid that he would escape her and she would somehow never know. 'Don't tek on like that. I was coming to tell you, wasn't I.' He stopped helplessly, looking from one to the other of his mates. 'Here – you tell her– '

They backed away, shaking their heads. Nell turned and stared at them. She looked into their faces, into their sliding eyes. She turned back and met Sam Brown's glance, and would not let it slide away. Slowly, she unclasped her fingers and let her hand drop from his arm.

'He's . . . dead, int he?' she said slowly, almost wonderingly. 'My Bill – as allus did his best to help, as wouldn't hurt a fly. He's dead . . .' She spoke the word as if it was one that she had never needed to speak before, tasting it like some foul fruit on her tongue. Then she looked at each man again, searching their faces as if hoping even now that it might not be the truth. 'Dead . . .' And then, with sudden anger: 'Well, int he? Int that what you come to tell me? Int it? My god, what's got into you all? Ent you got no tongues? Can't you just *tell* me?'

Lizzie Brown came forward and tried to take her in her arms, but Nellie broke free. Her eyes were wild and accusing as she swung round, staring once more at each man, and they all took an involuntary step back, glancing sidelong at each other again. Sam lifted his hand, palm towards her, and tried to speak soothingly, but it came hard to a tongue more accustomed to curse and swear.

'Look, Nell, 'twasn't none of our doing– '

'Then tell me whose 'twas.'

'It ent easy– '

'*Tell* me.'

'Best tell her what happened,' Lizzie advised. 'I'd want to know, if 'twas me.'

Sam snorted. 'You'd just want to mek sure so you

could sell me boots,' he retorted, and then looked down at the footwear. 'Well, all right, I never meant that . . . Look, Nellie, it were an accident, we're all sure of that. But old Billy Boycott, he wouldn't wait for the cavalry, see. He would have volunteers – armed men, firing into the crowd– '

'*Firing into the crowd?*'

'Well, over their heads, it were supposed to be. Only a shot or two didn't, you see. And your Bill – well, he copped one.' He stopped as Nellie gave a faint cry and sagged against her neighbour's scrawny bosom. 'It were over in a minute,' he said miserably. 'I don't reckon he ever felt a thing.'

'My Bill – shot!'

'Well, that's about the long and the short of it, yes.'

'But why didn't no one come and tell me?'

'Well, we hev done,' he pointed out. 'And there was a deal of folk milling about up there – getting the crowd cleared, getting a doctor to him and such– '

'I thought you said it were over in a minute.'

'Well, it were, but they still had to get a doctor in, say how he was killed, like– '

'Couldn't they *see* how he was killed?'

'Aye, they could,' he admitted unhappily. 'But they still had to get the doctor. The constable was there, and he said it had to be done that way. And they took Bill– '

'Where? Where did they tek him?'

'It ent no use you going there. There ent nothing you can do, and it ent a sight . . .' Sam caught sight of Nell's face, paper-white, and stopped abruptly. 'Look, there ent no more we can tell you now, Nell. Constable said he'd be along later, you can ask him anything else. I'm sorry to bring bad news.' He looked at Lizzie. 'Can't you give her nothing? Penn'orth of gin, help her sleep a bit?'

'Aye, there's some in the house seeing as you've been out all night,' Lizzie said caustically, and then

394

took Nell in her arms once more. 'Come on now, Nellie, you come in along of me for a bit. Them boys of yours can look after theirselves. You've had a bad shock, you needs a bit of rest and comfort.'

'Comfort!' Nell said bitterly. 'Precious little comfort to be had down this way. You're in as bad a way as we are, Liz.' But she did not pull away this time, and allowed Lizzie to lead her into the tumbledown cottage next door to her own. At the door, she stopped and looked back at the three men.

'Just one thing,' she said, and her voice was hard. 'Just tell me who done it? Who shot my Bill and killed him? Who was the bloody murderer who put him in his grave?'

Again, the men looked at Sam. He shuffled his feet, no more willing to answer this question than any other, but at last he mumbled the name and when Nellie, unable to believe what she had heard, asked him to repeat it, said more loudly: 'Farrell. It were Matt Farrell. He had some pistols he brought back from Americky and it was him as shot your Bill.'

'*Matt Farrell*? But he were Bill's friend!' She stood by the door for a moment, her hand on the jamb, swaying slightly. And then her unfocused eyes narrowed and hardened. 'At least, he allus *said* he was! Some friend!' Her fingers tightened on the door jamb, until the knuckles gleamed white. 'Well, I hopes they got him under lock and key,' she spat, 'for if they haven't there'll be murder done again before today's out. Matt Farrell! He'll swing for this, and I'll be in the front row cheering him on.'

Rebecca woke to the second clatter of hooves to be heard in Kidderminster that day. Sighing, opening her eyes with difficulty, she turned over in bed and stared at the window. The sun was streaming through the curtains and she wondered dizzily how this could be. It took half the day for the sun to reach this side of the house . . . And then she remembered. Vivian's baby daughter . . . Maria . . .

The memory of the night burst upon her. Maria's screams echoed once again in her ears, the grip of her hands crushed upon her fingers as they had done all through that terrible night. And all in vain, for now Maria was cold and her baby with her. Both lost, gone for ever.

She remembered Vivian's incredulous reaction, his anger, his grief. She was sure now that it was grief. She remembered holding him in her arms, letting her own strength flow into him, amazed that she had any left after the ordeal she had suffered with his wife. He had turned to her, holding her as if he were clinging to an anchor, afraid of being swept away on the tide. And when at last he had allowed himself to be led away to his own bed, he had gone only after she had promised to come back.

'Why?' she had asked Francis as they made their own weary way home. 'Why should he and Maria both turn to me?' She still found it difficult to believe that Maria could ever have been envious of her. 'They've never really accepted me – at least, I never thought they did. Was I mistaken, seeing slights where none were meant?'

Francis had shaken his head. 'People are strange when they're upset. But I think you belittle yourself. You don't realise how much the family have come to love you— '

'Love me! Sarah? Jane? Edith? Francis, none of them love me.'

'You never thought that Maria loved you,' he pointed out, 'but it was you she called for. And you that Vivian turned to as well. I've never seen him turn to anyone in that way before— '

'It was only grief,' she said quickly. 'You must believe that, Francis. I would not have held him if I had thought— '

396

'It's all right – I understand. It was plainly just what he needed, at that moment.' Francis patted her arm. 'And it shows that what I've been saying is true. The family *have* accepted you. Look how much Father thinks of you – when he can think at all,' he ended sadly.

They were silent for a moment, thinking of Jeremiah. His deterioration, once begun, had proceeded rapidly and he was now only seldom totally lucid. He moved through his days in a twilit world of bewilderment, repeating his few remarks over and over again, receiving the same answer and forgetting it a few moments later. He wandered around the house searching, but never quite certain what or whom he sought. Sometimes they thought it was his wife, sometimes his long-dead daughter. Isabel – Isabella – it hardly mattered. Within minutes, he might have forgotten his search and be asking for some employee to be brought to him from the loom shops, an employee as likely as not from years ago, in his grave now and forgotten by everybody else.

'Poor Polly,' Rebecca said sadly. 'She takes care of him almost every minute of the day, and he hardly seems to know who she is. He thought she was his nanny the other day, and then again he tried to turn her out, saying he'd never seen her before and she'd come to steal the silver. And yesterday— ' She stopped suddenly, and Francis looked at her with understanding.

'I know. He thought she was my mother, Mary. He asked her how the girls were doing with their lessons, and then— ' His voice broke, but after a few seconds he steadied himself and went on quietly: 'At least he was happy for those few minutes.'

'I suppose so. But it's so sad, to see him like that. And remember how he once used to be . . .' She was quiet for a moment, then said: 'At least he has forgotten his guilt – over Mary, and over little Geoffrey.'

'Has he? I wonder. I wonder sometimes if it comes back to torment him in the night, when there's nobody near. And if it wasn't what drove him mad to begin with.'

'Mad!' It was the first time anyone had used the word openly, and Rebecca shivered. 'Oh, Francis— '

'Ssh. I shouldn't have said that. I know what's in your mind – you think we'll have to have him taken to the asylum. But we'll never do that. We'll look after him until he dies. You know that.'

'I couldn't bear him to go there,' she said in a low voice. 'Locked up in a cage, for people to come and stare at and make fun of . . . It's like a zoo, Francis. And the poor souls inside – they can't help it. They need comfort, not trapping like animals. We can't let your poor father go there.'

'We never will.' They were at the door now and he opened it and ushered her inside. 'And now stop worrying about everyone else and go to bed and rest. I'll tell Mother you aren't to be disturbed. Sleep as long as you like.'

And so she had done, waking now to the afternoon sun and the noise of horses galloping through the town. She got out of bed and went to the window, drawing a wrapper around her. What was happening now?

The bedroom door opened softly and Tilly came in, carrying a tray.

'Oh, mum, you're up. Ain't it 'orrible? All the riots and poor Mrs Vivian and the baby and all. And now there's more soldiers come and they're just rushing about on their 'orses, driving people off the streets. And ain't it *awful* abut poor Mr Farrell! And your— '

'Mr Farrell?' Rebecca turned quickly. 'Why, what's happened to Mr Farrell? He's not hurt, is he?'

Tilly stopped in the act of pouring a cup of tea. Her hand flew to her mouth. 'Oh, mum, there, I shouldn't 'ave said nothing. I forgot you 'adn't 'eard. Well, 'ow could you, what with being asleep and all. Oh dear, now what shall I do? Cook'll kill me when she finds out I've— '

'*I* shall kill you,' Rebecca said grimly, 'if you don't tell me at once what's happened. And please don't start crying, Tilly. Tell me – *now*.'

'No, Tilly,' came Francis's voice from the doorway, 'don't say another word. You've done quite enough damage for one day. Leave that tea and go back to the kitchen.' He stood aside as the snivelling girl scurried from the room, and then came over to Rebecca. He put his arms around her and looked gravely down into her face. 'I wish you hadn't woken to this,' he said. 'I would have liked you to rest a little longer.'

'Well, I am awake and I know something's happened – something bad.' Rebecca was fighting to keep her voice under control. ' "Awful", Tilly said. So please, Francis – tell me what it is.'

He led her to the bed, sat her down. She sat upright, staring at him white-faced.

'Rebecca, you know that the rioting went on late into the night. We could hear it from Vivian's house – it's a mercy they didn't come to attack us there, and why they didn't I'll never know. They went to almost every other manufacturer in Kidderminster and stormed the factories too. Windows were broken, lamps smashed, paving stones torn up— '

'Yes, yes,' she interrupted. 'But what had this to do with Matthew? He was hurt in the morning, he wasn't out in the rioting.' She saw his face and added sharply: 'He wasn't, was he?'

'He went out later on,' Francis said quietly. 'Apparently Bill Bucknell – the man who lives with Nellie Foster— '

'Yes, yes, I know Bill and Nellie. Go on.'

'Bucknell was amongst those asked by Billy Boycott to gather together volunteers to help quell the riot. He went to Matthew and they went back to the town together. Matthew had his guns.'

'His *guns*?' Rebecca's face, already ashen, turned the colour of new-fallen snow. 'He's not— '

'They were supposed to fire above the heads of the crowd,' Francis went on dully. 'God knows what happened – perhaps someone jogged his arm, accidentally. Certainly it must have been an accident as far as Matthew was concerned. But at the second firing— ' He stopped and bowed his head, covering his eyes with one hand. Rebecca stared at him. She wanted to pull his hands away from his face, make him tell her. But it was clear that for a moment or two, Francis was beyond speech.

At last, he gathered himself together. He looked up into her face and in a flat, monotonous tone as if it were a lesson he had been forced against his will to learn, he said: 'One of Matthew's shots hit Bill Bucknell. He was killed at once. And Matthew has been accused of his murder.' He paused, as though he had stopped speaking for ever, but Rebecca waited, sensing that, terrible as the news was, there was yet more to come. And at last, Francis told her, still in that dreadful flat voice, devoid of all emotion because the emotion was too terrible to face. 'And Bessie . . . our Bessie . . . was with him . . .'

The few weeks that followed the riot were amongst the worst that Rebecca had ever known – worse even than the time she had spent in London, searching hopelessly for Tom and Bessie, believing she had lost Francis for ever. For, dreadful though that time had been, no one was in peril of their life, no one facing the ruin of all they had worked for.

And now, it seemed that the world was crashing down about her ears. She was losing all that she loved, all that she held most dear. And felt powerless to stop it.

'What will happen to them?' she asked Francis when he came home after trying to find a lawyer to defend Matthew and Bess. 'What will they do to them?'

Francis sat down to take off his boots. His face was grave and drawn; he looked ten, twenty years older. She looked at the burning spot of scarlet on his pale cheek and wondered if he were going to be ill again. But no, it was more likely to be the anxiety that had tormented them both ever since Matthew and Bessie had been arrested. It had kept them awake through the long, bleak hours of the night; they had talked until they had nothing new to say, yet still they went on, as if by repeating their words over and over again they might find some hidden nugget of wisdom, some small thing that had previously been overlooked. But there was nothing.

If only Matthew had not agreed to go out that night, she thought again, uselessly. If only Bill had not come to ask him. If only Bessie, determined to keep her master under her eye, so sure he would need her, had not followed them; if only she had not caught up with him at just the moment he had shot Bill.

'What will they do to them?' she asked again. 'Did you find a lawyer?'

'Yes, Godson will take the case. He's a good man. As for how the trial will go – who's to tell? It was plainly an accident, but feeling's running high and the whole thing could spark off another riot. Some of the weavers are for Matthew, some against him. Billy's wife, Nellie, is swearing that Matthew should— ' He stopped abruptly. 'Well, the poor woman's grief-stricken, she's not responsible for what she says.'

'Nell thinks they should hang, doesn't she,' Rebecca said in a low, trembling voice. 'Could – could it happen, Francis? Could they do that?' She caught at his arm and gazed into his face, horror looking out of her eyes. 'They'd never *hang Matthew*?' she whispered in tones of pure horror. 'And Bessie – poor Bessie – they'd never hang her?'

'Of course they wouldn't. The whole thing was a mistake, an accident, and they'll see it as soon as it's explained.' But Francis's tone was over-hearty and Rebecca's hand fell away from his arm. She shook her head and the tears felt hot in her eyes.

'But it's been explained. And Matthew and Bess are in Stafford Gaol.' Her voice broke. 'Oh, Francis, is it very dreadful in there? I've heard such tales. Prisoners dying of gaol fever, or starving, forced into hard labour, fighting amongst themselves . . . I can't bear to think of them in such a place.'

'It's not so bad now,' Francis said, trying to comfort her. 'Since the prisons were reformed a few years ago, things have been much improved. People aren't crowded together now as they used to be – each prisoner has his own cell, a bath every week and regular exercise. There'll be a mattress on the bed, with the straw changed regularly. And there's a chaplain and a surgeon, so they'll be well looked after spiritually and bodily.' He tried a smile. 'They'll be comfortable enough.'

But Rebecca did not smile back. Bessie, who had suffered so much during her short life. And Matthew – who had roamed the world, slept under the stars – confined to a prison cell . . . She shuddered and covered her face with her hands.

'When will the trial be held?' she asked at last.

Francis shook his head. 'Who knows? It might be soon, it might be late. It might not be in Kidderminster – remember, they tried Humphrey Price in Hereford last year because everyone agreed he would not get a fair trial here. Perhaps they'll do the same for Matthew and Bess.'

'A fair trial? That was no fair trial. It makes little difference where it's held,' she said bitterly. 'The point is that the magistrates, the judge, the jury will all see Matthew in just the same way as they saw Humphrey – as a traitor to his class. That's why Humphrey Price went to prison for a year and that's why they – why they'll – oh, *Francis*!'

'Rebecca, Rebecca, my love.' He took her in his arms, cradling her against his chest, rocking her gently. He kissed her hair, stroked her wet cheeks. He tried to think of something he could say that would calm her fears, take away the dreadful spectre of the gallows. He tried to think of some words of reassurance, to convince her that their loved ones would be safe, that they would be returned to them.

But there was nothing he could say. Nothing. Because he did not believe it himself. He felt miserably, desolately certain that both Matthew and Bessie would hang for the murder of Bill Bucknell.

Rebecca found Vivian in his library. He was sitting quite still, staring into the empty fireplace, a bottle of brandy and a glass at his side. He did not look up as she came in.

'Vivian.' She crossed the room swiftly and sat by his side on the couch. 'Vivian, how are you?'

He laughed shortly. 'How do you expect me to be?'

'Oh, Vivian.' She touched his arm, then laid her hand over his. 'Vivian, I'm so very, very sorry.'

He turned then and looked at her. His eyes were empty, his face devoid of expression. He might have been wearing a mask. She felt a chill on her heart, as if she had suddenly brushed hands with a phantom.

'Sorry,' he said, as if it were a new word to him. 'Well, thank you, Rebecca. It's good of you to feel sorry.'

'Please, Vivian,' she said quietly, and lifted his hand to hold it in both of hers. 'Please believe me.' And she sat without saying any more, simply holding his hand and looking at his empty face.

After a few moments, he let his eyes fall. He looked at their hands, entwined on his thigh, and a long, shuddering sigh broke from his lips. He shook his head like a blind man, and Rebecca disengaged one of her hands and lifted it to his cheek.

'Vivian, I understand,' she said softly. 'It's a terrible blow. And Maria was so brave. She must have known there was something wrong, yet she never complained. She was a good wife to you, Vivian.'

'Six daughters,' he said in a low voice. 'She bore me six daughters.'

'Six beautiful daughters. You must be very proud of them.' She hesitated, then went on, 'I know she badly wanted to give you a son, Vivian. But it wasn't to be. And we can only do God's will. We can't any of us decide what family we're to have. And you have the girls now, to comfort you.'

Vivian said nothing and she wondered if she had been tactless. Perhaps he didn't see his daughters as a comfort. He had complained often enough about what they cost him. But surely that was just the way a father talked. Surely even Vivian . . .

'It seems to me,' he said, 'that you are the best comfort a man could have, Rebecca.'

Startled, she looked into his face. The emptiness had gone but the expression there now was enigmatic, unreadable. She felt a little uneasy, but told herself that she was being foolish. The old Vivian, with all his faults, seemed to have gone these days. In his place was a new, mature Vivian who had six daughters and a responsible position in the town. This Vivian would no longer bother about the fact that he had never managed to make a conquest of the little housemaid, Rebecca. This Vivian saw her as his cousin's wife, a member of the family, come to comfort him when he needed it. A friend, offering friendship as he had offered her friendship when her son had been drowned.

'I know what it is like to lose someone you love,' she answered steadily, and was rewarded by the faintest of smiles.

'Yes. So you do.' He sat up a little straighter and turned to the small table at his side. 'Can I offer you a brandy?'

'No, thank you.' She waited while he poured himself a measure. 'Vivian, is there anything we can do, Francis and I? For you and the girls? I could come and oversee them if you like, until you make other arrangements— '

'Arrangements? What arrangements?'

'Why, for their welfare, their upbringing— '

He shrugged, dismissing the idea. 'They have their nurse and their governess. What more do they need?'

Rebecca stared at him. Did he really not understand?

'Vivian, they've lost their mother. They need someone to take her place— '

'Are you suggesting I should marry again? So soon, with Maria not yet cold in her grave?'

'No, of course not! But your daughters need someone to look after them, to make sure that their nurse and governess are doing their jobs properly. They can't be allowed to run wild.'

'Oh, they won't be.' He gazed at her but she had a feeling he wasn't really seeing her. 'Don't worry about that, Rebecca. I shall see to that myself.'

'You mean *you* will— '

'Take care of my own daughters. But of course. Why not? Although I would certainly be grateful— ' He looked at her again, properly this time, and gave her a sudden smile. 'I'd be grateful if you would give them some of your time and attention. They're fond of you – especially Lucy.'

'Of course I will.' She was glad to help, glad to think she could be of comfort. It might at least help her to stop thinking all the time of Bessie and Matthew, alone in their tiny cells, sleeping on straw mattresses, fed on bread and water and little else, not knowing whether they were to live or die.

'And if there's anything I can do for you,' he said carelessly, 'you know you have only to ask.'

There was a short pause. Rebecca felt her heart thud suddenly. She looked up at him, wondering whether she dared take him at his word. But why not? He'd shown himself to be different, hadn't he? Hadn't she just been telling herself how much he had changed, how different he was from the young man who had thought it sport to ravish the maids? And hadn't he already proved himself to be her friend?

Vivian glanced at her, as if wondering at her sudden silence.

'What is it, Rebecca?'

'Vivian,' she said, suddenly breathless, 'there is something you could do for me . . .'

'And what's that?' He sounded disinterested, watching from the window as the girls walked in the garden, small black shadows in their heavy mourning, their faces sober and downcast.

Rebecca hesitated, but she had gone too far to draw back now. Quickly, before she lost courage, she said, 'It's my sister, Vivian. Bessie. And – and Matthew Farrell. They're in Stafford Gaol— '

'I know. A shooting. One of the Union Committee.' He gave a short laugh. 'Imagine Farrell shooting one of his own side! Or do you think he's turned over to the masters? He had put money into Francis's co-operative, hadn't he?'

Rebecca bit her lip. Already, she was regretting her words. Vivian might be sympathetic towards her, but he had still not forgiven Bessie and Tom. She would say no more, she thought, but Vivian had turned his head and was looking at her.

'Well? So they're in Stafford Gaol. What do you want me to do – get them out? Help them escape?' He paused and then added in a very quiet voice. 'Again . . .'

Rebecca flushed a deep, plainful crimson. 'No, of course I don't want that. But Vivian – you're a magistrate now. Can't you do anything? You must know it was an accident. Matthew would never have shot Bill Bucknell. And Bessie – she just happened to be there— '

'Just as she "happened to be there" when Jabez Gast had his throat cut with his own terry wire,' Vivian said tersely, and she gasped. 'Yes, Rebecca, it sounds harsh, I know, but isn't it the truth? And isn't truth a strange thing when the same woman *just happens* to be by when two men are murdered? I'm afraid a good many people will see it that way. Not that the jury are likely to acquit her,' he added.

'But she never fired it! And Matthew meant to fire into the sky. It was because Bessie caught at his arm that the shot . . .' She gazed at him, desperate now. 'Vivian, please do something for them. At least try to ensure that they have a fair trial.'

'And are you suggesting that English justice is ever unfair?' he demanded. And then his face softened a little. 'Rebecca, don't look so tragic. They'll have a fair trial. And I'm only trying to point out to you the way most people will see the case. It's no use hiding from the truth – and the truth so often turns out to be a matter of majority decision, more than anything else. What most people believe must be true . . . even if you and I know it isn't.' He thought for a moment, tapping his teeth with a fingernail, and then seemed to come to a decision. He gave her a quick smile.

'I'll go and see your sister in prison,' he said. 'And Farrell too, if I can. I'll talk to them and I'll talk to my fellow magistrates. Perhaps there were mitigating circumstances after all. We'll see.' He smiled again as Rebecca caught at his hands, the tears falling on to his skin as she began to thank him. 'Now, don't get so emotional, there's a good girl. It's little enough, and I hold out no hope of any success – but I'll go and see them. There.'

'Oh, Vivian,' Rebecca said brokenly. 'I'm so relieved. They need help so badly and I didn't know which way to turn. But if you're willing . . .'

For the first time, she began to feel a glimmering of hope.

Chapter Nineteen

'They'll try to make an example of him, I'm afraid,' Richard Godson said. He looked up over his spectacles and Francis and Rebecca glanced at each other and then back across the desk. Francis lifted his hands and let them drop back on the polished leather, a gesture that Rebecca felt effectively expressed her own sense of helplessness.

'But why? Matthew was trying to help quell the riot. He'd already been injured, earlier in the day.'

'I know, but he's known to have been involved in the earlier dispute – the strike – and he was on the weavers' side then. Moreover, he was closely associated with Humphrey Price and the Committee. The manufacturers would have been pleased to see him behind bars too, along with Price, but there was nothing they could charge him with. Now, however . . .' He shrugged.

'But it was an accident!' Rebecca exclaimed. 'And Bill Bucknell was his friend! Nobody could possibly believe that Matthew intended to kill him.'

'Bucknell's own wife seems to think so,' Godson pointed out. 'She's determined that he should be brought to justice – or what she sees as justice.' He regarded them apologetically. 'She's beyond reason, I'm afraid. She won't be satisfied with anything less than – well, the ultimate sentence.'

'The gallows,' Francis said, and Rebecca gave a gasp of horror.

Francis made a movement of apology. 'I'm sorry, my love. But we knew it before we came here.'

'I know. But to hear you say it, aloud like that . . .'

She shuddered. 'And Nell Foster wants this for – for Matthew? And even for Bessie? But they were *friends*.'

The lawyer nodded.

'As far as your sister's concerned, she's been ill for the past week and trial may have to be postponed. But in Mr Farrell's case – yes, I'm afraid so. Not that Foster's wishes count for anything, of course – as I understand it, she wasn't even legally married to Bucknell. But she's going about getting support, and with the weavers *and* the masters against him . . .' He paused again, delicately, but there was really no need for him to continue. Rebecca shook her head and felt for a handkerchief.

'Poor Matthew,' she whispered. 'Francis – Mr Godson – we *must* do something.'

'I shall do whatever I can, of course,' the lawyer told her. 'But I felt you should be quite clear about the position. I never like to raise false hopes. It does nobody any good in the end.'

'That's quite right. It's always better to face facts.' Francis thought for a moment. 'So this is how things stand. Matthew will come up at Worcester Quarter Sessions at Michaelmas, along with the other weavers who were arrested that night. He'll be tried for murder and you think that both the masters and the justices will be against him because of his involvement in the strike, while the weavers will be against him because he killed Bill Bucknell. In other words, both sides are using him as a scapegoat.'

'That puts it very clearly,' Richard Godson nodded.

Francis sighed. 'It will need a very fair judge and jury for Matthew to have a chance of receiving true justice.' He looked soberly at Rebecca. 'It doesn't sound good, my love.'

Rebecca stared at him, scarcely able to believe what she was hearing. 'Francis – we're not going to *give in*?'

'Of course not! We shall do our best to fight his case. But you heard what Mr Godson says – everyone seems to be against him. We have to be prepared for the worst— '

'Prepared for the worst? I shall *never* be prepared for the worst!' Rebecca rose to her feet, gathering her cloak about her. 'Matthew is going to walk away from that trial a free man. I shall *not* see him hang. He didn't commit murder – it was an accident, and everyone knows it. I shall *not* allow them to use him as a – a scapegoat.' Her dark eyes flashed fire as she looked from one man to the other. 'You can sit here in your dusty office, looking at old books and writing on pieces of paper,' she said disdainfully. 'But *I* shall go out and *do* something. Starting with Nell Foster.'

'Nell Foster? But— '

'She'll not welcome you,' the lawyer warned. 'And I'm not at all sure that you ought— '

'Ought? *Ought*? What does "ought" have to do with it? *Ought* the masters to use him as a means of revenge for the strike? *Ought* the weavers to turn against him because he tried to keep the peace? *Ought* the jury to convict him and the judge sentence him, because they think he's a traitor to his class? No! So don't tell me I *ought* not to go and see Nell Foster, who I've known since I was a baby at my mother's breast, Mr Godson, and don't tell me I *ought* or *ought not* to do anything else that I may think fit. You do what you think will help Matthew and I shall do what I think, and between us we'll save him from the gallows.' She stepped quickly to the door and turned to face them both. 'Is that clearly understood?'

The door flew open in her grasp and her skirts billowed as she whisked out of the room. The two men gazed after her for a moment, then, blinking a little as if a tornado had suddenly swept by, looked at each other.

'Your wife is a very determined woman,' Richard Godson said carefully, and Francis nodded.

'She is. People don't realise it – most of the time

411

she's quiet and meek – but once she smells injustice, and particularly when it concerns someone she loves, then she's like a tigress. I wouldn't be surprised to see her stand up in court and tell the judge exactly how to conduct his own summing-up.'

'I very much hope she will not,' the lawyer said dryly. 'Your wife may impress us, she may even impress the weavers and masters of Kidderminster, but I doubt if she would impress the judge.' He thought for a moment, and then smiled a little and added: 'Though I should very much enjoy watching her try . . .'

As a magistrate, Vivian was well enough known at Staffordshire Gaol, and he passed the hard-faced wardresses with a nod. One of them directed him to Bessie's cell, and he went in, wrinkling his nose fastidiously at the smell of vomit, excreta and urine that hung about the small, bleak room. The door clanged shut behind him. The only light came filtering reluctantly through a small, grimy window set high up in the wall and he stood for a moment letting his eyes become accustomed to the dimness. Then he glanced at the narrow iron bed and at the woman who lay upon it.

Bess looked like a crone of sixty. Her once golden hair had turned a dirty grey, its curls no more now than a mass of tangles. Her skin was the sickly oatmeal of unbleached linen. Her eyes were dull pits in a face that had lost all curves, her nose sharp as a beak jutting from the thin, wasted cheeks.

She stared at Vivian and recognition crept slowly into her sunken eyes, followed by a dim fear. She struggled to sit up, stretching out one skeletal hand, but fell back again on the flat, lumpy pillow. Her body began to tremble and Vivian watched with a cynical smile on his lips. He bent over her and the trembling grew worse. She turned her head away, closing her eyes, and he laughed.

'You can't pretend I'm not here, Bess Himley. You

412

can't pretend I'm a dream.' He paused for a moment, watching as her eyes turned slowly back to him. 'So we meet again at last,' he said softly. 'And it can't be a surprise. You must have known that once you came back to Kidderminster I would find you. You even made it easy for me – housekeeping for Farrell!' He laughed. 'Did you think you'd be safe there? Didn't you realise that I would be able to take my time, leaving the day of reckoning for you until I had time to enjoy it?'

Bess's head shook as if she had an ague. Her lips moved and a faint whisper came out. Vivian bent closer, his mouth curling with distaste.

'Well, what is it? Speak up, woman – you don't imagine I want to risk my health by getting too near you, do you? What do you have to say?'

'Becky . . .' Bess's lips were cracked and dry, the words sounding rusty as if she had not used her voice for a long time. 'Becky said . . . you were good to her . . .'

'Good to her? To Rebecca?' Vivian laughed. 'Oh yes, I'm good to Rebecca. I have a feeling Rebecca's going to be very useful to me some day. But you're not.' His voice was cruel. 'You're not going to be any use to me at all. You never were. And now you're in here – to pay your debts – you may as well pay the ones you owe me.'

Bessie's head shook again and tears began to roll down her cheeks. 'But I can't pay . . . I've got nothing, nothing. I never did have. I can't pay you, Mr Vivian – not no way. Please – please don't do nothing to me. Don't hurt me, I hurt enough.'

She stopped, exhausted, and closed her eyes. Her body was clothed in prison rags, oversized and loose. He could see the painful rise and fall of her chest, almost imagined that he could see the beating of her heart. He gave an exclamation of disgust.

'You don't really imagine I'd want the sort of

payment you're accustomed to offer! No, there's nothing you can do for me now, Bess Himley. Nothing except suffer as I've always wanted you to suffer. Nothing except let me watch you, as I've always wanted to watch you. And, of course, to keep this visit between us purely private. I wouldn't want your sister, for instance, to know what's passed between us. She thinks I've come to help you – poor Rebecca, she never has quite lost her charming, innocent trust – and I wouldn't want her to think any differently. Do you understand? Because I can always make things . . . shall we say, less comfortable for you . . . if you do not.'

Bess nodded weakly. She did not speak again; perhaps, Vivian thought, she could not. She lay somewhere between waking and sleep, somewhere between life and death, each breath dragged into her lungs with a sound like a rasping saw. It was clear that her life hung by the thinnest of threads, but Vivian knew that she could last like this for weeks; even months.

He hoped that she would. He had long ago given up expecting his money to be repaid. But he had never given up his desire for revenge.

And here it was, dropped into his hand like a plum. Revenge on Bessie for eluding and humiliating him, and Rebecca for rejecting him, all in one delightful package. For, if he liked, Vivian could have ordered Bessie's release at once. He could have taken her home with him in his carriage, delivered her to her sister, let her spend her last days, weeks, months, in comfort at least, tended with love by people she knew and trusted.

Instead, he said nothing. He sat and watched for a while, as if to imprint the scene on his mind so that he need not come to this desolate place again, and then he left. With a nod and a brief, cold smile for the frozen-faced wardresses.

Humphrey Price was admitted to the gaol about three weeks before the trial was due to be heard. He came

414

into the cold, bare room where Matthew and a few other prisoners were waiting for visitors, and crossed to the bench where Matthew sat. He sat down beside him.

'Well, how are you? You're looking thinner.'

'Everyone looks thinner after a week or two in this place,' Matthew said. 'What food there is wouldn't fatten a cockroach – though there are plenty here to try. And we don't lie about resting and playing cards – though you know all about that.'

'I certainly do,' Price agreed. 'Walking the treadmill, sawing stone, polishing marble, scrubbing, cleaning, digging – there's no end to the tasks an ingenious prison governor can find to prevent boredom amongst the inmates.' He looked about him at the high stone walls with their small windows set too high for even the tallest prisoner to look through, at the green stains of damp and mould, the dirty straw that littered the cold flags of the floor. 'I thought I'd seen the last of places such as this,' he observed. 'And here I am, only a month or two after I shook the dust of the place off my shoes, back again.' He shot Matthew a look under his bristling brows. 'You're a fool, Matt.'

'It was an accident.'

'I know that! But to place yourself in a position whereby such an accident could happen . . .' He shook his head. 'What went wrong? Did they go stark, staring mad? After conducting the strike with such care to keep the peace, to let such madness run riot in the streets! And the manufacturers are no better. Imbeciles and oppressors, all of them. Well, almost all. Your friend Francis Pagnel seems to be trying hard to improve matters and set a new pattern. But I doubt if he'll succeed.'

'I hope he does,' Matthew said. 'It seems to me to be the only chance. Feeling is so bad now, I can't see the weavers ever regaining a good relationship with their masters. And the masters simply close their eyes to the conditions they're creating.'

'Well, I shall do my best to bring the truth home to them. I've written a pamphlet— '

'A pamphlet!' Matthew gave a short, unamused laugh. 'Don't you ever learn, Humphrey? Do you really want to join me back in here?'

'There's no law against writing pamphlets— '

'No, but they can soon find a law you *have* broken. Isn't that just what they did before? You were used as an instrument of revenge, just as I'm going to be. The manufacturers had their knives into us from the start and now they've got the weavers on their side too, as far as I'm concerned.' Matthew was silent for a moment, then said quietly, 'It's the high jump for me, Humphrey. The long drop.'

'Nonsense!'

'Of course it is. Murder always carries the death penalty. Well, there'll be a good audience from Kidderminster, no doubt. I only wish it could be done in private. I hate to be made a public show.'

'It won't come to that,' Price insisted, but Matthew shook his head.

'Well, we won't argue about it. We shall know soon enough. And I don't know that I'll be all that sorry in a way. Bill was a good friend and the thought that I killed him, even by accident . . . And poor Bess Himley too, escaped from the gallows once and now looks likely to end there all the same, all through me . . . My life's been a pretty useless one, on the whole.'

'Matthew . . .' Price said, concern in his voice. 'Matthew, you mustn't get despondent. It's the worst thing, in this place. At all costs, you must keep cheerful – it's the only way to survive.'

'Oh, I keep cheerful.' He glanced around the cell, at the men who sat or lay about, their bodies thin, their faces ravaged with hunger, disease and despair. An old man in the corner sat mumbling to himself, apparently unaware of anyone else, two young lads played apathetically with a few pebbles they had collected, a man sat talking to his wife who had come to visit him, their faces filled with desolation. 'You should see us when we're on our own here,' Matthew went on. 'We really begin to enjoy ourselves then. Why, we keep up the fun half the night.' He raised his voice, addressing the oblivious old man. 'Don't we, Jem? There, you see— ' as the rheumy eyes lifted for a moment in a blank, uncomprehending stare ' — Jem will tell you. A great one for a good time, is Jem.'

'Matthew . . .' Price said again, anxiously, and Matthew gave him a rueful look.

'Sorry, Humphrey. I know I'm feeling bitter, but wouldn't— ' He caught himself up and grinned a little more naturally. 'No, you wouldn't, would you? You've proved it. You spent a year in here – a year, my God! – and came out saying it had improved you. But we can't all be saints, Humphrey. I certainly can't.'

'Nobody's asking you to be a saint, Matthew – saints are difficult, prickly sort of folk anyway. Just patient.'

'And what do I get for being good?' Matthew said, sardonically. 'A free pardon? My liberty back?' His voice shook with sudden emotion. 'It's the only thing worth having, Humphrey, you know that. A few days without it are bad enough – but to think of weeks, months, *years*— ' He shuddered violently. 'I tell you, for someone like me the death penalty is the better choice.'

Humphrey Price was silent for a moment. Then he touched Matthew's knee and said quietly, 'I hope it won't come to either of those things, Matthew. You still have friends, you know that. And we're working all the time for justice, for your release. If it's possible at all— '

'I notice you say "if".'

'If it's possible at all,' Price went on, ignoring Matthew's interruption, 'we shall achieve it.'

'And who are "we"?'

'Why, myself, of course, and your friends the Pagnels – Francis and Rebecca. And— '

'Rebecca? How is Rebecca?' Matthew asked. 'She must be desperate about her sister.'

'And about you. But she's well. Well, and fighting for you. She's talking of going to see Nell Foster to convince her that it was an accident. She wants to talk to the weavers themselves, some of the rougher ones who are most against you. She— '

'But she mustn't do that! It's dangerous – those men are hard, unpleasant types, they're not to be trusted. Humphrey, you've got to stop her. What's Francis thinking of, to let her— '

'We tried to stop her. She simply reminded us that she had grown up amongst those weavers and knew them all by name. She's visited Nell Foster often enough in the past. She has their trust.'

'She had it once. Who's to say any of us has it now?'

'I believe she's right,' Humphrey said steadily. 'There's something about that young woman – something few of us had seen before. Something very strong and brave. I believe she can sway them, Matthew, and even if she can't I believe she should be allowed to try. Indeed, as I said, there doesn't seem to be any way of preventing her. She is very, very determined. She clearly thinks a great deal of you, Matt.'

Humphrey got to his feet.

'I have to go now.' He laid his hand on Matthew's head in blessing. 'I shall pray for you, my friend. Keep in good heart. Remember we're working for you. And I'll come in again soon.'

He departed, picking his way over the refuse-strewn floor. Matthew sat quite still, hardly noticing the clang of the heavy door. He gazed at the grey stone flags, barely aware of his surroundings.

Was this really how it was to end? The life he had lived so carelessly, strolling through it as if it were a game until he had become so passionately involved with the weavers? And had it really been so useless?

Not merely useless, he thought with savage remorse. It had been damaging. He had, through his own carelessness, brought an innocent woman to the trouble with him, and that woman the sister of his best friend. And yet, looking back, it all seemed so inevitable. Almost as if it had been predestined.

But that was nonsense. He didn't believe in Fate. He believed in having free will, in having choices and making them, rightly or wrongly.

At some point, he had made a wrong choice. Had it been when he had agreed to go out with his pistols? Or had it been much earlier than that – somewhere back in the past? When he had first met Humphrey Price – or perhaps that day when he had first come back to Kidderminster and seen Rebecca stepping, bright as a summer breeze, up the steep little street towards him. Perhaps it had all begun then.

He bowed his head and wished, more passionately than he had ever wished anything before, that he had never come back to Kidderminster.

A cold little wind lurked spitefully in alleyways and darted around the corners as Rebecca made her way through the narrow courts and backstreets to Nell Foster's home. All the more unkind after such a warm summer, it carried with it a flurry of rain and the low, steely clouds above threatened more before night.

The few people in the streets glanced curiously at Rebecca as she walked determinedly along the pavements, avoiding the holes where 'kidney' stones had been wrenched up to use as missiles on the night of the riot. She was aware of their stares, but didn't respond to them. They all knew who she was. Let them wonder where she was going and why. Let them stare and whisper. Let them – just let them *try* to stop her . . .

419

But nobody did try. The men were mostly at work, except for a few loungers outside the alehouses, and those women who were not also in the factories were too occupied with their daily chores to bother much about Rebecca. She saw them going about the tasks that took up their days: fetching water from the wells, washing a few clothes in a trough, coming back from some hedgerow with a bundle of sticks for their fire. Most of them had children with them too, small toddlers who ran and scampered ahead or trailed behind, each with his own little task – a few sticks to carry, a small pail of water, a younger child to look after.

None of them were as well fed and rosy as her own two boys. Nor as warmly clad or stoutly shod.

Rebecca came to Nellie's street and stopped at the broken door. For the first time, it occurred to her that Nellie might not be here. Didn't she work herself? And didn't she need money even more desperately, now that Bill was dead?

But before Rebecca had time to raise her hand to knock, the door was dragged open and Nell was there, her arms folded across her body, her mouth clamped in a thin, hard line, her eyes hostile.

'So it's you. I wondered if you'd show your face here again.'

Rebecca looked at her with pity. Nellie, once a ripe and sparkling girl, was now a thin wisp of a woman, looking twenty years more than her age. Her body was scrawny, her neck creased, her face grey. Bitter lines clustered around her lips and eyes, betraying the angry expression which seemed to have settled permanently on features that had once smiled and laughed. And the eyes that had once looked Vivian Pagnel up and down in bold appraisal, were now flat and stony.

'Well?' she demanded truculently. 'What d'you want?'

Rebecca found her voice.

'Can I come in, Nellie? I want to talk to you.'

'Talk, is it? Talk won't bring my Bill back.' But she shrugged and turned inside to the dark little cottage, leaving Rebecca to follow or not as she chose.

Rebecca closed the door behind her and let her eyes become accustomed to the gloom. It had changed very little since the first day she had come here, she thought, noting the rickety table, the mattress on the floor in the corner with its pile of old blankets and sacking, the black pot by the cold fireplace. Yet in the past year or two, Nellie and Bill had begun to improve it, get a few things together. There had been a rag rug, an old easy chair for Bill, stools for the children. Now these were gone.

Nell was watching her sardonically.

'It's all right,' she said, 'we haven't had the bailiffs in. Just had to sell a few bits and pieces to mek ends meet. Even funerals like my Bill's cost money.'

'Oh, Nell . . .' Pity rose in Rebecca's heart and she came forward quickly, impulsively, meaning to take Nell in her arms. But the other woman moved away.

'You don't hev to be sorry for me,' she said harshly. 'It ent me that's going to swing from the gallows and hang there for all to see. Be sorry for your sister what I thought was my friend, be sorry for your friend Matt Farrell, him that murdered Bill. Or maybe you don't need to be sorry for either of 'em,' she added, sinking down on one of the old kitchen chairs that stood around the littered table. 'They'll be out of it. They won't hev to struggle to keep the food in their children's bellies and the cold from freezing their poor little bones. They won't hev to watch 'em die like we had to watch our little Sammy die.'

Rebecca took the other chair and sat gazing at Nell. She hardly knew what to say. Such bitterness erected a wall between them, a wall too high and wide to be easily breached or even climbed. Yet she could not blame Nell for her reaction. She thought of how she would feel if it had been Francis, and shivered.

'Cold?' Nell asked. 'Afraid I can't offer you a fire. We has to keep the kindling for cooking. There's six of us in this row – we teks it in turns to hev a fire, this time of year when it ent too cold. It's Lizzie next door's turn today. We teks our broth in there for her to boil. So they'll be warm and cosy next door, if you'd rather go there. Ent my turn till Friday.'

'Nell, I came to see you. Not to sit beside Lizzie Brown's fire.' Rebecca hesitated, trying to choose her words. 'I came to say how sorry I am— '

'Sorry? I told you, sorry won't bring my Bill back.' The hard eyes filled suddenly with tears. 'Nothing's going to do that, is it, so what's the use of talking about it? It's done now and them that done it will pay, and that'll be an end to it and good riddance.'

'Nellie – please.' Rebecca leaned across the table. 'Nellie, listen to me. You know Matthew Farrell didn't shoot Bill deliberately. They were friends. It was an accident. And Bess— '

'Oh, so you was there? You saw it, did you?'

'No, of course I didn't, but— '

'So how d'you know it were an accident? How d'you know they didn't quarrel over something? Everyone was fighting and quarrelling that night.'

'But not Matthew and Bill. Bill went to Matthew's house, he *asked* him to go down with his guns.' Rebecca stopped, leaning her head on her hand. How often she had wished that Matthew had simply refused to go. He could so easily have said that he wasn't fit – hadn't he already been injured, that very morning? And to go again, armed . . . Why had he taken such a terrible risk? And why had Bessie followed them?

'So how was it Bill ended up getting shot?' Nell demanded. 'How did it come to be him? If it had been an accident, it could have been anyone. Why my Bill?'

'Why anyone at all?' Rebecca returned wearily. She looked across the table at the angry, unhappy face and spoke gently. 'Nellie, you're very upset. I know that.

But please don't let it make you bitter. Look, you know Matthew Farrell was on the weavers' side. He did all he could to help during the strike. He and Mr Price— '

'Aye, and there's another of 'em. Gentry!' Nell spat the word. 'George Hodgett saw the way the land was laying, years back. Don't never let gentry get involved, he used to say, they'll only bring trouble in the end. He were allus against them two being took up by the Committee. And he was right.'

'But they *did* help. And Mr Price spent a year in prison for what he did.'

'Yes, well . . .' Nellie's glance dropped to the table. She fiddled with a cup and didn't look up. Rebecca wondered if she were beginning to soften.

'And Matthew was trying to help again. He really did care about the weavers, Nell. He and Francis and Tom – you believe *they* care, don't you? You know about the co-operative, Bill knew about it and believed in it.'

'Oh yes. Mind, he didn't think it'd ever get took up by the other masters, but he thought it were a good idea right enough.'

'And Matthew was involved in that too. He helped set up the school and he was designing new houses for the workers. Why would he suddenly turn against your Bill? It doesn't make sense.'

'Nothing makes sense,' Nellie said with spirit. 'It don't do no good to expect it to, neither. I never been able to mek sense of anything yet. I just teks it as it comes, it's all anybody can do.'

'So why fight this? Nellie, I know that what happened was a terrible thing. You've lost Bill. But as you say, it's happened now and nothing can change it. So why let it make you bitter? Why try to punish Matthew? And Bess, poor Bess, who only went because she wanted to stop him getting hurt.' She paused but Nellie said nothing. 'It won't bring Bill back or help him in any way,' she said softly. 'Why not just admit that it was an accident – you know it must have been – and stop whipping up all this hatred against them?'

'And what good will *that* do?' Nell demanded, and at last raised her eyes to Rebecca's face.

Rebecca gave her a long, steady look.

'It may help to prevent another man dying unnecessarily. It could save Bess from dying in prison.'

'Bess?' Nell said uncertainly. 'She sick again, then?'

Rebecca nodded. 'She's desperately ill. They won't let me go to see her, but I've heard from others . . . And Vivian's been trying to get her released, but they won't let her go, and I'm afraid– ' her voice trembled and broke ' –I'm afraid she's going to die there, in such misery, and I'll never see her again. And she's had such a hard life, Nell. She hasn't even had the love that you've had. She's never even had a child.'

There was a long silence. Outside, they could hear the sounds of the street – boots clattering on the 'kidneys', women's voices, the clank of a bucket. Lizzie Brown was screeching at her children next door, and there was the sound of a slap. One of them began to wail.

Nellie looked down at the cup again, then back at Rebecca.

'It don't mek no difference what I says,' she muttered at last. 'I'm just a poor bobbin-winder, like your mam used to be. What do it matter what I thinks anyway?'

'It matters because a lot of the weavers are on your side. And they're the sort of men who will do anything to get back at the masters. They're like George Hodgett – they never liked people like Matthew and Mr Price helping them, and now this has happened they've turned against them completely. Nell, you know what they'll do – they'll bring false evidence at Matthew's trial. They'll swear that they saw Matthew shoot Bill

424

deliberately. You know they will.'

'Well, mebbe they did.'

'They *didn't*. It was an accident.' Rebecca's voice grew desperate. She could feel the knot of anxiety tightening in her stomach. Nell seemed to be in the brink of giving in, admitting the truth – but could she bring herself to do it, finally? What would it do to her? Were her bitterness and hatred the only things that kept her grief bearable?

'Nell, please. Think about it. Your Bill thought a lot of Matthew Farrell. He went to see him that night because he respected him – because he knew Matthew would help. He knew Matthew would stand by the weavers in trouble, just as he would have stood by Matthew. Do you think he would want to see Matthew punished – *hanged* – for an accident? Do you think he would want men to give false evidence? Do you think he would want *you* to let it happen? And Nell— ' her voice shook with tears ' —remember Bessie and the days when you were friends, when you used to go to work together in the mornings. And think of her now, lying sick in a prison cell, being punished for something that was never her fault.'

Polly, settling at last into her chair in the kitchen, took a cup of tea from Mrs Hudd and looked up at her, shaking her head.

'I do'know. He's getting worse every day now. I never seen anyone go downhill so fast.'

'It was the shock of that poor little boy drowning that brought it on,' the housekeeper said. 'My old granfer was the same. Cottage caught fire, Grandma caught in it and he was a little child from that day on. Hale and hearty up to that day, too. It was pitiful to see.'

Polly nodded. 'Pitiful's the word. Mind, there's times I could strangle him, when he keeps on asking me the same thing for an hour at a time. It was the fire this morning. "Put another coal on the fire, Mary" – I'm Mary today, or was this morning. God knows who I'll be when I go back, Admiral Nelson as like as not. And when I told him I'd only just put coals on, he says "all right". And then, not a minute later – "Put another coal on the fire, Mary". And so it goes on, till I could scream. And if it's not that, it's something else. Or else he loses something and says I've stolen it.'

'I don't know how you keep your patience,' the cook remarked. 'I couldn't.'

'Well, it isn't easy, Mrs Atkins, I allow. But then I looks at him, still a fine figure of a man as he is, and I remembers how he used to be – so kind, so good to Rebecca and those boys. And I just feels so sorry for him – well, he could do aught he liked and I couldn't find it in me heart to be cross with him. And he's never going to get any better – and the worst of it is, he knows it. He knows what he's like and you can see him sometimes, wondering how to get out of it. Poor old man.'

'Aye, it's a sad thing,' Mrs Atkins said. 'And none of us knows but what it might be our turn next. It's only Christian to be sorry for him.'

'Well, I hope you'll be as sorry for me if it's my turn next,' Mrs Hudd said grimly, 'for I won't have a fine house to live in and servants to look after me. It'll be the asylum for me. And any one of us. I'm only surprised Mr Vivian hasn't had him put away before now.'

'Rebecca would never let him,' Polly stated. 'Nor Mr Francis. They got too much to thank him for. They'd hev him living with them if it come to it. Even with the little boys.' She finished her tea. 'Well, I'd better go back, I know Edward don't like being with him for long, and Mr Pagnel don't tek too kindly to Edward neither. I thought if he seemed steady enough I might tek him for a walk. Out in the fields. It allus seems to settle him down, getting out in the air.'

The other servants watched as she went up the stairs

and back into the main part of the house. Then the cook sighed and poured herself another cup of tea.

'Aye, it's a queer business, life,' she mused. 'A man like Mr Pagnel, all the money he wants, fine house and furniture and all – and gone as simple as an old granfer down in the cottages. Don't seem to make any sense, does it?'

Mrs Hudd shook her head. But before she could answer, Edward, the footman, came bursting down the stairs and into the basement. His face was white, his hair on end, his uniform dishevelled. The two women started to their feet.

'What's amiss? What's happened? Is it the master?'

'Aye,' he panted. 'We'd best get Dr Curtis. I'm going for him right away. And Polly asks if someone can go up and help her.'

'What is it? Another fit?'

He shook his head. 'I do'know. Something worse nor a fit, I reckon. He's lying on the floor, fell down just before she come back. I was looking at him and his face went all queer and twisted – and he just fell down. Give his head a crack on the big table as he went, and just laid there, didn't move again.' He grabbed his jacket and dragged it on. 'Look, I got to go – one of you get up there and help Polly, for God's sake.'

'Here, that ent no way to talk to your betters,' Mrs Atkins began, but the housekeeper interrupted her.

'Never mind that. I'll go up – you get a kettle boiling. Doctors always need hot water. My heavens above, what a thing to happen,' she panted as she hurried up the stairs. 'As if the family hadn't got enough to do, what with all this trouble over Mr Farrell. And now Mr Pagnel taken ill again. And it sounds bad, too.' She paused at the top of the steps and looked back at the cook. 'You'd better get someone round to Mr Vivian and Mr Francis as well. And get that kettle on, quick!'

* * *

Jeremiah Pagnel's funeral was held three days later and the mourners came back to Pagnel House afterwards, to talk in low voices about the departed man, to drink his wine and to commiserate with his children.

Rebecca stood by the window. It was almost impossible to imagine that she would never see Jeremiah again. She remembered him as he had been when she first came to Pagnel House as a scullerymaid. She seldom saw him then, for her duties lay far beyond his daily round, but she had seen him about the town. A big, broad, awe-inspiring figure he had been to her, and she'd quailed at the thought of working in his house. Suppose she should meet him, she asked her mother, and Fanny had laughed.

'You'll not meet Mr Pagnel much. You'll be in the scullery, scrubbing, and I doubt he even knows where the scullery is – or what it is. You'll see him Christmas, mebbe, when him and the mistress comes down to give the servants their Christmas boxes, and if you gets as far as being housemaid you'll see him then. But you'll be a big girl by then, Becky, and trained, or Mrs Hudd'll never let you near the Family. You don't hev to worry about Mr Pagnel.'

And so it had been. In the years before Rebecca was promoted to housemaid, she saw Jeremiah Pagnel less than half a dozen times. And by the time she found herself answering his summons to stoke the fire or bring a tray of tea, she had learned not to tremble when a member of the Family deigned to notice her. You knew your place, you behaved with proper deference and all was well.

Thinking of all this, Rebecca had almost forgotten where she was. When a hand touched her shoulder, she jumped and turned quickly.

'Vivian! I didn't hear you coming.' She looked up into his face, thinking how sombre he looked. 'Vivian, I'm so sorry. Losing your father, and so soon after Maria and the baby . . . He was a good man.'

'I know.' Vivian stood beside her, staring down towards the town. The first few lights to be replaced after the riots were beginning to be lit and glimmered faintly through the dusk. 'It's been a sad month, Rebecca.'

'I was very fond of your father,' she said in a low voice. 'When I first came here, I was afraid of him – terrified of meeting him. But later – when Francis and I were married and he came to see us in London, he was so kind to me. And with the children, he was so good. He really seemed to love them.' She looked up again and wondered if she ought to have said that. Would Vivian take it as a slighting reference to the fact that she and Francis had sons, whereas he . . . But you couldn't go through life pretending that the situation was any different from what it was. And Jeremiah *had* loved her boys.

'I'm surprised you can take that view,' Vivian said, and she thought of little Geoffrey and looked down again, feeling the tears smart in her eyes.

'It was an accident. He couldn't help it. He was ill, Vivian.'

'And should never have been out with them.' Vivian's hand tightened on her shoulder. 'Rebecca, you don't have to pretend with me. I know just what it's like to lose a son.' She raised her eyes, suddenly incredulous, and he gave a short, abrupt laugh. 'Haven't I felt the same each time yet another daughter was born to me? I was surprised that you ever allowed Father near your boys again, after that. Had it been me, I would have wanted him in an asylum.'

'Oh, no! Never. Even in the last months . . .' She shook her head blindly. 'I loved him. The children loved him – and I was glad for them. They'll miss him as much as I will.'

'Well, perhaps.' But Vivian had clearly begun to think of something else. She glanced up at him, but he was still staring down into the gathering darkness. He must be grieving too, she thought with compassion. And had no one to turn to for comfort. Francis and she could turn to each other, but Vivian . . . Suddenly moved, she raised her hand to cover his, and he looked down at her and smiled.

'Vivian, I really am very sorry. If there's anything I can do . . .' The words sounded empty: what could she do to comfort him, after all? But Vivian's smile deepened and he looked into her eyes, holding her gaze.

'Rebecca,' he said, 'you're very sweet. Exactly the kind of sister-in-law a man would ask for. Your offer to help with the girls – I'm most grateful for your help there. It takes up a lot of your time, I know, and you're a busy woman, so I hear, gathering support for your friend Farrell over that business of the murdered weaver— '

'It wasn't murder,' Rebecca said quickly. 'It was an accident – Matthew is innocent. But you know that – you've been to see Bess.' She hesitated. 'Vivian – tell me again how she was. They say she's ill and they won't let me go. And Francis is so busy with the factory and the lawyers, and Tom – Tom's been but he won't tell me. He just says she's not very well.' She looked up at him. 'You'll tell me the truth, Vivian, won't you?'

'But why should you suspect your brother of lying to you? Rebecca, it's true that she isn't well, but it's nothing serious, I'm sure. But just in case – well, it's certainly best that you don't go there. Gaols aren't places for women.'

'But it's a woman's prison! And Bessie's there.'

'Bessie is used to living poorly,' he said bluntly. 'And you're not, Rebecca, not any more. There are all kinds of diseases drifting about in that place. It's best that you don't go.'

'Poor Bessie,' she whispered. 'If only we could get her home. Is there really no chance, Vivian? Is there nothing you can do?'

Vivian laid his hand on her arm and spoke softly, his eyes full of concern. 'Rebecca, believe me if there were any more I could do I'd be doing it. But . . . it isn't so easy, stopping the machinery of the law once it moves into action. Too many people want to see the affair come to trial. They want to make an example. I'm sorry.' His fingers stroked hers. 'But I won't give in. I'll go on trying. You'll have your Bess back, if it's humanly possible to get her back.' He stopped for a moment, as if thinking hard. 'Unfortunately, a good many people seem to believe that it *was* murder. And I suppose one can't blame them. Strange, isn't it, how history repeats itself. A weaver killed in suspicious circumstances which everyone supposes to be murder, yet it turns out to have been only an accident. And stranger still that it should happen twice with your sister close by, Rebecca . . . But I'm sure you're right. And I'm sure your efforts will be successful. The question is – will they leave you time to keep your promise to me and help with my motherless daughters?'

'I always keep my promises,' Rebecca said steadily. 'I'll be happy to do whatever I can for your daughters.'

'Then I shall always be grateful to you.' He took his hand away from her shoulder. 'And now I must go. The lawyer is here to read Father's will. I must ask you to excuse me.'

Rebecca nodded and watched him go. She saw Francis and the other male members of the family follow Vivian from the room, and then turned back again to her contemplation of the town.

It was fully dark now. The factories were all lit and their windows glimmered in straight rows, up and down, across. Down there, small boys and girls were working at the looms, drawing for the weavers, passing first the sword and then the terry wire through the loops in endless repetition, their hands and arms moving almost automatically, the muscles of their backs and legs screaming with pain and fatigue. Down there, men were working at their looms for tenpence a yard. And somewhere past them all, out in the darkness far beyond Kidderminster, Bessie lay sick in a cold prison cell, waiting for her trial. Waiting to hear if she was to live or die, when it seemed she was already halfway along Death's lonely road.

And not far from her sat Matthew, on his hard prison bed, waiting also, and perhaps wondering if he would ever look up and see the stars again.

The men were gone for a long time. Jeremiah's daughters moved about the room, speaking to the mourners who were beginning to depart. They summoned maids to clear away the remains of the food and drink that had been served, and then clustered around the fire, talking quietly. Rebecca moved to join them and sat silent, gazing into the fire, remembering the man who had lived here. None of them had known him as well as she, she thought. Daughters they might be, but none of them had either known or loved him as well as she.

'Ah, here they are at last!' Sarah cried as the door opened and the men filed back into the room. 'Well, and are we all rich?' Her laughter rippled across the room. 'Did Father apportion it all fairly?'

Rebecca turned and looked for Francis. He came quickly to her side and she stretched her hand out towards him. He took it and raised her to her feet.

'I'm afraid we have to leave now,' he said to his sisters. 'Rebecca likes to be home to see the boys before they go to sleep.' He gave Vivian a brief nod. 'I'll see you in the morning.'

Vivian did not reply, and Rebecca saw that his face was dark, as if suffused with an anger he could barely keep in check. She gazed at him in surprise. What could be wrong? It had always been known that he would be Jeremiah's heir, and she was certain that the promise, so long made, would not have been broken. What could have angered him?

What had Jeremiah done?

Chapter Twenty

'But I don't understand,' Rebecca said. 'Your father carried out his promise. He left the business to Vivian. So why did Vivian look so angry?'
. 'Because that was all he did leave him.' Francis poured himself a brandy and came back to the sofa. 'That and some money, of course – certainly enough to keep him comfortable. You see, that's just what he'd promised to do – make Vivian his heir *as far as the business was concerned*. That's where Isabella's fortune went, into the business. But the house – Pagnel House – was already Father's when he met her. So he evidently didn't consider that as part of the promise. And as for what happened to the business after Vivian dies – he evidently didn't consider that a part of it, either.'

'So what has he done?'

Francis sighed. He looked troubled. He found a cigar, clipped off the end and lit it. Then he looked again at Rebecca.

'He's left Pagnel House to me.'

Rebecca stared at him. 'To *you*?'

'Yes. And now you know why Vivian looked so disappointed. I don't know that he was exactly angry – after all, there's not much point in his being angry with me, is there? I had no idea— '

All the same, Rebecca thought, he certainly *was* angry. And if not with Francis, then with Jeremiah. It must be very uncomfortable, she thought, to be angry with someone who was dead and therefore out of reach of that anger. And she looked at Francis and feared for him.

'But why did he do it? Everyone's always expected Vivian to inherit.'

'Quite. But he explained in the will that Vivian already had a very satisfactory home, which Father built for him when he married Maria. So he considered that duty done. And you and I have no home of our own, we only rent this house, and our sons have very little to inherit.' He paused, then added: 'There's more. And this is probably what made Vivian most angry.'

'What's that?'

'The business. Yes, he kept his promise – Vivian inherits that outright. But – only for his lifetime. In effect, he holds it in trust for the next heir.'

Rebecca stared at him. 'And the next heir is?'

'Vivian's eldest son. And . . . if Vivian should have no sons . . . mine.'

'*Daniel?*'

'Daniel.'

They gazed at each other. We ought to be feeling joyful, Rebecca thought. We ought to be excited, happy. We've inherited a fine house and our son looks likely to inherit a business. So why are we staring at each other like this, as though something dreadful has happened?

'Of course, it's unlikely it will ever come about,' Francis said hastily. 'Vivian is almost certain to marry again, especially with this proviso hanging over him. The will was made before Maria died – Father was evidently as sure as Vivian that the child would be a boy at last. But there's plenty of time for Vivian to get his son. Daniel is never likely to find himself the owner of Pagnel Carpets.'

'I don't much mind if he doesn't. We've never thought of that for him, after all. But even if he doesn't, the damage has been done, Francis.'

'Damage?'

'Yes.' She looked at him, her eyes dark with concern. 'Don't you see – Vivian has always been so possessive about the business. He's always been desperate to make it his, and he's always feared you— '

'Vivian? Feared *me*?'

'He's always been afraid that you would usurp him,' Rebecca said soberly. 'And now, with your inheritance of the house and this condition about the business – and the fact that you already have sons and Vivian has none . . . Suppose he can't father sons, Francis? Some men can't – look at Henry the Eighth. Vivian must be wondering that himself. He might marry again, once, twice, six times and never have a son. And have to watch the business go to your children. Yours.'

'And me the illegitimate son, the by-blow,' Francis agreed. 'But he wouldn't actually see it happen – he'd be dead— '

Rebecca moved her hand impatiently. 'That's not the point. The point is that he would die knowing it was going to happen.' She shook her head. 'Francis, he's going to carry that bitterness with him all through his life. And you know that Vivian finds it hard to forgive old grudges.'

They were silent for a few moments. Francis finished his brandy and sat cradling the glass in his hands, staring into the fire. Then he said: 'Vivian hinted once that when he was in complete charge, I would find it difficult to stay. He talked about "changes" he meant to make – changes I wouldn't like. He advised me to make sure I had an income elsewhere.'

'He was telling you there'd be no place for you at Pagnel's.'

'I thought so. But now . . . You see, Rebecca, he can't actually turn me out now. Another of Father's conditions was that I should have a very strong interest in the business. It isn't entirely Vivian's, even now. And with the possibility that the business might come

437

to Daniel eventually, I'm obliged to keep that interest. Otherwise, I might leave. But I have to look after Daniel.'

A coal shifted in the fire and sent up a little cluster of sparks. Rebecca leaned forward and lifted the poker to settle it.

'Your father has us tied, doesn't he?' she said quietly. 'I'm sure he meant it all for the best. But that's what he's done. He's bound us, hand and foot.' She turned her head, and the sparks from the fire were reflected in her eyes. '*Why* do you have to retain that interest?' she demanded. 'Why do you have to look after Daniel – in that way? You've already said he might never inherit. Vivian could marry next month, he could have a son by this time next year. Or he could live until he was seventy years old and *then* father a boy! You know that's possible. Are you to spend your life "looking after Daniel" and waiting for an inheritance that might never come? Is *he* to spend his life waiting for something that might never be his?'

'It's not a matter of waiting. We shall be building the business all the time.'

'No, Francis. Leave it, now. Concentrate on your own business, the co-operative, which you know Daniel *can* inherit— '

'Rebecca, nobody inherits a co-operative— '

'They can inherit the spirit of it,' she retorted. 'They can inherit the beliefs that make it work. But only if you yourself have those beliefs to hand on, Francis. And if you turn away now, if you stay with Vivian at Pagnel's because you feel you must make it a success just in case Daniel might inherit – you will have betrayed those beliefs.'

Francis stared at her. He got up abruptly, ramming the end of his cigar into a dish. His normally pale face was flushed, his jaw tight.

'Francis— ' Rebecca began, but he whipped round and stared down at her.

'Do you know what you're saying, Rebecca? *Betray my beliefs*? Do you really think that of me? Because if you do, it seems that we have never really known each other at all.' She saw that he was trembling. 'Don't you have any idea of what it means to be a father? To know that your children's destiny rests in your hands, that what you do with your life will follow them through theirs? Don't you understand the responsibility?'

'I understand that you see it as a responsibility,' she answered. 'But you're wrong about destiny, Francis. We each of us hold our destiny in our own hands. We have to take our own responsibility. You can't go through life blaming your misfortunes on your father.'

'I don't— '

'No, you don't. That's just what I'm saying – don't you see? Your father made mistakes, mistakes that have affected you – and made them right up to the moment of his death. Oh, he made every one out of love and kindness and concern – but they were mistakes, just the same.' She stopped and looked into the fire, trying to work out what she wanted to say. 'But look at each of those mistakes, Francis, and see what really happened. From his love affair with Mary, you were born. From her death, you came to live with Geoffrey and Enid and brought them happiness, just as they gave you love and care. From— '

'Are you going to find something good from little Geoffrey's death?' he asked quietly, and she flinched.

'No. I can't do that. But that wasn't his *mistake*, Francis, it was his misfortune. He was ill, he couldn't help it. He wasn't even aware of his illness – he never knew he'd had those small fits before, the ones I told you about. *I* knew, you knew, Polly knew – but we did nothing about them, so if that was anyone's mistake, it was ours. And now this will— '

'That's a mistake too? You don't believe I should

have inherited the house, or Daniel have an interest in the firm?'

Rebecca sighed. 'I don't know. But I do know that it would be wrong for you to forget about the co-operative and concentrate on Pagnel's. And if you truly believe that Daniel's future rests in your hands, it would be the very *worst* thing you could do.' She lifted her hands towards him. 'Francis, the most important inheritance we can pass on to our children is our beliefs. And if you turn away from the co-operative, Daniel will think you no longer believe in it.'

'But I'm not turning away. Of course I believe in the co-operative – nothing's going to change that. But Daniel may one day inherit a business, the biggest in Kidderminster. And although everything you say about Vivian is true, there are other possibilities too. He might not marry again. He might never have a son. He might die himself – tomorrow, next week. And it's up to me to make sure that if Daniel does inherit, he inherits something worth having and not a business that could be a millstone round his neck.' He sat down again, taking both her hands in his, gazing into her eyes. 'Don't you understand, Rebecca, that Daniel could turn that business into a co-operative and change the fortunes of every weaver in Kidderminster? We've always said that if only one of the big manufacturers would do that, they would all follow suit? I've begun it – Daniel could make it *really* work.'

Rebecca returned his look, but her heart was heavy. Had he not heard any of her words about destiny, responsibility? Did he really believe that Daniel's future must lie with Pagnel Carpets?

Francis's words were logical, well reasoned. Too logical, too well reasoned for argument. And he might be right. Perhaps Daniel could do as he suggested and turn Pagnel Carpets into the biggest co-operative in Kidderminster, in the country, leading the way into the future. Perhaps she was wrong to feel this sense of doom, this cold dismay.

But as she looked into Francis's eyes, she detected a new expression in them. A faint glitter of excitement. An excitement she had never seen in him before, but recognised. And her heart sank a little further.

Francis was, after all, a Pagnel. Could he too have been infected by the sense of dynasty that seemed to have been so important to Jeremiah and was still so vital to Vivian? Did he see his sons, his grandsons, marching ahead into a future that would bring the name of Pagnel into the forefront of carpet manufacturing, regardless of how it was produced? Was he tempted by the idea of prestige?

To Rebecca, the weaver's daughter, it was a concept even more ominous than the pursuit of riches.

It had long been the custom for Tom and Nancy to dine with Francis and Rebecca on Saturday evenings. With the week behind them, it was a good time to review the progress of the co-operative, which interested the women as much as it did the men. Rebecca was always keen to know the latest details and Nancy saw no reason to be left out of the discussions simply because she was a woman. Tom remarked once that he hoped these meetings were kept a secret – 'as secret as a freemasons' lodge' – for what the other manufacturers would think of this petticoat government, he dreaded to think.

'Government, you call it!' Nancy had exclaimed scornfully. 'Why, you and Francis take no more notice of Rebecca and me than that fly on the wall does.' But in fact, she knew that the two men did listen to their words, and had more than once taken their advice over conditions in the factories. For both Rebecca and Nancy had known what it was to work long hours for a living, and Tom could vouch for the truth of their words. And Francis knew that it was this that made the co-operative a success.

Tonight, however, the talk had not been of business, but of Bessie, still desperately ill in prison, and of Matthew Farrell's impending trial.

'I must go to see her,' Rebecca said. 'Francis – Tom – you've got to do something. Vivian's tried, but there must be some way.' She looked at her brother. 'She's dying, isn't she?'

Tom met her eyes. His own were dark, filled with sadness for the sister with whom he had shared so much.

'Yes, she is,' he said simply. 'And all I can hope is that it won't be too long coming.'

There was silence among the four of them. Rebecca felt the heat of tears burning her eyes, and she looked down at her plate. Poor, poor Bessie. What sort of a life had she had? Why was it all so unfair?

'I am going to see her,' she said at last. 'I don't care what anyone says. Nobody is going to stop me from going to see my sister before she dies. If I have to go to the King himself . . .' She looked up and although her eyes still glittered, her mouth was firm. 'I shall go.'

'And so shall I,' Tom said. 'I stuck by her all those years when we were in London, and she stuck by me. She needs us now.' He gave Francis a challenging look. 'First thing in the morning we'll go and see that cousin of yours, and we'll *make* him get them to let us in. I don't believe he's even tried. I don't believe he wants Rebecca to see her sister.'

'Oh, I'm sure you're wrong,' Rebecca exclaimed. 'Vivian has tried very hard. He's told me. But Bessie's only allowed certain visitors and they won't agree to my being one of them. If he could do anything about it, he would. Tom, I know you've never trusted him, but he *did* help you to get away all those years ago, and he's never made trouble for you since you came back. And he's been a good friend to me. Don't you think you're mistaken about him? He's had troubles of his own, you know, and he does seem to have changed.'

'Well, I'm not so sure. Leopards don't change their spots and there's a look in his eye sometimes . . . But we'll try him.'

'We will,' Francis said. 'I feel rather the same way as Tom – I've never entirely trusted Vivian. And since Father died and he's known about the inheritance, he's been even less friendly towards me. But Rebecca's right, he never has actually made trouble. So perhaps it's worth it.'

'Well, we've got to do something,' Tom said, and got up from the table. 'And we'd better go home now, Nancy. We've sat here talking long enough. You're looking tired and our Rebecca's worn out. We all needs our strength.'

'If you are going to see Vivian in the morning,' Rebecca said, 'I'm coming with you. I don't really believe there's any more he can do – but he may be able to tell us who can help. And if there's any chance at all . . .'

The other three looked at her. Pale, thin, exhausted, her mouth was as determined as ever, her eyes steady. Francis opened his mouth as if to object, and then slowly nodded.

'We'll go early, while he is still at breakfast,' he said, and Rebecca smiled.

'If I'm not visiting Bessie in Staffordshire Gaol by nightfall tomorrow,' she declared, 'I shall camp at their gates. I'll stay there until they *have* to let me in. And I shall tell Vivian that myself.'

Vivian was indeed just finishing his breakfast when the small deputation arrived to see him next morning.

Rebecca was the first one to come into the breakfast room as the maid announced them. She came straight to the table and stood before Vivian. He looked up and saw the determination in her eyes, and was instantly wary. But why should he be wary of her? He knew she trusted him. He knew she believed in his powers.

'Well,' he said easily, wiping his lips on a napkin, 'and what is all this about? A little early for social visiting, isn't it?'

'This isn't a social visit, Vivian,' Francis said, coming to stand beside Rebecca. 'We've come to ask your help.'

'My help! Why, is the famous co-operative in trouble? You knew when you started that it was entirely your own venture— '

'It's nothing to do with the co-operative,' Francis said quietly. 'It's about Rebecca's sister, Bess.'

'Bess? Bess Himley?' His eyes moved towards Rebecca and then away again. 'But I've already done all I can about Bess. What more are you expecting?'

Rebecca stepped forwards. She stood close to Vivian, looked down into his eyes, spoke imploringly. 'Vivian, you know what case Bess is in. You've seen her. She's seriously ill – Tom's seen her too and he thinks – he thinks she's dying. Please, *please*, isn't there any way you can make them let me in to see her? Or let her out, so that I can look after her? What use is it to keep her there, if she's never going to live to be tried? What harm would it do if she were allowed to come home and be nursed through her last few weeks, or perhaps only days? Please, Vivian – won't you try again?'

He looked at her thoughtfully. So she had come to beg, she and her husband, the woman who had once been his mother's housemaid and the by-blow who had thrust him aside and stolen his inheritance. He felt again the smouldering anger that had seethed within him ever since he had sat in the library at Pagnel House and heard the reading of his stepfather's will. And he wanted nothing more than to turn them out of his house, to see them grovel in the streets, to see them both lying on pallets of straw in cold prison cells, slowly dying . . .

'But you know I've done all I can, Rebecca, my dear,' he said reasonably. 'And really, you know, it's not a very pleasant place to visit. I think you're far better— '

'It's not a pleasant place to *be*!' she cried passionately and fell to her knees beside his chair, clutching his hands in hers. 'Vivian, I beg you – try again! Bessie's dying. She may be dead at this very moment. But if she lives, I must see her again, I must be with her. I don't care how dreadful it is in there – do you think I am not used to dreadful scenes, do you think I can't stand it? Am I so weak, in your eyes? Vivian, if you make them let me in, if you get Bessie released so that she can spend her last days in some measure of comfort, I will be grateful to you for the rest of my life. I mean it. You'll have my gratitude always and I'll do my best to repay you, I promise.' The torrent of words ceased and she sank her forehead down on to her hands, and he felt the tears seep hot through her fingers to wet his own. 'Please . . .' she whispered, and he knew she was spent.

Vivian sat quite still, looking down at the bent head, the smooth chestnut hair. It was a moment of triumph. The proud Rebecca who had defied him as a girl, reduced to this. The young housemaid who had looked at him with scorn in her eyes, who had fought off his advances, who had let his cousin Francis make love to her instead . . . reduced now to kneeling at his feet, begging and pleading for her sister's life. Offering him her gratitude always. Placing herself for ever in his debt.

It was a pleasant thought. And he remembered the will his stepfather had made, the loss of the house he had always believed to be his, the even worse prospect of the business he had also considered his passing to

445

Francis's son. Yes, Rebecca's gratitude might be very well worth while earning.

Gently, he pulled one hand away from her feverish clutch and stroked her smooth hair. There was no doubt about it, Rebecca was an attractive woman. Her hair was like silk, her skin smooth velvet. He let his mind play for a moment with the forms her gratitude might take.

But that was all in the future. Just now, he must balance his own immediate sense of vengeance, which was well satisfied by the present situation, with the possibility of future manipulations. A game which could go on for the rest of his life; whereas once Bessie had died . . .

'Get up, Rebecca,' he said quietly, and took her hands to raise her to her feet. He sat her in a chair by the table and poured coffee for her to drink. His movements were careful, his touch gentle. And when her sobs had ceased a little, he looked first at her, then at Francis and Tom.

'I'll try again,' he said, knowing well that he would be successful, for it was by his orders that Rebecca had never been admitted. 'We'll go to Stafford this morning, and I'll do my very best to see that you are with your sister within an hour. And let's not talk of gratitude or debts. Let's call it simple friendship. After all, it's I who should be grateful to you, for all you've done for me.'

Rebecca raised her tear-stained face. 'Do you really mean it, Vivian? Do you really think I might see Bessie today?'

He smiled at her, and thought of that undying gratitude, continuing through life. Yes, it was a better way. Bess Himley was no further use to him now. But in this last throw of the dice, she could serve him well.

'I mean it, Rebecca,' he said.

And so, at last, Rebecca was admitted to Stafford

Gaol and guided to the cell where Bessie lay near to death.

With Francis and Tom close behind her, she stepped through the door. The wardress, her face like stone, clanged the iron door shut behind them as if expecting them to remove Bessie by force. And oh, Rebecca thought, if only they could do just that. If only they could take her away, out of this horrible place, and bring her to a clean, warm room where she could lie on a comfortable bed between fresh sheets and be tended night and day.

It was almost impossible to stifle her shock as she looked down at the wasted figure. Could this really be Bessie? Could this really be the woman who had begun to blossom as Matthew's housekeeper, whose skin had begun to regain its colour, even its bloom? Whose hair might never wholly regain its bright gold but had at least begun to curl again and attain a pale silveriness that in itself promised a certain beauty? Who had begun to smile again, even to laugh, whose life it seemed had turned a corner and started to discover better things?

It was difficult to believe. This woman lying here, her body shrunken, her skin the colour of ashes, was surely an old woman. Bessie was barely thirty. There must be some mistake.

But even as she turned in dismay to Francis and Tom, there was a cracked whisper from the bed and she heard her own name spoken in tones that chilled her blood and brought a prickle to her flesh.

'Becky . . . Is that you, our Becky?'

Rebecca turned back swiftly and knelt by the bed, ignoring the grime that encrusted the stone floor. She laid her hand gently on the cold brow and looked into the hollow eyes, and knew that this was indeed her sister Bessie. A lump came into her throat.

'Bessie . . . Bessie. Yes, it's me, it's Becky. And Tom's here too, look, and Francis. We've come— '

she hesitated, then plunged on. 'We've come to take you home . . .'

Behind her, she felt the sudden stir of the two men. But she went on, determined now. 'We're going to take you back to Kidderminster, Bessie, and look after you and make you better again. Do you understand? You're going to be better.' She gazed down at the blank eyes, wondering if Bessie were capable of understanding, would ever be capable again. But the dry lips moved again and she bent closer to listen.

'. . . won't let me go,' Bessie whispered hopelessly. '. . . dying anyway . . . and if I wasn't . . . they'd . . . hang me . . .'

'No!' Rebecca restrained herself from gripping Bessie's thin, bony hands. 'No, you're not dying, Bessie – remember how ill you were when Tom and I came to see you in London and how you got better then? You can get better again – you *will* get better again.' You must, she thought agonisingly. You can't die here in this terrible place.

Bessie was whispering again. '. . . oughter hev let me go then . . . my time was up . . . only meks trouble if you . . . keeps folk alive past their time . . .' Her brow was damp with sweat but when Rebecca touched it, the skin was icy cold. 'Let me go, Becky . . . just let me slip away . . .'

She closed her eyes and Rebecca stared at her, panic kicking at her heart. Was she dying now? Had that been her last breath? But no, her chest was rising still, very slightly, there was breath still going into her lungs. And while there was breath, there must still be hope. She stood up quickly and turned to face her husband and brother.

'We've got to get her out of here. No one could survive in this awful place. The air's stinking, there's filth everywhere and it's clear nobody has washed poor Bess or done anything for her for days. They're just leaving her here to rot.' She pushed past them and began to beat on the door and call for the wardress.

Francis caught at her arm. 'Rebecca— '

Angrily, she shook him off. 'Don't try to stop me, Francis. I'm going to get my sister out of this hell-hole. I shan't leave unless I leave with her, and nothing you can do will— ' The door swung open and she stalked out. 'You stay with her, Tom,' she flung over her shoulder. 'She may wake and she'll be worried and frightened if nobody's there. Tell her I'm coming back as soon as I can.' She turned to Francis. 'Well? Are you coming with me?'

'Of course I'm coming with you.' He was beside her as they marched swiftly along the narrow stone corridor. 'Rebecca, I'm not trying to stop you. I'm as determined as you are to get Bessie out of this place. I only wish I'd come before and seen the condition she was in. Vivian never gave me any idea it was that bad— '

'Vivian!' Rebecca stopped suddenly. 'Of course! *He* can order Bessie to be released. He has influence here, he's part of the Board who govern the place – and more shame to him,' she added bitterly. 'Why didn't he tell us, Francis?' And then, not waiting for a reply, 'And where is he now? We must find him at once.'

Vivian was with the governor of the prison. He came to his feet as Rebecca marched in with Francis close behind her. Rebecca flung him a glance that made him stagger, and then turned her flashing eyes on the Governor.

'My sister Bess Himley is dying in the most appalling conditions in this slum you call a prison,' she declared. 'And I want her out of it. You have no right to keep innocent people in such a state. I thought the prisons were supposed to have been reformed – I don't like to imagine what they must have been like before.'

The Governor rose to his feet. His small, cold eyes moved briefly over Rebecca and then he looked over her head and addressed Francis.

'Do you have any complaint to make, sir? I understand you've been visiting a relative – one of your wife's relatives, is that right? The prisoner Himley?'

Rebecca gasped, but Francis gave her a warning glance and stepped forwards.

'That's correct. And yes, I do have a complaint to make.' His voice was firm and cool. 'My wife is quite right in what she says. Her sister is dangerously ill and appears to be receiving no care at all. The cell she is in is filthy, and the bed is crawling with lice and other insects. I want your authority to remove her, so that we can look after her properly at home and either nurse her back to health or make her last few days at least more comfortable.'

The Governor stared at him, then laughed abruptly.

'You want my authority, do you? By your tone, sir, I'm surprised that you even bother to ask for it. Why not march in and remove all my prisoners because you don't happen to like the way they're living? May I remind you, sir, that these people are criminals, the lowest of the low, and would not be here at all if they hadn't committed some felony? As for filth, they cause that themselves. They're no more than animals, most of them.'

Rebecca's face blazed.

'My sister's neither a criminal nor an animal! She's innocent of any charge and you have no right to keep her here at all. Now – please give us authority to remove her and we'll bother you no more.'

Again, the Governor addressed Francis.

'Sir, I have no jurisdiction over which prisoners are brought here and how long they should be kept. I merely administer them while they are here. Whether your wife's sister is innocent or not is not for me to say – I'm neither judge nor jury.'

'Then who can say?' Rebecca cried bitterly. 'Or does she have to wait for a trial, and probably die before a jury even sees her.'

450

The Governor glanced at Vivian and hesitated. Vivian stepped forwards.

'In the circumstances,' he said smoothly, 'I can order Bess's release. At least until she's fit to face trial and so long as I approve of the place she goes to and the people who are to take care of her.'

Rebecca stared at him. Her lips parted, but before she could speak Francis said, 'And do you order this, Vivian? Can we take Bessie home?'

'But of course,' he said as if there had never been any question of it. 'Her condition has clearly deteriorated since I last saw her, and her cell too if what you say is true. When I came here a week or so ago, she was clean and well cared for.' He turned to the Governor. 'It seems that not all your wardresses are as kindly as the one who was looking after Bessie then. Perhaps you should look into that.'

The Governor bowed his head. He glanced again, briefly, at Rebecca and then at Francis. Then he opened the door.

'I'll take you back to the cell myself,' he said, leading the little procession through the maze of corridors. 'You can take the prisoner immediately.'

But when they reached the small stone dungeon where Bessie lay, the door was already open. Tom was standing beside it, his whole body drooping with sorrow. And as soon as Rebecca saw him, she knew.

'Tom?'

He nodded. 'She's gone, Becky. Only a few minutes ago. She just opened her eyes for a minute and looked at me. And then she sort of shivered – and almost smiled.' There was a touch of wonder in his voice. 'Just as if she saw something good at the last – something that made her feel really happy. I ent seen Bessie look like that in years.' He was silent for a moment, and then he went on. 'And then she lifted up her hands and reached out, like . . . and then it was all over. She just stopped breathing. And she was . . . gone.'

451

For a few minutes, nobody spoke. Then Rebecca felt the tears come. She turned to Francis and he laid his arm about her shoulder and drew her close. Soundlessly, held firmly against him, she wept for her sister.

Poor, poor Bessie, whose life had been so harsh, so cruel. And yet – Tom had said she seemed happy in those last few minutes. Happier than she'd been for years.

If that were true, then perhaps it wasn't so important that Bessie had died here, in the squalor of a prison cell. But she wished, she wished very much indeed, that she could have been here too.

Bess Himley was buried on a cool, windy afternoon, with more people to mourn her than she had ever known in life.

The family were there: Rebecca, Francis, Tom, Nancy, Enid. Vivian was there, standing back a little as if to dissociate himself from the proceedings. The servants from Unicorn Street and from Matthew's house were there.

And so were the weavers. Dozens of them, gathering in small knots which merged and grew to a crowd. Men and women who remembered Bessie as a child, who had played with her in the yard, who had worked with her. And many who had never met her at all, but knew the story of her life and knew that it could so very easily have been theirs. Who saw her as a symbol of the cruelty of a weaver's life: from the harshness of twelve and twelve working, with the risks that attended any young girl working late into the night with an unscrupulous master, to the injustice of the blame that was meted out to a woman who just happened to be nearby when a man died, and had no one to defend her.

Rebecca looked at the crowd and her heart ached. So poor, all of them. It seemed that nothing had changed since she was a child, a draw-girl working for her father while he wove at his own loom. In fact, some of them were even worse off now than they had been then. Wages had been reduced, trade worsened and many weavers were idle – 'playing' as it had been called – and had nothing but the few pence the Friendly Society could pay them. She and her wives' association did the best they could, but a soup kitchen did no more than keep body and soul together by the frailest of threads. And the task was so great . . .

'I wonder if things will ever be any better,' she said later on to Francis. They were alone at last, sitting by the fire, resting after a day that had been a peculiar strain. 'The poor people . . . I felt so sorry for them, Francis. And there seems to be nothing more we can do.'

'I know.' He took her hand in his and she looked up into his face. During these past few days they had begun to grow closer again, as if realising that the love they had shared was too precious to be allowed to die. And Rebecca, always aware of her need for Francis, had begun to sense an answering need in him. As if, at last, he had begun to cast off whatever restraints he had imposed upon himself.

'Francis,' she said, 'please hold me.'

He met her eyes. His own, so blue still, were darkened as she remembered seeing them during those mornings in the library when they had first fallen in love. Her heart beat a little faster. Almost without realising what she did, she lifted her face and her lips parted softly.

'Francis . . .'

'Oh, Rebecca,' he murmured. '*Rebecca* . . .'

He drew her into his arms and held her close against his heart. There was no need for words. The touch of his cheek against hers, the strength of his arms about her, the strong beating of his heart close to hers, all these were enough to tell her that the love was still there, that it had never died.

'Francis, what's happened to us?' she whispered. 'Why did we grow so far apart? It's so long since you held me like this – so long since you loved me.'

He shook his head. 'Rebecca, I can't tell you why— '

'But you know.' Something in his voice made her lift her head, look at him more sharply. 'You know why it is. And you must tell me, Francis! Don't you think I have a right to know? Isn't it my life too? Isn't it my *love*?'

He looked at her helplessly. She sat up, straight and proud, challenging him with her bright, dark eyes, and he thought of how much she had done, how far she had come in her life. From a weaver's daughter living in a poor, bare hovel, through service in his father's house, to the woman she was now, not only wife and mother but helping to run one of the most advanced businesses in Kidderminster. He thought of the factory with its Jacquard looms, their rolls of thin card punched with designs Rebecca had drawn; the co-operative, where every man or woman in the carpet shop knew and worshipped her. The weavers' cottages, where she went so often and had so many friends, and the school where she visited the children and helped to teach them their letters.

All this, and yet he had denied her not only his love, but the right to know why she must be denied. And he felt a great shame. Rebecca was right. It was her life too, and her love, and he had taken away her right to make her own choice.

'Rebecca, it was never because I had stopped loving you,' he said in a low voice. 'It was because I loved you so much . . . It was when William was born. You were so ill. And the doctor told me . . . he told me that you must never have any more children.' His eyes were dark now with sorrow, with remembered pain. 'Rebecca, my love, I dared not risk losing you. I couldn't take the risk of loving you, when I knew it might end in . . . in that. I knew that if I lost you, I might as well lose my own life. I just wouldn't have wanted to go on if you had died, and I had been the cause of it.'

He stopped, overcome by emotion he had thought long buried. Rebecca stared at him. It was several moments before she spoke, and she seemed to be working the idea through in her own mind.

'You stopped loving me because you thought another child would kill me? But . . . I might not have conceived again.'

'The doctor told me it was possible that you would be barren. But there was no way of telling. And – and I couldn't take the risk. God knows, I wanted to – there were times when my longing for you nearly drove me mad, when I had to stay away from you or I would have succumbed.' He paused. 'I want you still,' he said in a low voice.

Rebecca looked at him. She could feel his longing, his desire, just as she had always been able to feel it, and her own yearning grew to match it. But there were still things to say. Now that they had, at last, begun to talk, the opportunity must not be lost.

'You should have told me,' she said at last. 'You should have given me the choice.'

'I know. But I was afraid – I was afraid you would want to take the risk, Rebecca. And I dared not. I dared not lose you.'

Rebecca took his hands in hers and held them fast. She looked into his eyes and would not let him look away. He faced their darkness and knew what she was about to tell him.

'You were right, Francis. I would have taken the risk, and taken it gladly. And I don't believe I would have died. But you were wrong not to tell me. I had a right to know, a right to make that choice. And I still have that right.'

She stopped and drew in a deep breath. Francis

watched her. He knew that Rebecca meant what she said, that she believed in her rights over her own body even though in law her body belonged to him. And he knew that whatever decision she made now, he would comply, because he believed in Rebecca herself. In her strength and in her wisdom.

'We almost lost each other anyway,' she said quietly. 'Not through death, but through the death of our love. Wasn't that just as bad a loss, Francis? It has been to me. I tell you this – I would rather die in your arms, knowing that you loved me, than live with a gulf between us and never understand why.' She let go of his hands and wound her arms around his neck, pressing herself close against him. 'Love me, Francis,' she whispered against his lips. 'Love me as you used to. Let us have that at least.'

His face turned against hers. His lips found her mouth and shaped it to his. He caught her against him with a groan and the desire that had smouldered in them both for so long, damped down like a fire banked up so that no flame could consume it, suddenly burst from its confinement.

The fire in the hearth burned and died down and had begun to cool before Francis and Rebecca had completed their new loving.

Chapter Twenty-One

The bells of Worcester Cathedral rang out across the city, declaring the opening of a new day, and Rebecca turned over in bed and opened her eyes.

Francis was already at the window. She saw his profile against the light, still as slender as a boy, his head bent in contemplation. Pushing back the covers, she slipped out of bed and padded across to join him.

Francis put his arm around her. They stood together, looking down into the narrow street below the inn. It was already crowded, with horses dragging their carts to the market at the end of the road, shopkeepers opening their doors and taking down their shutters, and people hurrying about their early morning business. Women with baskets over their arms, anxious to get their shopping done before setting off for the glove factories or the porcelain works. Men sweeping the road, making deliveries, thrusting their way through the crowd with baskets of bread or vegetables or meat balanced on their heads.

'What a busy place Worcester is,' Rebecca said. 'And very grand too – the Cathedral's beautiful. Did you know King John's tomb is in there? I thought kings and queens were all buried in London.' She turned in the circle of Francis's arm and looked up into his face. 'Francis – how do you think it will go?'

'The trial?' He shrugged. 'How can I say? The prosecution will begin with their evidence. And it won't sound good. But it will be Godson's turn later and I'm sure he'll be able to show that Matthew would never have shot Bucknell deliberately. After all, there's no clear evidence – nobody saw it happen.'

Rebecca nodded. After Bessie's death, she had at last won Nell's acceptance of the fact that Bill's death had been an accident, and persuaded her to lend her support to Matthew's cause. The two had spent a large part of their time on the streets, telling anyone who would listen that Matthew Farrell was innocent.

'Not that it'll mek any difference,' Nellie had said. 'Who's going to listen to folk like us?'

But Rebecca had insisted that it might. 'You were sure enough that you could get him condemned. Why not be as sure that he could be acquitted?' But she had sensed Nell's doubts and, try as she might to resist them, had inevitably picked up the feeling of hopelessness that hung around the little cottage. 'Nell, we must *believe* in Matthew,' she said desperately. 'Otherwise he has no chance at all.'

She looked around the bare, damp little room and thought of Matthew living in circumstances not so very different. Except that she and Nell could get up at any moment and walk out of the door, walk to wherever they liked – while Matthew was confined, trapped, and with no prospect of ever walking free again.

'Come on,' she said, jumping up. 'We'll do no good sitting in here. Let's go out and talk to some more people. There must have been some witnesses, someone who could swear that Matthew didn't fire deliberately.'

'And if there were,' Nell said wearily, getting to her feet as well, 'don't you reckon they'd hev come forward by now. There can't be a body in Kidder don't know about Bill Bucknell and Matt Farrell by now. I tell you, Becky, you're flogging a dead horse.'

'Not dead, no.' Rebecca tied the strings of her bonnet firmly under chin. 'It may yet get up and walk, Nell. Until the very last moment, until the trial itself is over, it may yet get up and walk.' And she led the way out into the street, determined to find her vital witness.

But if he existed, he never came forward. And now, listening to Francis's words, Rebecca shivered.

'That doesn't mean they won't bring witnesses who are ready to swear that they did. Francis, what could we do if they did that? Matthew would be doomed.'

She felt Francis's arm tighten around her. 'My love, we mustn't even think that way. Just hope and pray and *believe* that all will be well. And now, it's getting late. We'd better get dressed and ready.' He bent his head and kissed her on the lips. 'Matthew will survive this. He didn't travel all around the world to die in an English prison. He'll live to travel again.'

'I hope so. He must.' She clung to him for a moment, thinking of Matthew taking that last, lonely walk to the gallows.

'Oh, *Francis* . . .' She bent her head against him, unable to stop the tears, and he held her close for a few minutes and then lifted her face with one hand and kissed the tears tenderly away.

'Be brave, my love. You're going to see Matthew in court in an hour or two, and he mustn't see that you've been crying. We've got to give him hope and strength. If we don't do that, we'd be better to stay away.'

'Yes.' She sniffed and wiped her eyes. It was little enough that she and Francis could do, but who knew what might be significant? Who knew what might tip the balance?

Now she sat between him and Humphrey Price in the crowded courtroom, watching the door. The courtroom was crowded with weavers who had walked from Kidderminster to attend the trials. Some had gone home after the main trial, jubilant with the release of their mates, bringing them back in triumph. But a good many had stayed to hear Matthew's trial, and she saw that most of the members of the Committee were there – Fred Holloway, George Hodgett and the others. Nell had not come; she had children to attend to, she said,

459

and a living to earn. She'd hear soon enough, and none of it would bring back her Bill anyway.

There were carpet manufacturers as well, amongst them William Cooper, John Broom, the manager from Brinton's, several others. And masters of other trades too, for the Union movement was affecting them all now and the outcome of this trial was an important one. And that too, Rebecca thought, could affect the jury. Was there – could there ever be – such a thing as true, impartial justice?

Rebecca had a clear view to the dock where Matthew would stand. The lawyers began to filter through, carrying their papers, looking solemn. Slowly, unhurriedly, they settled themselves in their places. They were waiting now for Richard Godson. During the past few days he had defended eleven Kidderminster weavers accused of offences varying from 'Riot and Assault' to 'Tumultuous Assembly'. And secured the acquittal of all but four, she thought with a sudden lightening of her heart, and those four sentenced lightly – no more than a few months in prison. If he could be as clever with Matthew . . .

'It was mostly lack of evidence that helped them,' Francis had told her. 'No one had actually *seen* anything being damaged or any person being attacked. Or would admit to having seen it! The jury had no choice but to acquit. And I suspect that the unfairness of Humphrey Price's trial last year may have had something to do with it, too. There was a good deal of uneasiness about that.'

'Will it help Matthew too?' Rebecca asked eagerly.

But Francis shook his head. 'It's impossible to say. Matthew faces a much more serious charge. And since it was a weaver who died, and that weaver a member of the Union Committee . . . well, it might even go against him. I'm sorry, my love— ' as he saw her stricken face ' —but we can't hide from it. We can't escape it.'

'We can only hope,' she said in a low voice, and he nodded.

'We can only hope.'

Rebecca felt Francis lean across her to speak to Humphrey.

'Where's Godson?'

The clergyman shook his head. 'He must have been delayed. He'll be here in a moment – he's never been known to be late for a case. Don't worry.'

Rebecca looked from one to the other. 'What will happen if he doesn't come?'

Francis squeezed her arm. 'He'll come. Why, that's probably him now.'

There was a slight disturbance at the door. People had been arriving all the time and it was especially crowded there now, with more and more trying to squeeze in. Rebecca craned her neck to see who was causing the flurry. Was it Richard Godson? She felt a sudden anxiety. Suppose he *didn't* come? Suppose something had happened to him? They were depending on him. Matthew was depending on him.

The crowd was shifting in order to let someone through. There were mutters and complaints, but at last they parted and a man strode past them and marched straight to the desk where Richard Godson's assistant, John Pascal, was sorting out papers. Pascal looked up as he approached and Rebecca felt a chill touch her body, as if someone had opened a door to an icy wind. The two men conferred for a few minutes.

'He isn't coming,' she said, and this time Francis did not contradict her.

Humphrey stood up. 'I'll go and see.' He made his way past the other people who were seated in their row, and down into the body of the court. He broke into the two men's conversation, courteously but firmly, and they turned towards him. Their faces were grave.

461

'He isn't coming,' Rebecca said again, and clenched her hands into small, tight fists.

And now Humphrey was coming back, and his face too was grave. He climbed back into his seat, and Francis and Rebecca turned to him at once. Rebecca felt sick with apprehension. She could not speak.

'What's happened?' Francis asked.

'It's Godson. He's been taken ill – some kind of food poisoning, apparently. There's no possibility of his being able to come today, nor for several days in all likelihood. The doctor attending him can't say.' He paused and his mouth turned downwards. 'He won't be able to defend Matthew after all.'

'But what will they do? Postpone the trial?'

'No. Pascal will have to do it.' Humphrey looked at them both. 'It isn't as bad as all that, you know. Pascal is very good. He's been with Godson for some years and knows his ways, he'll present as good a defence. We must have faith in him.'

'Yes, of course.' But Francis sounded despondent, and Rebecca felt her heart sink as if it were a leaden weight in her breast. They had come to rely so much on Richard Godson, seeing him as Matthew's saviour, the only man who could save him from the gallows. And now he had been snatched from them. And, clever though John Pascal might be, he didn't have the presence, the charisma, of Richard Godson.

'We must have faith,' Humphrey repeated. 'He can't work properly if he doesn't have all our belief and encouragement to spur him on. He needs our faith, Rebecca – he needs us as much as we need him.'

She looked at him. Was it true? Could their belief, their faith, do anything positive to help John Pascal in this task that had been thrust upon him? Would it really make a difference to him that they believed in his ability? Would it matter what they thought?

Pascal had turned his head in their direction and she met his eyes. And knew that it mattered very much.

John Pascal was an experienced lawyer, accustomed to conducting cases like this, accustomed to presenting a good defence to the judge and jury, accustomed to winning his cases. But he still needed the will and faith of those he defended, and of their families and friends. He still needed the strength that they could give him.

A long, steady look passed between them, and Rebecca felt a strange new sensation creeping through her veins. It was as if, for a brief space, she had been allowed into John Pascal's mind. Not the thinking, reasoning part of it, but into some deeper recess. Or perhaps their minds had met on some different level, some higher plane. Whichever it was, there had been a moment of complete communication between them. It was like a white light, shining into her heart. And then it was gone, and she sat quite still for a moment and then relaxed.

'Yes,' she said to Humphrey. 'You're right. Pascal needs our belief, our faith in him.'

And now the ushers were calling for silence. The lawyers were all there, bewigged and gowned, the jury sworn in and in their seats. The judge had entered with all due pomp and now there was only one person to come.

Matthew.

The courtroom was hushed. Rebecca held her breath. She watched the door as if willing it to open.

Slowly, it moved. Slowly, the dark gap grew. Slowly, it came fully open and revealed a prison guard who stepped out of the shadows with someone close behind him.

Rebecca caught her breath. She twined her fingers within Francis's and felt his other hand on her arm, soothing her. She craned forward.

He was thinner. His face, robbed of its exposure to sun and wind and air, was sallow and drawn. His chestnut hair had lost its brightness; it was longer and hung dull and lank about his ears. His clothes were dusty and crumpled.

A murmur ran round the crowded courtroom, and Rebecca turned anxiously to Humphrey Price.

'Are they for him or against him? What does it mean?'

He pulled down the corners of his mouth. 'It's difficult to say. To some, he might appear the very embodiment of a ruthless murderer. Others might simply look on his appearance as a case for more prison reform. It all depends on the prejudices they came in with.'

Rebecca looked at the people who filled the courtroom. There were weavers, some of them for Matthew, others against. But there were also a great many people whom she had never seen before. People who didn't come from Kidderminster, who had just come in for the entertainment of seeing a man tried for murder. Or perhaps they were interested in the workings of justice and didn't really care what trial they heard.

None of them knew Matthew for the man he was. None of them really cared about him.

The sound of the gavel brought everyone turning to the Bench. The trial had begun.

Vivian strode through his biggest carpet shop and looked about him with satisfaction.

They were working at full strength again. The riots of September had been quelled and the ringleaders tried in Worcester, though he wasn't best pleased by the fact that most of them had been released. That was Godson's doing. But since it was widely believed that Richard Godson was destined for greater things, possibly even Parliament, Vivian was not inclined to challenge him. Better to let the matter drop.

And the weavers would not be likely to riot, nor to strike again. With the 14th Light Dragoons now firmly stationed in the town and talk of a permanent barracks being built, peace would be kept in the town and the manufacturers able to pursue their plans without all this talk of unions and strikes and 'a fair day's wage for a fair day's work'. Why, they'd been getting that all along. Demanding more was just plain greed.

He looked up into the high roof of the carpet shop. The Jacquard looms had been installed here soon after Broom had brought the system to Kidderminster, and the great machinery clattered constantly, the long rolls of thin card rolling down over the heddles to guide the different coloured wools into their design. It had been a major step forward, this Jacquard system, but it had been expensive to instal and had still not paid for itself. Broom, the innovator, was said to be in financial difficulties, and other manufacturers were hesitating over installing it themselves.

Well, Pagnel's would not go to the wall over it. Vivian had been careful not to plunge all his savings into the new system, and to keep the more traditional Brussels weave going as well. And Francis's designs were second to none. They alone would keep Pagnel's customers loyal.

At the thought of Francis, Vivian frowned. For years, he had been conscious of his need to stay one step ahead of Francis – preferably several. Yet he had never quite understood why. He had always known himself to be Jeremiah's heir. He had known that one day the business would be his. He had looked forward to that day, when he would be able to dispense with Francis, dismiss him from the business and leave him to sink or swim according to his own ability.

As he should always have been doing, Vivian thought. A by-blow, born the wrong side of the blanket – why should Francis have expected to be feather-bedded through life? Yet he'd been cosseted and cared for since birth. Found a home with Jeremiah's own brother, educated, brought into the business. And even when he disgraced himself with a little housemaid and brought further shame on the family by actually marrying her, he'd been helped to set up a business in London, given a job managing the warehouse there, and eventually brought back to Kidderminster and into the family business again.

A true parallel with the story of the Prodigal Son! While Vivian, who had stayed at home, who had worked industriously, married well and done his best to provide further heirs for the Pagnel dynasty, had been given nothing.

And now, when he ought to have been coming into his own, when he should have been able to turn Francis away without a second thought, all was changed and his hands were tied as tightly as ever.

Vivian turned and strode out of the carpet shop. He walked rapidly down to the river and stared into the muddy waters. With no dyeing in progress at present, the colour was a dark, rusty red, stained with waste from the iron works further upstream. It swirled beneath him as he leaned over the bridge and he wondered how long it had been since any fish had been bold enough to swim in these waters.

No, he could not dismiss Francis now. For one thing his cousin, half-brother, call him what you would, had too strong an interest in the business now. He owned Pagnel House and, unless Vivian were yet to father a son of his own, he held a position of trust in the company. In fact, whether Jeremiah had intended it or not, Francis was in effect the true heir, and Vivian held only a life interest.

Vivian turned to walk up the hill to Mount Pleasant. He wondered how the trial was proceeding. Had they produced the witnesses who would testify to having seen Matthew Farrell take aim at Bucknell and deliberately gun him down? Had Godson's defence crumbled?

He was almost home. The trees he had planted in his garden when he first married Maria were tall now, their leaves turning to red and gold. He could hear the voices of his daughters as they played on the other side of the wall. A few days ago, Rebecca had been there with them, talking to them, losing her hat in a game of tag, laughing like a girl. He had stood at the windows and watched.

And that was when he had seen the truth. And understood at last what had been wrong with his life, all these years.

I should have been the one to marry Rebecca, he thought with a sudden bitter, savage regret. Those occasions when I caught her and tried to force her to submit to me – those were opportunities I missed. I should have been gentle with her, as Frank must have been, I should have seen the gold that lay beneath the housemaid's cap. I should have coaxed her and courted her and made her love me. I should have taken her into my bed and made love to her, and I should have married her.

Rebecca's sons would then have been mine. Pagnel House would have been mine. Pagnel Carpets would have been mine, and my son's after me, with no rival. Frank would have been left some money, enough to run his own business, and he would have been out of my life.

Rebecca should have been *my* woman. Her sons, my sons.

Vivian unfastened the gate and went into his garden. In a few days, the trial would be over, Farrell disposed of and Rebecca back in Kidderminster. There was still Francis to be considered, of course, but Francis was delicate, always had been. He was like old Geoffrey. And he didn't look after himself. That cough . . .

One day, Vivian thought, Rebecca is going to need someone to turn to. And I shall be here. Waiting.

John Pascal spoke the last few words of his defence and sat down. The courtroom was silent.

Once more, Rebecca met Matthew's eyes across the space between them. He looked tired, she thought, tired and a little dispirited. Mentally she urged him to straighten his shoulders, lift his head. Don't give in now, Matthew, she prayed. For God's sake – for *my* sake – don't give in now . . .

'What will happen now?' she whispered.

Humphrey answered her. 'The jury will go out to deliberate on their verdict. But I expect the judge will adjourn the court soon anyway – it's getting late in the day and they're not likely to come to any quick conclusion. He'll probably give them an hour and then send us all away till tomorrow.'

'Tomorrow!' Rebecca thought of yet another night in the hotel room, waiting and wondering. And for Matthew, another night in the prison cell, still not knowing whether he was to live or die. But there was nothing to be done about it. Humphrey was right. Just at that moment, it was announced that the court was adjourning until the next day, and everyone started to prepare to leave.

Rebecca watched as Matthew was led away down the little staircase which led to the cells. In her imagination, she went with him, down the narrow stone steps, along the passage somewhere below the building, into the small, cold room where he would spend the night. Not for Matthew the comfortable inn room with the blazing fire to sit beside. Not for him the tea that she would have to comfort her after the long, gruelling day, the whisky and hot water that Francis would drink. Not for him the hot water to wash his face and hands, the fresh clothes to wear, the good hot meal placed in front of him before it was time to sink into the soft feather mattress of a big double bed. Not for him the comfort of someone to turn to in the night, someone to love and hold and draw comfort from.

'How do you think the jury will decide?' she asked as she and Francis and Humphrey sat over their meal that evening.

The two men looked at each other.

'It's impossible to say,' Humphrey said slowly. 'The prosecution played some unpleasant tricks. Those witnesses who swore they had seen Matthew take aim – they were difficult to dislodge, and who could say for certain whether they were truthful or not? Pascal did well to discredit them as much as he did – and anyone could see what kind of men they were, thugs and felons each one. Not even weavers, by all accounts, so what were they doing there anyway? And known troublemakers . . . But none of that is proof that they *didn't* see anything. That's the problem with such evidence. It's no more than their word against that of the defence witnesses who say that Matthew did *not* take aim.'

'And they're not so certain,' Francis said gloomily.

'No, because they're honest men and honest men understand that in such confusion nothing *is* certain.' Humphrey sighed and reached for the sauce. 'Rebecca, my dear, I'm sorry I can't answer your question. I too would like to sleep easily tonight, confident that Matthew would be coming back to Kidderminster with us tomorrow. But . . . I can't.'

The meal finished, they pushed back their chairs. Rebecca felt suddenly very tired. She went up to the room she and Francis shared, and sat at the window, gazing out at the lights of the city.

Somewhere out there, Matthew sat in his cell, waiting for tomorrow's verdict. Did he have faith in the outcome, the faith she had felt that morning and tried to convey to him across the crowded courtroom? Did she even have that faith herself?

The door opened and Francis came quietly into the room. He came across and drew her to her feet and into his arms, holding her close and tenderly.

'Come to bed, my love,' he murmured, beginning to unfasten the buttons on her dress. 'Come to bed and let me hold you. It will help the time pass, even if we don't sleep.'

Rebecca nodded and allowed him to undress her. He slipped off her dress, her shift, her bodice. He smoothed her stockings from her legs and wrapped her nightgown around her. He laid her in the bed, slipped quickly out of his own clothes, and stretched himself beside her.

There was no passion between them as they lay close, holding each other, treasuring each other's warmth. But there was a great, shining tenderness that seemed to encompass them both in a translucent shell of protecting love. And Rebecca imagined that tenderness stretching itself to enfold Matthew as well, somewhere out in the city, deep in his underground cell. She saw him joining the two of them in their protective cocoon, untouchable, safe from all harm. And she felt again the faith that had upheld her in the morning.

The courtroom was filling again, to a buzz of excited chatter. All morning, they had waited for the jury to return, until the judge announced they would adjourn for lunch. Only then had Rebecca been persuaded to leave the court, knowing that nothing could happen while she was away. Now, after toying with a lunch she did not want, she was back in her seat, her eyes bright with anxiety. Surely the jury would be back soon? Surely they couldn't take much longer?

But it was another two hours before there was a stir at the door and the twelve men filed back into their seats.

Rebecca found Francis's hand and held it tightly. She saw Matthew brought back from his cell, met his eyes again, sent him her last message of hope. And then the foreman of the jury was speaking.

And her heart sank deeply in her breast.

'Transportation!' she said to Francis. 'I never expected that – I never even thought of it. It's as bad as the death sentence. Francis, I've heard such terrible things of those ships. The long voyage, the disease, the overcrowding . . . he'll never survive it. He'll die after all, Francis! I know he will.'

'No!' Francis was pale, but his mouth was set with determination. He caught her shoulders, almost shaking her. 'What's happened to your faith, your belief? Darling, I know you wanted him freed – we all did. But this – it sounds terrible I know, but don't you see, it could mean a new life for Matthew? Yes, he'll be transported to the other side of the world – but once there, he'll have a chance. He can work, he can earn a pardon, he can come back to England once his sentence expires. And who better than Matthew to survive transportation? He's used to travelling, he's used to hardship, to hard work. Rebecca, don't you see – this is the best thing that could have happened.' He looked at her soberly. 'We all knew that he could never be acquitted. He was never able to deny that he shot Bucknell.'

'But . . . transportation,' she said faintly. 'Australia . . . Francis, we may never see him again.'

'Perhaps not,' Francis said quietly. 'But at least we'll know he's alive. At least we'll know he's living the active kind of life he enjoys, perhaps on a sheep farm somewhere, or working with timber. He may not be free, but he won't be rotting in some cold prison cell.'

As Bessie had done. The words hung unspoken in the air between them. And slowly, Rebecca nodded.

The sadness was still there. But Francis was right. At least Matthew was still alive.

They were allowed to see Matthew once before he was taken away. They went in together, the three of them, to the bare little room where prisoners were allowed to say their final goodbyes. They sat together in a little group, at a loss for words.

'Let's hold each other's hands,' Humphrey Price said, and they moved their chairs together and each put out both hands. They clasped their fingers together like the hub of a wheel, their arms forming the spokes. Rebecca felt Matthew's fingers in hers, as warm and strong as they had ever been. She lifted her eyes and gazed into his face, and he met her look with a steady smile that told her that he was hopeful about the future. That he was glad not to be facing the gallows; that he meant, one day, to return.

Once again, they were back in Kidderminster. Once again, Francis and Tom were working together in the co-operative, while Vivian seemed to have overcome his anger and bitterness at Jeremiah's will and to have accepted the situation in Pagnel Carpets. Once again, life was settling into a rhythm and the future was looking brighter.

'Not that we can afford to be complacent,' Francis warned Rebecca. 'Trade still isn't good, and we shall have to be very careful. But with caution, we ought to pull through.' He sighed. 'I'm afraid the same can't be said of some of the others. They say poor John Broom is going to go bankrupt. And he was the first to bring Jacquard to Kidderminster, too.'

'Perhaps that's why,' Rebecca observed. 'Perhaps he overstretched in the early days. But your father would never allow that.'

'No, and we're grateful for his caution now. Even Vivian seems to have settled down.' Francis sipped his brandy thoughtfully. 'He's changed, Rebecca. He's not so harsh. He's easier to work with.'

'Easier to live with, too.' Rebecca said. 'I see him most days now, when I go to see the girls. He pays them more attention, and they seem happier.'

'So . . .' Francis put down his glass and smiled at her. 'So all's well with our world. We've had our troubles – we'll never forget our little Geoffrey, or Bessie, or Father. We've had our difficult times. But just at the moment, it seems that everything is going well. We've had word that Matthew is in Australia, safe and well. And next week we move into Pagnel House.'

'And start a new stage in our lives.' Rebecca moved over to the window and looked down over the town. She thought of all that had happened during the past few years, all the people who had come into their lives and passed through, some to return, some never to be seen again. Jeremiah, Maria, Bessie, Bill Bucknell – and her precious Geoffrey, all gone for ever. And others who had stayed for just a while, yet each had his effect – Humphrey Price, Richard Godson, Matthew himself.

And those who remained. Vivian and his daughters, who were so large a part of her life now. Her own sons, Daniel and William.

And – most of all, and most enduring – the husband she loved more deeply, more tenderly with every passing day.

Francis.

AUTHOR'S NOTE

The events in this book are based upon true events taking place in Kidderminster during the years 1824–31.

During this time, the carpet industry experienced considerable problems and unrest. The formation of the Union and the secret societies with their initiation rituals are factual; so is the Great Strike and the subsequent riots. The Reverend Humphrey Price was very active in campaigning on the weavers' behalf and was imprisoned for a year. Richard Godson defended eleven weavers in Worcester and gained acquittal for all but four of them; he later became Kidderminster's first Member of Parliament.

Other characters and events are from my own imagination, and all errors are my own.